Case Studies in Contemporary Criticism

JOSEPH CONRAD

The Secret Sharer

Case Studies in Contemporary Criticism

SERIES EDITOR: Ross C Murfin

Case Studies in Contemporary Criticism

SERIES EDITOR: Ross C Murfin, *Southern Methodist University*

JOSEPH CONRAD
The Secret Sharer

**Complete, Authoritative Text with
Biographical and Historical Contexts,
Critical History, and Essays from
Five Contemporary Critical Perspectives**

EDITED BY

Daniel R. Schwarz
Cornell University

Bedford Books
BOSTON ⚎ NEW YORK

For Bedford Books
President and Publisher: Charles H. Christensen
General Manager and Associate Publisher: Joan E. Feinberg
Managing Editor: Elizabeth M. Schaaf
Developmental Editor: Stephen A. Scipione
Assistant Managing Editor: John Amburg
Production Editors: Tony Perriello and Maureen Murray
Copyeditor: Barbara Price
Text Designer: Sandra Rigney, The Book Department
Cover Design: Richard Emery Design, Inc.
Cover Art: Barry Masteller. *Natural Occurrence 37,* © 1993. Tempera
on board. From Lisa Parker Fine Art, NY.

Library of Congress Catalog Card Number: 96–84946

Manufactured in the United States of America.

2   1   0   9   8   7
f   e   d   c   b   a

For information, write: Bedford Books, 75 Arlington Street, Boston, MA 02116
(617–426–7440)

ISBN: 0–312–11224–6 (paperback)
ISBN: 0–312–16291–X (hardcover)

Published and distributed outside North America by:

MACMILLAN PRESS LTD.
Houndmills, Basingstoke, Hampshire RG21 2XS and London
Companies and representatives throughout the world.

ISBN: 0–333–69092–3

Acknowledgments

Edouard Manet. *Déjeuner sur l'herbe (Luncheon on the Grass)*, 1863. Oil on canvas.
Musée d'Orsay, Paris, France. Erich Lessing/Art Resource, NY.
J. Hillis Miller, "Reading Secrets." Copyright © 1997 by J. Hillis Miller.

About the Series

Volumes in the Case Studies in Contemporary Criticism series provide college students with an entree into the current critical and theoretical ferment in literary studies. Each volume reprints the complete text of a classic literary work and presents critical essays that approach the work from different theoretical perspectives, together with the editors' introductions to both the literary work and the critics' theoretical perspectives.

The volume editor of each Case Study has selected and prepared an authoritative text of the classic work, written an introduction to the work's biographical and historical contexts, and surveyed the critical responses to the work since its initial publication. Thus situated biographically, historically, and critically, the work is examined in five critical essays, each representing a theoretical perspective of importance to contemporary literary studies. These essays, prepared especially for undergraduates, show theory in praxis; whether written by established scholars or exceptional young critics, they demonstrate how current theoretical approaches can generate compelling readings of great literature.

As series editor, I have prepared introductions, with bibliographies, to the theoretical perspectives represented in the five critical essays. Each introduction presents the principal concepts of a particular theory in their historical context and discusses the major figures and key works that have influenced their formulation. It is my hope that these introductions will reveal to students that effective criticism is informed by a set of coherent assumptions, and will encourage them to recognize and examine their own assumptions about literature. After each introduction, a selective bibliography presents a partially annotated list of important works from the literature of the particular theoretical perspective, including the most recent and readily available editions and translations of the works cited in the introduction. Finally, I have compiled a glossary of key terms that recur in these volumes and in the discourse of contemporary theory and criticism. We hope that the Case Studies in Contemporary Criticism series will reaffirm the richness of its literary works, even as it introduces invigorating new ways to mine their apparently inexhaustible wealth.

Ross C Murfin
Series Editor
Southern Methodist University

About This Volume

Part One reprints the 1924 Doubleday Edition of "The Secret Sharer"—which appears in the volume *'Twixt Land and Sea*—preceded by my biographical and historical introduction. Part Two begins with my critical history of "The Secret Sharer" and includes five essays written from different theoretical perspectives: psychological (mine), reader-response (James Phelan), new historicism (Michael Levenson), feminist and gender (Bonnie Kime Scott), and deconstructive (J. Hillis Miller). Each of these essays—written especially for this volume and placed in theoretical context by Ross Murfin's introductions—addresses both the experience of reading "The Secret Sharer" and the critical, scholarly, and pedagogical issues that "The Secret Sharer" presents to the contemporary critical mindscape. I chose the four other contributors because for years I have been learning from their work. Each of them plays an important role in the dialogue within the profession and is recognized as a master teacher by students and colleagues. That the contributors often address similar issues from different perspectives creates a community of inquiry that teachers and students will, I hope, wish to enter.

Acknowledgments

I wish to thank Anne Marie Ellis for her insight and editorial acumen, and Irene Perciali and Tim Hoekstra for their splendid research assistance. Lisa Melton provided invaluable secretarial support. It has been a pleasure working with the four contributors: James Phelan, Michael Levenson, Bonnie Kime Scott, and J. Hillis Miller. My high-spirited collegial relationship and friendship with Ross Murfin, general editor, helped make the project a delight. At Bedford Books, Steve Scipione provided sensitive guidance and direction; I am also grateful for the warm support of Charles Christensen and Joan Feinberg. As always I want to acknowledge the input of my Cornell students from whom I have continually learned over the past twenty-nine years when teaching "The Secret Sharer," as well as the stimulation of my five NEH summer seminars for college teachers and four NEH summer seminars for secondary school teachers.

Daniel R. Schwarz
Cornell University

Contents

Case Studies in Contemporary Criticism

JOSEPH CONRAD

The Secret Sharer

PART ONE

"The Secret Sharer":
The Complete Text

Introduction:
Biographical and
Historical Contexts

Conrad is not only one of the greatest novelists who wrote in English, but he is particularly important for understanding twentieth-century British culture. Although English was his third language, Conrad's unique background as a Polish emigré and a seaman combined with the traditions of his adopted country to change permanently the English novel. He recognized the role of repressed desires, unconscious motives, and unacknowledged impulses in human conduct and brought a new psychological and moral intensity to the English novel's traditions of manners and morals. Because he wanted to dramatize how a writer comes to terms with words and meaning, he focused on the teller as much as the tale. To achieve a more intense presentation of theme and a more thorough analysis of characters' moral behavior, he adopted innovative techniques, including the use of non-linear chronology and the invention of the meditative, self-dramatizing narrator he called Marlow. Focusing on the problems of how we understand, communicate, and signify experience, Conrad anticipated essential themes in the philosophy, linguistics, criticism, and literature of our era. He understood the potential of the novel for political and historical insights and thus enlarged its subject matter. In dramatizing the search for meaning in an amoral universe, he addressed the central epistemological problem of the twentieth century.

Conrad was born December 31, 1857, as Józef Teodor Konrad

Korzeniowski. His father, Apollo Korzeniowski, was imprisoned and then sent into exile in Russia for his political activities in opposition to the Russian occupation of Poland. His mother died in 1865 while in exile, and his father died in 1868 after returning to Poland. Conrad then lived with his uncle, Tadeusz Bobrowski, who supervised his up-bringing, until Conrad left Poland in 1874 for Marseilles, where he worked as a seaman. In 1877 Conrad made a suicide attempt. In 1878 he joined his first British ship and in 1886 became a British subject. His career as British merchant seaman climaxed with his passing his Captain's examination in 1888. Conrad's captaincy of the *Otago*, his only command, was a source for "The Secret Sharer" (1910) as well as *The Shadow-Line* (1916). In 1890 he visited the Congo and kept a diary of his experiences that formed the kernel of *Heart of Darkness* (1899). Fatherless, a bachelor until age thirty-eight, an exile from his native land who felt guilty for deserting not only his homeland but his father's political heritage, Conrad was particularly concerned with loneliness and isolation. Perhaps the passage from the German writer Novalis that serves as the epigraph to *Lord Jim* (1900) and is repeated in *A Personal Record* (1912) should serve as the epigraph to Conrad's whole career: "It is certain my conviction gains infinitely the moment another soul will believe in it." The desperate reaching out to an alter ego who might sympathetically respond to his frustrations (as exempli-fied by his letters to Edward Garnett and R. B. Cunninghame-Graham) defines a central structural and thematic component of his work: a lonely soul—be it Marlow, Jim, the captain in "The Secret Sharer," Razumov, Heyst, or Captain Anthony—reaches out for another who he hopes will recognize, understand, and authenticate him.

From 1890 to 1930, the author's struggle to define form and val-ues became a major determinant of the modernist novel. Thus, in the 1898–1900 Marlow tales, and in D. H. Lawrence's *The Rainbow* (1915), James Joyce's *Ulysses* (1922), and Virginia Woolf's *Mrs. Dal-loway* (1925), the author wrote to define himself or herself. The writer did not strive for the rhetorical finish of earlier novels but, instead, like Rodin in such sculptures as *Balzac* (1895), invited the reader to per-ceive a relationship between the creator and the artistic work and to experience the dialogue between the creative process and the raw ma-terial. Whereas the Victorian novelists believed that they had coherent selves and that their characters could achieve coherence, modernists were conscious of disunity in their own lives and the world in which they lived. The novelist became a divided self: both the creator and seeker, the prophet who would convert others and the agonizing doubter who would convince himself while engaging in introspective self-examination. Even while the writer stands detached, inventing characters, we experience his or her urgent effort to invent a self. Thus the reader must maintain a double vision, apprehending both the narrative and the process of constructing it. In such diverse works as the Marlow tales, *The Rainbow,* and Woolf's *To the Lighthouse* (1927), the process of writing, of defining the subject, of evaluating character, of searching for truth, becomes part of the novel. Yet, as Woolf writes in "Mr. Bennett and Mrs. Brown" (1924), "Where so much strength is spent on finding a way of telling the truth, the truth itself is bound to reach us in rather an exhausted and chaotic condition" (117). "Finding a way"—the quest for values and for aesthetic form—became a major modernist subject.

Conrad believed that "another man's truth is a dismal lie to me" (Letters 1: 253). To understand why Conrad thought that we are all locked into our own perceptions and that all values are ultimately illusions, we should examine Conrad's ironic image of the cosmos as created by an indifferent knitting machine—an image which he proposed in an 1897 letter to his optimistic socialist friend Cunninghame-Graham:

> There is a—let us say—a machine. It evolved itself (I am severely scientific) out of a chaos of scraps of iron and behold!—it knits. I am horrified at the horrible work and stand appalled. I feel it ought to embroider,—but it goes on knitting. You come and say: "this is all right; it's only a question of the right kind of oil. Let us use this,—for instance—celestial oil and the machine shall embroider a most beautiful design in purple and gold." Will it? Alas no. You cannot by any special lubrication make embroidery with a knitting machine. And the most withering thought is that the infamous thing has made itself; made itself without thought, without conscience, without foresight, without eyes, without heart. . . .
>
> It knits us in and it knits us out. It has knitted time, space, pain, death, corruption, despair and all the illusions—and nothing matters. I'll admit however that to look at the remorseless process is sometimes amusing. (Letters 1: 425)

Conrad used this elaborate ironic trope to speak to the late-Victorian social Darwinist belief that the industrial revolution represented evolutionary progress. According to Conrad, humankind would like to believe in a providentially ordered world vertically descending from a benevolent God—that is, to believe in an embroidered world. But we actually inhabit a temporally defined horizontal dimension—troped by the inexorable knitting process within an amoral, indifferent universe—a process Conrad calls "remorseless."

In Conrad's works, especially in first-person narrations such as "The Secret Sharer," Conrad dramatizes that humans always judge one another in terms of their own current psychic and moral needs. But notwithstanding the fallibility of all judgments, Conrad makes clear the need to be objective and to sustain values and ideals, even though people will always fall short of them. Thus, when Conrad writes that all is illusion, he means that all we can do is make working arrangements with the cosmos and that there are no absolute values derived from an external source. He does not, however, mean that all values are equal. By affirming the value of the search for meaning in the lives of his characters within his imagined world, Conrad is rhetorically enacting the value of our search for meaning in our reading of texts.

Conrad's first two novels, *Almayer's Folly* (1895) and *An Outcast of the Islands* (1896), reflect his state of mind and reveal his values. In these early novels, narrated by a conventional omniscient narrator, Conrad tests and refines themes and techniques that appear in his later fiction. Characteristic of Conrad's early works, he used factual material from his own adventures as his source. Conrad visited the Malay Archipelago while sailing as first mate on the steamer *Vidar* (1887–88), and he not only drew upon his Malay experience but based the title character of his first novel on a man he actually knew.

Sambir, the setting for *Almayer's Folly* and *An Outcast of the Islands,* is the first of Conrad's symbolic settings. Like the Congo in *Heart of Darkness* and Patusan in *Lord Jim,* Sambir becomes a metaphor for actions that occur there. It is also a projection of Conrad's state of mind as revealed in his 1894–96 letters: exhaustion and ennui alternating with spasmodic energy. Conrad's narrator is in the process of creating a myth out of Sambir, but the process is never quite completed. Like Egdon Heath in Thomas Hardy's *The Return of the Native* (1878), Sambir is a resistant topography that can be controlled neither by one's endeavors nor imagination. The demonic energy that seethes within its forests is a catalyst for the perverse sexuality of the novel's white people and their subsequent moral deterioration. Sambir refutes the Romantic myth that beyond civilization lie idyllic cultures in a state of innocence. Sambir's river, the Pantai, is a prototype for the Congo River in *Heart of Darkness;* the atavistic influence it casts upon white men, drawing out long repressed and atrophied libidinous energies, anticipates the Congo River's effect on Kurtz. Sambir's primordial jungle undermines the illusion shared by the major characters in *Almayer's Folly* and *An Outcast of the Island:* that passionate love can transform the world. Sambir's tropical setting seems steeped in the processes of death and destruction; the jungle's uncontrollable fecundity expresses itself in devolution rather than evolution. Through the dominance of the Pantai and the forest, Conrad reveals a vision of a cosmos indifferent to human aspirations—much like the cosmos Hardy created in *Jude the Obscure,* published the same year.

Before he created Marlow, Conrad had difficulty controlling the personal turmoil we see in his 1894–96 letters. In these letters, Conrad feels isolated in a meaningless universe; he is cynical about humankind's motives and purposes; he senses that he is an artistic failure; he doubts his ability to communicate, even while expressing his desperate need to be understood. If in Conrad's early work his speaker's commentary is not always appropriate to the dramatic action that evokes it, it is because Conrad is using his conventional omniscient speaker to explore his own bafflement in a universe he regards as amoral, indifferent, and at times hostile. In the first two novels, when Conrad's narrator-surrogate places an episode in an intellectual and moral context, he is often testing and probing to discover what an episode means. In subsequent works, Conrad learned to capitalize on his reluctance to be dogmatic; "Youth" (1898), *Heart of Darkness,* and *Lord Jim* dramatize Marlow's process of moral discovery and show how Marlow continually formulates, discards, and redefines his beliefs through experience. Because in 1894–95 Conrad had difficulty in embracing a consistent set of values, however, his narrator's commentary does not always move toward a consistent philosophic position, but rather may posit contradictory perspectives. Quite frequently, the omniscient voice of the first two novels, *Almayer's Folly* and *An Outcast of the Islands,* explores characters and action from the perspective of a man committed to family ties, the work ethic, sexual constraint, individual responsibility, and racial understanding. Yet these basic humanistic values are often at odds with the artistic tentativeness and moral confusion that derive from Conrad's uncertainty and anxiety. The unresolved tension between Conrad's personal concerns and his attempt to objectify moral issues is revealed in the conflict between the values expressed by the narrator and the implications of the plot and setting.

Conrad's life in the British merchant marine and his travels to the East played an important role in his fiction. He not only fused stories he had heard with accounts of his own journeys, but because, when writing *The Nigger of "Narcissus"* (1897) he had actually sailed on a ship named the *Narcissus* in 1884, he could draw upon romantic memories of a successfully completed voyage at a time when his creative impulses were stifled by doubts. Conrad sought an appropriate plot structure and point of view with which to organize his subject matter. By imagining the voyage of the *Narcissus* as a structural principle, he overcame writing paralysis. After he had committed himself completely to literature (The literary profession is therefore my sole means of support [Letters 1: 266]), he became bogged down with the early version of "The Rescuer." Agonizing about his inability to make progress on "The Rescuer," he wrote to Garnett: "Now I've got all my people together I don't know what to do with them. The progressive episodes of the story *will* not emerge from the chaos of my sensations. I feel nothing clearly" (Letters 1: 288). The imagined voyage of the *Narcissus* became at once the material for a plot to examine ethical and political questions of fundamental importance to Conrad and a private metaphor for the process of creating significance. Frustrated by his inability to write, the voyage of the *Narcissus* provided Conrad with an imaginative escape to the space and time of past successes. He discovered that remembering his experiences at sea could free him from the debilitating restraints of shore life and be an ordering principle for his new career as a writer. Although he last sailed in 1894, Conrad used the fantasy of returning to sea to deal with writer's block and with the disappointment of meager economic returns from his new career.

Conrad's early artistic code, the 1897 preface to *The Nigger of the "Narcissus"* is remarkable for its emphasis on creating a community of readers. Seen in the context of his own fear of loneliness and of not communicating, it reflects his hope that fiction will not only enable him to arrest the flux and turmoil within himself but that it will relieve him of his sense of isolation. Conrad in the preface to *The Nigger of the "Narcissus"* defines art "as a single-minded attempt to render the highest kind of justice to the visible universe, by bringing to light the truth, manifold and one, underlying its every aspect" (*NN* xi). The artist's *mission* is to reveal the experience that unites all men and, in particular, to make the reader aware of the common humanity each shares with mankind. Conrad hopes for a community of responsive temperaments to verify the effectiveness of *his* creation; this hope may be behind the intensity of the famous but elusive assertion, "My task which I am trying to achieve is, by the power of the written word, to make you hear, to make you feel—it is, before all, to make you *see*" (*NN* xiv).

Conrad's 1914 preface to the American edition of *The Nigger of the "Narcissus"* makes clear that he meant the tale's focus to be on the crew's response to Wait, a black crew member and malingerer: "In the book [Wait] is nothing; he is merely the centre of the ship's collective psychology and the pivot of the action" (ix). Sentimentalism is the peculiar form of egotism that preys upon the crew's response to Wait and to Donkin, another misfit on board the *Narcissus*. The men sacrifice their integrity in a desperate and pathetic effort to forestall Wait's inevitable death. Neither Wait nor Donkin has an identity independent of that conferred by the crew's sentimentalism; they flourish *because* the crew responds to them. Wait is in a parasitic relationship with the crew: "Each, going out, seemed to leave behind a little of his own vitality, surrender some of his own strength, renew the assurance of life—the indestructible thing!" (165; ch. 5). Once the crew responds to Donkin with a "wave of sentimental pity" (26; ch. 1), "the development of the destitute Donkin aroused interest" (27; ch. 1). When he responds to Wait and Donkin against his better judgment, the sailor-speaker embodies Conrad's own fear of sentimentalism. After he had completed *The Nigger* but before it had begun to appear in *The New Review,* Conrad wrote, "I feel horribly sentimental. . . . I want to rush into print whereby my sentimentalism, my incorrect attitude to life . . . shall be disclosed to the public gaze" (Letters 1: 347). Just as the eternal truths of Singleton and Allistoun triumph over the "temporary formulas" of Donkin and the crew's misguided sentimentalism, the fiction writer must eschew fashionable aesthetic philosophies. As Conrad writes in the preface to *The Nigger of the "Narcissus,"* "Realism, Romanticism, Naturalism, even the unofficial Sentimentalism . . . all these gods must . . . abandon him . . . to the stammerings of his conscience and to the outspoken consciousness of the difficulties of his work" (*NN* xv).

Conrad was concerned with transforming the "freedom" of living in a purposeless world from a condition into a value. Marlow enabled him to examine this issue in "Youth," *Heart of Darkness,* and *Lord Jim.* Writing enabled Conrad to define his own values and his own character: he uses his narrators and dramatic personae to objectify his feelings and values. Marlow is a surrogate through whom Conrad works out his own epistemological problems, psychic turmoil, and moral confusion. Marlow's search for values echoes Conrad's; thus he is a means by which Conrad orders his world. He is defining not only the form of the story but the relation between Conrad's past and present self. The younger Marlow was explicitly committed to the same conventional values of the British merchant marine to which Conrad had devoted his early adulthood, but the mature Marlow has had experiences that have caused him to re-evaluate completely his moral beliefs. That Marlow is a vessel for some of Conrad's doubts and anxieties and for defining the problems that made his own life difficult is clear not only from Conrad's 1890 Congo diary and the 1890s correspondence with his aunt, Marguerite Poradowska, but even more so from the letters of the 1897–99 period, selections from which have already been quoted.

The meanings of several novels, most notably *The Nigger of the "Narcissus"* and *The Rescue* (1919), depend in part on our understanding of the way Conrad's emotional life is embodied in the texts. In *Nostromo* (1904) the suicidal despair of Decoud, a skeptic whose values are often close to Conrad's, reflects a mood that Conrad had known many times in his novel-writing years and recalls his own suicide attempt. As we shall see, "The Secret Sharer" becomes more meaningful once we recognize that it has an autobiographical element. At the outset of his voyage, the captain not only relives emotions Conrad felt during his first command but reflects the uncertainty and anxiety Conrad experienced in the period when he wrote it.

"Youth" is a story that transforms Conrad's experiences as second mate aboard the *Palestine* in 1881–82. In "Youth," Conrad addresses the dour view of European life presented in his first collection of short stories, *Tales of Unrest* (1898). Marlow is the heir of the white men of such early Conrad stories as "The Lagoon" (1896) and "Karain: A Memory" (1897)—those sensitive, if disillusioned men, who neither live passionately like the natives nor believe in any sustaining ideals. "Youth" is about Marlow's efforts to create a significant yesterday so that his life will not seem a meaningless concatenation of durational events. Marlow's narrative in "Youth" reflects his need "to arrest" time and preempt the future. Somewhere past the middle of his life, he attempts to discover a symbolic meaning in the past voyage of the *Judea*. He wishes to believe that his first journey to the East was one of "those voyages that seem ordered for the illustration of life, that might stand for a symbol of existence ("Youth" 3). As Marlow recalls his great adventure, he discovers that in spite of the voyage's failure, it not only contains great significance for him, but enables him to recapture on occasion his feeling of youthful energy. Conrad takes a good-natured, ironic view of the supposedly mature Marlow's attempts to expose his own youthful illusions. While he purports to take an objective and detached view of a meaningful experience of his youth, the mature Marlow is revealed as a nostalgic romantic. Conrad shows us that reality is partly subjective and that our illusions and oversimplifications are as real to us as so-called objective facts.

The subject of Conrad's next work, *Heart of Darkness,* is primarily Marlow, but the presence of Conrad is deeply engraved on every scene. Conrad first examined his 1890 Congo journey—the source of *Heart of Darkness*—in his short story, "An Outpost of Progress" (1896). When we study his 1890 Congo diary, reprinted in his posthumous *Last Essays* (1926), we see how Conrad's anterior reality informs a text and how the imagination creates the reality of place to meet the thematic needs of a text. Note the diary entries:

> *Friday, 4th of July.* . . . Saw another dead body lying by a path in an attitude of meditative repose. At night when the moon rose heard shouts and drumming in distant villages. Passed a bad night. (165)

> *Monday, 7th July.* . . . Hot, thirsty and tired. At eleven arrived on the mket place. About 200 people. No water. No camp place. After remaining for one hour left in search of a resting place. Row with carriers. No water. . . . Sun heavy. Wretched. (166)

Conrad's 1896 letter to Fisher T. Unwin makes clear that "An Outpost of Progress" is an intense response to his Congo experience: "All the bitterness of those days, all my puzzled wonder as to meaning of all I saw—all my indignation at masquerading philanthropy have been with me again while I wrote" (quoted in Karl, *Joseph Conrad: The Three Lives* 379). In *Heart of Darkness* Marlow's effort to come to terms with the Congo experience, especially Kurtz—the epitome of European civilization who reverts to savagery—is the crucial activity that engaged Conrad's imagination. Marlow's consciousness is the arena of the tale, and the interaction between his verbal behavior—his effort to find the appropriate words—and his memory is as much the pivotal action as his Congo journey. Both the epistemological quest for a context or perspective with which to interpret the experience and the semiological quest to discover the signs and symbols which make the experience intelligible are central to the tale.

Probably influenced by Paul Gauguin's Tahitian paintings and his *Noa, Noa* (excerpts of which were published in 1897), *Heart of Darkness* needs to be placed in its cultural context. *Heart of Darkness* speaks to major turn-of-the-century concerns: the breakdown of moral certainty, the sense that each of us lives in a closed circle, and the consequent fear of solipsism. Conrad feared that we are all locked in our own perceptions and despaired in his letters that even language will not help us communicate to others. Thus, Conrad's fear that "we live, as we dream—alone" (*Heart of Darkness* 527) is also an idea that recurs throughout the period of early modernism, a period in which European intellectuals felt, to quote the philosopher F. H. Bradley's *Appearance and Reality,* that "my experience is a closed circle; a circle closed from the outside. . . . In brief . . . the whole world for each is peculiar and private to that soul" (346). That the frame narrator, after listening to Marlow, can retell the story to his audience shows that Marlow has communicated with someone and offers a partial antidote to the fear of isolation and silence that haunted Conrad. Conrad's narrative demonstrates the common humanity of the Africans and Europeans: the English were once natives conquered by the Romans, and England was once one of the dark places of the earth. Moreover, the Europeans not only require laws and rules to restrain their atavistic impulses, but they become more monstrous than those they profess to civilize. Finally, terms such as *savage* and *barbarian* are arbitrary designations by imperialists who in fact deserve these epithets more than the natives.

Conrad takes issue with Victorian assumptions about univocal truth and a divinely ordered world. His use of Marlow's dramatized consciousness reflects his awareness that no one perspective is enough to grasp the whole. One can see that just as in modern painting, the fauvists and cubists were freeing traditional ideas of representation from the morphology of color, Conrad, too, was freeing black and white from the traditional expectations of color. Conrad was also freeing his language from the expectations of representation—as in his use of adjectives for purely affective rather than descriptive reasons. Conrad's use of allegorized rather than nominalistic adjectives, such as *subtle* and *unspeakable,* invite the frame narrator and Conrad's readers to respond in terms of their own experiences and to validate in their responses that they, too, dream alone. Like Gauguin and Picasso, Conrad explores ancient voices and the presence of primitive cultures in modernist texts through the savage mistress and the other natives.

In 1900 Conrad produced his masterpiece *Lord Jim,* which he originally began as a short story. *Lord Jim* includes elements of an actual sea disaster involving a pilgrim ship, the steamship *Jeddah,* abandoned at sea in 1880, as well as some of Conrad's experiences during his three visits to eastern seas between 1883 and 1888. The title character, Jim, an officer of the *Patna,* abandons the ship's human cargo. After disgracing himself, he wanders around the colonial ports until Marlow makes arrangements, with the help of a prophetic figure named Stein, to send Jim to a primitive island, Patusan, where for a time he succeeds beyond his wildest dreams.

Lord Jim involves the reader in the "remorseless process" of responding to different judgments of Jim's behavior. First, there is the judgment of the omniscient narrator that precedes not only our meeting Marlow, but also our learning what happens on the *Patna*. Does the reader ever forget this narrator's original rigorous judgment of Jim in the first three chapters—a judgment that is based on adherence to absolute standards? Does not that judgment accompany the reader as he or she proceeds through Marlow's narrative of his own efforts to find some terms with which to understand Jim's terrible failure on the *Patna*, when Jim, along with the rest of the white officers, abandons the native crew and passengers? And of course the reader must sort out the significance of Stein's oracular but hazy pronouncements. We hear Marlow's initial judgment, based on his knowledge that Jim has succeeded on Patusan, and we learn that Marlow believes his confidence in Jim was justified; then we are confronted with Marlow's final, inconclusive judgment after Jim has failed. This judgment is halfway between the omniscient narrator's rigorous one and Marlow's earlier empathetic one.

Not all of Conrad's novels deal with the lonely struggle of isolated individuals to understand themselves and their world. *Nostromo, The Secret Agent* (1907), and *Under Western Eyes* (1911) address the politics of Europe and the implications of imperialism, colonialism, and ultranationalism. Yet while the subjects of these novels are often political, their values are not. The novels affirm the primacy of family, the sanctity of the individual, the value of love, and the importance of sympathy and understanding in human relations. Conrad married Jessie George in 1896 and became the father of a son, Borys, in 1898; another son, John, was born eight years later.

Conrad's friendships with R. B. Cunninghame-Graham, writer H. G. Wells, and playwright George Bernard Shaw, all of whose views were far more liberal than his, show that he put personal relationships before political ideology. His concern for the working class derived not from political theory but from his experience as a seaman and from his imaginative response to the miseries of others. Conrad's humanism informed his political vision. In his political writings, the abstractions upholding private virtues carry conviction. He wrote in "Autocracy and War" (1905) that it is to "our sympathetic imagination" that we must "look for the ultimate triumph of concord and justice" (*Notes on Life and Letters,* 84). In "Autocracy and War" the paramount values threatened by Russian autocracy—which as a Pole he detested— are "dignity," "truth," "rectitude," and "all that is faithful in human nature" (99). Thus, Russia is "a yawning chasm open between East and West; a bottomless abyss that has swallowed up every hope of mercy, every aspiration towards personal dignity, towards freedom, towards knowledge, every ennobling desire of the heart, every redeeming whisper of conscience" (100).

Nostromo shows how Conrad used his reading and a brief visit to the West Indies in 1878 to create an imaginary nation with its own history and landscape. The pain of exile and the feeling of marginality are important in Conrad. It is not necessary to agree fully with those critics who believe that Costaguana is a disguised version of Poland to understand *Nostromo* as a sublimated act of self-justification. Conrad was deeply troubled over accusations that he had abandoned Poland; he questioned his own motives for settling in England and turning his back on both his country and his family heritage. The justification that living in Poland was incompatible with a career as a seaman was difficult to sustain once he had become a writer.

It may be that *Nostromo* also reflects Conrad's subconscious resentment toward a father who neglected his family for politics and, after inflicting exile, disgrace, and economic hardship upon his family, ultimately left Conrad an orphan. If *Nostromo* is Conrad's subconscious atonement for turning his back on his father's tradition, it is hardly surprising that the catalytic act that generates the novel's plot and the decisive act in the history of Costaguana is the capitalist Gould's return to the land of his father's defeat for the purpose of reviving the mine. By repudiating the possibility of change through politics, Conrad justified his own decision to desert Poland, to which his father had made a complete political commitment. Given his father's zealotry and Conrad's awareness of it, it seems reasonable to say that politics became a paternal abstraction to which Conrad must atone, palliate, and explain to himself. The means of palliation are his political novels. *Nostromo* justifies the choice of personal fulfillment over political involvement because it shows politics as a maelstrom that destroys those it touches and, more important, shows that a crucial part of one's personality is inevitably surrendered in committing oneself to ideology.

Decoud, the character in *Nostromo* who is most like Conrad and from whom Conrad is at times barely able to separate himself, is alternately cynic and romantic, pragmatist and idealist. His perceptive analysis of others often goes beyond the narrator's understanding. He uses the written word—the art of writing—to give shape to his identity. Decoud is Conrad's surrogate, and the distance between Conrad's voice and his character dissolves when Conrad narrates Decoud's complete inability to cope with his solitude. Decoud's final crisis approaches states of mind that Conrad experienced from 1895 to 1898. Thus, in 1896 Conrad wrote to Edward Garnett:

> I am paralyzed by doubt and have just enough sense to feel the agony but am powerless to invent a way out of it. . . . I knock about blindly in it till I am positively, physically sick—and then I give up saying—tomorrow! And tomorrow comes—and brings only the renewed and futile agony. I ask myself whether I am breaking up mentally. . . . Everything seems so abominably stupid. You see *the belief* is not in me—and without the belief—the brazen thick headed, thick skinned immovable belief nothing good can be done. (Letters 1: 296–97).

Decoud's suicidal urges, nihilism, and self-hate objectify qualities that Conrad despised in himself.

In *The Secret Agent,* Conrad takes issue with a common Edwardian view that time inevitably equals progress. Writers such as Samuel Butler and Shaw proposed the concept of an upwardly evolving life force. Conrad regarded as cant the political euphoria of the Fabians and of his socialist friend Cunninghame-Graham, that a "benign" and "congenial" future awaits us once we locate and ameliorate the problems of civilization. Conrad's sense of history as inexorably indifferent to man's aspirations was shaped partly by his despair and indignation at the suppression of Polish freedom. Thus, even the book's dedication to the utopian H. G. Wells has an ironic aspect. *The Secret Agent* proposes no solutions for the oppressive economic system and negligent political system.

The Secret Agent depends on a tension between disintegration of content (Conrad's perception of turn-of-the-century London) and integration and cohesion of form (the language and the tightly unified narrative). Conrad creates a language that is moral, civilized, and rational, and a narrator with the intelligence and moral energy to suggest alternatives to the cynicism, amorality, and hypocrisy that dominate political relationships within London. Although the narrator, to whom the entire language of the book is assigned, at first seems isolated and detached from a world he abhors, he gradually reveals himself as a multidimensional figure whose concern and sympathy for those trapped within the cosmic chaos become part of the novel's values. The major character is the narrator; his *action* is to attack a world he despises. The satire in *The Secret Agent* depends on the immense ironic distance between a civilized voice that justifiably conceives of itself as representing sanity, rationality, and morality, and the people of London, who are for the most part caught in a maelstrom of violence and irrationality beyond their control.

Conrad's next novel, *Under Western Eyes,* depends on a juxtaposition of Geneva and Russia. Conrad had a deep, abiding hatred for Russia because he believed it had exploited and terrorized Poland and was responsible for the deaths of his parents. He followed events in Russia and, through his friends the Garnett family, knew Russian refugees and revolutionaries. In the novel's author note, he writes that the plot and characters "owe their existence to no special experience but to the general knowledge of the condition of Russia" (x).

In Conrad's depiction of Russia, autocratic politics create a world in which personal lives are distorted by the political abstractions served by proponents and antagonists. Each Russian creates the fiction of a receptive counterpart who understands his or her every thought and feeling. Russia finally emerges as primitive and atavistic, a kind of European version of the Congo, where possibilities exist that have all but been discarded by Western countries.

Conrad's Geneva is a civilization in which libidinous energies and the atavistic impulses may be squelched, but violence and anarchy are under control. In some ways Geneva is a metaphor for London and England. Conrad had once visited Geneva in the 1890s, and had taken his son Borys there in 1907 for hydropathic treatment of suspected tuberculosis, the disease that took Conrad's parents' lives. He claimed that the catalyst for *Under Western Eyes* was a story he had been told by a man he had met in Geneva. It is very much to the point that the people of Geneva (other than the revolutionaries) are engaged in shopkeeping, teaching, picnicking, and walking. Unlike in Russia, these quite ordinary activities can take place without bombs and intimidation. Geneva may have its materialistic aspect, epitomized by the rather tasteless Chateau Borel that now stands abandoned by its owners, but Geneva allows the cultivation of personal affections and the fulfillment of private aspirations, which the autocratic and violent Russian world blunts.

In December 1909 Conrad interrupted his work on *Under Western Eyes* to write "The Secret Sharer." Commenting on Conrad's original plan to call the story either "The Second Self" or "The Other Self," Conrad's biographer Frederick R. Karl writes, "His psychological need to share his situation with those close to him is a personal manifestation of what he had just been writing. . . . He displayed now his familiar pattern of dependency, seeking supports as he was being deserted, first by [his friend, the writer Ford Madox Ford], then by [his agent, James] Pinker" (675–76).

"The Secret Sharer" owes its origins to events that took place on the *Cutty Sark* in 1880, when the first mate killed a man under his supervision. Conrad's author's note to the volume *'Twixt Land and Sea* (1912) explains that the story was based on a tale he heard less than two months after the crime on the *Cutty Sark* was committed. Indeed, in July–August 1882, he probably read about the trial in the London *Times,* since he was in Falmouth at the time.

Norman Sherry's *Conrad's Eastern World* is a useful resource for contexts and backgrounds, and Zdzislaw Najder and Jocelyn Baines have examined the biographical aspects of "The Secret Sharer." Baines writes:

> The story is based on an incident which happened on board the *Cutty Sark* in 1880. The *Cutty Sark* had put in to Singapore on 18 September, three days after the chief officer of the *Jeddah* (the *Patna* in *Lord Jim*) had arrived there. In Conrad's adaptation of the *Cutty Sark* incident, Leggatt, the mate of the *Sephora,* kills a disobedient member of the crew during a storm and is put under arrest by his captain. But he escapes and swims to another ship of which the narrator of the story is captain. The captain is a young, comparatively inexperienced man who has just been given his first command—here Conrad seems to draw on his own experiences on the *Otago*—"a stranger to the ship" and "somewhat of a stranger to myself." (355)

Apparently Conrad had performed the kind of maneuver he describes (taking the ship perilously close to land before changing direction) as skipper of the *Otago* in 1888 during the first days of his only command.

Basil Lubbock's *The Log of the "Cutty Sark"* is an important background source. Excerpts from chapter five are reprinted in *Conrad's Secret Sharer and the Critics,* edited by Bruce Harkness. Harkness also reprints crucial articles from the London *Times* about the arrest and trial of Sidney Smith, chief mate on the *Cutty Sark,* the character on whose murderous behavior Leggatt is based. In their essay "Morality and Psychology in 'The Secret Sharer,'" Royal Gettmann and Bruce Harkness stress the importance of both sources:

> In respect to the world of external appearances—the world of things, places, and actions—there are numerous parallels between the short story and the actual events aboard the *Cutty Sark* as narrated in Lubbock's "A Hell-Ship Voyage." The same is true of the possible source material from the London *Times.* (125)

But they stress how Conrad's art transformed the story:

> Conrad felt obliged to penetrate much more deeply: to show that the universe and human nature are so constituted that any man innocently passing the time of night anywhere may have thrust upon him a moral dilemma that can be resolved only at the cost of a bitter struggle. (Gettmann and Harkness 127)

The source material enables them to argue that Leggatt represents atavistic, amoral behavior:

> This, then, is what Leggatt symbolizes: the instinct for violence in the Captain; his acknowledging Leggatt as his double means just that, for to acknowledge Leggatt is to acknowledge violence. . . . The hate then combines the expression of the Captain's pity and the dark impulse of Leggatt. It is, finally, a symbol of integration. It saves the present ship by permitting the Captain to navigate his ship safely past the rocks. The dark side of man saved the *Sephora,* as well as all hands aboard the new ship. (Gettmann and Harkness 130, 131)

'Twixt Land and Sea contains three long stories written for magazines from 1909 to 1911. "The Secret Sharer" is one of the great tales in the English language, and the others—"Freya of the Seven Isles" and "A Smile of Fortune"—although not major works, deserve to be read more than they are. All three tales examine a young captain under stress. Conrad returns to a world he had left behind: the lonely, bachelor world of the sea with its homosocial ship bonding and its absolute moral code. Although in this period of renewed personal and financial turmoil Conrad's imagination turns nostalgically to life at sea, the sea is no longer the simplified world of *Typhoon* (1902) or *The End of the Tether* (1902), where moral distinctions are clear.

In *'Twixt Land and Sea,* a young captain is faced with circumstances and emotional traumas for which neither the maritime code nor his experience has prepared him. Both "Freya of the Seven Isles" and "A Smile of Fortune" provide evidence that Conrad is interested in the heterosexual relationships of inexperienced young adults. In each story an ingenuous and imperceptive man ceases to function effectively in his career because of his passionate involvement with an immature young woman. "A Smile of Fortune" is the more autobiographical and revealing of the two. In fact, it may suffer from Conrad's inability to separate himself from the captain-narrator. But "The Secret Sharer" is personal in the way great lyrical poetry is personal, drawing from experience that is at once individual (Conrad's assuming the captaincy of the *Otago* in 1888) and universal (fear and self-doubt in the face of challenge).

After 1910 Conrad wanted to demonstrate that he was an English novelist, not a Slav writing in English, as some reviewers implied. The diffident, self-effacing narrator of *Under Western Eyes* owes something to this impulse. In a sense, *Under Western Eyes, Chance* (1912), and *Victory* (1915) are Conrad's English trilogy. Married for fifteen years and the father of two sons, Conrad had given up the fantasy of returning to sea and had expanded his interests. *Chance* and *Victory* represent Conrad's attempt to write English novels of manners and to explore the intricacies of personal relationships in the context of contemporary customs and values. He regarded *Victory* as a "strictly proper" work "meant for cultured people," and he even thought that "The Secret Sharer" was English "in moral atmosphere, feeling and even in detail" (qtd. and paraphrased in Karl 717, 725).

In *Chance* and *Victory,* Conrad's subject matter is less his own life than the external world. The form and narrative technique stress his detachment and withdrawal. Even when he revives Marlow in *Chance,* that figure is no longer a surrogate who echoes Conrad's anxieties and doubts. Although we certainly see important resemblances between Conrad and his characters Heyst and Captain Anthony, he is not primarily writing fictional versions of himself.

Chance, Conrad's first novel after his three major political novels, sustains and intensifies the stress on private life and passionate love as the only alternatives to a world threatened by materialism, political ideology, and uncontrollable historical forces. As in Conrad's earlier novels, each major character is lonely, isolated, and separate and requires the recognition of another as friend, lover, parent, child, or counsel to be complete. If there is an alternative in *Chance* to repression, isolation, and self-imprisonment, it is in the possibility of sympathy and understanding, and most significantly, passionate love. Once one perceives the prominence of the prison metaphor within the texture of the novel, one realizes that Conrad's indictment of English life has the harshness and bitterness of *The Secret Agent. Chance* discovers a heart of darkness beneath the civilized exteriors of Edwardian London, just as *The Secret Agent* discovers it in the political machinations not only of anarchists and reactionaries, but also of those charged with upholding the status quo. In *Chance,* the London of *The Secret Agent* exists in all its shabby, ugly decadence, and people are separated by individual dreams and illusions.

Although London is its setting, *Victory* is the last of Conrad's novels to analyze contemporary European culture. Beginning with *The Shadow-Line* (1916), the subsequent novels beat a retreat from confronting the crisis of values that Conrad believed was undermining Western civilization. For Conrad, the crisis was epitomized by imperialism, capitalism, the decline of family and national ties, and the replacement of personal relationships with economic ones. *Victory* depicts an "age in which we are camped like bewildered travelers in a garish, unrestful hotel" (3; ch. 1). *Victory* is about the decline in civility and morality not only on an obscure island, but in Western civilization. Conrad perceived, as Thomas Mann had in *Death in Venice* (1912), that something had gone wrong with the amenities and proprieties that hold civilization together.

From 1912 to 1914, when Conrad wrote *Victory*, the stable, secure England in which Conrad had found a home was in danger of disintegrating. Beset by political turmoil in the form of labor unrest, the women's movement, and the excesses and zeal of the Conservative opposition which threatened to undermine parliamentary government, England must have seemed to Conrad increasingly in danger of becoming like his native Poland. The ironically titled *Victory* is Conrad's response to an England torn by powerful conflicting enclaves and suffering a loss of esteem in its own eyes as well as in those of other nations.

Heyst, the major figure in *Victory*, may represent Conrad's perception that a certain kind of man—polished, tolerant, polite, considerate of others, with impeccable integrity and the highest personal standards—was becoming obsolete in England. For all his quirks, Heyst adheres to Edwardian propriety and decorum with the single exception of his elopement. The negativism of Heyst's father may echo the anonymous 1905 pamphlet "The Decline and Fall of the British Empire"; in any case, his outlook is a rejection of the more optimistic of the social Darwinists and may also be a criticism of *A Commentary* by Conrad's friend John Galsworthy. *Victory* attacks imperialistic pretensions, decadent aristocracy, and business morality, only to give those forces the laurels of victory. The title finally implies the triumph of materialism and greed over feelings and personal relationships. By using the word *business* interchangeably with *game*, Conrad emphasizes the Edwardian effort to disguise competitive and aggressive impulses in understatements.

After *Chance* and *Victory*, Conrad often turned from contemporary issues back to his own memories. *The Shadow-Line* and *The Arrow of*

Gold (1919), like "The Secret Sharer" and "A Smile of Fortune," express Conrad's emotions and passions, but unlike in the Marlow tales, Conrad recreates past emotions more than he objectifies present inner turmoil. Whereas *The Shadow-Line* and *The Arrow of Gold* reach into his past, *The Rescue* (1919) was finally completed primarily to settle his long-standing anxiety about a work that had been stalled for two decades. *The Rescue* returns to the romance world of Malay, which provided the setting of his first two novels, *Almayer's Folly* and *An Outcast of the Islands,* as well as such early tales as "Karain" and "The Lagoon." It is a nostalgic look at both Conrad's personal and literary pasts and provides something of an escape from his present anxieties and harsher memories.

Based, like "The Secret Sharer," on his command of the *Otago* in 1888, *The Shadow-Line* explores the difference between merely practicing skills and providing leadership to a community. Conrad had written in Richard Curle's copy of the novel, "This story had been in my mind for some years. Originally I used to think of it under the name of *First Command.* When I managed in the second year of war to concentrate my mind sufficiently to begin working I turned to this subject as the easiest. But in consequence of my changed mental attitude to it, it became *The Shadow-Line*" (Curle 94). In contrast, the seemingly similar "The Secret Sharer" emphasized the captain-narrator's psychological development rather than his ability to do his job. By fulfilling the moral requirements of a clearly defined position, the captain-narrator fulfills himself; he overcomes ennui, anxiety, and anomie and merges his psychological life with the demands of the external world. To oversimplify, perhaps: *The Shadow-Line* affirms that hyperconsciousness is a moral rather than a psychological problem and demonstrates how hyperconsciousness and its symptoms can be overcome by discovering the authentic self that exists beneath self-doubt and anxiety.

Conrad died August 3, 1924. His last novel, *The Rover* (1923), incorporates a number of major themes from his previous work. He had hoped to appeal to a wide audience. Conrad spoke of *The Rover* in terms that suggest its special importance to him: "I have wanted for a long time to do a seaman's 'return' (before my own departure)" (Jean-Aubry 2: 339). The principal character, Peyrol, an aging seaman and an outsider, is a fictional counterpart of Conrad. Peyrol's desire to merge his destiny with his nation's in his final voyage may reflect Conrad's desire as he approached death to contribute meaningfully to Poland's destiny. Conrad's fantasy of a significant political act is embodied in Peyrol. Conrad's life as embodied in his imagination reveals that he was never comfortable with having turned his back on politics and the heritage of his father, whom he recalled as an idealistic patriot. The novel's title also refers to himself, the twice transplanted alien who finally found a home in England and no longer felt himself something of an outsider. Peyrol recreates himself at fifty-eight when circumstances connive with his own weariness to deprive him of his past; he creates a new identity just as surely as a younger Conrad did when he left Poland to go to sea and, later, when he turned from the sea to a writing career.

Daniel R. Schwarz

WORKS CITED

Baines, Jocelyn. *Joseph Conrad: A Critical Biography*. New York: McGraw, 1960.

Bradley, F. H. *Appearance and Reality: A Metaphysical Essay*, 2nd ed. London: Swan, 1906.

Conrad, Joseph. *Heart of Darkness. The Portable Conrad*. Ed. Morton Dauwen Zabel. New York: Viking, 1969.

———. *Last Essays*. Kent Edition. Garden City: Doubleday, 1926.

———. *The Nigger of the "Narcissus."* Kent Edition. Garden City: Doubleday, 1926.

———. *Notes on Life and Letters*. Kent Edition. Garden City: Doubleday, 1926.

———. *'Twixt Land and Sea*. Kent Edition. Garden City: Doubleday, 1926.

———. *Under Western Eyes*. Kent Edition. Garden City: Doubleday, 1926.

———. *Victory*. Kent Edition. Garden City: Doubleday, 1926.

———. *Youth and Two Other Stories*. Kent Edition. Garden City: Doubleday, 1926.

Curle, Richard. *The Last Twelve Years of Joseph Conrad*. Garden City: Doubleday, 1928.

Fleishman, Avrom. *Conrad's Politics: Community and Anarchy in the Fiction of Joseph Conrad*. Baltimore: Johns Hopkins UP, 1967.

Fogel, Aaron. *Coercion to Speak: Conrad's Poetics of Dialogue*. Cambridge: Harvard UP, 1985.

Galsworthy, John. *A Commentary*. London: Grant Richards, 1908.

Garnett, Edward. *Letters from Joseph Conrad 1895–1924.* Indianapolis: Bobbs, 1928.

Gettmann, Royal A., and Bruce Harkness. "Morality and Psychology in 'The Secret Sharer.'" *Conrad's Secret Sharer and the Critics.* Ed. Bruce Harkness. Belmont, CA: Wadsworth, 1962. 125–132.

Guerard, Albert J. *Conrad the Novelist.* Cambridge: Harvard UP, 1958.

Harkness, Bruce. *Conrad's "The Secret Sharer" and the Critics.* Belmont, CA: Wadsworth, 1962.

Hay, Eloise Knapp. *The Political Novels of Joseph Conrad.* Chicago: University of Chicago Press, 1963.

Jean-Aubry, G., ed. *Joseph Conrad: Life and Letters.* 2 vols. Garden City: Doubleday, 1927.

Karl, Frederick. *Joseph Conrad: The Three Lives.* New York: Farrar, 1979.

Karl, Frederick, and Lawrence Davies, eds. *The Collected Letters of Joseph Conrad.* Vol. 1. Cambridge, Eng.: Cambridge UP, 1983.

Lubbock, Basil. "A Hell-Ship Voyage." *Conrad's Secret Sharer and the Critics.* Ed. Bruce Harkness. 39–52. Rpt. of *The Log of the "Cutty Sark."* Glasgow, Scot.: Brown, 1960. 142–192.

Miller, J. Hillis. *Poets of Reality: Six Twentieth Century Writers.* Cambridge: Belknap-Harvard UP, 1965.

Moser, Thomas. *Joseph Conrad: Achievement and Decline.* Cambridge: Harvard UP, 1967.

Murfin, Ross, ed. *Heart of Darkness: A Case Study in Contemporary Criticism.* Boston: Bedford Books, 1989.

Najder, Zdzislaw. *Joseph Conrad: A Chronicle.* New Brunswick: Rutgers UP, 1983.

Rosenfield, Clair. *Paradise of Snakes: An Archetypal Analysis of Conrad's Political Novels.* Chicago: University of Chicago Press, 1967.

Schwarz, Daniel R. *Conrad: "Almayer's Folly" Through "Under Western Eyes."* London: Macmillan; Ithaca: Cornell UP, 1980.

———. *Conrad: The Later Fiction.* London: Macmillan, 1982.

Sherry, Norman. *Conrad's Eastern World.* Cambridge, Eng.: Cambridge UP, 1966.

Watt, Ian. *Conrad in the Nineteenth Century.* Berkeley and Los Angeles: University of California Press, 1979.

Woolf, Virginia. "Mr. Bennett and Mrs. Brown." *The Captain's Deathbed and Other Essays.* New York: Harcourt, 1950. 94–119.

"The Secret Sharer"

On my right hand there were lines of fishing-stakes resembling a mysterious system of half-submerged bamboo fences, incomprehensible in its division of the domain of tropical fishes, and crazy of aspect as if abandoned for ever by some nomad tribe of fishermen now gone to the other end of the ocean; for there was no sign of human habitation as far as the eye could reach. To the left a group of barren islets, suggesting ruins of stone walls, towers, and blockhouses, had its foundations set in a blue sea that itself looked solid, so still and stable did it lie below my feet; even the track of light from the westering sun shone smoothly, without that animated glitter which tells of an imperceptible ripple. And when I turned my head to take a parting glance at the tug which had just left us anchored outside the bar, I saw the straight line of the flat shore joined to the stable sea, edge to edge, with a perfect and unmarked closeness, in one levelled floor half brown, half blue under the enormous dome of the sky. Corresponding in their insignificance to the islets of the sea, two small clumps of trees, one on each side of the only fault in the impeccable joint, marked the mouth of the river Meinam we had just left on the first preparatory stage of our homeward journey; and, far back on the inland level, a larger and loftier mass, the grove surrounding the great Paknam pagoda, was the only thing on which the eye could rest from the vain task of exploring the monotonous sweep of the horizon. Here and there gleams as of a few scattered pieces of silver marked the windings of the great river; and on the nearest of them, just within the bar, the tug steaming right into the land became lost to my sight, hull and funnel and masts, as though the impassive earth had swallowed her up without an effort, without a tremor. My eye followed the light cloud of her smoke, now here, now there, above the plain, according to the devious curves of the stream, but always fainter and farther away, till I lost it at last behind the mitre-shaped hill of the great pagoda. And then I was left alone with my ship, anchored at the head of the Gulf of Siam.

She floated at the starting-point of a long journey, very still in an immense stillness, the shadows of her spars flung far to the eastward by the setting sun. At that moment I was alone on her decks. There was not a sound in her—and around us nothing moved, nothing lived, not a canoe on the water, not a bird in the air, not a cloud in the sky. In this breathless pause at the threshold of a long passage we seemed to be measuring our fitness for a long and arduous enterprise, the appointed task of both our existences to be carried out, far from all human eyes, with only sky and sea for spectators and for judges.

There must have been some glare in the air to interfere with one's sight, because it was only just before the sun left us that my roaming eyes made out beyond the highest ridge of the principal islet of the group something which did away with the solemnity of perfect solitude. The tide of darkness flowed on swiftly; and with tropical suddenness a swarm of stars came out above the shadowy earth, while I lingered yet, my hand resting lightly on my ship's rail as if on the shoulder of a trusted friend. But, with all that multitude of celestial bodies staring down at one, the comfort of quiet communion with her was gone for good. And there were also disturbing sounds by this time—voices, footsteps forward; the steward flitted along the main-deck, a busily ministering spirit; a hand-bell tinkled urgently under the poop-deck. . . .

I found my two officers waiting for me near the supper table, in the lighted cuddy.° We sat down at once, and as I helped the chief mate, I said:

"Are you aware that there is a ship anchored inside the islands? I saw her mastheads above the ridge as the sun went down."

He raised sharply his simple face, overcharged by a terrible growth

cuddy: Cabin.

of whisker, and emitted his usual ejaculations: "Bless my soul, sir! You don't say so!"

My second mate was a round-cheeked, silent young man, grave beyond his years, I thought; but as our eyes happened to meet I detected a slight quiver on his lips. I looked down at once. It was not my part to encourage sneering on board my ship. It must be said, too, that I knew very little of my officers. In consequence of certain events of no particular significance, except to myself, I had been appointed to the command only a fortnight before. Neither did I know much of the hands forward. All these people had been together for eighteen months or so, and my position was that of the only stranger on board. I mention this because it has some bearing on what is to follow. But what I felt most was my being a stranger to the ship; and if all the truth must be told, I was somewhat of a stranger to myself. The youngest man on board (barring the second mate), and untried as yet by a position of the fullest responsibility, I was willing to take the adequacy of the others for granted. They had simply to be equal to their tasks; but I wondered how far I should turn out faithful to that ideal conception of one's own personality every man sets up for himself secretly.

Meantime the chief mate, with an almost visible effect of collaboration on the part of his round eyes and frightful whiskers, was trying to evolve a theory of the anchored ship. His dominant trait was to take all things into earnest consideration. He was of a painstaking turn of mind. As he used to say, he "liked to account to himself" for practically everything that came in his way, down to a miserable scorpion he had found in his cabin a week before. The why and the wherefore of that scorpion—how it got on board and came to select his room rather than the pantry (which was a dark place and more what a scorpion would be partial to), and how on earth it managed to drown itself in the inkwell of his writing-desk—had exercised him infinitely. The ship within the islands was much more easily accounted for; and just as we were about to rise from table he made his pronouncement. She was, he doubted not, a ship from home lately arrived. Probably she drew too much water to cross the bar except at the top of spring tides. Therefore she went into that natural harbour to wait for a few days in preference to remaining in an open roadstead.

"That's so," confirmed the second mate, suddenly, in his slightly hoarse voice. "She draws over twenty feet. She's the Liverpool ship *Sephora* with a cargo of coal. Hundred and twenty-three days from Cardiff."

We looked at him in surprise.

"The tugboat skipper told me when he came on board for your letters, sir," explained the young man. "He expects to take her up the river the day after tomorrow."

After thus overwhelming us with the extent of his information he slipped out of the cabin. The mate observed regretfully that he "could not account for that young fellow's whims." What prevented him telling us all about it at once, he wanted to know.

I detained him as he was making a move. For the last two days the crew had had plenty of hard work, and the night before they had very little sleep. I felt painfully that I—a stranger—was doing something unusual when I directed him to let all hands turn in without setting an anchor-watch. I proposed to keep on deck myself till one o'clock or thereabouts. I would get the second mate to relieve me at that hour.

"He will turn out the cook and the steward at four," I concluded, "and then give you a call. Of course at the slightest sign of any sort of wind we'll have the hands up and make a start at once."

He concealed his astonishment. "Very well, sir." Outside the cuddy he put his head in the second mate's door to inform him of my unheard-of caprice to take a five hours' anchor-watch on myself. I heard the other raise his voice incredulously—"What? The Captain himself?" Then a few more murmurs, a door closed, then another. A few moments later I went on deck.

My strangeness, which had made me sleepless, had prompted that unconventional arrangement, as if I had expected in those solitary hours of the night to get on terms with the ship of which I knew nothing, manned by men of whom I knew very little more. Fast alongside a wharf, littered like any ship in port with a tangle of unrelated things, invaded by unrelated shore people, I had hardly seen her yet properly. Now, as she lay cleared for sea, the stretch of her main-deck seemed to me very fine under the stars. Very fine, very roomy for her size, and very inviting. I descended the poop and paced the waist, my mind picturing to myself the coming passage through the Malay Archipelago, down the Indian Ocean, and up the Atlantic. All its phases were familiar enough to me, every characteristic, all the alternatives which were likely to face me on the high seas—everything! . . . except the novel responsibility of command. But I took heart from the reasonable thought that the ship was like other ships, the men like other men, and that the sea was not likely to keep any special surprises expressly for my discomfiture.

Arrived at that comforting conclusion, I bethought myself a cigar and went below to get it. All was still down there. Everybody at the after end of the ship was sleeping profoundly. I came out again on the quarter-deck, agreeably at ease in my sleeping-suit on that warm breathless night, barefooted, a glowing cigar in my teeth, and, going forward, I was met by the profound silence of the fore end of the ship. Only as I passed the door of the forecastle I heard a deep, quiet, trustful sigh of some sleeper inside. And suddenly I rejoiced in the great security of the sea as compared with the unrest of the land, in my choice of that untempted life presenting no disquieting problems, invested with an elementary moral beauty by the absolute straightforwardness of its appeal and by the singleness of its purpose.

The riding-light in the fore-rigging burned with a clear, untroubled, as if symbolic, flame, confident and bright in the mysterious shades of the night. Passing on my way aft along the other side of the ship, I observed that the rope side-ladder, put over, no doubt, for the master of the tug when he came to fetch away our letters, had not been hauled in as it should have been. I became annoyed at this, for exactitude in small matters is the very soul of discipline. Then I reflected that I had myself peremptorily dismissed my officers from duty, and by my own act had prevented the anchor-watch being formally set and things properly attended to. I asked myself whether it was wise ever to interfere with the established routine of duties even from the kindest of motives. My action might have made me appear eccentric. Goodness only knew how that absurdly whiskered mate would "account" for my conduct, and what the whole ship thought of that informality of their new captain. I was vexed with myself.

Not from compunction certainly, but, as it were mechanically, I proceeded to get the ladder in myself. Now a side-ladder of that sort is a light affair and comes in easily, yet my vigorous tug, which should have brought it flying on board, merely recoiled upon my body in a totally unexpected jerk. What the devil! . . . I was so astounded by the immovableness of that ladder that I remained stock-still, trying to account for it to myself like that imbecile mate of mine. In the end, of course, I put my head over the rail.

The side of the ship made an opaque belt of shadow on the darkling glassy shimmer of the sea. But I saw at once something elongated and pale floating very close to the ladder. Before I could form a guess a faint flash of phosphorescent light, which seemed to issue suddenly from the naked body of a man, flickered in the sleeping water with the elusive, silent play of summer lightning in a night sky. With a gasp I saw revealed to my stare a pair of feet, the long legs, a broad livid back immersed right up to the neck in a greenish cadaverous glow. One hand, awash, clutched the bottom rung of the ladder. He was complete but for the head. A headless corpse! The cigar dropped out of my gaping mouth with a tiny plop and a short hiss quite audible in the absolute stillness of all things under heaven. At that I suppose he raised up his face, a dimly pale oval in the shadow of the ship's side. But even then I could only barely make out down there the shape of his black-haired head. However, it was enough for the horrid, frost-bound sensation which had gripped me about the chest to pass off. The moment of vain exclamations was past, too. I only climbed on the spare spar and leaned over the rail as far as I could, to bring my eyes nearer to that mystery floating alongside.

As he hung by the ladder, like a resting swimmer, the sea-lightning played about his limbs at every stir; and he appeared in it ghastly, silvery, fish-like. He remained as mute as a fish, too. He made no motion to get out of the water, either. It was inconceivable that he should not attempt to come on board, and strangely troubling to suspect that perhaps he did not want to. And my first words were prompted by just that troubled incertitude.

"What's the matter?" I asked in my ordinary tone, speaking down to the face upturned exactly under mine.

"Cramp," it answered, no louder. Then slightly anxious, "I say, no need to call any one."

"I was not going to," I said.

"Are you alone on deck?"

"Yes."

I had somehow the impression that he was on the point of letting go the ladder to swim away beyond my ken—mysterious as he came. But, for the moment, this being appearing as if he had risen from the bottom of the sea (it was certainly the nearest land to the ship) wanted only to know the time. I told him. And he, down there, tentatively:

"I suppose your captain's turned in?"

"I am sure he isn't," I said.

He seemed to struggle with himself, for I heard something like the low, bitter murmur of doubt. "What's the good?" His next words came out with a hesitating effort.

"Look here, my man. Could you call him out quietly?"

I thought the time had come to declare myself.

"*I* am the captain."

I heard a "By Jove!" whispered at the level of the water. The phosphorescence flashed in the swirl of the water all about his limbs, his other hand seized the ladder.

"My name's Leggatt."

The voice was calm and resolute. A good voice. The self-possession of that man had somehow induced a corresponding state in myself. It was very quietly that I remarked:

"You must be a good swimmer."

"Yes. I've been in the water practically since nine o'clock. The question for me now is whether I am to let go this ladder and go on swimming till I sink from exhaustion, or—to come on board here."

I felt this was no mere formula of desperate speech, but a real alternative in the view of a strong soul. I should have gathered from this that he was young; indeed, it is only the young who are ever confronted by such clear issues. But at the time it was pure intuition on my part. A mysterious communication was established already between us two—in the face of that silent, darkened tropical sea. I was young, too; young enough to make no comment. The man in the water began suddenly to climb up the ladder, and I hastened away from the rail to fetch some clothes.

Before entering the cabin I stood still, listening in the lobby at the foot of the stairs. A faint snore came through the closed door of the chief mate's room. The second mate's door was on the hook, but the darkness in there was absolutely soundless. He, too, was young and could sleep like a stone. Remained the steward, but he was not likely to wake up before he was called. I got a sleeping-suit out of my room and, coming back on deck, saw the naked man from the sea sitting on the main-hatch, glimmering white in the darkness, his elbows on his knees and his head in his hands. In a moment he had concealed his damp body in a sleeping-suit of the same grey-stripe pattern as the one I was wearing and followed me like my double on the poop. Together we moved right aft, barefooted, silent.

"What is it?" I asked in a deadened voice, taking the lighted lamp out of the binnacle,° and raising it to his face.

"An ugly business."

He had rather regular features; a good mouth; light eyes under somewhat heavy, dark eyebrows; a smooth, square forehead; no growth on his cheeks; a small, brown moustache, and a well-shaped, round chin. His expression was concentrated, meditative, under the inspecting light of the lamp I held up to his face; such as a man thinking hard in solitude might wear. My sleeping-suit was just right for his size. A well-knit young fellow of twenty-five at most. He caught his lower lip with the edge of white, even teeth.

binnacle: Compass stand.

"Yes," I said, replacing the lamp in the binnacle. The warm, heavy tropical night closed upon his head again.

"There's a ship over there," he murmured.

"Yes, I know. The *Sephora*. Did you know of us?"

"Hadn't the slightest idea. I am the mate of her—" He paused and corrected himself. "I should say I *was*."

"Aha! Something wrong?"

"Yes. Very wrong indeed. I've killed a man."

"What do you mean? Just now?"

"No, on the passage. Weeks ago. Thirty-nine south. When I say a man—"

"Fit of temper," I suggested, confidently.

The shadowy, dark head, like mine, seemed to nod imperceptibly above the ghostly grey of my sleeping-suit. It was, in the night, as though I had been faced by my own reflection in the depths of a sombre and immense mirror.

"A pretty thing to have to own up to for a Conway° boy," murmured my double, distinctly.

"You're a Conway boy?"

"I am," he said, as if startled. Then, slowly . . . "Perhaps you too—"

It was so; but being a couple of years older I had left before he joined. After a quick interchange of dates a silence fell; and I thought suddenly of my absurd mate with his terrific whiskers and the "Bless my soul—you don't say so" type of intellect. My double gave me an inkling of his thoughts by saying: "My father's a parson in Norfolk. Do you see me before a judge and jury on that charge? For myself I can't see the necessity. There are fellows that an angel from heaven— And I am not that. He was one of those creatures that are just simmering all the time with a silly sort of wickedness. Miserable devils that have no business to live at all. He wouldn't do his duty and wouldn't let anybody else do theirs. But what's the good of talking! You know well enough the sort of ill-conditioned snarling cur—"

He appealed to me as if our experiences had been as identical as our clothes. And I knew well enough the pestiferous danger of such a character where there are no means of legal repression. And I knew well enough also that my double there was no homicidal ruffian. I did not think of asking him for details, and he told me the story roughly in brusque, disconnected sentences. I needed no more. I saw it all going on as though I were myself inside that other sleeping-suit.

Conway: Officer training ship in the British merchant marine.

"It happened while we were setting a reefed foresail, at dusk. Reefed foresail! You understand the sort of weather. The only sail we had left to keep the ship running; so you may guess what it had been like for days. Anxious sort of job, that. He gave me some of his cursed insolence at the sheet. I tell you I was overdone with this terrific weather that seemed to have no end to it. Terrific, I tell you—and a deep ship. I believe the fellow himself was half crazed with funk. It was no time for gentlemanly reproof, so I turned round and felled him like an ox. He up and at me. We closed just as an awful sea made for the ship. All hands saw it coming and took to the rigging, but I had him by the throat, and went on shaking him like a rat, the men above us yelling, 'Look out! look out!' Then a crash as if the sky had fallen on my head. They say that for over ten minutes hardly anything was to be seen of the ship—just the three masts and a bit of the forecastle head and of the poop all awash driving along in a smother of foam. It was a miracle that they found us, jammed together behind the forebits. It's clear that I meant business, because I was holding him by the throat still when they picked us up. He was black in the face. It was too much for them. It seems they rushed us aft together, gripped as we were, screaming 'Murder!' like a lot of lunatics, and broke into the cuddy. And the ship running for her life, touch and go all the time, any minute her last in a sea fit to turn your hair grey only a-looking at it. I understand that the skipper, too, started raving like the rest of them. The man had been deprived of sleep for more than a week, and to have this sprung on him at the height of a furious gale nearly drove him out of his mind. I wonder they didn't fling me overboard after getting the carcass of their precious ship-mate out of my fingers. They had rather a job to separate us, I've been told. A sufficiently fierce story to make an old judge and a respectable jury sit up a bit. The first thing I heard when I came to myself was the maddening howling of that endless gale, and on that the voice of the old man. He was hanging on to my bunk, staring into my face out of his sou'wester.

"'Mr. Leggatt, you have killed a man. You can act no longer as chief mate of this ship.'"

His care to subdue his voice made it sound monotonous. He rested a hand on the end of the skylight to steady himself with, and all that time did not stir a limb, so far as I could see. "Nice little tale for a quiet tea-party," he concluded in the same tone.

One of my hands, too, rested on the end of the skylight; neither did I stir a limb, so far as I knew. We stood less than a foot from each other. It occurred to me that if old "Bless my soul—you don't say so" were to put his head up the companion and catch sight of us, he would think he was seeing double, or imagine himself come upon a scene of weird witchcraft; the strange captain having a quiet confabulation by the wheel with his own grey ghost. I became very much concerned to prevent anything of the sort. I heard the other's soothing undertone.

"My father's a parson in Norfolk," it said. Evidently he had forgotten he had told me this important fact before. Truly a nice little tale.

"You had better slip down into my stateroom now," I said, moving off stealthily. My double followed my movements; our bare feet made no sound; I let him in, closed the door with care, and, after giving a call to the second mate, returned on deck for my relief.

"Not much sign of any wind yet," I remarked when he approached.

"No, sir. Not much," he assented, sleepily, in his hoarse voice, with just enough deference, no more, and barely suppressing a yawn.

"Well, that's all you have to look out for. You have got your orders."

"Yes, sir."

I paced a turn or two on the poop and saw him take up his position face forward with his elbow in the ratlines of the mizzen-rigging before I went below. The mate's faint snoring was still going on peacefully. The cuddy lamp was burning over the table on which stood a vase with flowers, a polite attention from the ship's provision merchant—the last flowers we should see for the next three months at the very least. Two bunches of bananas hung from the beam symmetrically, one on each side of the rudder-casing. Everything was as before in the ship—except that two of her captain's sleeping-suits were simultaneously in use, one motionless in the cuddy, the other keeping very still in the captain's stateroom.

It must be explained here that my cabin had the form of the capital letter L the door being within the angle and opening into the short part of the letter. A couch was to the left, the bed-place to the right; my writing-desk and the chronometers' table faced the door. But any one opening it, unless he stepped right inside, had no view of what I call the long (or vertical) part of the letter. It contained some lockers surmounted by a bookcase; and a few clothes, a thick jacket or two, caps, oilskin coat, and such like, hung on hooks. There was at the bottom of that part a door opening into my bath-room, which could be entered also directly from the saloon. But that way was never used.

The mysterious arrival had discovered the advantage of this particular shape. Entering my room, lighted strongly by a big bulkhead lamp swung on gimbals° above my writing-desk, I did not see him anywhere till he stepped out quietly from behind the coats hung in the recessed part.

"I heard somebody moving about, and went in there at once," he whispered.

I, too, spoke under my breath.

"Nobody is likely to come in here without knocking and getting permission."

He nodded. His face was thin and the sunburn faded, as though he had been ill. And no wonder. He had been, I heard presently, kept under arrest in his cabin for nearly seven weeks. But there was nothing sickly in his eyes or in his expression. He was not a bit like me, really; yet, as we stood leaning over my bed-place, whispering side by side, with our dark heads together and our backs to the door, anybody bold enough to open it stealthily would have been treated to the uncanny sight of a double captain busy talking in whispers with his other self.

"But all this doesn't tell me how you came to hang on to our side-ladder," I inquired, in the hardly audible murmurs we used, after he had told me something more of the proceedings on board the *Sephora* once the bad weather was over.

"When we sighted Java Head I had had time to think all those matters out several times over. I had six weeks of doing nothing else, and with only an hour or so every evening for a tramp on the quarter-deck."

He whispered, his arms folded on the side of my bed-place, staring through the open port. And I could imagine perfectly the manner of this thinking out—a stubborn if not a steadfast operation; something of which I should have been perfectly incapable.

"I reckoned it would be dark before we closed with the land," he continued, so low that I had to strain my hearing, near as we were to each other, shoulder touching shoulder almost. "So I asked to speak to the old man. He always seemed very sick when he came to see me —as if he could not look me in the face. You know, that foresail saved the ship. She was too deep to have run long under the bare poles. And it was I that managed to set it for him. Anyway, he came. When I had him in my cabin—he stood by the door looking at me as if I had the halter round my neck already—I asked him right away to leave my cabin door unlocked at night while the ship was going through Sunda Straits. There would be the Java coast within two or three miles, off

gimbals: Device for keeping objects horizontal despite the rocking of a ship.

Angier Point. I wanted nothing more. I've had a prize for swimming my second year in the Conway."

"I can believe it," I breathed out.

"God only knows why they locked me in every night. To see some of their faces you'd have thought they were afraid I'd go about at night strangling people. Am I a murdering brute? Do I look it? By Jove! if I had been he wouldn't have trusted himself like that into my room. You'll say I might have chucked him aside and bolted out, there and then—it was dark already. Well, no. And for the same reason I wouldn't think of trying to smash the door. There would have been a rush to stop me at the noise, and I did not mean to get into a confounded scrimmage. Somebody else might have got killed—for I would not have broken out only to get chucked back, and I did not want any more of that work. He refused, looking more sick than ever. He was afraid of the men, and also of that old second mate of his who had been sailing with him for years—a grey-headed old humbug; and his steward, too, had been with him devil knows how long—seventeen years or more—a dogmatic sort of loafer who hated me like poison, just because I was the chief mate. No chief mate ever made more than one voyage in the *Sephora*, you know. Those two old chaps ran the ship. Devil only knows what the skipper wasn't afraid of (all his nerve went to pieces altogether in that hellish spell of bad weather we had)—of what the law would do to him—of his wife, perhaps. Oh, yes! she's on board. Though I don't think she would have meddled. She would have been only too glad to have me out of the ship in any way. The 'brand of Cain'° business, don't you see. That's all right. I was ready enough to go off wandering on the face of the earth—and that was price enough to pay for an Abel of that sort. Anyhow, he wouldn't listen to me. 'This thing must take its course. I represent the law here.' He was shaking like a leaf. 'So you won't?' 'No!' 'Then I hope you will be able to sleep on that,' I said, and turned my back on him. 'I wonder that *you* can,' cries he, and locks the door.

"Well, after that, I couldn't. Not very well. That was three weeks ago. We have had a slow passage through the Java Sea; drifted about Carimata for ten days. When we anchored here they thought, I suppose, it was all right. The nearest land (and that's five miles) is the ship's destination; the consul would soon set about catching me; and there would have been no object in bolting to these islets there. I

---

brand of Cain: In the Bible, God marked Cain, who murdered his brother Abel, to prevent anyone from killing him (Gen. 4.15).

don't suppose there's a drop of water on them. I don't know how it was, but to-night that steward, after bringing me my supper, went out to let me eat it, and left the door unlocked. And I ate it—all there was, too. After I had finished I strolled out on the quarter-deck. I don't know that I meant to do anything. A breath of fresh air was all I wanted, I believe. Then a sudden temptation came over me. I kicked off my slippers and was in the water before I had made up my mind fairly. Somebody heard the splash and they raised an awful hullabaloo. 'He's gone! Lower the boats! He's committed suicide! No, he's swimming.' Certainly I was swimming. It's not so easy for a swimmer like me to commit suicide by drowning. I landed on the nearest islet before the boat left the ship's side. I heard them pulling about in the dark, hailing; and so on, but after a bit they gave up. Everything quieted down and the anchorage became as still as death. I sat down on a stone and began to think. I felt certain they would start searching for me at daylight. There was no place to hide on those stony things— and if there had been, what would have been the good? But now I was clear of that ship, I was not going back. So after a while I took off all my clothes, tied them up in a bundle with a stone inside, and dropped them in the deep water on the outer side of that islet. That was suicide enough for me. Let them think what they liked, but I didn't mean to drown myself. I meant to swim till I sank—but that's not the same thing. I struck out for another of these little islands, and it was from that one that I first saw your riding-light. Something to swim for. I went on easily, and on the way I came upon a flat rock a foot or two above water. In the daytime, I dare say, you might make it out with a glass from your poop. I scrambled up on it and rested myself for a bit. Then I made another start. That last spell must have been over a mile."

His whisper was getting fainter and fainter, and all the time he stared straight out through the port-hole, in which there was not even a star to be seen. I had not interrupted him. There was something that made comment impossible in his narrative, or perhaps in himself; a sort of feeling, a quality, which I can't find a name for. And when he ceased, all I found was a futile whisper: "So you swam for our light?"

"Yes—straight for it. It was something to swim for. I couldn't see any stars low down because the coast was in the way, and I couldn't see the land, either. The water was like glass. One might have been swimming in a confounded thousand-feet deep cistern with no place for scrambling out anywhere; but what I didn't like was the notion of swimming round and round like a crazed bullock before I gave out;

and as I didn't mean to go back . . . No. Do you see me being hauled back, stark naked, off one of these little islands by the scruff of the neck and fighting like a wild beast? Somebody would have got killed for certain, and I did not want any of that. So I went on. Then your ladder—"

"Why didn't you hail the ship?" I asked, a little louder.

He touched my shoulder lightly. Lazy footsteps came right over our heads and stopped. The second mate had crossed from the other side of the poop and might have been hanging over the rail, for all we knew.

"He couldn't hear us talking—could he?" My double breathed into my very ear, anxiously.

His anxiety was an answer, a sufficient answer, to the question I had put to him. An answer containing all the difficulty of that situation. I closed the port-hole quietly, to make sure. A louder word might have been overheard.

"Who's that?" he whispered then.

"My second mate. But I don't know much more of the fellow than you do."

And I told him a little about myself. I had been appointed to take charge while I least expected anything of the sort, not quite a fortnight ago. I didn't know either the ship or the people. Hadn't had the time in port to look about me or size anybody up. And as to the crew, all they knew was that I was appointed to take the ship home. For the rest, I was almost as much of a stranger on board as himself, I said. And at the moment I felt it most acutely. I felt that it would take very little to make me a suspect person in the eyes of the ship's company.

He had turned about meantime; and we, the two strangers in the ship, faced each other in identical attitudes.

"Your ladder—" he murmured, after a silence. "Who'd have thought of finding a ladder hanging over at night in a ship anchored out here! I felt just then a very unpleasant faintness. After the life I've been leading for nine weeks, anybody would have got out of condition. I wasn't capable of swimming round as far as your rudder-chains. And, lo and behold! there was a ladder to get hold of. After I gripped it I said to myself, 'What's the good?' When I saw a man's head looking over I thought I would swim away presently and leave him shouting—in whatever language it was. I didn't mind being looked at. I—I liked it. And then you speaking to me so quietly—as if you had expected me—made me hold on a little longer. It had been a confounded lonely time—I don't mean while swimming. I was glad to talk a little to somebody that didn't belong to the *Sephora*. As to asking for the captain, that was a mere impulse. It could have been no use, with all the ship knowing about me and the other people pretty certain to be round here in the morning. I don't know—I wanted to be seen, to talk with somebody, before I went on. I don't know what I would have said. . . . 'Fine night, isn't it?' or something of the sort."

"Do you think they will be round here presently?" I asked with some incredulity.

"Quite likely," he said, faintly.

He looked extremely haggard all of a sudden. His head rolled on his shoulders.

"H'm. We shall see then. Meantime get into that bed," I whispered. "Want help? There."

It was a rather high bed-place with a set of drawers underneath. This amazing swimmer really needed the lift I gave him by seizing his leg. He tumbled in, rolled over on his back, and flung one arm across his eyes. And then, with his face nearly hidden, he must have looked exactly as I used to look in that bed. I gazed upon my other self for a while before drawing across carefully the two green serge curtains which ran on a brass rod. I thought for a moment of pinning them together for greater safety, but I sat down on the couch, and once there I felt unwilling to rise and hunt for a pin. I would do it in a moment. I was extremely tired, in a peculiarly intimate way, by the strain of stealthiness, by the effort of whispering and the general secrecy of this excitement. It was three o'clock by now and I had been on my feet since nine, but I was not sleepy; I could not have gone to sleep. I sat there, fagged out, looking at the curtains, trying to clear my mind of the confused sensation of being in two places at once, and greatly bothered by an exasperating knocking in my head. It was a relief to discover suddenly that it was not in my head at all, but on the outside of the door. Before I could collect myself the words "Come in" were out of my mouth, and the steward entered with a tray, bringing in my morning coffee. I had slept, after all, and I was so frightened that I shouted, "This way! I am here, steward," as though he had been miles away. He put down the tray on the table next the couch and only then said, very quietly, "I can see you are here, sir." I felt him give me a keen look, but I dared not meet his eyes just then. He must have wondered why I had drawn the curtains of my bed before going to sleep on the couch. He went out, hooking the door open as usual.

I heard the crew washing decks above me. I knew I would have been told at once if there had been any wind. Calm, I thought, and I was doubly vexed. Indeed, I felt dual more than ever. The steward reappeared suddenly in the doorway. I jumped up from the couch so quickly that he gave a start.

"What do you want here?"

"Close your port, sir—they are washing decks."

"It is closed," I said, reddening.

"Very well, sir." But he did not move from the doorway and returned my stare in an extraordinary, equivocal manner for a time. Then his eyes wavered, all his expression changed, and in a voice unusually gentle, almost coaxingly:

"May I come in to take the empty cup away, sir?"

"Of course!" I turned my back on him while he popped in and out. Then I unhooked and closed the door and even pushed the bolt. This sort of thing could not go on very long. The cabin was as hot as an oven, too. I took a peep at my double, and discovered that he had not moved, his arm was still over his eyes; but his chest heaved; his hair was wet; his chin glistened with perspiration. I reached over him and opened the port.

"I must show myself on deck," I reflected.

Of course, theoretically, I could do what I liked, with no one to say nay to me within the whole circle of the horizon; but to lock my cabin door and take the key away I did not dare. Directly I put my head out of the companion I saw the group of my two officers, the second mate barefooted, the chief mate in long india-rubber boots, near the break of the poop, and the steward half-way down the poop-ladder talking to them eagerly. He happened to catch sight of me and dived, the second ran down on the main-deck shouting some order or other, and the chief mate came to meet me, touching his cap.

There was a sort of curiosity in his eye that I did not like. I don't know whether the steward had told them that I was "queer" only, or downright drunk, but I know the man meant to have a good look at me. I watched him coming with a smile which, as he got into point-blank range, took effect and froze his very whiskers. I did not give him time to open his lips.

"Square the yards by lifts and braces before the hands go to breakfast."

It was the first particular order I had given on board that ship; and I stayed on deck to see it executed, too. I had felt the need of asserting myself without loss of time. That sneering young cub got taken down a peg or two on that occasion, and I also seized the opportunity of having a good look at the face of every foremast man as they filed past me to go to the after braces. At breakfast time, eating nothing myself, I presided with such frigid dignity that the two mates were only too glad to escape from the cabin as soon as decency permitted; and all the time the dual working of my mind distracted me almost to the point of insanity. I was constantly watching myself, my secret self, as dependent on my actions as my own personality, sleeping in that bed, behind that door which faced me as I sat at the head of the table. It was very much like being mad, only it was worse because one was aware of it.

I had to shake him for a solid minute, but when at last he opened his eyes it was in the full possession of his senses, with an inquiring look.

"All's well so far," I whispered. "Now you must vanish into the bath-room."

He did so, as noiseless as a ghost, and then I rang for the steward, and facing him boldly, directed him to tidy up my stateroom while I was having my bath—"and be quick about it." As my tone admitted of no excuses, he said, "Yes, sir," and ran off to fetch his dust-pan and brushes. I took a bath and did most of my dressing, splashing, and whistling softly for the steward's edification, while the secret sharer of my life stood drawn up bolt upright in that little space, his face looking very sunken in daylight, his eyelids lowered under the stern, dark line of his eyebrows drawn together by a slight frown.

When I left him there to go back to my room the steward was finishing dusting. I sent for the mate and engaged him in some insignificant conversation. It was, as it were, trifling with the terrific character of his whiskers; but my object was to give him an opportunity for a good look at my cabin. And then I could at last shut, with a clear conscience, the door of my stateroom and get my double back into the recessed part. There was nothing else for it. He had to sit still on a small folding stool, half smothered by the heavy coats hanging there. We listened to the steward going into the bath-room out of the saloon, filling the water-bottles there, scrubbing the bath, setting things to rights, whisk, bang, clatter—out again into the saloon—turn the key —click. Such was my scheme for keeping my second self invisible. Nothing better could be contrived under the circumstances. And there we sat; I at my writing-desk ready to appear busy with some papers, he behind me out of sight of the door. It would not have been prudent to talk in daytime; and I could not have stood the excitement of that queer sense of whispering to myself. Now and then, glancing over my shoulder, I saw him far back there, sitting rigidly on the low stool, his bare feet close together, his arms folded, his head hanging on his breast—and perfectly still. Anybody would have taken him for me.

I was fascinated by it myself. Every moment I had to glance over my shoulder. I was looking at him when a voice outside the door said:

"Beg pardon, sir."

"Well!" . . . I kept my eyes on him, and so when the voice outside the door announced, "There's a ship's boat coming our way, sir," I saw him give a start—the first movement he had made for hours. But he did not raise his bowed head.

"All right. Get the ladder over."

I hesitated. Should I whisper something to him? But what? His immobility seemed to have been never disturbed. What could I tell him he did not know already? . . . Finally I went on deck.

II

The skipper of the *Sephora* had a thin red whisker all round his face, and the sort of complexion that goes with hair of that colour; also the particular, rather smeary shade of blue in the eyes. He was not exactly a showy figure; his shoulders were high, his stature but middling—one leg slightly more bandy than the other. He shook hands, looking vaguely around. A spiritless tenacity was his main characteristic, I judged. I behaved with a politeness which seemed to disconcert him. Perhaps he was shy. He mumbled to me as if he were ashamed of what he was saying; gave his name (it was something like Archbold—but at this distance of years I hardly am sure), his ship's name, and a few other particulars of that sort, in the manner of a criminal making a reluctant and doleful confession. He had had terrible weather on the passage out—terrible—terrible—wife aboard, too.

By this time we were seated in the cabin and the steward brought in a tray with a bottle and glasses. "Thanks! No." Never took liquor. Would have some water, though. He drank two tumblerfuls. Terrible thirsty work. Ever since daylight had been exploring the islands round his ship.

"What was that for—fun?" I asked, with an appearance of polite interest.

"No!" He sighed. "Painful duty."

As he persisted in his mumbling and I wanted my double to hear every word, I hit upon the notion of informing him that I regretted to say I was hard of hearing.

"Such a young man, too!" he nodded, keeping his smeary blue, unintelligent eyes fastened upon me. "What was the cause of it—some disease?" he inquired, without the least sympathy and as if he thought that, if so, I'd got no more than I deserved.

"Yes; disease," I admitted in a cheerful tone which seemed to shock him. But my point was gained, because he had to raise his voice to give me his tale. It is not worth while to record that version. It was just over two months since all this had happened, and he had thought so much about it that he seemed completely muddled as to its bearings, but still immensely impressed.

"What would you think of such a thing happening on board your own ship? I've had the *Sephora* for these fifteen years. I am a well-known shipmaster."

He was densely distressed—and perhaps I should have sympathised with him if I had been able to detach my mental vision from the unsuspected sharer of my cabin as though he were my second self. There he was on the other side of the bulkhead, four or five feet from us, no more, as we sat in the saloon. I looked politely at Captain Archbold (if that was his name), but it was the other I saw, in a grey sleeping-suit, seated on a low stool, his bare feet close together, his arms folded, and every word said between us falling into the ears of his dark head bowed on his chest.

"I have been at sea now, man and boy, for seven-and-thirty years, and I've never heard of such a thing happening in an English ship. And that it should be my ship. Wife on board, too."

I was hardly listening to him.

"Don't you think," I said, "that the heavy sea which, you told me, came aboard just then might have killed the man? I have seen the sheer weight of a sea kill a man very neatly, by simply breaking his neck."

"Good God!" he uttered, impressively, fixing his smeary blue eyes on me. "The sea! No man killed by the sea ever looked like that." He seemed positively scandalised at my suggestion. And as I gazed at him, certainly not prepared for anything original on his part, he advanced his head close to mine and thrust his tongue out at me so suddenly that I couldn't help starting back.

After scoring over my calmness in this graphic way he nodded wisely. If I had seen the sight, he assured me, I would never forget it as long as I lived. The weather was too bad to give the corpse a proper sea burial. So next day at dawn they took it up on the poop, covering its face with a bit of bunting; he read a short prayer, and then, just as it was, in its oilskins and long boots, they launched it amongst those mountainous seas that seemed ready every moment to swallow up the ship herself and the terrified lives on board of her.

"That reefed foresail saved you," I threw in.

"Under God—it did," he exclaimed fervently. "It was by a special mercy, I firmly believe, that it stood some of those hurricane squalls."

"It was the setting of that sail which—" I began.

"God's own hand in it," he interrupted me. "Nothing less could have done it. I don't mind telling you that I hardly dared give the order. It seemed impossible that we could touch anything without losing it, and then our last hope would have been gone."

The terror of that gale was on him yet. I let him go on for a bit, then said, casually—as if returning to a minor subject:

"You were very anxious to give up your mate to the shore people, I believe?"

He was. To the law. His obscure tenacity on that point had in it something incomprehensible and a little awful; something, as it were, mystical, quite apart from his anxiety that he should not be suspected of "countenancing any doings of that sort." Seven-and-thirty virtuous years at sea, of which over twenty of immaculate command, and the last fifteen in the *Sephora,* seemed to have laid him under some pitiless obligation.

"And you know," he went on, groping shamefacedly amongst his feelings, "I did not engage that young fellow. His people had some interest with my owners. I was in a way forced to take him on. He looked very smart, very gentlemanly, and all that. But do you know—I never liked him, somehow. I am a plain man. You see, he wasn't exactly the sort for the chief mate of a ship like the *Sephora.*"

I had become so connected in thoughts and impressions with the secret sharer of my cabin that I felt as if I, personally, were being given to understand that I, too, was not the sort that would have done for the chief mate of a ship like the *Sephora.* I had no doubt of it in my mind.

"Not at all the style of man. You understand," he insisted, superfluously, looking hard at me.

I smiled urbanely. He seemed at a loss for a while.

"I suppose I must report a suicide."

"Beg pardon?"

"Sui-cide! That's what I'll have to write to my owners directly I get in."

"Unless you manage to recover him before to-morrow," I assented, dispassionately. . . . "I mean, alive."

He mumbled something which I really did not catch, and I turned my ear to him in a puzzled manner. He fairly bawled:

"The land—I say, the mainland is at least seven miles off my anchorage."

"About that."

My lack of excitement, of curiosity, of surprise, of any sort of pronounced interest, began to arouse his distrust. But except for the felicitous pretence of deafness I had not tried to pretend anything. I had felt utterly incapable of playing the part of ignorance properly, and therefore was afraid to try. It is also certain that he had brought some ready-made suspicions with him, and that he viewed my politeness as a strange and unnatural phenomenon. And yet how else could I have received him? Not heartily! That was impossible for psychological reasons, which I need not state here. My only object was to keep off his inquiries. Surlily? Yes, but surliness might have provoked a point-blank question. From its novelty to him and from its nature, punctilious courtesy was the manner best calculated to restrain the man. But there was the danger of his breaking through my defence bluntly. I could not, I think, have met him by a direct lie, also for psychological (not moral) reasons. If he had only known how afraid I was of his putting my feeling of identity with the other to the test! But, strangely enough—(I thought of it only afterwards)—I believe that he was not a little disconcerted by the reverse side of that weird situation, by something in me that reminded him of the man he was seeking—suggested a mysterious similitude to the young fellow he had distrusted and disliked from the first.

However that might have been, the silence was not very prolonged. He took another oblique step.

"I reckon I had no more than a two-mile pull to your ship. Not a bit more."

"And quite enough, too, in this awful heat," I said.

Another pause full of mistrust followed. Necessity, they say, is mother of invention, but fear, too, is not barren of ingenious suggestions. And I was afraid he would ask me point-blank for news of my other self.

"Nice little saloon, isn't it?" I remarked, as if noticing for the first time the way his eyes roamed from one closed door to the other. "And very well fitted out, too. Here, for instance," I continued, reaching over the back of my seat negligently and flinging the door open, "is my bath-room."

He made an eager movement, but hardly gave it a glance. I got up, shut the door of the bath-room, and invited him to have a look round, as if I were very proud of my accommodation. He had to rise and be shown round, but he went through the business without any raptures whatever.

"And now we'll have a look at my stateroom," I declared, in a voice as loud as I dared to make it, crossing the cabin to the starboard side with purposely heavy steps.

He followed me in and gazed around. My intelligent double had vanished. I played my part.

"Very convenient—isn't it?"

"Very nice. Very comf . . ." He didn't finish and went out brusquely as if to escape from some unrighteous wiles of mine. But it was not to be. I had been too frightened not to feel vengeful; I felt I had him on the run, and I meant to keep him on the run. My polite insistence must have had something menacing in it, because he gave in suddenly. And I did not let him off a single item; mate's room, pantry, store-rooms, the very sail-locker which was also under the poop—he had to look into them all. When at last I showed him out on the quarter-deck he drew a long, spiritless sigh, and mumbled dismally that he must really be going back to his ship now. I desired my mate, who had joined us, to see to the captain's boat.

The man of whiskers gave a blast on the whistle which he used to wear hanging round his neck, and yelled, "*Sephora*'s away!" My double down there in my cabin must have heard, and certainly could not feel more relieved than I. Four fellows came running out from somewhere forward and went over the side, while my own men, appearing on deck too, lined the rail. I escorted my visitor to the gangway ceremoniously, and nearly overdid it. He was a tenacious beast. On the very ladder he lingered, and in that unique, guiltily conscientious manner of sticking to the point:

"I say . . . you . . . you don't think that—"

I covered his voice loudly:

"Certainly not. . . . I am delighted. Good-bye."

I had an idea of what he meant to say, and just saved myself by the privilege of defective hearing. He was too shaken generally to insist, but my mate, close witness of that parting, looked mystified and his face took on a thoughtful cast. As I did not want to appear as if I wished to avoid all communication with my officers, he had the opportunity to address me.

"Seems a very nice man. His boat's crew told our chaps a very extraordinary story, if what I am told by the steward is true. I suppose you had it from the captain, sir?"

"Yes. I had a story from the captain."

"A very horrible affair—isn't it, sir?"

"It is."

"Beats all these tales we hear about murders in Yankee ships."

"I don't think it beats them. I don't think it resembles them in the least."

"Bless my soul—you don't say so! But of course I've no acquaintance whatever with American ships, not I, so I couldn't go against your knowledge. It's horrible enough for me. . . . But the queerest part is that those fellows seemed to have some idea the man was hidden aboard here. They had really. Did you ever hear of such a thing?"

"Preposterous—isn't it?"

We were walking to and fro athwart the quarter-deck. No one of the crew forward could be seen (the day was Sunday), and the mate pursued:

"There was some little dispute about it. Our chaps took offence. 'As if we would harbour a thing like that,' they said. 'Wouldn't you like to look for him in our coal-hole?' Quite a tiff. But they made it up in the end. I suppose he did drown himself. Don't you, sir?"

"I don't suppose anything."

"You have no doubt in the matter, sir?"

"None whatever."

I left him suddenly. I felt I was producing a bad impression, but with my double down there it was most trying to be on deck. And it was almost as trying to be below. Altogether a nerve-trying situation. But on the whole I felt less torn in two when I was with him. There was no one in the whole ship whom I dared take into my confidence. Since the hands had got to know his story, it would have been impossible to pass him off for any one else, and an accidental discovery was to be dreaded now more than ever. . . .

The steward being engaged in laying the table for dinner, we could talk only with our eyes when I first went down. Later in the afternoon we had a cautious try at whispering. The Sunday quietness of the ship was against us; the stillness of air and water around her was against us; the elements, the men were against us—everything was against us in our secret partnership; time itself—for this could not go on forever. The very trust in Providence was, I suppose, denied to his guilt. Shall I confess that this thought cast me down very much? And as to the chapter of accidents which counts for so much in the book of success, I could only hope that it was closed. For what favourable accident could be expected?

"Did you hear everything?" were my first words as soon as we took up our position side by side, leaning over my bed-place.

He had. And the proof of it was his earnest whisper, "The man told you he hardly dared to give the order."

I understood the reference to be to that saving foresail.

"Yes. He was afraid of it being lost in the setting."

"I assure you he never gave the order. He may think he did, but he never gave it. He stood there with me on the break of the poop after the maintopsail blew away, and whimpered about our last hope—positively whimpered about it and nothing else—and the night coming on! To hear one's skipper go on like that in such weather was enough to drive any fellow out of his mind. It worked me up into a sort of desperation. I just took it into my own hands and went away from him, boiling, and— But what's the use telling you? *You* know! . . . Do you think that if I had not been pretty fierce with them I should have got the men to do anything? Not it! The bo's'n perhaps? Perhaps! It wasn't a heavy sea—it was a sea gone mad! I suppose the end of the world will be something like that; and a man may have the heart to see it coming once and be done with it—but to have to face it day after day—I don't blame anybody. I was precious little better than the rest. Only— I was an officer of that old coal-wagon, anyhow—"

"I quite understand," I conveyed that sincere assurance into his ear. He was out of breath with whispering; I could hear him pant slightly. It was all very simple. The same strung-up force which had given twenty-four men a chance, at least, for their lives, had, in a sort of recoil, crushed an unworthy mutinous existence.

But I had no leisure to weigh the merits of the matter—footsteps in the saloon, a heavy knock. "There's enough wind to get under way with, sir." Here was the call of a new claim upon my thoughts and even upon my feelings.

"Turn the hands up," I cried through the door. "I'll be on deck directly."

I was going out to make the acquaintance of my ship. Before I left the cabin our eyes met—the eyes of the only two strangers on board. I pointed to the recessed part where the little camp-stool awaited him and laid my finger on my lips. He made a gesture—somewhat vague— a little mysterious, accompanied by a faint smile, as if of regret.

This is not the place to enlarge upon the sensations of a man who feels for the first time a ship move under his feet to his own independent word. In my case they were not unalloyed. I was not wholly alone with my command; for there was that stranger in my cabin. Or rather,

I was not completely and wholly with her. Part of me was absent. That mental feeling of being in two places at once affected me physically as if the mood of secrecy had penetrated my very soul. Before an hour had elapsed since the ship had begun to move, having occasion to ask the mate (he stood by my side) to take a compass bearing of the Pagoda, I caught myself reaching up to his ear in whispers. I say I caught myself, but enough had escaped to startle the man. I can't describe it otherwise than by saying that he shied. A grave, preoccupied manner, as though he were in possession of some perplexing intelligence, did not leave him henceforth. A little later I moved away from the rail to look at the compass with such a stealthy gait that the helmsman noticed it—and I could not help noticing the unusual roundness of his eyes. These are trifling instances, though it's to no commander's advantage to be suspected of ludicrous eccentricities. But I was also more seriously affected. There are to a seaman certain words, gestures, that should in given conditions come as naturally, as instinctively as the winking of a menaced eye. A certain order should spring on to his lips without thinking; a certain sign should get itself made, so to speak, without reflection. But all unconscious alertness had abandoned me. I had to make an effort of will to recall myself back (from the cabin) to the conditions of the moment. I felt that I was appearing an irresolute commander to those people who were watching me more or less critically.

And, besides, there were the scares. On the second day out, for instance, coming off the deck in the afternoon (I had straw slippers on my bare feet) I stopped at the open pantry door and spoke to the steward. He was doing something there with his back to me. At the sound of my voice he nearly jumped out of his skin, as the saying is, and incidentally broke a cup.

"What on earth's the matter with you?" I asked, astonished.

He was extremely confused. "Beg your pardon, sir. I made sure you were in your cabin."

"You see I wasn't."

"No, sir. I could have sworn I had heard you moving in there not a moment ago. It's most extraordinary . . . very sorry, sir."

I passed on with an inward shudder. I was so identified with my secret double that I did not even mention the fact in those scanty, fearful whispers we exchanged. I suppose he had made some slight noise of some kind or other. It would have been miraculous if he hadn't at one time or another. And yet, haggard as he appeared, he looked always perfectly self-controlled, more than calm—almost invulnerable. On my suggestion he remained almost entirely in the bath-room, which, upon the whole, was the safest place. There could be really no shadow of an excuse for any one ever wanting to go in there, once the steward had done with it. It was a very tiny place. Sometimes he reclined on the floor, his legs bent, his head sustained on one elbow. At others I would find him on the camp-stool, sitting in his grey sleeping-suit and with his cropped dark hair like a patient, unmoved convict. At night I would smuggle him into my bed-place, and we would whisper together, with the regular footfalls of the officer of the watch passing and repassing over our heads. It was an infinitely miserable time. It was lucky that some tins of fine preserves were stowed in a locker in my stateroom; hard bread I could always get hold of; and so he lived on stewed chicken, paté de foie gras, asparagus, cooked oysters, sardines—on all sorts of abominable sham delicacies out of tins. My early morning coffee he always drank; and it was all I dared do for him in that respect.

Every day there was the horrible manœuvring to go through so that my room and then the bath-room should be done in the usual way. I came to hate the sight of the steward, to abhor the voice of that harmless man. I felt that it was he who would bring on the disaster of discovery. It hung like a sword over our heads.

The fourth day out, I think (we were then working down the east side of the Gulf of Siam, tack for tack, in light winds and smooth water)—the fourth day, I say, of this miserable juggling with the unavoidable, as we sat at our evening meal, that man, whose slightest movement I dreaded, after putting down the dishes ran up on deck busily. This could not be dangerous. Presently he came down again; and then it appeared that he had remembered a coat of mine which I had thrown over a rail to dry after having been wetted in a shower which had passed over the ship in the afternoon. Sitting stolidly at the head of the table I became terrified at the sight of the garment on his arm. Of course he made for my door. There was no time to lose.

"Steward," I thundered. My nerves were so shaken that I could not govern my voice and conceal my agitation. This was the sort of thing that made my terrifically whiskered mate tap his forehead with his forefinger. I had detected him using that gesture while talking on the deck with a confidential air to the carpenter. It was too far to hear a word, but I had no doubt that this pantomime could only refer to the strange new captain.

"Yes, sir," the pale-faced steward turned resignedly to me. It was this maddening course of being shouted at, checked without rhyme or reason, arbitrarily chased out of my cabin, suddenly called into it, sent flying out of his pantry on incomprehensible errands, that accounted for the growing wretchedness of his expression.

"Where are you going with that coat?"

"To your room, sir."

"Is there another shower coming?"

"I'm sure I don't know, sir. Shall I go up again and see, sir?"

"No! never mind."

My object was attained, as of course my other self in there would have heard everything that passed. During this interlude my two officers never raised their eyes off their respective plates; but the lip of that confounded cub, the second mate, quivered visibly.

I expected the steward to hook my coat on and come out at once. He was very slow about it; but I dominated my nervousness sufficiently not to shout after him. Suddenly I became aware (it could be heard plainly enough) that the fellow for some reason or other was opening the door of the bath-room. It was the end. The place was literally not big enough to swing a cat in. My voice died in my throat and I went stony all over. I expected to hear a yell of surprise and terror, and made a movement, but had not the strength to get on my legs. Everything remained still. Had my second self taken the poor wretch by the throat? I don't know what I could have done next moment if I had not seen the steward come out of my room, close the door, and then stand quietly by the sideboard.

"Saved," I thought. "But, no! Lost! Gone! He was gone!"

I laid my knife and fork down and leaned back in my chair. My head swam. After a while, when sufficiently recovered to speak in a steady voice, I instructed my mate to put the ship round at eight o'clock himself.

"I won't come on deck," I went on. "I think I'll turn in, and unless the wind shifts I don't want to be disturbed before midnight. I feel a bit seedy."

"You did look middling bad a little while ago," the chief mate remarked without showing any great concern.

They both went out, and I stared at the steward clearing the table. There was nothing to be read on that wretched man's face. But why did he avoid my eyes I asked myself. Then I thought I should like to hear the sound of his voice.

"Steward!"

"Sir!" Startled as usual.

"Where did you hang up that coat?"

"In the bath-room, sir." The usual anxious tone. "It's not quite dry yet, sir."

For some time longer I sat in the cuddy. Had my double vanished as he had come? But of his coming there was an explanation, whereas his disappearance would be inexplicable. . . . I went slowly into my dark room, shut the door, lighted the lamp, and for a time dared not turn round. When at last I did I saw him standing bolt-upright in the narrow recessed part. It would not be true to say I had a shock, but an irresistible doubt of his bodily existence flitted through my mind. Can it be, I asked myself, that he is not visible to other eyes than mine? It was like being haunted. Motionless, with a grave face, he raised his hands slightly at me in a gesture which meant clearly, "Heavens! what a narrow escape!" Narrow indeed. I think I had come creeping quietly as near insanity as any man who has not actually gone over the border. That gesture restrained me, so to speak.

The mate with the terrific whiskers was now putting the ship on the other tack. In the moment of profound silence which follows upon the hands going to their stations I heard on the poop his raised voice: "Hard alee!" and the distant shout of the order repeated on the main-deck. The sails, in that light breeze, made but a faint fluttering noise. It ceased. The ship was coming round slowly; I held my breath in the renewed stillness of expectation; one wouldn't have thought that there was a single living soul on her decks. A sudden brisk shout, "Mainsail haul!" broke the spell, and in the noisy cries and rush overhead of the men running away with the main-brace we two, down in my cabin, came together in our usual position by the bed-place.

He did not wait for my question. "I heard him fumbling here and just managed to squat myself down in the bath," he whispered to me. "The fellow only opened the door and put his arm in to hang the coat up. All the same — "

"I never thought of that," I whispered back, even more appalled than before at the closeness of the shave, and marvelling at that something unyielding in his character which was carrying him through so finely. There was no agitation in his whisper. Whoever was being driven distracted, it was not he. He was sane. And the proof of his sanity was continued when he took up the whispering again.

"It would never do for me to come to life again."

It was something that a ghost might have said. But what he was alluding to was his old captain's reluctant admission of the theory of suicide. It would obviously serve his turn — if I had understood at all the view which seemed to govern the unalterable purpose of his action.

"You must maroon me as soon as ever you can get amongst these islands off the Cambodge° shore," he went on.

"Maroon you! We are not living in a boy's adventure tale," I protested. His scornful whispering took me up.

"We aren't indeed! There's nothing of a boy's tale in this. But there's nothing else for it. I want no more. You don't suppose I am afraid of what can be done to me? Prison or gallows or whatever they may please. But you don't see me coming back to explain such things to an old fellow in a wig and twelve respectable tradesmen, do you? What can they know whether I am guilty or not—or of *what* I am guilty, either? That's my affair. What does the Bible say? 'Driven off the face of the earth.'° Very well. I am off the face of the earth now. As I came at night so I shall go."

"Impossible!" I murmured. "You can't."

"Can't? . . . Not naked like a soul on the Day of Judgment. I shall freeze on to this sleeping-suit. The Last Day is not yet—and . . . you have understood thoroughly. Didn't you?"

I felt suddenly ashamed of myself. I may say truly that I understood—and my hesitation in letting that man swim away from my ship's side had been a mere sham sentiment, a sort of cowardice.

"It can't be done now till next night," I breathed out. "The ship is on the off-shore tack and the wind may fail us."

"As long as I know that you understand," he whispered. "But of course you do. It's a great satisfaction to have got somebody to understand. You seem to have been there on purpose." And in the same whisper, as if we two whenever we talked had to say things to each other which were not fit for the world to hear, he added, "It's very wonderful."

We remained side by side talking in our secret way—but sometimes silent or just exchanging a whispered word or two at long intervals. And as usual he stared through the port. A breath of wind came now and again into our faces. The ship might have been moored in dock, so gently and on an even keel she slipped through the water, that did not murmur even at our passage, shadowy and silent like a phantom sea.

At midnight I went on deck, and to my mate's great surprise put the ship round on the other tack. His terrible whiskers flitted round me in silent criticism. I certainly should not have done it if it had been only a question of getting out of that sleepy gulf as quickly as possible.

Cambodge: Cambodian.   **Driven off the face of the earth:** Reference to Cain's
words (Gen. 4.13–14).

I believe he told the second mate, who relieved him, that it was a great want of judgment. The other only yawned. That intolerable cub shuffled about so sleepily and lolled against the rails in such a slack, improper fashion that I came down on him sharply.

"Aren't you properly awake yet?"

"Yes, sir! I am awake."

"Well, then, be good enough to hold yourself as if you were. And keep a look-out. If there's any current we'll be closing with some islands before daylight."

The east side of the gulf is fringed with islands, some solitary, others in groups. On the blue background of the high coast they seem to float on silvery patches of calm water, arid and grey, or dark green and rounded like clumps of evergreen bushes, with the larger ones, a mile or two long, showing the outlines of ridges, ribs of grey rock under the dank mantle of matted leafage. Unknown to trade, to travel, almost to geography, the manner of life they harbour is an unsolved secret. There must be villages—settlements of fishermen at least—on the largest of them, and some communication with the world is probably kept up by native craft. But all that forenoon, as we headed for them, fanned along by the faintest of breezes, I saw no sign of man or canoe in the field of the telescope I kept on pointing at the scattered group.

At noon I gave no orders for a change of course, and the mate's whiskers became much concerned and seemed to be offering themselves unduly to my notice. At last I said:

"I am going to stand right in. Quite in—as far as I can take her."

The stare of extreme surprise imparted an air of ferocity also to his eyes, and he looked truly terrific for a moment.

"We're not doing well in the middle of the gulf," I continued, casually. "I am going to look for the land breezes to-night."

"Bless my soul! Do you mean, sir, in the dark amongst the lot of all them islands and reefs and shoals?"

"Well—if there are any regular land breezes at all on this coast one must get close inshore to find them, mustn't one?"

"Bless my soul!" he exclaimed again under his breath. All that afternoon he wore a dreamy, contemplative appearance which in him was a mark of perplexity. After dinner I went into my stateroom as if I meant to take some rest. There we two bent our dark heads over a half-unrolled chart lying on my bed.

"There," I said. "It's got to be Koh-ring. I've been looking at it ever since sunrise. It has got two hills and a low point. It must be inhabited. And on the coast opposite there is what looks like the mouth of a biggish river—with some town, no doubt, not far up. It's the best chance for you that I can see."

"Anything. Koh-ring let it be."

He looked thoughtfully at the chart as if surveying chances and distances from a lofty height—and following with his eyes his own figure wandering on the blank land of Cochin-China, and then passing off that piece of paper clean out of sight into uncharted regions. And it was as if the ship had two captains to plan her course for her. I had been so worried and restless running up and down that I had not had the patience to dress that day. I had remained in my sleeping-suit, with straw slippers and a soft floppy hat. The closeness of the heat in the gulf had been most oppressive, and the crew were used to see me wandering in that airy attire.

"She will clear the south point as she heads now," I whispered into his ear. "Goodness only knows when, though, but certainly after dark. I'll edge her in to half a mile, as far as I may be able to judge in the dark—"

"Be careful," he murmured, warningly—and I realised suddenly that all my future, the only future for which I was fit, would perhaps go irretrievably to pieces in any mishap to my first command.

I could not stop a moment longer in the room. I motioned him to get out of sight and made my way on the poop. That unplayful cub had the watch. I walked up and down for a while thinking things out, then beckoned him over.

"Send a couple of hands to open the two quarter-deck ports," I said, mildly.

He actually had the impudence, or else so forgot himself in his wonder at such an incomprehensible order, as to repeat:

"Open the quarter-deck ports! What for, sir?"

"The only reason you need concern yourself about is because I tell you to do so. Have them opened wide and fastened properly."

He reddened and went off, but I believe made some jeering remark to the carpenter as to the sensible practice of ventilating a ship's quarter-deck. I know he popped into the mate's cabin to impart the fact to him because the whiskers came on deck, as it were by chance, and stole glances at me from below—for signs of lunacy or drunkenness, I suppose.

A little before supper, feeling more restless than ever, I rejoined, for a moment, my second self. And to find him sitting so quietly was surprising, like something against nature, inhuman.

I developed my plan in a hurried whisper.

"I shall stand in as close as I dare and then put her round. I will presently find means to smuggle you out of here into the sail-locker, which communicates with the lobby. But there is an opening, a sort of square for hauling the sails out, which gives straight on the quarter-deck and which is never closed in fine weather, so as to give air to the sails. When the ship's way is deadened in stays and all the hands are aft at the main-braces you will have a clear road to slip out and get over-board through the open quarter-deck port. I've had them both fastened up. Use a rope's end to lower yourself into the water so as to avoid a splash—you know. It could be heard and cause some beastly complication."

He kept silent for a while, then whispered, "I understand."

"I won't be there to see you go," I began with an effort. "The rest . . . I only hope I have understood, too."

"You have. From first to last"—and for the first time there seemed to be a faltering, something strained in his whisper. He caught hold of my arm, but the ringing of the supper bell made me start. He didn't, though; he only released his grip.

After supper I didn't come below again till well past eight o'clock. The faint, steady breeze was loaded with dew; and the wet, darkened sails held all there was of propelling power in it. The night, clear and starry, sparkled darkly, and the opaque, lightless patches shifting slowly against the low stars were the drifting islets. On the port bow there was a big one more distant and shadowily imposing by the great space of sky it eclipsed.

On opening the door I had a back view of my very own self looking at a chart. He had come out of the recess and was standing near the table.

"Quite dark enough," I whispered.

He stepped back and leaned against my bed with a level, quiet glance. I sat on the couch. We had nothing to say to each other. Over our heads the officer of the watch moved here and there. Then I heard him move quickly. I knew what that meant. He was making for the companion; and presently his voice was outside my door.

"We are drawing in pretty fast, sir. Land looks rather close."

"Very well," I answered. "I am coming on deck directly."

I waited till he was gone out of the cuddy, then rose. My double moved too. The time had come to exchange our last whispers, for neither of us was ever to hear each other's natural voice.

"Look here!" I opened a drawer and took out three sovereigns. "Take this anyhow. I've got six and I'd give you the lot, only I must keep a little money to buy some fruit and vegetables for the crew from native boats as we go through Sunda Straits."

He shook his head.

"Take it," I urged him, whispering desperately. "No one can tell what—"

He smiled and slapped meaningly the only pocket of the sleeping-jacket. It was not safe, certainly. But I produced a large old silk handkerchief of mine, and tying the three pieces of gold in a corner, pressed it on him. He was touched, I suppose, because he took it at last and tied it quickly round his waist under the jacket, on his bare skin.

Our eyes met; several seconds elapsed, till, our glances still mingled, I extended my hand and turned the lamp out. Then I passed through the cuddy, leaving the door of my room wide open. . . . "Steward!"

He was still lingering in the pantry in the greatness of his zeal, giving a rub-up to a plated cruet stand the last thing before going to bed. Being careful not to wake up the mate, whose room was opposite, I spoke in an undertone.

He looked round anxiously. "Sir!"

"Can you get me a little hot water from the galley?"

"I am afraid, sir, the galley fire's been out for some time now."

"Go and see."

He flew up the stairs.

"Now," I whispered, loudly, into the saloon—too loudly, perhaps, but I was afraid I couldn't make a sound. He was by my side in an instant—the double captain slipped past the stairs—through a tiny dark passage . . . a sliding door. We were in the sail-locker, scrambling on our knees over the sails. A sudden thought struck me. I saw myself wandering barefooted, bareheaded, the sun beating on my dark poll. I snatched off my floppy hat and tried hurriedly in the dark to ram it on my other self. He dodged and fended off silently. I wonder what he thought had come to me before he understood and suddenly desisted. Our hands met gropingly, lingered united in a steady, motionless clasp for a second. . . . No word was breathed by either of us when they separated.

I was standing quietly by the pantry door when the steward returned.

"Sorry, sir. Kettle barely warm. Shall I light the spirit-lamp?"

"Never mind."

I came out on deck slowly. It was now a matter of conscience to shave the land as close as possible—for now he must go overboard whenever the ship was put in stays. Must! There could be no going back for him. After a moment I walked over to leeward and my heart flew into my mouth at the nearness of the land on the bow. Under any other circumstances I would not have held on a minute longer. The second mate had followed me anxiously.

I looked on till I felt I could command my voice.

"She will weather," I said then in a quiet tone.

"Are you going to try that, sir?" he stammered out incredulously.

I took no notice of him and raised my tone just enough to be heard by the helmsman.

"Keep her good full."

"Good full, sir."

The wind fanned my cheek, the sails slept, the world was silent. The strain of watching the dark loom of the land grow bigger and denser was too much for me. I had shut my eyes—because the ship must go closer. She must! The stillness was intolerable. Were we standing still?

When I opened my eyes the second view started my heart with a thump. The black southern hill of Koh-ring seemed to hang right over the ship like a towering fragment of the everlasting night. On that enormous mass of blackness there was not a gleam to be seen, not a sound to be heard. It was gliding irresistibly towards us and yet seemed already within reach of the hand. I saw the vague figures of the watch grouped in the waist, gazing in awed silence.

"Are you going on, sir?" inquired an unsteady voice at my elbow.

I ignored it. I had to go on.

"Keep her full. Don't check her way. That won't do now," I said, warningly.

"I can't see the sails very well," the helmsman answered me, in strange, quavering tones.

Was she close enough? Already she was, I won't say in the shadow of the land, but in the very blackness of it, already swallowed up as it were, gone too close to be recalled, gone from me altogether.

"Give the mate a call," I said to the young man who stood at my elbow as still as death. "And turn all hands up."

My tone had a borrowed loudness reverberated from the height of the land. Several voices cried out together: "We are all on deck, sir."

Then stillness again, with the great shadow gliding closer, towering higher, without a light, without a sound. Such a hush had fallen on the ship that she might have been a bark of the dead floating in slowly under the very gate of Erebus.°

Erebus: Entrance to Hades.

"My God! Where are we?"

It was the mate moaning at my elbow. He was thunderstruck, and as it were deprived of the moral support of his whiskers. He clapped his hands and absolutely cried out, "Lost!"

"Be quiet," I said, sternly.

He lowered his tone, but I saw the shadowy gesture of his despair. "What are we doing here?"

"Looking for the land wind."

He made as if to tear his hair, and addressed me recklessly.

"She will never get out. You have done it, sir. I knew it'd end in something like this. She will never weather, and you are too close now to stay. She'll drift ashore before she's round. O my God!"

I caught his arm as he was raising it to batter his poor devoted head, and shook it violently.

"She's ashore already," he wailed, trying to tear himself away.

"Is she? . . . Keep good full there!"

"Good full, sir," cried the helmsman in a frightened, thin, child-like voice.

I hadn't let go the mate's arm and went on shaking it. "Ready about, do you hear? You go forward"—shake—"and stop there"—shake—"and hold your noise"—shake—"and see these head-sheets properly overhauled"—shake, shake—shake.

And all the time I dared not look towards the land lest my heart should fail me. I released my grip at last and he ran forward as if fleeing for dear life.

I wondered what my double there in the sail-locker thought of this commotion. He was able to hear everything—and perhaps he was able to understand why, on my conscience, it had to be thus close—no less. My first order "Hard alee!" re-echoed ominously under the towering shadow of Koh-ring as if I had shouted in a mountain gorge. And then I watched the land intently. In that smooth water and light wind it was impossible to feel the ship coming-to. No! I could not feel her. And my second self was making now ready to slip out and lower himself overboard. Perhaps he was gone already . . . ?

The great black mass brooding over our very mastheads began to pivot away from the ship's side silently. And now I forgot the secret stranger ready to depart, and remembered only that I was a total stranger to the ship. I did not know her. Would she do it? How was she to be handled?

I swung the mainyard and waited helplessly. She was perhaps stopped, and her very fate hung in the balance, with the black mass of

Koh-ring like the gate of the everlasting night towering over her taffrail. What would she do now? Had she way on her yet? I stepped to the side swiftly, and on the shadowy water I could see nothing except a faint phosphorescent flash revealing the glassy smoothness of the sleeping surface. It was impossible to tell—and I had not learned yet the feel of my ship. Was she moving? What I needed was something easily seen, a piece of paper, which I could throw overboard and watch. I had nothing on me. To run down for it I didn't dare. There was no time. All at once my strained, yearning stare distinguished a white object floating within a yard of the ship's side. White on the black water. A phosphorescent flash passed under it. What was that thing? . . . I recognised my own floppy hat. It must have fallen off his head . . . and he didn't bother. Now I had what I wanted—the saving mark for my eyes. But I hardly thought of my other self, now gone from the ship, to be hidden for ever from all friendly faces, to be a fugitive and a vagabond on the earth, with no brand of the curse on his sane forehead to stay a slaying hand . . . too proud to explain.

And I watched the hat—the expression of my sudden pity for his mere flesh. It had been meant to save his homeless head from the dangers of the sun. And now—behold—it was saving the ship, by serving me for a mark to help out the ignorance of my strangeness. Ha! It was drifting forward, warning me just in time that the ship had gathered sternway.

"Shift the helm," I said in a low voice to the seaman standing still like a statue.

The man's eyes glistened wildly in the binnacle light as he jumped round to the other side and spun round the wheel.

I walked to the break of the poop. On the overshadowed deck all hands stood by the forebraces waiting for my order. The stars ahead seemed to be gliding from right to left. And all was so still in the world that I heard the quiet remark, "She's round," passed in a tone of intense relief between two seamen.

"Let go and haul."

The foreyards ran round with a great noise, amidst cheery cries. And now the frightful whiskers made themselves heard giving various orders. Already the ship was drawing ahead. And I was alone with her. Nothing! no one in the world should stand now between us, throwing a shadow on the way of silent knowledge and mute affection, the perfect communion of a seaman with his first command.

Walking to the taffrail, I was in time to make out, on the very edge of a darkness thrown by a towering black mass like the very gateway of

Erebus—yes, I was in time to catch an evanescent glimpse of my white hat left behind to mark the spot where the secret sharer of my cabin and of my thoughts, as though he were my second self, had lowered himself into the water to take his punishment: a free man, a proud swimmer striking out for a new destiny.

PART TWO

"The Secret Sharer": A Case Study in Contemporary Criticism

A Critical History of "The Secret Sharer"

The critical history of "The Secret Sharer" reflects the history of Anglo-American criticism in the postwar period. In the 1950s and 1960s, two types of formalism prevailed: the New Criticism, which eschewed biography and the reader's response and emphasized the *isness* of the text, and Aristotelian criticism, which stressed what we might call the *doesness* of the text—that is, the effects of the author's creation, whether intended or unintended, on the reader. The New Critics focused more on poetry and the Aristotelians on the novel. Anglo-American criticism of British fiction is in part derived from the very tradition of manners and morals this genre addresses. Perhaps from a historical perspective this criticism should be seen as a response to British fiction's interest in content and its moral effects on readers. Thus Anglo-American criticism of British fiction has tended to focus on moral issues, while viewing aesthetic matters as subservient.

Even when Anglo-American criticism is primarily interested in aesthetic characteristics, it never really abandons humanism. Its concerns are the accuracy, inclusiveness, maturity, and sincerity of a novel's representation of life. Anglo-American criticism has subscribed to the view that art is about something other than art and that subject matter is important. This criticism does acknowledge the importance of form, but its interest in form is tied to the belief that the "doing" (narrative technique, structure, and style) is important *because* it reveals the meaning inherent in the subject.

The differences that separate various strands of Anglo-American criticism prior to the theoretical revolution of the 1970s seem less significant than they once did. Now we are able to see that the formalists, historicists, New Critics, Aristotelians, the *Partisan Review* group, contextualists, and literary historians share a number of important assumptions: authors write to express their ideas and emotions; people's lives and values are of fundamental interest to authors and readers; literature expresses insights about the human condition—and that human focus is the main reason we read, teach, and think about literature. While the emphasis varies from critic to critic, we can identify several concepts that define Anglo-American criticism in general and we can see that until the theoretical revolution of the 1970s—structuralism, poststructuralism, cultural criticism—all shared similar humanistic assumptions:

1. The form of the novel—style, structure, narrative technique—expresses its value system. Put another way, form discovers the meaning of content.
2. A work of literature is also a creative gesture of the author and the result of its historical context. Understanding the author's process of imitating the external world gives us insight into the artistry and meaning of the work.
3. The work of fiction imitates a world that precedes the text, and the critic should recapture that world primarily by formal analysis of the text, although knowledge of the historical context and the author is often important.
4. The work has an original meaning, a center, which can be approached and often almost reached by perceptive reading. The goal is to discover what authors said to their intended audience *then,* as well as what they say to us now. Subtle, lucid, inclusive, perceptive interpretation can bring that goal into sight.
5. Human behavior is central to most works and should be the major concern of analysis: How do people behave? What do they fear, desire, doubt, and need? Although modes of characterization differ, the psychology and morality of characters must be understood as if they were real people, for understanding others helps us to understand ourselves.
6. The inclusiveness of the novel's vision in terms of depth and range is a measure of the work's quality.

In the Introduction, I have spoken of the parallels between Conrad's life and "The Secret Sharer" and have mentioned the important work of biographers Jocelyn Baines, Frederick Karl, and Zdzislaw Najder. Thus I will begin this discussion with thematic criticism which focuses on the reflection of broad issues and concerns of writers and their times in literary works. In the late 1940s when thematic criticism competed with more formal criticism, and concomitantly, when formal criticism was used to probe for thematic implications, Walter Wright stressed the theme of self-knowledge and community necessary on-board ship:

> But what causes the struggle here is that the very bond which should tie him to his fellowmen—the secret of man's emotional and impulsive nature, of his fear and irresolution, of his unpredictability to himself—this bond is pulling him further away from the kinship which he must achieve with humanity as the master of a crew and a ship. (49)

One might note that in the 1940s the value of fellowship among a group of men pursuing a common purpose was in the forefront during and in the years immediately following World War II. Success on board ship, like in battle, depended on the efficiency of an interdependent community in which each male could be depended to take care of his fellows. Following from that was the credo that each member of a unit had to know himself to do one's duty and that such self-knowledge often derived from the Christian ethical imperative of placing the community's needs before one's own. Typical of the Christian humanism of the postwar criticism, Wright contends,

> The motif of the kind act's saving the doer is at least as old as Christianity. Conrad objected to Tolstoy for making the Christian religion his basis; yet he himself not infrequently arrived at a resolution of a paradox in accord with Christian sentiments . . . to do one's duty. It came when a man apprehended the mysterious nature of personality and destiny and found a dream that gave his world a center. When he did this, however far he might be estranged from actual men, he was true to the life of man. (50)

A later version of a thematic approach—fertilized by F. R. Leavis's stress on bracing moralism and tangible realism as the values to be discovered and valued by close reading—can be found in H. M. Daleski's characteristically humanistic and sensitive perspective in *Joseph Conrad: The Way of Dispossession*. Daleski sees the story in terms of the development and maturation of the captain as a result of his contact with Leggatt. One of the most interesting humanistic discussions in the 1980s was Steve Ressler's *Consciousness and Integrity in*

Joseph Conrad. As have a number of other critics, including Sherlyn Abdoo, he argues that:

> Conrad provides numerous signs that Leggatt is to be regarded as a symbolic manifestation of the captain's unconscious, his being a physical double both suggesting and reinforcing unconscious connections. . . . In the sense that the visitor corresponds uncannily to the wished-for male image, one might say that the captain has dreamed Leggatt into existence. (Ressler 82)

But the problem with this position, that Leggatt is a dream of the captain's, is that unlike, say, in Hawthorne's "Young Goodman Brown," the dream is not embedded within the text as a suggestion that a dream is taking place. And where does the dream begin and end? In other words, where do we put the brackets that signify the dream, as opposed to the waking experience? Archbold would surely have to be part of the dream, and if the whole story is a dream, how and why is it different from other works of fiction? It seems odd to argue that because he is alone on deck and Leggatt wears his sleeping-suit, that the captain has fallen asleep. Within a text's system of language, we need specific formal indications that the text is a dream narrative.

Perhaps one of the best early formalist (as opposed to thematic) studies is that of R. W. Stallman, a significant figure in the New Critical movement, who writes in his essay "Conrad and 'The Secret Sharer' ":

> The fact is that Conrad's theory of the novel is no other than the modern canon that every work of art is symbolic. Every great novel has a symbolic meaning, imparts a significance which transcends mere plot or fable. Symbolism, it has been aptly said, does not deny Realism; it extends it. . . . Because a novel is a product of language, a novel depends for its very life upon the word. What we term the characters of a novel are nothing more that the author's verbal arrangements. (276)

Stallman discusses the relationship between Leggatt and the captain, stressing how they are counterparts or doubles of one another:

> It is this mutual, sympathetic understanding of what the other's plight means to him that bolsters and morally fortifies their spiritual being, Leggatt's no less than the captain's. . . . Through Leggatt that initial mood of calm and resolute self-confidence with which the captain begins and ends his arduous enterprise is gradually reinstated. (280)

Stallman perceptively notes that each is the secret sharer of the other. He also implies that were Leggatt to tell the tale, he would have a vastly different version of events, and the reader would experience a vastly different structure of effects. Emphasizing, as so many of the New Critics do, the ethical and humanistic implications of formalist readings, Stallman continues:

> In terms of the ethical allegory, Leggatt is the embodiment of the captain's moral consciousness. . . . The captain's subconscious mind has anticipated, in the fiction of the symbolic flame, the idea of a second self—the appearance, that is, of someone untroubled, unyielding, self-confident. (The captain is just the opposite, being of a mind troubled and filled with self-doubt.) The symbolic flame materializes in human form. Leggatt bodies forth the very commonplace upon which the whole story is built: no man is alone in the world, for he is always with himself. Leggatt, this other self, becomes the psychological embodiment of the reality, the destiny, the ideal of selfhood which the captain must measure up to. He provides him the utmost test. (280–81)

Daniel Curley's 1962 essay "Legate of the 'Ideal'" is an important discussion of the doubling theme in formalist terms. While contending that Leggatt is not really guilty, Curley writes, "He [Conrad] had to find a way of separating his protagonist's legal and moral responsibilities, and he had to invent for Leggatt an action that would be a crime in form but not a crime in fact" (77). But Curley's and Stallman's fine formalist readings show the problem of ignoring both the source material and the maritime code discussed in the Introduction. They do not pay sufficient attention to the *Cutty Sark* or Conrad's maritime values. If one sees, as Curley does, the captain as a surrogate for Conrad, one tends to sympathize with the captain's identification with the murderous Leggatt. But later critics had difficulty seeing Leggatt as an ideal, particularly in view of Conrad's strict allegiance in his fiction to maritime ethics, which requires that the first mate be responsible for the welfare of those serving under him. Within the benign autocracy of the ship, the captain has the full allegiance and full responsibility for all those under his command, and the first mate, his second in command, is responsible in the same way for all but the captain. Put another way: Leggatt can no more be killing his crew members—no matter how much they misbehave—than a first grade teacher can toss an unruly child down the stairwell during a fire drill. Louise K. Barnett views

Leggatt as a social misfit rather than a murderer, more a primitive than a criminal.

Stallman and Curley are typical of a generation of postwar formalists who, influenced by such figures as Dorothy Van Ghent and F. R. Leavis, used formal analysis to ask questions not merely about the structure and language of the text but about the author's psyche and philosophy.

Among the landmarks of Conrad criticism is Albert Guerard's important study *Conrad the Novelist,* which provides what is still one of the most illuminating commentaries on "The Secret Sharer." Guerard wrote at a time when the archetypal-myth theories of Carl Jung were extremely influential. Using the concept of the Jungian "night journey," Guerard sees "The Secret Sharer," along with Conrad's two other great symbolist masterpieces, *Heart of Darkness* and *The Shadow Line,* as quest journeys within the dark, dimly acknowledged parts of the psyche:

> I refer to the archetypal myth dramatized in much great literature since the Book of Jonah: the story of an essentially solitary journey involving profound spiritual change in the voyager. In its classical form the journey is a descent into the earth, followed by a return to light. (15)

In addition to focusing on the archetypal dimension of "The Secret Sharer," Guerard writes compellingly about the narrative perspective:

> The point of view is not, as it happens, Conrad's usual one when employing the first person. His normal manner is to employ a retrospective first person, free to move where he wished in time, and therefore free to foreshadow his conclusion. (27)

He stresses how the self-dramatizing telling is a critical issue of the captain-narrator understanding the story: "The nominal narrative past is, actually, a harrowing present which the reader too must explore and survive" (Guerard 27). Although Guerard's view may not adequately account for the retrospective nature of the narrator in "The Secret Sharer," who tells us that he speaks at a distance of years, it began a process of seeing the telling as a central *agon* of the tale and of analyzing the teller's psyche and values in terms of his soliloquy.

Guerard discusses how *The Shadow Line*—another of Conrad's first-person accounts of a captain on his maiden voyage—can be read as a sequel to "The Secret Sharer." Also wanting to see "The Secret Sharer" as a precursor to *The Shadow Line* is Carl Benson, whose 1954 essay "Conrad's Two Stories of Initiation" is characteristic of humanistic formalism—a criticism that, as noted before, believes that literary criticism addresses the inextricable relation within texts of formal aesthetic issues and ethical implications. According to Benson, "The Secret Sharer" is not a story of full initiation into mature responsibilities. It is the beginning of the initiation, but it remains for *The Shadow Line* to show the passage from egocentric youth to human solidarity. Unlike the pure New Critics who exclude the author from their discussion, Benson uses Conrad's other works to decode his "conscious interest" and to stress the relationship between Conrad and the captain:

> It is not, I think, remarkable that a reader who turns to the short novel after the long story should ask: For what reason, or reasons, did Conrad decide to handle the same problem (initiation), same ship, same crew, same captain twice? Is not *The Shadow Line* in a sense a peculiarly significant rewriting, done because Conrad realized that the initiation of the captain of "The Secret Sharer" was humanly abortive—and this despite the last phrase, more applicable to the captain than to Leggatt, about "a free man, striking out for a new destiny"? (46)

At the time when the captain-narrator's telling was becoming a particular focus of readers in the 1950s and 1960s, Wayne Booth was formulating rigorous "narratological" methods for such an approach. In *The Rhetoric of Fiction* Booth shows that the "autonomous" text derives from the conscious or unconscious decisions made by the author to shape the reader's response: "Nothing is real for the reader until the author makes it so, and it is for the reader that the author chooses to make this scene as powerful as possible" (*Rhetoric* 108). Booth insists that an author affects the reader as the author intends and communicates human emotions and values to an audience. The reader in turn responds to the presence of a human voice within the text (152, 159). In a retrospective essay on *The Rhetoric of Fiction*, Booth differentiates between a poetics ("study of what the work *is*, what it has been made to *be*") and a rhetoric ("what the work is made to *do*"): "*The kinds of actions authors perform on readers* differ markedly, though subtly, from *the kinds of imitations of objects they are seen as making,* in the poetic mode" ("Rhetoric and Poetics" 115). Booth believed the New Critics focused on poetics—the ontology of a text as a well-wrought urn—and minimized rhetoric in the form of the author-reader relationship; by contrast, the neo-Aristotelian Booth defined the relationship among author, text, and audience.

One of Booth's major legacies is his distinction between reliable and unreliable narrators: "I have called a narrator *reliable* when he speaks for or acts in accordance with the norms of the work (which is to say, the implied author's norms), *unreliable* when he does not" (158–59). (I prefer the terms *perceptive* and *imperceptive* since a narrator might be reliable and yet be unaware of the implications of his or her behavior.) Following Booth's insistence on asking, "Who is speaking to whom?" and "For what purpose?," other critics have pursued the captain-narrator's motives. Although critics such as Michael Murphy have discussed the possibility of an unreliable narrator, it might be more to the point to understand the narrator as more imperceptive than unreliable. Other essays pursuing this line of discussion focusing on narrative point of view include J. D. O'Hara's "Unlearned Lessons in 'The Secret Sharer'" and Robert D. Wyatt's "Joseph Conrad's 'The Secret Sharer': Point of View and Mistaken Identities."

One of the best discussions of "The Secret Sharer" is Louis H. Leiter's 1960 essay "Echo Structures: Conrad's 'The Secret Sharer,'" which speaks of the way patterns of narrative formations—what he calls the "echo structures"—create meaning by displaying major similarities but crucial and revealing differences.

> Structures not only of character but also of narrative action, parable, metaphor, and the like, become a fundamental means for achieving aesthetic and thematic effects. . . . An echo structure implies one or more structures similar to itself. The tautology which is the echo structure may be a repeated symbol, metaphor, scene, pattern of action, state of being, myth, fable, or archetype. If viewed within the perspective of Biblical story or classical myth, either directly stated in the text of the story or implied, that perspective may suffuse the echo structures of similar construction with additional meanings. (159)

In this dense essay influenced by Joseph Frank's famous 1975 three-part piece on spatial form in modern literature, Leiter concludes,

> The action of the echo structure implies, it seems to me, a moral judgment of Leggatt, although it does not state the judgment openly. It dramatizes it and by doing so makes the reader psychologically aware of it. At the same time the echo scene declares the moral superiority of the consciously aware narrator-captain who has come to face his secret inner self, to conquer it, and to control it. (162)

The scene in which the captain disciplines his first mate by shaking his arm departs radically from Leggatt's disciplining his crew member by killing him and implies a strong judgment of Leggatt. Like Stallman, Leiter was influenced by the theories of Kenneth Burke—especially his *Philosophy of Literary Form*. Burke argues that

> a poem's structure is to be described most accurately by thinking always of the poem's function. . . . [A] poem is designed to "do something" for the poet and his readers, and . . . we can make the most relevant observations about its design by considering the poem as the embodiment of this act. In the poet, we might say, the poetizing existed as a physiological function. The poem is its corresponding anatomic structure. And the reader, in participating in the poem, breathes into this anatomic structure a new physiological vitality that resembles, though with a difference, the act of its maker, the resemblance being in the overlap between writer's and reader's situation, the difference being in the fact that these two situations are far from identical. (75–76)

Leiter also stresses mythopoeic parallels. In addition to following Guerard by drawing a parallel between the captain's descent into himself and the Jonah story, Leiter discusses the important Cain-Abel resonances:

> The Cain-Abel archetype circumscribes the narrator-Leggatt relationship as well, the longest pattern of action and most important relationship of the novel, for the narrator, in a role comparable to that of Cain, figuratively kills his Abel-Leggatt when he consigns him to the sea. (168–69)

Others who have discussed parallels between "The Secret Sharer" and the Bible include Mark A. R. Facknitz and Daphna Erdinast-Vulcan.

The focus on mythopoeic issues reflects not only the influence of T. S. Eliot's mythic method (articulated in his famous 1923 review of *Ulysses* in *The Dial* and demonstrated in his poetry). It also reflects Northrop Frye's archetypal theories (related to but different from Jung's view that we share a collective unconscious) in the late 1950s and early 1960s. In his *Anatomy of Criticism* Frye creates a literary analogue to the Bible, which he describes as a "definitive myth, a single archetypal structure extending from creation to apocalypse" (315). His description of the biblical cycle is useful in understanding his work:

> The Bible as a whole . . . presents a gigantic cycle from creation to apocalypse, within which is the heroic quest of the Messiah from

incarnation to apotheosis. Within this again are three other cyclical movements, expressed or implied: individual from birth to salvation: sexual from Adam and Eve to the apocalyptic wedding; social from the giving of the law to the established kingdom of the law, the rebuilt Zion of the Old Testament and the milennium of the New. (Frye 316–17)

Like the work of Franz Kafka, Sigmund Freud, James Joyce, Bertolt Brecht, or Jackson Pollock, Frye's *Anatomy* attempts to question the possibility and significance of temporality, progress, and indeed any concept of unity that is dependent on movement.

Traditional formalism—biographical and contextual criticism and myth criticism—all share the assumption that the author has consciously, and on rare occasions unconsciously, made the narrative what it is and almost always *intended* the mythical, biblical, and biographical parallels the text contains. More recently, readers have sought perspectives of which the author may have been unaware, sometimes because his or her historical situation prevented such awareness. One model for such reading has derived from psychoanalysis. In their essay "Secret Sharing: Reading Conrad Psychoanalytically," Barbara Johnson and Marjorie Garber have used "The Secret Sharer" to explore varieties of psychoanalytic criticism. Influenced by Freud's *Interpretation of Dreams* and most notably by the work of Jacques Lacan, they examine the text in terms of "the pathology of the author," "the pathology of the protagonist," "the pathology (or symptomology, or symptomography) of the text," "the text as a theory of a symptom or complex," and "the text as an allegory of psychoanalysis." Johnson and Garber differentiate between psychological and psychoanalytic reading:

> Psychological readings often posit intentions and beliefs in the author, and then apply them to the story told by the text. . . . A psychoanalytical reading, in contrast, sees conscious attitudes and beliefs as unstable constructions resulting from an ongoing struggle with conflicting forces within the self. Consciousness is only one part of a complex signifying dynamic. A hypothesis about Conrad's probable attitude toward Leggatt's crime can thus in no way be determining for an interpretation. This does not mean that the question of Leggatt's moral status is irrelevant, but that the question of morality in the story is more complex than can be accounted for through a simple innocent/guilty opposition. (Johnson and Garber 631)

They use "The Secret Sharer" as a paradigm of psychoanalytic process, arguing that the "relation between concealment and doubleness" articulated in the text is not the "relation between a mystery and its solution or a symbol and its meaning" but rather a "way of investigating that which psychoanalysis, too, investigates" (Johnson and Garber 629).

Johnson and Garber's interest in the psychology of the captain-narrator as a model of psychoanalytic countertransference is hardly new to criticism of "The Secret Sharer," but they take it in new directions:

> When we turn to the second paradigm of psychoanalytic reading, the pathology of the character, we discover a very similar Oedipal conflict in Conrad's "The Secret Sharer." If by Oedipal we mean competition with or rivalry with a father or father figure, or, by extension, threatening figures who wield power and seem to disempower the protagonist, the story has more than enough such conflicts to offer. There are several candidates for the role of father, notably the chief mate on the ship, an older man with "a terrible growth of whisker," "round eyes and frightful whiskers," like many emblems of castration in Freud (e.g., "The Head of the Medusa," "The Uncanny"), and, later, the skipper of the *Sephora,* also older, also whiskered, a married man whose name might be Archbold (a splendidly potent name) but the narrator isn't sure—he has repressed it, and explains away the repression: "at this distance of years I hardly am sure." . . . "Captain Archbold (if that was his name)." . . . In the end, having harbored and released the fugitive, the young captain can be alone with the ship, with the command. He has come out the other end of the Oedipal crisis by accepting the necessity of losing part of himself: his fantasy of guilty omnipotence. In essence he has arrived at a new, revisionary version of castration as *enabling.* (632, 634)

For them the ship represents the mother. When they discuss what they call the symptomology of the text, one sees how in the recent criticism the critic has become more of a focus figure than the author:

> There is another way to read the scene of Leggatt's appearance from the water, a way that accords more readily with what we have called the symptomology of the text than of the narrator. Viewed mythically or archetypally, the dangling rope ladder, though it may in one way signal vulnerability to castration, in another resembles an umbilicus, and the scene is a birth scene, the naked infant emerging from the water clinging to the cord. (Johnson and Garber 634)

They conclude their ingenious and subtle reading by suggesting that,

> [t]he narrator seems at last to have renounced both the potency
> and the terror of infantile omnipotence, and to be ready to recog-
> nize that control of his fate is neither his nor not his. Rather, his
> fate is somehow henceforth tied to the course of a floating signi-
> fier. (Johnson and Garber 639)

We should realize that like formalists—or for that matter, myth
critics—of a prior generation, Johnson and Garber look for patterns of
iteration, including those of prior myths, such as the Oedipus story.
Are they not emphasizing the ontological reality of the text—the sentences and words themselves as objects, units of energy, textures,
sounds, visual surfaces, spaces, and even distinct letters—as well as the
perceiver's role in making sense of that reality?

Yet for older generations of formalists, Johnson and Garber's spec-
ulations may be troubling. Their brilliant essay testifies to a fundamental shift *from* trying to render the author's conscious or unconscious
intention and the effects the author was trying to create for readers *to*
resistant readings which empower critics to create patterns of meaning
of which the author was unaware. These critics use the text to illustrate
psychoanalytic models even while deconstruing (or deconstructing)
the *construed* text that the author intended for his audience. Garber
and Johnson speak also to the extraordinary influence of Lacanian psychoanalysis in the past decade. In their deconstructive model, text may
be open, unresolved, and problematic, and readers need not choose
one reading. An urge for order may falsify a text, and we need be at-
tentive to gaps, fissures, and enigmas.

Joyce Wexler, in "Conrad's Dream of a Common Language: Lacan
and 'The Secret Sharer,'" uses Conrad's text to illuminate "Lacan's
theory of the subject's entry into the Symbolic order" (599). For her it
is Leggatt who is the catalyst for the narrator's movement:

> In Lacanian terms, the captain does not project the double as an
> aspect of himself; instead, he views the other as his double so that
> he can introject him. According to Lacan, soon after birth a pri-
> mordial form of subjectivity inaugurates the Imaginary, which
> dominates from six to eighteen months but never entirely disap-
> pears. In this early period, the child only partially and intermit-
> tently differentiates itself from the outside world. . . . Although
> most of Conrad's fiction recognizes the constraints of the Sym-
> bolic, in "The Secret Sharer," the narrator, a young captain uneasy
> with his first command, regains access to the Imaginary world of

direct identification with the other. . . . [Finally,] relinquishing the Symbolic for a more primitive kind of connection with Leggatt, the captain relies on intuition and gesture to perform what words cannot do. (Wexler 602, 603)

Josiane Paccaud's Freudian and Lacanian reading underlines the story's kinship to *Under Western Eyes*. In language indebted to Lacan, she writes,

My contention is that the ritual initiation performed in "The Secret Sharer" is no less than the subject's accession to the symbolic after inner divisiveness and the unbridgeable gap between desire and its impossible object, between signifier and signified, between the speaking "I" and the psychic self, have been acknowledged. Unlike Jim, the captain has realized that the step from the name to the thing must not be walked, for fear one should stumble into the realm of imaginary, albeit romantic, fantasies.[1] (Paccaud 62)

As gender and gay studies and, more recently, queer theory have become important factors in reading, interest has turned to the male bonding in Conrad. Building on suggestions in Thomas Moser's excellent *Joseph Conrad: Achievement and Decline* and Bernard Meyer's idiosyncratic but valuable *Joseph Conrad: A Psychoanalytic Biography*, Robert Hodges writes in "Deep Fellowship: Homosexuality and Male Bonding in the Life and Fiction of Joseph Conrad" that Leggatt represents the captain's homosexual side:

A young ship's captain falls in love with the fugitive whom he hides in his cabin, and later risks both his ship and his career to help his lover escape. . . . The sexual connotations are prominent. Leggatt appears at night and is completely naked until the captain somewhat hastily finds clothing for him. He is always clad in a sleeping suit and is hidden in the captain's bedroom and bathroom. . . . The moment of their parting has intense sexual overtones. The two men crouch together in the sail locker from which Leggatt intends to drop into the sea unnoticed. The captain wants to give Leggatt a hat to protect him from the tropical sun. . . . The obvious suggestion here is of a sexual approach at first misunderstood, perhaps even construed as an attempt at murder, but finally accepted as a loving gesture of farewell. (384, 386)

---

[1] Using the different approach of Jungian psychology, James White locates the theme of fertility in his essay "The Third Theme in 'The Secret Sharer.'" *Conradiana* 21.1 (Spring 1989) 37–46.

Our discussion demonstrates that the interpretative history of a text—in particular "The Secret Sharer"—is a trialogue among the text as object which critics write about, the subjective interests of individual critics, and the cultural context in which those critics write. The various strands of criticism coalesce around similar psychological, formal, and moral issues: how Leggatt and the Captain behave and how they *should* behave; the narrator's point of view and how it is shaped by events of his life; and how the narrative iterations shape the reader's response. We see a continuing pattern of interest in "The Secret Sharer" as a tale of initiation, of individual guilt and collective responsibility, and as a journey into self from which the speaker emerges with great self-knowledge—a tale aesthetically organized to stress the transformation of the narrator. The critical history of "The Secret Sharer" is not only a critical history of Anglo-American criticism and of kinds of responses to literary modernism, but a continuing and vital conversation about how we make sense of a text that talks to us about our fear of failure, our need to communicate, and our desire to understand ourselves and be understood by others.

Daniel R. Schwarz

WORKS CITED

Abdoo, Sherlyn. "Ego Formation and the Land/Sea Metaphor in Conrad's 'Secret Sharer.'" *Poetics of the Elements in the Human Condition: The Sea: From Elemental Stirrings to Symbolic Inspiration, Language, and Life-Significance in Literary Interpretation and Theory.* Ed. Anna-Theresa Tymieniecka. *Analecta Husserliana* 19 (1985): 67–76.

Baines, Jocelyn. *Joseph Conrad: A Critical Biography.* New York: McGraw, 1960.

Barnett, Louise K. "'The Whole Circle of the Horizon': The Circumscribed Universe of 'The Secret Sharer.'" *Studies in the Humanities* 8.2 (1981): 5–9.

Benson, Carl. "Conrad's Two Stories of Initiation." *PMLA* 69 (March 1954): 46–56.

Booth, Wayne C. *The Rhetoric of Fiction.* Rev. ed. Chicago: U of Chicago P, 1983.

———. "The Rhetoric of Fiction and the Poetics of Fiction." *Novel* 1.2 (1968): 105–17.

Burke, Kenneth. *The Philosophy of Literary Form*. Rev. ed. New York: Vintage, 1957.

Curley, Daniel. "Legate of the Ideal." *Conrad's 'Secret Sharer' and the Critics*. Ed. Bruce Harkness. Belmont, CA: Wadsworth, 1962. 75–82.

Daleski, H. M. *Joseph Conrad: The Way of Dispossession*. New York: Holmes, 1976.

Eliot, T. S. "Ulysses, Order, and Myth." *The Dial* 75 (1923): 480–83.

Erdinast-Vulcan, Daphna. *Joseph Conrad and the Modern Temper*. Oxford: Clarendon, 1991.

Facknitz, Mark A. R. "Cryptic Allusions and the Moral of the Story: The Case of Joseph Conrad's 'The Secret Sharer,'" *The Journal of Narrative Technique* 17.1 (Winter 1987): 115–30.

Frank, Joseph. "Spatial Form in Modern Literature." *Sewanee Review* 53 (1945): 221–40, 433–56, 643–53.

Freud, Sigmund. *The Interpretation of Dreams*. Trans. A. A. Brill. New York: Random, 1950.

Frye, Northrop. *Anatomy of Criticism: Four Essays*. Princeton: Princeton UP, 1957.

Guerard, Albert J. *Conrad the Novelist*. Cambridge: Harvard UP, 1958.

Hodges, Robert. "Deep Fellowship: Homosexuality and Male Bonding in the Life and Fiction of Joseph Conrad." *Journal of Homosexuality* 4.4 (1979): 379–87.

Johnson, Barbara, and Marjorie Garber. "Secret Sharing: Reading Conrad Psychoanalytically." *College English* 49.6 (1987): 628–40.

Karl, Frederick R. *Joseph Conrad: The Three Lives: A Biography*. New York: Farrar, 1979.

Leiter, Louis H. "Echo Structures: Conrad's 'The Secret Sharer.'" *Twentieth Century Literature* 5.4 (1960): 159–75.

Meyer, Bernard C. *Joseph Conrad: A Psychoanalytic Biography*. Princeton: Princeton UP, 1967.

Moser, Thomas. C. *Joseph Conrad: Achievement and Decline*. Cambridge: Harvard UP, 1957.

Murphy, Michael. "'The Secret Sharer': Conrad's Turn of the Winch." *Conradian* 18.3 (1986): 193–200.

Najder, Zdzislaw. *Joseph Conrad: A Chronicle*. New Brunswick: Rutgers UP, 1983.

O'Hara, J. D. "Unlearned Lessons in 'The Secret Sharer.'" *College English* 26 (1965): 444–50.

Paccaud, Josiane. "Under the Other's Eyes: Conrad's 'The Secret Sharer.'" *Conradian* 12.1 (1987): 59–73.

Ressler, Steve. *Joseph Conrad: Consciousness and Integrity.* New York: New York UP, 1988.

Stallman, R. W. "Conrad and 'The Secret Sharer.'" *Accent* 9 (1949): 131–43. Rpt. in *The Art of Joseph Conrad: A Critical Symposium.* Ed. R. W. Stallman. East Lansing: Michigan State UP, 1969. 275–88.

Wexler, Joyce. "Conrad's Dream of a Common Language: Lacan and 'The Secret Sharer.'" *Psychoanalytic Review* 78.4 (1991): 599–606.

White, James F. "The Third Theme in 'The Secret Sharer.'" *Conradiana* 21.1 (1989): 37–46.

Wright, Walter F. *Romance and Tragedy in Joseph Conrad.* Lincoln: U of Nebraska P, 1949.

Wyatt, Robert D. "Joseph Conrad's 'The Secret Sharer.'" *Conradiana* 5:1 (1973): 12–26.

Psychoanalytic Criticism
and
"The Secret Sharer"

WHAT IS PSYCHOANALYTIC CRITICISM?

It seems natural to think about literature in terms of dreams. Like dreams, literary works are fictions, inventions of the mind that, although based on reality, are by definition not literally true. Like a literary work, a dream may have some truth to tell, but, like a literary work, it may need to be interpreted before that truth can be grasped. We can live vicariously through romantic fictions, much as we can through daydreams. Terrifying novels and nightmares affect us in much the same way, plunging us into an atmosphere that continues to cling, even after the last chapter has been read — or the alarm clock has sounded.

The notion that dreams allow such psychic explorations, of course, like the analogy between literary works and dreams, owes a great deal to the thinking of Sigmund Freud, the famous Austrian psychoanalyst who in 1900 published a seminal study, *The Interpretation of Dreams.* But is the reader who feels that Emily Brontë's *Wuthering Heights* is dreamlike — who feels that Mary Shelley's *Frankenstein* is nightmarish — necessarily a Freudian literary critic? To some extent the answer has to be yes. We are all Freudians, really, whether or not we have read a single work by Freud. At one time or another, most of us have referred to ego, libido, complexes, unconscious desires, and sexual repression. The premises of Freud's thought have changed the way the Western world thinks about itself. Psychoanalytic criticism has influenced the teachers our teachers studied with, the works of scholarship and criticism they read, and the critical and creative writers *we* read as well.

What Freud did was develop a language that described, a model that explained, a theory that encompassed human psychology. Many of the elements of psychology he sought to describe and explain are present in the literary works of various ages and cultures, from Sophocles' *Oedipus Rex* to Shakespeare's *Hamlet* to works being written in our own day. When the great novel of the twenty-first century is written, many of these same elements of psychology will probably inform its discourse as well. If, by understanding human psychology according to Freud, we can appreciate literature on a new level, then we should acquaint ourselves with his insights.

Freud's theories are either directly or indirectly concerned with the nature of the unconscious mind. Freud didn't invent the notion of the unconscious; others before him had suggested that even the supposedly "sane" human mind was conscious and rational only at times, and even then at possibly only one level. But Freud went further, suggesting that the powers motivating men and women are *mainly* and *normally* unconscious.

Freud, then, powerfully developed an old idea: that the human mind is essentially dual in nature. He called the predominantly passional, irrational, unknown, and unconscious part of the psyche the *id,* or "it." The *ego,* or "I," was his term for the predominantly rational, logical, orderly, conscious part. Another aspect of the psyche, which he called the *superego,* is really a projection of the ego. The superego almost seems to be outside of the self, making moral judgments, telling us to make sacrifices for good causes even though self-sacrifice may not be quite logical or rational. And, in a sense, the superego *is* "outside," since much of what it tells us to do or think we have learned from our parents, our schools, or our religious institutions.

What the ego and superego tell us *not* to do or think is repressed, forced into the unconscious mind. One of Freud's most important contributions to the study of the psyche, the theory of repression, goes something like this: much of what lies in the unconscious mind has been put there by consciousness, which acts as a censor, driving underground unconscious or conscious thoughts or instincts that it deems unacceptable. Censored materials often involve infantile sexual desires, Freud postulated. Repressed to an unconscious state, they emerge only in disguised forms: in dreams, in language (so-called Freudian slips), in creative activity that may produce art (including literature), and in neurotic behavior.

According to Freud, all of us have repressed wishes and fears; we all have dreams in which repressed feelings and memories emerge disguised, and thus we are all potential candidates for dream analysis. One of the unconscious desires most commonly repressed is the childhood wish to displace the parent of our own sex and take his or her place in the affections of the parent of the opposite sex. This desire really involves a number of different but related wishes and fears. (A boy — and it should be remarked in passing that Freud here concerns himself mainly with the male — may fear that his father will castrate him, and he may wish that his mother would return to nursing him.) Freud referred to the whole complex of feelings by the word *oedipal,* naming the complex after the Greek tragic hero Oedipus, who unwittingly killed his father and married his mother.

Why are oedipal wishes and fears repressed by the conscious side of the mind? And what happens to them after they have been censored? As Roy P. Basler puts it in *Sex, Symbolism, and Psychology in Literature* (1975), "from the beginning of recorded history such wishes have been restrained by the most powerful religious and social taboos, and as a result have come to be regarded as 'unnatural,'" even though "Freud found that such wishes are more or less characteristic of normal human development":

> In dreams, particularly, Freud found ample evidence that such wishes persisted. . . . Hence he conceived that natural urges, when identified as "wrong," may be repressed but not obliterated. . . . In the unconscious, these urges take on symbolic garb, regarded as nonsense by the waking mind that does not recognize their significance. (14)

Freud's belief in the significance of dreams, of course, was no more original than his belief that there is an unconscious side to the psyche. Again, it was the extent to which he developed a theory of how dreams work — and the extent to which that theory helped him, by analogy, to understand far more than just dreams — that made him unusual, important, and influential beyond the perimeters of medical schools and psychiatrists' offices.

The psychoanalytic approach to literature not only rests on the theories of Freud; it may even be said to have *begun* with Freud, who was interested in writers, especially those who relied heavily on symbols.

Such writers regularly cloak or mystify ideas in figures that make sense only when interpreted, much as the unconscious mind of a neurotic disguises secret thoughts in dream stories or bizarre actions that need to be interpreted by an analyst. Freud's interest in literary artists led him to make some unfortunate generalizations about creativity; for example, in the twenty-third lecture in *Introductory Lectures on Psycho-Analysis* (1922), he defined the artist as "one urged on by instinctive needs that are too clamorous" (314). But it also led him to write creative literary criticism of his own, including an influential essay on "The Relation of a Poet to Daydreaming" (1908) and "The Uncanny" (1919), a provocative psychoanalytic reading of E. T. A. Hoffmann's supernatural tale "The Sandman."

Freud's application of psychoanalytic theory to literature quickly caught on. In 1909, only a year after Freud had published "The Relation of a Poet to Daydreaming," the psychoanalyst Otto Rank published *The Myth of the Birth of the Hero*. In that work, Rank subscribes to the notion that the artist turns a powerful, secret wish into a literary fantasy, and he uses Freud's notion about the oedipal complex to explain why the popular stories of so many heroes in literature are so similar. A year after Rank had published his psychoanalytic account of heroic texts, Ernest Jones, Freud's student and eventual biographer, turned his attention to a tragic text: Shakespeare's *Hamlet*. In an essay first published in the *American Journal of Psychology*, Jones, like Rank, makes use of the oedipal concept: he suggests that Hamlet is a victim of strong feelings toward his mother, the queen.

Between 1909 and 1949, numerous other critics decided that psychological and psychoanalytic theory could assist in the understanding of literature. I. A. Richards, Kenneth Burke, and Edmund Wilson were among the most influential to become interested in the new approach. Not all of the early critics were committed to the approach; neither were all of them Freudians. Some followed Alfred Adler, who believed that writers wrote out of inferiority complexes, and others applied the ideas of Carl Gustav Jung, who had broken with Freud over Freud's emphasis on sex and who had developed a theory of the *collective* unconscious. According to Jungian theory, a great work of literature is not a disguised expression of its author's personal, repressed wishes; rather, it is a manifestation of desires once held by the whole human race but now repressed because of the advent of civilization.

It is important to point out that among those who relied on Freud's models were a number of critics who were poets and novelists as well. Conrad Aiken wrote a Freudian study of American literature, and poets such as Robert Graves and W. H. Auden applied Freudian insights when writing critical prose. William Faulkner, Henry James, James Joyce, D. H. Lawrence, Marcel Proust, and Toni Morrison are only a few of the novelists who have either written criticism influenced by Freud or who have written novels that conceive of character, conflict, and creative writing itself in Freudian terms. The poet H.D. (Hilda Doolittle) was actually a patient of Freud's and provided an account of her analysis in her book *Tribute to Freud*. By giving Freudian theory credibility among students of literature that only they could bestow, such writers helped to endow earlier psychoanalytic criticism with a largely Freudian orientation that has begun to be challenged only in the last two decades.

The willingness, even eagerness, of writers to use Freudian models in producing literature and criticism of their own consummated a relationship that, to Freud and other pioneering psychoanalytic theorists, had seemed fated from the beginning; after all, therapy involves the close analysis of language. René Wellek and Austin Warren included "psychological" criticism as one of the five "extrinsic" approaches to literature described in their influential book, *Theory of Literature* (1942). Psychological criticism, they suggest, typically attempts to do at least one of the following: provide a psychological study of an individual writer; explore the nature of the creative process; generalize about "types and laws present within works of literature"; or theorize about the psychological "effects of literature upon its readers" (81). Entire books on psychoanalytic criticism began to appear, such as Frederick J. Hoffman's *Freudianism and the Literary Mind* (1945).

Probably because of Freud's characterization of the creative mind as "clamorous" if not ill, psychoanalytic criticism written before 1950 tended to psychoanalyze the individual author. Poems were read as fantasies that allowed authors to indulge repressed wishes, to protect themselves from deep-seated anxieties, or both. A perfect example of author analysis would be Marie Bonaparte's 1933 study of Edgar Allan Poe. Bonaparte found Poe to be so fixated on his mother that his repressed longing emerges in his stories in images such as the white spot on a black cat's breast, said to represent mother's milk.

A later generation of psychoanalytic critics often paused to analyze the characters in novels and plays before proceeding to their authors — but not for long, since characters, both evil and good, tended to be seen by these critics as the author's potential selves or projections of various repressed aspects of his or her psyche. For instance, in *A Psychoanalytic Study of the Double in Literature* (1970), Robert Rogers begins with the view that human beings are double or multiple in nature. Using this assumption, along with the psychoanalytic concept of "dissociation" (best known by its result, the dual or multiple personality), Rogers concludes that writers reveal instinctual or repressed selves in their books, often without realizing that they have done so.

In the view of critics attempting to arrive at more psychological insights into an author than biographical materials can provide, a work of literature is a fantasy or a dream — or at least so analogous to daydream or dream that Freudian analysis can help explain the nature of the mind that produced it. The author's purpose in writing is to gratify secretly some forbidden wish, in particular an infantile wish or desire that has been repressed into the unconscious mind. To discover what the wish is, the psychoanalytic critic employs many of the terms and procedures developed by Freud to analyze dreams.

The literal surface of a work is sometimes spoken of as its "manifest content" and treated as a "manifest dream" or "dream story" by a Freudian analyst. Just as the analyst tries to figure out the "dream thought" behind the dream story — that is, the latent or hidden content of the manifest dream — so the psychoanalytic literary critic tries to expose the latent, underlying content of a work. Freud used the words *condensation* and *displacement* to explain two of the mental processes whereby the mind disguises its wishes and fears in dream stories. In condensation, several thoughts or persons may be condensed into a single manifestation or image in a dream story; in displacement, an anxiety, a wish, or a person may be displaced onto the image of another, with which or whom it is loosely connected through a string of associations that only an analyst can untangle. Psychoanalytic critics treat metaphors as if they were dream condensations; they treat metonyms — figures of speech based on extremely loose, arbitrary associations — as if they were dream displacements. Thus figurative literary language in general is treated as something that evolves as the writer's conscious mind resists what the unconscious tells it to picture or describe. A symbol is, in Daniel Weiss's words, "a meaningful concealment of truth as the truth promises to emerge as some frightening or forbidden idea" (20).

In a 1970 article entitled "The 'Unconscious' of Literature," Norman Holland, a literary critic trained in psychoanalysis, succinctly sums up the attitudes held by critics who would psychoanalyze authors, but without quite saying that it is the *author* that is being analyzed by the psychoanalytic critic. "When one looks at a poem psychoanalytically," he writes, "one considers it as though it were a dream or as though some ideal patient [were speaking] from the couch in iambic pentameter." One "looks for the general level or levels of fantasy associated with the language. By level I mean the familiar stages of childhood development — oral [when desires for nourishment and infantile sexual desires overlap], anal [when infants receive their primary pleasure from defecation], urethral [when urinary functions are the locus of sexual pleasure], phallic [when the penis or, in girls, some penis substitute is of primary interest], oedipal." Holland continues by analyzing not Robert Frost but Frost's poem "Mending Wall" as a specifically oral fantasy that is not unique to its author. "Mending Wall" is "about breaking down the wall which marks the separated or individuated self so as to return to a state of closeness to some Other" — including and perhaps essentially the nursing mother ("'Unconscious'" 136, 139).

While not denying the idea that the unconscious plays a role in creativity, psychoanalytic critics such as Holland began to focus more on the ways in which authors create works that appeal to *our* repressed wishes and fantasies. Consequently, they shifted their focus away from the psyche of the author and toward the psychology of the reader and the text. Holland's theories, which have concerned themselves more with the reader than with the text, have helped to establish another school of critical theory: reader-response criticism. Elizabeth Wright explains Holland's brand of modern psychoanalytic criticism in this way: "What draws us as readers to a text is the secret expression of what we desire to hear, much as we protest we do not. The disguise must be good enough to fool the censor into thinking that the text is respectable, but bad enough to allow the unconscious to glimpse the unrespectable" (117).

Holland is one of dozens of critics who have revised Freud significantly in the process of revitalizing psychoanalytic criticism. Another such critic is R. D. Laing, whose controversial and often poetical writings about personality, repression, masks, and the double or "schizoid" self have (re)blurred the boundary between creative writing and psychoanalytic discourse. Yet another is D. W. Winnicott, an "object-relations" theorist who has had a significant impact on literary criticism. Critics influenced by Winnicott and his school have questioned the tendency to see reader/text as an either/or construct; instead, they have seen reader and text (or audience and play) in terms of a *relationship* taking place in what Winnicott calls a "transitional" or "potential" space — space in which binary terms such as *real* and *illusory, objective* and *subjective,* have little or no meaning.

Psychoanalytic theorists influenced by Winnicott see the transitional or potential reader/text (or audience/play) space as being *like* the space entered into by psychoanalyst and patient. More important, they also see it as being similar to the space between mother and infant: a space characterized by trust in which categorizing terms such as *knowing* and *feeling* mix and merge and have little meaning apart from one another.

Whereas Freud saw the mother-son relationship in terms of the son and his repressed oedipal complex (and saw the analyst-patient relationship in terms of the patient and the repressed "truth" that the analyst could scientifically extract), object-relations analysts see both relationships as *dyadic* — that is, as being dynamic in both directions. Consequently, they don't depersonalize analysis or their analyses. It is hardly surprising, therefore, that contemporary literary critics who apply object-relations theory to the texts they discuss don't depersonalize critics or categorize their interpretations as "truthful," at least not in any objective or scientific sense. In the view of such critics, interpretations are made of language — itself a transitional object — and are themselves the mediating terms or transitional objects of a relationship.

Like critics of the Winnicottian school, the French structuralist theorist Jacques Lacan focuses on language and language-related issues. He treats the unconscious *as* a language and, consequently, views the dream not as Freud did (that is, as a form and symptom of repression) but rather as a form of discourse. Thus we may study dreams psychoanalytically to learn about literature, even as we may study literature to learn more about the unconscious. In Lacan's seminar on Poe's "The Purloined Letter," a pattern of repetition like that used by psychoanalysts in their analyses is used to arrive at a reading of the story. According to Wright, "the new psychoanalytic structural approach to literature" employs "analogies from psychoanalysis . . . to explain the workings of the text as distinct from the workings of a particular author's, character's, or even reader's mind" (125).

Lacan, however, did far more than extend Freud's theory of dreams, literature, and the interpretation of both. More significantly, he took Freud's whole theory of psyche and gender and added to it a crucial third term — that of language. In the process, he both used and significantly developed Freud's ideas about the oedipal stage and complex.

Lacan points out that the pre-oedipal stage, in which the child at first does not even recognize its independence from its mother, is also a pre*verbal* stage, one in which the child communicates without the medium of language, or — if we insist on calling the child's communications a language — in a language that can only be called *literal*. ("Coos," certainly, cannot be said to be figurative or symbolic.) Then, while still in the pre-oedipal stage, the child enters the *mirror* stage.

During the mirror period, the child comes to view itself and its mother, later other people as well, *as* independent selves. This is the stage in which the child is first able to fear the aggressions of another, to desire what is recognizably beyond the self (initially the mother), and, finally, to want to compete with another for the same desired object. This is also the stage at which the child first becomes able to feel sympathy with another being who is being hurt by a third, to cry when another cries. All of these developments, of course, involve projecting beyond the self and, by extension, constructing one's own self (or "ego" or "I") as others view one — that is, as *another*. Such constructions, according to Lacan, are just that: constructs, products, artifacts — fictions of coherence that in fact hide what Lacan calls the "absence" or "lack" of being.

The mirror stage, which Lacan also refers to as the *imaginary* stage, is fairly quickly succeeded by the oedipal stage. As in Freud, this stage begins when the child, having come to view itself as self and the father and mother as separate selves, perceives gender and gender differences between its parents and between itself and one of its parents. For boys, gender awareness involves another, more powerful recognition, for the recognition of the father's phallus as the mark of his difference from the mother involves, at the same time, the recognition that his older and more powerful father is also his rival. That, in turn, leads to the understanding that what once seemed wholly his and even indistinguishable from himself is in fact someone else's: something properly desired only at a distance and in the form of socially acceptable *substitutes*.

The fact that the oedipal stage roughly coincides with the entry of the child into language is extremely important for Lacan. For the linguistic order is essentially a figurative or "Symbolic" order; words are not the things they stand for but are, rather, stand-ins or substitutes for those things. Hence boys, who in the most critical period of their development have had to submit to what Lacan calls the "Law of the Father" — a law that prohibits direct desire for and communicative intimacy with what has been the boy's whole world — enter more easily into the realm of language and the Symbolic order than do girls, who have never really had to renounce that which once seemed continuous with the self: the mother. The gap that has been opened up for boys, which includes the gap between signs and what they substitute — the gap marked by the phallus and encoded with the boy's sense of his maleness — has not opened up for girls, or has not opened up in the same way, to the same degree.

For Lacan, the father need not be present to trigger the oedipal stage; nor does his phallus have to be seen to catalyze the boy's (easier) transition into the Symbolic order. Rather, Lacan argues, a child's recognition of its gender is intricately tied up with a growing recognition of the system of names and naming, part of the larger system of substitutions we call language. A child has little doubt about who its mother is, but who is its father, and how would one know? The father's claim rests on the mother's *word* that he is in fact the father; the father's relationship to the child is thus established through language and a system of marriage and kinship — names — that in turn is basic to rules of everything from property to law. The name of the father (*nom du père,* which in French sounds like *non du père*) involves, in a sense, nothing of the father — nothing, that is, except his word or name.

Lacan's development of Freud has had several important results. First, his seemingly sexist association of maleness with the Symbolic order, together with his claim that women cannot therefore enter easily into the order, has prompted feminists not to reject his theory out of hand but, rather, to look more closely at the relation between language and gender, language and women's inequality. Some feminists have gone so far as to suggest that the social and political relationships between male and female will not be fundamentally altered until language itself has been radically changed. (That change might begin dialectically, with the development of some kind of "feminine language" grounded in the presymbolic, literal-to-imaginary communication between mother and child.)

Second, Lacan's theory has proved of interest to deconstructors and other poststructuralists, in part because it holds that the ego (which in Freud's view is as necessary as it is natural) is a product or construct. The ego-artifact, produced during the mirror stage, *seems* at once unified, consistent, and organized around a determinate center. But the unified self, or ego, is a fiction, according to Lacan. The yoking together of fragments and destructively dissimilar elements takes its psychic toll, and it is the job of the Lacanian psychoanalyst to "deconstruct," as it were, the ego, to show its continuities to be contradictions as well.

In the psychoanalytic reading of "The Secret Sharer" that follows, Daniel R. Schwarz approaches the tale as one in which a "young captain is faced with circumstances and emotional traumas for which neither the maritime code nor his experience has prepared him" (95). Schwarz concentrates on the captain as perceiver and teller, for in order to understand how the captain reacts and responds to traumatic moral circumstances we must explore "not only why he behaves as he does but how the original experience is reflected, refracted, displaced, and projected in the retrospective telling" (95). In analyzing "The Secret Sharer," Schwarz focuses not only on "seeing" and "being seen" but also on memory, which Schwarz calls "another kind of seeing — retrospective seeing" — one that "creates its own distortions" (97). Those distortions occur, Schwarz suggests, because "the retrospective retelling" is "a *painful* act," one that "has the potential to be deeply disruptive to the captain's current sense of self" (97).

In reading Conrad's tale, Schwarz makes considerable use of Freud's psychoanalytic theory. At one point, he applies the distinctions Freud drew between the id, ego, and superego ("Leggatt is a man of unrestrained id and underdeveloped superego. The captain is his opposite") (102). At another point, he alludes to the "repetition-compulsion," a concept Freud used to explain "a patient's need to repeat partly forgotten and repressed material." The captain's need to tell of his past encounter with Leggatt is grounded in his "guilt" over having "broken the seaman's code," Schwarz suggests. Additionally, Schwarz utilizes the Freudian idea of the double, arguing that, like Thomas Mann's Gustave von Aschenbach and the governess who narrates Henry James's *The Turn of the Screw*, Conrad's captain-narrator is a "stranger to himself" (98).

Schwarz's essay, while greatly informed by Freud's psychoanalytic theory, is not strictly Freudian throughout. At times it offers a straightforward, relatively untheorized psychological reading of a story about a mind under moral stress; at other times it utilizes the controversial ideas set forth by R. D. Laing in *The Divided Self*. In addition, it employs Lacanian terms and concepts ("the gaze" and the "mirror stage") to elucidate a story about a man who "gains a sense of wholeness and identity" through his encounter with a heretofore unknown mirror self (98).

Schwarz's allusions, moreover, range beyond Freud, Laing, and Lacan — and even beyond psychoanalytic theory and criticism. Ultimately, Schwarz places Conrad's tale in the context of other modernist novels and even paintings that involve seeing and being seen, autoeroticism and homoeroticism (the captain-narrator's crisis is not unrelated to the role of the bachelor in a family-oriented culture, Schwarz argues), and "recollection" that is "informed by an insight that was lacking when the original event took place" (102). (The captain's observations, like those of character-narrators in other modernist works, are in Schwarz's view self-reflections.) Indeed, Conrad's captain-narrator is viewed by Schwarz almost as a paradigm for the modernist literary protagonist and indeed even the modern individual: he has been effectively split by historical, social, and cultural forces into a socialized public self and an instinctual other who is hardly known — but with whom the public self must somehow be reconciled.

Ross C Murfin

PSYCHOANALYTIC CRITICISM: A SELECTED BIBLIOGRAPHY

Some Short Introductions to Psychological and Psychoanalytic Criticism

Holland, Norman. "The 'Unconscious' of Literature." *Contemporary Criticism.* Ed. Norman Bradbury and David Palmer. Stratford-upon-Avon Ser. 12. New York: St. Martin's, 1970. 131–54.

Natoli, Joseph, and Frederik L. Rusch, comps. *Psychocriticism: An Annotated Bibliography.* Westport: Greenwood, 1984.

Scott, Wilbur. *Five Approaches to Literary Criticism.* London: Collier-Macmillan, 1962. See the essays by Burke and Gorer as well as Scott's introduction to the section "The Psychological Approach: Literature in the Light of Psychological Theory."

Wellek, René, and Austin Warren. *Theory of Literature.* New York: Harcourt, 1942. See the chapter "Literature and Psychology" in pt. 3, "The Extrinsic Approach to the Study of Literature."

Wright, Elizabeth. "Modern Psychoanalytic Criticism." *Modern Literary Theory: A Comparative Introduction.* Ed. Ann Jefferson and David Robey. Totowa: Barnes, 1982. 113–33.

Freud, Lacan, and Their Influence

Basler, Roy P. *Sex, Symbolism, and Psychology in Literature.* New York: Octagon, 1975. See especially 13–19.

Clément, Catherine. *The Lives and Legends of Jacques Lacan.* Trans. Arthur Goldhammer. New York: Columbia UP, 1983.

Freud, Sigmund. *Introductory Lectures on Psycho-Analysis*. Trans. Joan Riviere. London: Allen, 1922.

Gallop, Jane. *Reading Lacan*. Ithaca: Cornell UP, 1985.

Hoffman, Frederick J. *Freudianism and the Literary Mind*. Baton Rouge: Louisiana State UP, 1945.

Hogan, Patrick Colm, and Lalita Pandit, eds. *Lacan and Criticism: Essays and Dialogue on Language, Structure, and the Unconscious*. Athens: U of Georgia P, 1990.

Kazin, Alfred. "Freud and His Consequences." *Contemporaries*. Boston: Little, 1962. 351–93.

Lacan, Jacques. *Écrits: A Selection*. Trans. Alan Sheridan. New York: Norton, 1977.

———. *Feminine Sexuality: Lacan and the École Freudienne*. Ed. Juliet Mitchell and Jacqueline Rose. Trans. Rose. New York: Norton, 1985.

———. *The Four Fundamental Concepts of Psychoanalysis*. Trans. Alan Sheridan. London: Penguin, 1980.

Macey, David. *Lacan in Contexts*. New York: Verso, 1988.

Meisel, Perry, ed. *Freud: A Collection of Critical Essays*. Englewood Cliffs: Prentice, 1981.

Muller, John P., and William J. Richardson. *Lacan and Language: A Reader's Guide to "Écrits."* New York: International, 1982.

Porter, Laurence M. *"The Interpretation of Dreams": Freud's Theories Revisited*. Twayne's Masterwork Studies Ser. Boston: G. K. Hall, 1986.

Reppen, Joseph, and Maurice Charney. *The Psychoanalytic Study of Literature*. Hillsdale: Analytic, 1985.

Schneiderman, Stuart. *Jacques Lacan: The Death of an Intellectual Hero*. Cambridge: Harvard UP, 1983.

———. *Returning to Freud: Clinical Psychoanalysis in the School of Lacan*. New Haven: Yale UP, 1980.

Selden, Raman. *A Reader's Guide to Contemporary Literary Theory*. 2nd ed. Lexington: U of Kentucky P, 1989. See "Jacques Lacan: Language and the Unconscious."

Sullivan, Ellie Ragland. *Jacques Lacan and the Philosophy of Psychoanalysis*. Champaign: U of Illinois P, 1986.

Sullivan, Ellie Ragland, and Mark Bracher, eds. *Lacan and the Subject of Language*. New York: Routledge, 1991.

Trilling, Lionel. "Art and Neurosis." *The Liberal Imagination*. New York: Scribner's, 1950. 160–80.

Wilden, Anthony. "Lacan and the Discourse of the Other." Lacan, *Speech and Language in Psychoanalysis*. Trans. Wilden. Baltimore: Johns Hopkins UP, 1981. (Published as *The Language of the Self* in 1968.) 159–311.

Psychoanalysis, Feminism, and Literature

Chodorow, Nancy. *The Reproduction of Mothering: Psychoanalysis and the Sociology of Gender*. Berkeley: U of California P, 1978.

Gallop, Jane. *The Daughter's Seduction: Feminism and Psychoanalysis*. Ithaca: Cornell UP, 1982.

Garner, Shirley Nelson, Claire Kahane, and Madelon Sprengnether. *The (M)other Tongue: Essays in Feminist Psychoanalytic Interpretation*. Ithaca: Cornell UP, 1985.

Irigaray, Luce. *The Speculum of the Other Woman*. Trans. Gillian C. Gill. Ithaca: Cornell UP, 1985.

———. *This Sex Which Is Not One*. Trans. Catherine Porter. Ithaca: Cornell UP, 1985.

Jacobus, Mary. "Is There a Woman in This Text?" *New Literary History* 14 (1982): 117–41.

Kristeva, Julia. *The Kristeva Reader*. Ed. Toril Moi. New York: Columbia UP, 1986. See especially the selection from *Revolution in Poetic Language*, 89–136.

Mitchell, Juliet. *Psychoanalysis and Feminism*. New York: Random, 1974.

Mitchell, Juliet, and Jacqueline Rose. "Introduction I" and "Introduction II." Lacan, *Feminine Sexuality: Jacques Lacan and the École Freudienne*. New York: Norton, 1985. 1–26, 27–57.

Sprengnether, Madelon. *The Spectral Mother: Freud, Feminism, and Psychoanalysis*. Ithaca: Cornell UP, 1990.

Psychological and Psychoanalytic Studies of Literature

Bettelheim, Bruno. *The Uses of Enchantment: The Meaning and Importance of Fairy Tales*. New York: Knopf, 1976. Although this book is about fairy tales instead of literary works written for publication, it offers model Freudian readings of well-known stories.

Crews, Frederick C. *Out of My System: Psychoanalysis, Ideology, and Critical Method*. New York: Oxford UP, 1975.

———. *Relations of Literary Study*. New York: MLA, 1967. See the chapter "Literature and Psychology."

Diehl, Joanne Feit. "Re-Reading *The Letter:* Hawthorne, the Fetish, and the (Family) Romance." *Nathaniel Hawthorne, "The Scarlet Letter."* Ed. Ross C Murfin. Case Studies in Contemporary Criticism Ser. Ed. Ross C Murfin. Boston: Bedford–St. Martin's, 1991. 235–51.

Hallman, Ralph. *Psychology of Literature: A Study of Alienation and Tragedy.* New York: Philosophical Library, 1961.

Hartman, Geoffrey, ed. *Psychoanalysis and the Question of the Text.* Baltimore: Johns Hopkins UP, 1978. See especially the essays by Hartman, Johnson, Nelson, and Schwartz.

Hertz, Neil. *The End of the Line: Essays on Psychoanalysis and the Sublime.* New York: Columbia UP, 1985.

Holland, Norman N. *Dynamics of Literary Response.* New York: Oxford UP, 1968.

———. *Poems in Persons: An Introduction to the Psychoanalysis of Literature.* New York: Norton, 1973.

Kris, Ernest. *Psychoanalytic Explorations in Art.* New York: International, 1952.

Lucas, F. L. *Literature and Psychology.* London: Cassell, 1951.

Natoli, Joseph, ed. *Psychological Perspectives on Literature: Freudian Dissidents and Non-Freudians: A Casebook.* Hamden: Archon Books–Shoe String, 1984.

Phillips, William, ed. *Art and Psychoanalysis.* New York: Columbia UP, 1977.

Rogers, Robert. *A Psychoanalytic Study of the Double in Literature.* Detroit: Wayne State UP, 1970.

Skura, Meredith. *The Literary Use of the Psychoanalytic Process.* New Haven: Yale UP, 1981.

Strelka, Joseph P. *Literary Criticism and Psychology.* University Park: Pennsylvania State UP, 1976. See especially the essays by Lerner and Peckham.

Weiss, Daniel. *The Critic Agonistes: Psychology, Myth, and the Art of Fiction.* Ed. Eric Solomon and Stephen Arkin. Seattle: U of Washington P, 1985.

Lacanian Psychoanalytic Studies of Literature

Collings, David. "The Monster and the Imaginary Mother: A Lacanian Reading of *Frankenstein.*" *Mary Shelley, "Frankenstein."* Ed. Johanna M. Smith. Case Studies in Contemporary Criticism Ser. Ed. Ross C Murfin. Boston: Bedford–St. Martin's, 1992. 245–58.

Davis, Robert Con, ed. *The Fictional Father: Lacanian Readings of the Text*. Amherst: U of Massachusetts P, 1981.

———. "Lacan and Narration." *Modern Language Notes* 5 (1983): 843–1063.

Felman, Shoshana, ed. *Jacques Lacan and the Adventure of Insight: Psychoanalysis in Contemporary Culture*. Cambridge: Harvard UP, 1987.

———, ed. *Literature and Psychoanalysis: The Question of Reading: Otherwise*. Baltimore: Johns Hopkins UP, 1982.

Froula, Christine. "When Eve Reads Milton: Undoing the Canonical Economy." *Canons*. Ed. Robert von Hallberg. Chicago: U of Chicago P, 1984. 149–75.

Homans, Margaret. *Bearing the Word: Language and Female Experience in Nineteenth-Century Women's Writing*. Chicago: U of Chicago P, 1986.

Muller, John P., and William J. Richardson, eds. *The Purloined Poe: Lacan, Derrida, and Psychoanalytic Reading*. Baltimore: Johns Hopkins UP, 1988. Includes Lacan's seminar on Poe's "The Purloined Letter."

Psychoanalytic Approaches to Conrad

Gettmann, Royal A., and Bruce Harkness. "Morality and Psychology in 'The Secret Sharer.'" *Conrad's Secret Sharer and the Critics*. Ed. Bruce Harkness. Belmont, CA: Wadsworth, 1962.

Guerard, Albert J. *Conrad the Novelist*. Cambridge: Harvard UP, 1958.

Johnson, Barbara, and Marjorie Garber. "Secret Sharing: Reading Conrad Psychoanalytically." *College English* 49.6 (1987): 628–40.

Meyer, Bernard C. *Joseph Conrad: A Psychoanalytic Biography*. Princeton: Princeton UP, 1967.

Moser, Thomas C. *Joseph Conrad: Achievement and Decline*. Cambridge: Harvard UP, 1957.

Najder, Zdzislaw. *Joseph Conrad: A Chronicle*. New Brunswick: Rutgers UP, 1983.

Paccaud, Josiane. "Under the Other's Eyes: Conrad's 'The Secret Sharer.'" *Conradian* 12.1 (1987): 59–73.

Wexler, Joyce. "Conrad's Dream of a Common Language: Lacan and 'The Secret Sharer.'" *Psychoanalytic Review* 78.4 (1991): 599–606.

A PSYCHOANALYTIC PERSPECTIVE

DANIEL R. SCHWARZ
"The Secret Sharer" as an Act of Memory

"The Secret Sharer" is personal in the way great lyrical poetry is personal, drawing from experience that is at once individual (Conrad's assuming the captaincy of the *Otago* in 1888) and representative of the deepest strains of human experience, especially fear and self-doubt in the face of challenge. Although in this period of renewed personal and financial turmoil Conrad's imagination turned nostalgically to life at sea, the sea is no longer the simplified world of "Typhoon" or "The End of the Tether," where moral distinctions are clear. A young captain is faced with circumstances and emotional traumas for which neither the maritime code nor his experience has prepared him.

Conrad's narrative reveals as it conceals, but conceals as it reveals. The captain-narrator recounts a tale of initiation in which he successfully overcomes debilitating emotional insecurity to command his ship. The sensitive and intelligent captain discovers within himself the *ability to act* decisively. Initially the captain doubts himself, feels a "stranger" to his ship and crew, and wonders if he should "turn out faithful to that ideal conception of one's own personality every man sets up for himself secretly" (26). His concern *now* in telling the story is to convey what Leggatt meant to him. Although he certainly knows that harboring an escaped murderer represents a threat to maritime civilization and violates his own legal and moral commitment, his retelling ignores this. In our psychological critique of "The Secret Sharer" we need to explore the complex psyche and values of the captain-narrator and to understand not only why he behaves as he does but how the original experience is reflected, refracted, displaced, and projected in the retrospective telling.

The act of observing is a crucial focus of modernism. For example, borrowing from astronomy, James Joyce makes the theme of parallax (how the same phenomenon looks different depending on the angle of vision or perspective) central to *Ulysses* (1922). Cubism is about the need to see from multiple perspectives. Conrad's "The Secret Sharer," like Henry James's *The Turn of the Screw* (1898), is about seeing and being seen, which plays such an important role in impressionism and postimpressionism, especially in the tradition of still life. Leggatt likes to be looked at:

> "When I saw a man's head looking over I thought I would swim
> away presently and leave him shouting—in whatever language it
> was. I didn't mind being looked at. I—I liked it. And then you
> speaking to me so quietly—as if you had expected me—made me
> hold on a little longer." (37)

As in this passage, the self-reflection and narcissism of "The Secret
Sharer" are reflected in the verbal style of both the captain and Leggatt. The "I" is not here the "I" of a strong ego; rather, as the *object*
of observation, "I" becomes the subject.

Conrad's experiments with the dramatized narrator show how, in
the act of interpreting the subject, modernism has shifted the emphasis
from the subject itself to the perceiver's mind. With some complaining
irony, Virginia Woolf remarks in "Mr. Bennett and Mrs. Brown" that
"where so much strength is spent on finding a way of telling the truth,
the truth itself is bound to reach us in rather an exhausted and chaotic
condition" (117). In the modern period, "finding a way—the quest
for values and for the appropriate style and form—becomes the subject. And is not finding our way another version of seeing? In my discussion I want to examine the importance of seeing and being seen.
When Conrad wrote eloquently in the preface to *The Nigger of the
"Narcissus"* about his purpose as a writer, he wrote with the fervor of
a man who believes in the capacity of art to shape our responses to
life: "My task which I am trying to achieve is, by the power of the
written word, to make you hear, to make you feel—it is, before all,
to make you *see*" (14). He was speaking of the power of the written
word to create within the reader's mind an experience—a visual experience—that would belong to the reader but still be a version of
Conrad's own:

> Fiction—if it at all inspires to be art—appeals to temperament.
> And in truth it must be, like painting, like music, like all art, the
> appeal of one temperament to all the other innumerable tempera-
> ments whose subtle and resistless power endows passing events
> with their true meaning, and creates the moral, the emotional at-
> mosphere of the place and time. (13)

In many ways "to make you see" is also the subject of James's *The
Turn of the Screw*, another story that revolves around the psychological
complexity of simultaneously observing and being observed. The governess learns how to see differently in part because of her need to be
seen; Douglas wants to be the center of attention as narrator, and
James is using his tale to discuss the subjective nature of optics. Using

the governess as a paradigm of what happens when reality becomes subordinated to self-indulgence, James explores the way a teller becomes a painter of souls whose telling always has a strong autobiographical dimension. It may be that the governess—the unreliable narrator whose perceptions are psychotic—is a self-parody of extreme and self-indulgent aestheticism.

Memory is another kind of seeing—retrospective seeing—and as we know, memory creates its own distortions. The captain-narrator, separated by a "distance of years" from the meeting with Leggatt, delivers a retrospective monologue:

> On my right hand there were lines of fishing-stakes resembling a mysterious system of half-submerged bamboo fences, incomprehensible in its division of the domain of tropical fishes, and crazy of aspect as if abandoned for ever by some nomad tribe of fishermen now gone to the other end of the ocean; for there was no sign of human habitation as far as the eye could reach. (24)

But despite the past tense, the reader often forgets that the events have already occurred; as Albert Guerard has written, "The nominal narrative past is, actually, a harrowing present which the reader too must explore and survive" (27).

The oblique style disguises as much as it reveals: the "fishing-stakes resembling a mysterious system of half-submerged bamboo fences" anticipate the "headless corpse" that the captain pulls out of the water. When Leggatt appears he is "silvery, fish-like. He remained as mute as a fish, too" (29). Leggatt is aligned with the atavistic and primitive, whereas the captain is a hyperconscious modern man, retreating to his psychic laboratory to sift through his feelings. Appropriately, at the end Leggatt asks to be abandoned to the primitive world. Words such as *incomprehensible* and *crazy* are the available and feeble semiotic tools with which the captain is trying to come to terms with his behavior—behavior that even at the distance of years eludes explanation. He is well aware *now* of the stakes and knows that in the past he jeopardized his future by harboring an escaped murderer; Leggatt violated every tenet of the maritime code when he strangled a man under his command.

We need to understand that the narrative is a *painful* act of memory that has the potential to be deeply disruptive to the captain's current sense of self. In a way we are in the position of an analyst hearing about an incomprehensible, even traumatic experience. Indeed, we might recall that the act of telling is a version of "repetition-compulsion," which Freud describes in his 1920 essay "Beyond the Pleasure Principle":

> It must be explained that we are able to postulate the principle of a repetition-compulsion in the unconscious mind, based upon instinctual activity and inherent in the very nature of the instincts—a principle powerful enough to overrule the pleasure-principle, lending to certain aspects of the mind their daemonic character, and still very clearly expressed in the tendencies of small children; a principle, too, which is responsible for a part of the course taken by the analysis of neurotic patients. Taken in all, the foregoing prepares us for the discovery that whatever reminds us of this inner repetition-compulsion is perceived as uncanny. (qtd. in Hertz 300)

Freud is describing a patient's need to repeat partly forgotten and repressed material. In "The Secret Sharer" the speaker has a burden of guilt because he has broken the seaman's code. His excuses make up much of the story, and his narrative iterates that he is still a stranger to himself. In a sense, the captain's telling allows him to relive the original experience. As Neil Hertz has observed in his discussion of trauma in "Freud and the Sandman,"

> Repetition becomes "visible" when it is colored or tinged by something being repeated, which itself functions like vivid or heightened language, lending a kind of rhetorical consistency to what is otherwise quite literally unspeakable. Whatever it is that is repeated—an obsessive ritual, perhaps, or a bit of acting-out in relation to one's analyst—will, then, feel most compellingly uncanny when it is seen as *merely* coloring, that is, when it comes to seem most gratuitously rhetorical. (301)

The act of watching and being watched is a theme that became increasingly prominent in the nineteenth century, as paintings such as Édouard Manet's *Déjeuner sur l'herbe* and works such as *The Turn of the Screw* and Thomas Mann's *Death in Venice* illustrate. Lacan has focused on the importance of the gaze:

> Is there no satisfaction in being under that gaze . . . that gaze that circumscribes us, and . . . which in the first instance makes us beings who are looked at, but without showing this. The spectacle of the world, in this sense, appears to us as all-seeing. . . . The world is all-seeing, but it is not exhibitionistic—it does not provoke our gaze. When it begins to provoke it, the feeling of strangeness begins too. (75)

Isn't the captain reenacting the developmental stage (called the "mirror stage" by Lacan) in which the baby recognizes the image in the mirror and gains a sense of wholeness and identity? Interestingly, Conrad entitled his reminiscence *The Mirror and the Sea* (1906).

Let us consider how mirrors function in modernism. The captain observes, "The shadowy, dark head, like mine, seemed to nod imperceptibly above the ghostly grey of my sleeping-suit. It was, in the night, as though I had been faced by my own reflection in the depths of a sombre and immense mirror" (31). Mirrors always distort, for we see only what we want to see; we see only the part of the body on which we focus. In *The Turn of the Screw,* the governess sees herself for the first time "from head to foot" in the mirror in the long, impressive room to which she is assigned (631). Identity is dependent on what one sees, how one sees, and how one is seen. And does the mirror not focus on ourselves creating what we see and so call attention to the self-reflexivity of reading in the modern era and the continuity between reading texts and reading lives? Specter experiences may reveal that one is perceiving myopically *or* perspicaciously. There can be little doubt that the captain sees Leggatt—if he did not, where would the specter/dream experience begin? (After all, Captain Archbold comes looking for Leggatt.)

Let us consider Manet's *Déjeuner sur l'Herbe* (1863), a parody of the pastoral as seen from an urban perspective (see Figure 1). Manet's painting is a narrative of voyeurism, one that anticipates Henry James's *The Turn of the Screw* and the obsession in "The Secret Sharer" with seeing and being seen. Two young urban males—the tasseled cap was worn by students—are picnicking with a naked woman. Meanwhile, in the background—recalling ironically Botticelli's *Birth of Venus* (1480)—a woman emerges from a stream. But the flat background landscape might be another picture ironically commenting on the foregrounded picnic. Or we might say the "middle-grounded picnic" because foregrounded on the left is a still life; only the still life has a sense of depth. Isn't Manet calling attention to the painter's ability to mix genres however he pleases and to defy conventions of genre and perspective?

Neither woman—the one sitting on her wrap or the one emerging from the stream—pays attention to the men or to each other. Each is in her own space. Note how the naked woman is un-self-consciously looking away from her companions, perhaps to catch the attention of other men or women who are not within the scene. In a sense, we the audience are engaged frankly by her as voyeurs in a libidinal

Figure 1. Déjeuner sur l'herbe (1863)

interchange in which she both looks and is looked at. If we think of *The Turn of the Screw,* the foregrounded woman is the governess's suppressed libidinal self and the self-absorbed woman in the background is the mysterious, ghostly presence that exists beyond the conscious level. We follow the phallic cane as it calls attention to her nakedness. As Francoise Cachin notes, "The still life accentuates the nudity of the woman, who becomes, in the presence of this heap of fashionable raiment, undressed rather than nude" (*Manet* 169). Yet the picnic lunch—with cherries of June, the figs of September—is not realistic. We see the influence of Titian's "Concert Champetre" and Raimondi's engraving—inspired by a Raphael composition—"The Judgment of Paris." (Manet would have enjoyed the classical echo of his city's name.) But in Manet's realistic Paris sexual frankness dominates.

I want to consider "The Secret Sharer" in the tradition of Joris-Karl Huysman's *À Rebours* (*Against the Grain,* 1884) and Oscar Wilde's *The Picture of Dorian Gray* (1891). As Richard Sieburth notes, the bachelor has no place in a family-oriented culture:

The bachelor cuts a somewhat pathetic figure in a nineteenth century given over to the ideological consolidation of the social and economic virtues of family life. Sexually, he is viewed with both condescension and trepidation, for while his legitimate recourse to prostitution is more or less condoned, he nonetheless threatens the social order as a possible agent of adultery, criminal seduction, or unnatural perversion. Economically, he is considered at most a marginal entity, for he plays no role in the transmission of property through inheritance or dowry. Civically, he is seen as an embarrassment to community values, a case of arrested development, narcissistically clinging to the prerogatives of his self-centered individualism. (5)

The bachelor motif plays a role in the sea tales of Conrad, in the male bonding between Marlow and Kurtz in *Heart of Darkness* and, in particular, between the captain and Leggatt in "The Secret Sharer," where the word *secret* (which implied sexuality—as in the anonymous text *My Secret Life*—to the Victorians) gives the male bonding a strong sexual implication. The captain-narrator never mentions a woman in his life, and Leggatt is disturbed that Captain Archbold of the *Sephora* has brought his wife aboard. The captain is a sometimes introverted bachelor, wedded to his routines, desperately lonely, and he creates his own company by reaching out for a lonely male figure— a supposedly empathetic other in the form of Leggatt.

"The Secret Sharer," like James's *The Turn of the Screw*, emphasizes looking and seeing as a mode of perception that reveals the inner workings of character; the captain's and Leggatt's loneliness help to create what they see. The captain becomes imprisoned by a nightmare of his own choosing. Leggatt destabilizes the captain as the captain's obsession with Leggatt undermines his capacity to command his ship.

Among other things, homoeroticism is a metaphor for the inversion of art. In *The Turn of the Screw* the apparitions, particularly Quint's female companion and counterpart, Miss Jessel, become the governess's secret sharers, and she speaks of Quint as a stranger the way the captain-narrator speaks of Leggatt in "The Secret Sharer." Particularly to a contemporary reader, does the male bonding in Conrad's story not have a homoerotic aspect? After all, they are in bed together and communicate like lovers: "And in the same whisper, as if we two whenever we talked had to say things to each other which were not fit for the world to hear, he added, 'It's very wonderful'" (52). Note the parallel between the unmarried governess when she encounters her predecessor—or, rather, her ghost—in the schoolroom: "She had looked at me long enough to appear to say that her right to sit at my table was as good as mine to sit at hers" (707). The captain's looking at the naked Leggatt and realizing him as other—as a potentially fulfilling and sexualized other—is a male version of the kind of gazing we see in *Déjeuner sur l'Herbe*. It is this looking at and being seen which suggest homoerotic interest on the captain's part. Like Gabriel Conroy, Joyce's paralytically self-conscious figure in "The Dead," the captain often regards himself as strangely detached, the object of his own gaze.

Let us return to the captain's act of memory. Perhaps we can draw upon Louis L. Martz's conception of a meditative poem to clarify what is happening. The intense reflective process in which the speaker's past comes alive in his memory and offers a moment of illumination by which he can order his life recalls Martz's definition of the meditative process: "The mind grasps firmly a problem or situation deliberately evoked by the memory, brings it forward toward the full light of consciousness, and concludes with a moment of illumination, where the speaker's self has, for a time, found an answer to his conflicts" (330). A meditative poem, such as George Herbert's "The Collar," recollects a vital episode in which the speaker experiences spiritual growth by conquering the secular demands of his ego. In both "The Collar" and "The Secret Sharer," the recollection is informed by insight that was lacking when the original event took place. That the captain can give meaning and structure to an experience which included neurotic immobilization demonstrates his emotional and moral development and his present psychic health.

One of Conrad's recurring themes is that each man interprets events according to his moral and emotional needs. Because one's version of events reflects an interaction between, on the one hand, experience and perception, and, on the other, memories and psychic needs, interpretation always has a subjective element. The captain's interpretation of his experience dramatizes the process of his coming to terms with what Leggatt symbolizes. In somewhat reductive but apt Freudian terms, Leggatt is a man of unrestrained id and underdeveloped superego. The captain is his opposite: a hyperconscious modern man who fastidiously thinks of the consequences of every action to the point where he cannot *do* anything. Self-doubt and anxiety create an illogical identification with Leggatt as his double. He risks his future to hide the man he regards as his other self. To avoid discovery, he begins to act desperately and instinctively without conscious examination of the consequences of each action. Leggatt's presence creates situations where the luxury of introspection is no longer possible. Symbolically, the captain completes himself. He finds within himself the potential to act instinctively and boldly that his double exemplifies. It can be said that his adult ego is created by appeasing the contradictory demands of the id and superego. Listening to the narrator, we tentatively suspend our moral perspective and fail to condemn him for giving refuge to a suspected murderer. We react this way because as his words engage us and we become implicated as his confessor, we come to share his perspective.

Conrad wants us to perceive Leggatt and the captain as representatives of a modern split between mind and instinct. Leggatt's Conradian predecessors are Falk ("Falk: A Reminiscence") and Kurtz, the demonic figure who reverts to savagery in *Heart of Darkness;* the Captain recalls the narrators of "Il Conde," "The Informer," and "An Anarchist"—three of Conrad's political short stories collected in his *Set of Six* (1908)—and anticipates the language-teacher of *Under Western Eyes,* to which Conrad returned after finishing "The Secret Sharer." The effect of Leggatt's presence is to disrupt the ship's community and to raise further doubts in the minds of the captain's officers about his own self-control and sanity. The captain becomes more neurotic because he has to consider whether his every sentence might reveal his secret. He now has twin loyalties, mutually exclusive, to his ship and to the man he is harboring and with whom he identifies. Paradoxically, the desperation of his paranoia, of his belief that he is constantly being scrutinized by his subordinates, leads him to give his "first particular order." When threatened, he "felt the need of asserting myself." The pressure of circumstances makes it increasingly difficult for him to distinguish between himself and Leggatt:

> All the time the dual working of my mind distracted me almost to the point of insanity. I was constantly watching myself, my secret self, as dependent on my actions as my own personality, sleeping in that bed, behind that door which faced me as I sat at the head of the table. It was very much like being mad, only it was worse because one was aware of it. (40)

His distinction between self and other threatens to collapse; he had the "mental feeling of being in two places at once [which] affected me physically as if the mood of secrecy had penetrated my very soul" (48). Like Eliot's J. Alfred Prufrock and Joyce's Gabriel Conroy in "The Dead," the captain has a personality, the integrity of which is threatened by a disbelief in the authenticity of self. R. D. Laing's *The*

Divided Self aptly describes this phenomenon of modern literature. The terms in which this existential psychologist describes schizoid conditions are directly related to the crisis of identity that Conrad analyzes:

> If one experiences the other as a free agent, one is open to the possibility of experiencing oneself as an *object* of his experience and thereby of feeling one's own subjectivity drained away. One is threatened with the possibility of becoming no more than a thing in the world of the other, without any life for oneself, without any being for oneself. . . . One may find oneself enlivened and the sense of one's own being enhanced by the other, or one may experience the other as deadening and impoverishing. (47)

In retrospect it is clear that the captain has been "enlivened" by his experience of Leggatt, although at first Leggatt's appearance—like the presence of the threatening first mate, whose whiskers and manner intimidate the captain—has the effect of "deadening" the captain by making him doubt his own capacity.

The captain's *creation* of Leggatt is a major part of the original experience. By "creation," I do not mean that the captain invents or dreams up Leggatt but that he constructs Leggatt for his own psychological purposes. Before Leggatt's appearance, the captain is immobilized by self-consciousness and self-doubt: "My position was that of the only *stranger* on board. I mention this because it has some bearing on what is to follow. But what I felt most was my being a *stranger* to the ship; and if all the truth must be told, I was somewhat a *stranger* to myself" (26, emphasis added). That "stranger" carries the meaning of "alien" and "outside" from the French word *étranger* is an instance of how the richness of Conrad's language is occasionally increased by his appropriating French definitions for similarly spelled English words.

Humorless, insecure, and claustrophobic, the captain needs to be on deck to avoid the discomfort and awkwardness fed by his feelings of inadequacy. Leggatt fulfills the captain's need for someone with whom to share the burdens of loneliness and anxiety. The captain's impulse is to completely integrate Leggatt into his social and moral fabric, and to totemize him as part of himself. But Leggatt is one of what Melville calls *Isolatoes,* one who "not acknowledging the common continent of men . . . [lives] on a separate continent of his own" (108; ch. 27). When the captain hears of Leggatt's alternatives (to keep swimming until he drowns or is welcomed aboard), he responds, "I felt this was no mere formula of desperate speech, but a real alternative in the view of a strong soul. . . . A mysterious communication was established already between us two—in the face of that silent, darkened tropical sea" (30). The captain recalls, "The voice was calm and resolute. A good voice. The *self-possession* of that man had somehow induced a corresponding state in myself" (30, emphasis added).

But this contrasts with his original assessment only seconds before: "He seemed to struggle with himself, for I heard something like the low, bitter murmur of doubt. 'What's the good?' His next words come out with a hesitating effort" (29). Jumping from one assertion to another without empirical data, the captain continues to convince himself of Leggatt's resemblance to himself on such flimsy grounds as that they are both "young." Although he tells us that they looked identical, he later admits that Leggatt "was not a bit like me, really" (34). His flattering description of Leggatt is continually modified until it is almost contradicted. Before Leggatt even begins to explain how he killed a man, the captain has excused him: "'Fit of temper,' I suggested, confidently" (31). Insisting on the value of his second self enables the captain to discover himself morally and psychologically; but the process of idealizing his double, his other self, into a model of self-control, self-confidence, and sanity is arbitrary and noncognitive. Perhaps we can better understand the extent of the narrator's surrender of self if we recall Laing's analysis of a man who suffered from what he calls "ontological insecurity": "In contrast to his own belittlement of uncertainty about himself, he was always on the brink of being overawed and crushed by the formidable reality that other people contained. In contrast to his own . . . uncertainty, and insubstantiality, *they* were solid, decisive, emphatic, and substantial" (48). Despite the evidence that Leggatt murdered another man in a fit of passion, the captain holds to a belief in Leggatt's control and sanity and insists that the killing was an act of duty. But the reader does not forget that Leggatt commits a horribly immoral act which *he does not regret*.

Conrad emphasizes how the destructive relationship between the doubting crew and the insecure captain shapes the captain's attitude toward Leggatt. The captain never criticizes Leggatt (despite his penchant for criticizing everybody else, from the ratiocinative first mate to the "impudent second mate" and "unintelligent" Captain Archbold) because believing himself a stranger on the ship, he desperately needs an ally against self-doubt and the hostility of the crew. He identifies with Leggatt not as a criminal, but as an outcast: "I felt that it would take very little to make me a suspect person in the eyes of the ship's company" (37). Because in *the captain's own mind* Leggatt is the picture of resolute self-confidence, he becomes in some respects an ideal to be studied: "And yet, haggard as he *appeared,* he *looked* always perfectly self-controlled, more than calm—almost invulnerable" (48, emphasis added). The fetal position that Leggatt assumes as he hides in the cabin hardly suggests invulnerability. Indeed, it suggests his moral immaturity and his inability to distinguish between self and world, either from an ethical or psychological perspective. The now mature captain *believes* he learned from his second self qualities of courage, self-confidence, and psychological wholeness—qualities which became his means of achieving maturity.

Paradoxically, Leggatt disrupts the captain's psychic health, and hence the order of the ship, at the same time as he is a catalyst for a more efficient integration of both the captain's personality and his fitness to command. As we have seen, the captain projects onto Leggatt a confidence he himself lacks and an ability to face crises he does not yet possess. Yet Leggatt's struggle with the crewman came when he was himself highly excited, and he shows considerable emotion several times in discussions with the captain.

The captain is as much Leggatt's secret sharer as Leggatt is the captain's: each plays the role of analyst and analysand. Indeed, each of the two men has a partial understanding of the other, but each *believes* the other's partial understanding to be complete. In this sense, too, Leggatt is the captain's double. Leggatt says, "As long as I know that you understand," before adding, "But of course you do," because he too needs to believe he is understood (52). Leggatt desperately reaches out for someone to share his psychic burden. He likes to be looked at and spoken to, and even stammers when recalling their first meeting. At one point he says, "I wanted to be seen, to talk with somebody, before I went on" (38). As R. W. Stallman says, "it is this mutual, sympathetic understanding of what the other's plight means to him that bolsters and morally fortifies their spiritual being" (99). They both create a buffer to protect themselves from their feelings of excruciating loneliness in a hostile world. In each other, they find the intimacy of a captain-mate relationship that they both pathetically lack. The first mate's suspicion of the captain echoes Leggatt's opinion of *his* captain. And Archbold, the captain of the *Sephora,* the boat on which Leggatt killed a man, is the type of captain—or, rather, Leggatt and the captain's version of him—that the narrator might have become if he had not engaged in this process of self-development. Archbold, whose name has resonances of traditional descriptions of Satan as *Archbold,* is an embodiment of the maritime tradition of authority. He represents a father figure whom the captain oedipally rejects.

Leggatt hides in the captain's L-shaped room. As Johnson and Garber remark in "Secret Sharing: Reading Conrad Psychoanalytically,"

> The cabin is L-shaped. It is shaped like a signifier, and what it signifies is what it contains and what contains it, the man whose name begins with L: Leggatt. Even Leggatt's name is doubled, two g's, two t's, two vowels—only the L stands alone, and it too is doubled in the form of the cabin. The capital L stands for Leggatt, but also for letter, for the "agency of the letter in unconscious" (Lacan), for the fact that what is innermost (concealed) in the mind is in a sense its other. (636)

While experiencing Leggatt's objective world—that is, seeing the world through Leggatt's perspective—the captain adopts Leggatt's perspective. Therefore he has no hesitation or ambivalence in his attitude toward Archbold. Not only does he compare Archbold, who stands, however poignantly, as an upholder of the moral order, to a criminal, but in addition he describes him as "a tenacious beast." Speaking of an exchange with Archbold, the captain recalls, "I had been too frightened not to feel *vengeful;* I felt I had him on the run, and I meant to keep him on the run. My polite insistence must have had something menacing in it because he gave in suddenly" (45, emphasis added). However, the reader knows that the captain's judgment of Archbold is really Leggatt's and cannot exclude the possibility—indeed the probability—that Archbold is everything *he* says he is.

Nor can we accept the captain's belief that Leggatt deserves the allegorical identity of Truth, and Captain Archbold that of Falsehood. His recollection of Leggatt's captain is consistent with his present mythmaking. Although he does not remember his name, he assigns a pejorative name that we realize would be far more appropriate to Leggatt, a figure whose *arch boldness* defies conventional morality: "He mumbled to me as if he were ashamed of what he was saying; gave his name (it was something like Archbold—but at this distance of years I hardly am sure), his ship's name, and a few other particulars of that sort, in the manner of a criminal making a reluctant and doleful confession" (41). Although the captain is certain that Archbold suspects him, he offers no real evidence to support this notion; since he has told us how *different* from Leggatt he looked, it is unlikely that he would be the object of Archbold's transference of the antagonism he feels toward Leggatt. When he implies that Archbold does not like him, he is describing perhaps his own guilt: "I had become so connected in thoughts and impressions with the secret sharer of my cabin that I felt as if I, personally, were given to understand that I, too, was not the sort that would have done for the chief mate of a ship like the *Sephora*. I had no doubt of it in my mind" (43). Conrad hardly expected his readers to believe the captain's assertion that he reminded Archbold of Leggatt.

If we regard "The Secret Sharer" as a drama about the problems and interrelationships of people, we must ask why Leggatt requests to be abandoned. Does he sense that the captain cannot continue to operate as a split personality? Probably, but defined by his murderous, impulsive act, Leggatt also needs to assert his own independence and to accept the role of exiled wanderer, as outcast to the universe where civilized values, embodied by the benign autocracy of maritime life, prevail. The narrator, of course, puts the best possible interpretation on Leggatt's behavior and implicitly invites us to do the same. Certainly, when the character with whom we identify and whose judgment is practically beyond reproach enlists our sympathy, it is not surprising that our first response is to accept his evaluation. He admires Leggatt both as a self-controlled man who can accept the consequences of his actions and as a man whose instinctive behavior saved the *Sephora*. For him, Leggatt is not a mutineer and a murderer, but an effective officer who is the victim of circumstances beyond his control.

The captain's final view of Leggatt is significant: "I was in time to catch an evanescent glimpse of my white hat left behind to mark the spot where the secret sharer of my cabin and of my thoughts, as though he were my second self, had lowered himself into the water to take his punishment: a *free* man, a *proud* swimmer striking out for a new destiny" (60, emphasis added). The only way for the captain to satisfy his conscience now that he has released Leggatt is to create the myth of a triumphant departure, for even retrospectively he cannot admit that he might have sacrificed Leggatt in order to preserve his own position. Yet for the reader, Leggatt is a tragic, lonesome figure, branded as an outsider destined to wander the earth not only by the standards of civilization but by the captain himself.

Why does the captain take Leggatt so close to land? For one thing he needs to assuage his conscience; for another, he has to prove to himself that he has grown into the role of captain; he needs to assert himself in the role of command. Indeed, the telling is that of a retrospective analysis and probing into a crucial crossing from youth to maturity. Although we cannot be sure of the tale's authenticity, its value to the speaker is incontestable.

It is the teller who has fulfilled the implied prophecy of a new destiny. He has lived up to an ideal conception of himself by proving his ability to command and by establishing his hierarchical position as captain. And Leggatt, abandoned to a world where the captain's epistemology is irrelevant, no longer exists within the civilized community except as part of the captain's consciousness. As soon as Leggatt has departed, the captain "hardly thought of my other self, now gone from the ship, to be hidden for ever from all friendly faces, to be a fugitive and a vagabond on the earth, with no brand of the curse on his sane forehead to stay a slaying hand . . . too proud to explain" (59). It is almost as the captain can now cast aside the man who once threatened his identity (although the telling shows that he regards the experience as crucial to his personal development). With hindsight it seems that Leggatt represents his own potential for evil, which must be expurgated before he can become morally, as well as psychologically, whole. The narrator clearly knows that he has behaved quite differently from the man he regarded as a double when confronted with a similar situation. When we as readers finish the story we understand the story's iterative, structure. As Louis H. Leiter perceptively argues,

> Leggatt seizes the man by the throat at the climax of his archetypal trial by storm and kills him in a fit of uncontrolled passion; the narrator also seizes the Chief Mate under similar circumstances, his archetypal trial by silence, but by controlling himself, controlling the frightened, disbelieving man, he controls the ship and consequently saves her from destruction, while saving his reputation and winning the respect of his crew. (142)

The captain finds within himself the confidence to act entirely without the paralytic self-consciousness that interfered at the outset with his ability to command the ship.

Leggatt is flippantly conscious of his similarity to Cain: "The 'brand of Cain' business, don't you see. That's all right. I was ready enough to go off wandering on the face of the earth—and that was price enough to pay for an Abel of that sort" (35). Ironically, although Leggatt proclaims indifference to legal and religious standards, he cannot avoid responding to them:

> "You don't suppose I am afraid of what can be done to me? . . . [Y]ou don't see me coming back to explain such things to an old fellow in a wig and twelve respectable tradesmen, do you? What can they know whether I am guilty or not—or of *what* I am

guilty, either? That's my affair. What does the Bible say? 'Driven off the face of the earth?' Very well. I am off the face of the earth now." (52)

It disturbs the conventional morality of the captain to be on the side of Cain. "The very trust in Providence was, I suppose, denied to his guilt. Shall I confess that this thought cast me down very much?" (46). Most of the time he acts as an Abel figure—his brother's keeper—in protecting Leggatt. Yet it is soon clear that the two men contain elements of both Cain and Abel. Leggatt plays the role of Abel when he willingly leaves the ship and thus helps the captain through the crisis. The captain's Cain identity derives from our realization that, to fulfill his own aspirations, he must abandon Leggatt.

The captain's use of Leggatt has its analogy in the creative process of art. Leggatt comes into his experience as a fact of the objective world; he transforms him into a fiction only partially congruent with the objective data of Leggatt's real identity; and then he releases him back into the objective world. Unwilling to risk his future, the captain *sacrifices* Leggatt for the unity of his own personality, just as the artist may sacrifice moral engagement for his artistic purposes. Conrad believed that all men have a Cain aspect to their personalities in the sense that physical and psychic survival is dependent on conscious and unconscious decisions that jeopardize the best interests of others. Likewise the artist withdraws into the imagination at the expense of immediate participation in the community. The persistent allusions to the Cain-Abel myth suggest that each man must continually confront an unresolvable conflict between self-fulfillment and commitment to others. In an early letter to his aunt, Marguerite Poradowska, Conrad writes, "Charity . . . is a gift straight from the Eternal to the elect. . . . For Charity is eternal and universal Love, the divine virtue, the sole manifestation of the Almighty which may in some manner justify the act of creation." But later in the same letter he writes:

> Abnegation carried to an extreme . . . becomes not a fault but a crime, and to return good for evil is not only profoundly immoral but dangerous, in that it sharpens the appetite for evil in the malevolent and develops (perhaps unconsciously) that latent human tendency towards hypocrisy in the . . . let us say, benevolent. (Lee 42)

The captain understands that it would be "sham sentiment"—what Conrad calls "abnegation carried to an extreme"—to sacrifice his future by indefinitely harboring Leggatt.

WORKS CITED

Conrad, Joseph. Preface. *The Nigger of the "Narcissus."* Garden City: Doubleday, 1959.

Guerard, Albert. *Conrad the Novelist.* Cambridge: Harvard UP, 1958.

Hertz, Neil. "Freud and the Sandman." *Textual Strategies: Perspectives in Post-Structuralist Criticism.* Ed. Josué V. Harari. Ithaca: Cornell UP, 1979. 296–321.

Johnson, Barbara, and Marjorie Garber. "Secret Sharing: Reading Conrad Psychoanalytically." *College English* 49.6 (1987): 628–40.

Lacan, Jacques. *The Four Fundamental Concepts of Psycho-Analysis.* Ed. Jacques-Alain Miller. Trans. Alan Sheridan. New York: Norton, 1981.

Laing, R. D. *The Divided Self: An Existential Study in Sanity and Madness.* Baltimore: Penguin, 1965.

Lee, John A., and Paul J. Sturm, eds. *Letters of Joseph Conrad to Marguerite Poradowska, 1890–1920.* New Haven: Yale, 1940.

Leiter, Louis H., "Echo Structures: Conrad's 'The Secret Sharer.'" *Twentieth Century Literature* 5.4 (1960): 169–75. Rpt. in *Conrad's "The Secret Sharer" and the Critics.* Ed. Bruce Harkness. Belmont, CA: Wadsworth, 1962. 133–50.

Martz, Louis L. *The Poetry of Meditation.* 2nd ed. New Haven: Yale UP, 1962.

Melville, Herman. *Moby-Dick.* New York: Norton, 1967.

Sieburth, Richard. "Dabbling in Damnation: The Bachelor, the Artist and the Dandy in Huysman." *TLS* 4652 (1992): 3–5.

Stallman, Robert W. "Conrad and 'The Secret Sharer.'" *The Art of Joseph Conrad: A Critical Symposium.* East Lansing: Michigan State UP, 1960. 275–88. Rpt. in *Conrad's "The Secret Sharer" and the Critics.* Ed. Bruce Harkness. Belmont, CA: Wadsworth, 1962. 94–109.

Woolf, Virginia. "Mr. Bennett and Mrs. Brown." *The Captain's Death Bed and Other Stories.* New York: Harcourt, 94–119.

Reader-Response Criticism
and
"The Secret Sharer"

WHAT IS READER-RESPONSE CRITICISM?

Students are routinely asked in English courses for their reactions to the texts they are reading. Sometimes there are so many different reactions that we may wonder whether everyone has read the same text. And some students respond so idiosyncratically to what they read that we say their responses are "totally off the wall." This variety of response interests reader-response critics, who raise theoretical questions about whether our responses to a work are the same as its meanings, whether a work can have as many meanings as we have responses to it, and whether some responses are more valid than others. They ask what determines what is and what isn't "off the wall." What, in other words, is the wall, and what standards help us define it?

In addition to posing provocative questions, reader-response criticism provides us with models that aid our understanding of texts and the reading process. Adena Rosmarin has suggested that a literary text may be likened to an incomplete work of sculpture: to see it fully, we must complete it imaginatively, taking care to do so in a way that responsibly takes into account what exists. Other reader-response critics have suggested other models, for reader-response criticism is not a monolithic school of thought but, rather, an umbrella term covering a variety of approaches to literature.

Nonetheless, as Steven Mailloux has shown, reader-response critics *do* share not only questions but also goals and strategies. Two of the basic goals are to show that a work gives readers something to do and to describe what the reader does by way of response. To achieve those goals, the critic may make any of a number of what Mailloux calls "moves." For instance, a reader-response critic might typically (1) cite direct references to reading in the text being analyzed, in order to justify the focus on reading and show that the world of the text is continuous with the one in which the reader reads; (2) show how other non-reading situations in the text nonetheless mirror the situation the reader is in ("Fish shows how in *Paradise Lost* Michael's teaching of Adam in Book XI resembles Milton's teaching of the reader throughout the poem"); and (3) show, therefore, that the reader's response is, or is analogous to, the story's action or conflict. For instance, Stephen Booth calls *Hamlet* the tragic story of "an audience that cannot make up its mind" (Mailloux, "Learning" 103).

Although reader-response criticism is often said to have emerged in the United States in the 1970s, it is in one respect as old as the foundations of Western culture. The ancient Greeks and Romans tended to view literature as rhetoric, a means of making an audience react in a certain way. Although their focus was more on rhetorical strategies and devices than on the reader's (or listener's) response to those methods, the ancients by no means left the audience out of the literary equation. Aristotle thought, for instance, that the greatness of tragedy lay in its "cathartic" power to cleanse or purify the emotions of audience members. Plato, by contrast, worried about the effects of artistic productions, so much so that he advocated evicting poets from the Republic on the grounds that their words "feed and water" the passions!

In our own century, long before 1970, there were critics whose concerns and attitudes anticipated those of reader-response critics. One of these, I. A. Richards, is usually associated with formalism, a supposedly objective, text-centered approach to literature that reader-response critics of the 1970s roundly attacked. And yet in 1929 Richards managed to sound surprisingly *like* a 1970s-vintage reader-response critic, writing in *Practical Criticism* that "the personal situation of the reader inevitably (and within limits rightly) affects his reading, and many more are drawn to poetry in quest of some reflection of their latest emotional crisis than would admit it" (575). Rather than deploring this fact, as many of his formalist contemporaries would have done, Richards argued that the reader's feelings and experiences provide a kind of reality check, a way of testing the authenticity of emotions and events represented in literary works.

Approximately a decade after Richards wrote *Practical Criticism,* an American named Louise M. Rosenblatt published *Literature as Exploration* (1938). In that seminal book, now in its fourth edition (1983), Rosenblatt began developing a theory of reading that blurs the boundary between reader and text, subject and object. In a 1969 article entitled "Towards a Transactional Theory of Reading," she sums up her position by writing that "a poem is what the reader lives through under the guidance of the text and experiences as relevant to the text" (127). Rosenblatt knew her definition would be difficult for many to accept: "The idea that a *poem* presupposes a *reader* actively involved with a *text,*" she wrote, "is particularly shocking to those seeking to emphasize the objectivity of their interpretations" ("Transactional" 127).

Rosenblatt implicitly and generally refers to formalists (also called the "New Critics") when she speaks of supposedly objective interpreters shocked by the notion that a "poem" is something cooperatively produced by a "reader" and a "text." Formalists spoke of "the poem itself," the "concrete work of art," the "real poem." They had no interest in what a work of literature makes a reader "live through." In fact, in *The Verbal Icon* (1954), William K. Wimsatt and Monroe C. Beardsley defined as fallacious the very notion that a reader's response is relevant to the meaning of a literary work:

> The Affective Fallacy is a confusion between the poem and its *results* (what it *is* and what it *does*). . . . It begins by trying to derive the standards of criticism from the psychological effects of a poem and ends in impressionism and relativism. The outcome . . . is that the poem itself, as an object of specifically critical judgment, tends to disappear. (21)

Reader-response critics have taken issue with their formalist predecessors. Particularly influential has been Stanley Fish, whose early work is seen by some as marking the true beginning of contemporary reader-response criticism. In "Literature in the Reader: Affective Stylistics" (1970), Fish took on the formalist hegemony, the New Critical establishment, by arguing that any school of criticism that would see a work of literature as an object, claiming to describe what it *is* and never what it *does,* is guilty of misconstruing the very essence of literature and reading. Literature exists when it is read, Fish suggests, and its force is an affective force. Furthermore, reading is a temporal process. Formalists assume it is a spatial one as they step back and survey the literary work as if it were an object spread out before them. They may find elegant patterns in the texts they examine and reexamine, but they fail to take into account that the work is quite different to a reader who is turning the pages and being moved, or affected, by lines that appear and disappear as the reader reads.

In a discussion of the effect that a sentence penned by the seventeenth-century physician Thomas Browne has on a reader reading, Fish pauses to say this about his analysis and also, by extension, about his critical strategy: "Whatever is persuasive and illuminating about [it] is the result of my substituting for one question — what does this sentence mean? — another, more operational question — what does this sentence do?" He then quotes a line from John Milton's *Paradise Lost,* a line that refers to Satan and the other fallen angels: "Nor did they not perceive their evil plight." Whereas more traditional critics might say that the "meaning" of the line is "They did perceive their evil plight," Fish relates the uncertain movement of the reader's mind *to* that half-satisfying interpretation. Furthermore, he declares that "the reader's inability to tell whether or not 'they' do perceive and his involuntary question . . . are part of the line's *meaning,* even though they take place in the mind, not on the page" (*Text* 26).

The stress on what pages *do* to minds (and what minds do in response) pervades the writings of most, if not all, reader-response critics. Stephen Booth, whose book *An Essay on Shakespeare's Sonnets* (1969) greatly influenced Fish, sets out to describe the "reading experience that results" from a "multiplicity of organizations" in a sonnet by Shakespeare (*Essay* ix). Sometimes these organizations don't make complete sense, Booth points out, and sometimes they even seem curiously contradictory. But that is precisely what interests reader-response critics, who, unlike formalists, are at least as interested in fragmentary, inconclusive, and even unfinished texts as in polished, unified works. For it is the reader's struggle to *make sense* of a challenging work that reader-response critics seek to describe.

The German critic Wolfgang Iser has described that sense-making struggle in his books *The Implied Reader* (1972) and *The Act of Reading: A Theory of Aesthetic Response* (1976). Iser argues that texts are full of "gaps" (or "blanks," as he sometimes calls them). These gaps powerfully affect the reader, who is forced to explain them, to connect what they separate, to create in his or her mind aspects of a poem or novel or play that aren't *in* the text but that the text incites. As Iser puts it in *The Implied Reader,* the "unwritten aspects" of a story "draw the reader into the action" and "lead him to shade in the many outlines suggested by the given situations, so that these take on a reality of their own." These "outlines" that "the reader's imagination animates" in turn "influence" the way in which "the written part of the text" is subsequently read (276).

In *Self-Consuming Artifacts: The Experience of Seventeenth-Century Literature* (1972), Fish reveals his preference for literature that makes readers work at making meaning. He contrasts two kinds of literary presentation. By the phrase "rhetorical presentation," he describes literature that reflects and reinforces opinions that readers already hold; by "dialectical presentation," he refers to works that prod and provoke. A dialectical text, rather than presenting an opinion as if it were truth, challenges readers to discover truths on their own. Such a text may not even have the kind of symmetry that formalist critics seek. Instead of offering a "single, sustained argument," a dialectical text, or self-consuming artifact, may be "so arranged that to enter into the spirit and assumptions of any one of [its] . . . units is implicitly to reject the spirit and assumptions of the unit immediately preceding" (*Artifacts* 9). Whereas a critic of another school might try to force an explanation as to why the units are fundamentally coherent, the reader-response critic proceeds by describing how the reader deals with the sudden twists and turns that characterize the dialectical text, returning to earlier passages and seeing them in an entirely new light.

"The value of such a procedure," Fish has written, "is predicated on the idea of meaning as *an event,*" not as something "located (presumed to be embedded) *in* the utterance" or "verbal object as a thing in itself" (*Text* 28). By redefining meaning as an event rather than as something inherent in the text, the reader-response critic once again locates meaning in time: the reader's time. A text exists and signifies while it is being read, and what it signifies or means will depend, to no small extent, on *when* it is read. (*Paradise Lost* had some meanings for a seventeenth-century Puritan that it would not have for a twentieth-century atheist.)

With the redefinition of literature as something that exists meaningfully only in the mind of the reader, with the redefinition of the literary work as a catalyst of mental events, comes a concurrent redefinition of the reader. No longer is the reader the passive recipient of those ideas that an author has planted in a text. "The reader is *active,*" Rosenblatt insists ("Transactional" 123). Fish begins "Literature in the Reader" with a similar observation: "If at this moment someone were to ask, 'what are you doing,' you might reply, 'I am reading,' and thereby acknowledge that reading is . . . something *you do*" (*Text* 22). Iser, in focusing critical interest on the gaps in texts, on what is not expressed, similarly redefines the reader as an active maker.

Amid all this talk of "the reader," it is tempting and natural to ask, "Just who *is* the reader?" (Or, to place the emphasis differently, "Just who is *the* reader?") Are reader-response critics simply sharing their own idiosyncratic responses when they describe what a line from *Paradise Lost* does in and to the reader's mind? "What about my responses?" you may want to ask. "What if they're different? Would reader-response critics be willing to say that my responses are equally valid?"

Fish defines "the reader" in this way: "*the* reader is the *informed* reader." The informed reader (whom Fish sometimes calls "the *intended* reader") is someone who is "sufficiently experienced as a reader to have internalized the properties of literary discourses, including everything from the most local of devices (figures of speech, etc.) to whole genres." And, of course, the informed reader is in full possession of the "semantic knowledge" (knowledge of idioms, for instance) assumed by the text (*Artifacts* 406).

Other reader-response critics define "*the* reader" differently. Wayne C. Booth, in *A Rhetoric of Irony* (1974), uses the phrase "the implied reader" to mean the reader "created by the work." (Only "by agreeing to play the role of this created audience," Susan Suleiman explains, "can an actual reader correctly understand and appreciate the work" [8].) Gerard Genette and Gerald Prince prefer to speak of "the narratee, . . . the necessary counterpart of a given narrator, that is, the person or figure who receives a narrative" (Suleiman 13). Like Booth, Iser employs the term "the implied reader," but he also uses "the educated reader" when he refers to what Fish called the "informed reader."

Jonathan Culler, who in 1981 criticized Fish for his sketchy definition of the informed reader, set out in *Structuralist Poetics* (1975) to describe the educated or "competent" reader's education by elaborating those reading conventions that make possible the understanding of poems and novels. In retrospect, however, Culler's definitions seem sketchy as well. By "competent reader," Culler meant competent reader of "literature." By "literature," he meant what schools and colleges mean when they speak of literature as being part of the curriculum. Culler, like his contemporaries, was not concerned with the fact that curricular content is politically and economically motivated. And "he did not," in Mailloux's words, "emphasize how the literary competence he described was embedded within larger formations and traversed by political ideologies extending beyond the academy" ("Turns" 49). It remained for a later generation of reader-oriented critics to do those things.

The fact that Fish, following Rosenblatt's lead, defined reader-response criticism in terms of its difference from and opposition to the New Criticism or formalism should not obscure the fact that the formalism of the 1950s and early 1960s had a great deal in common with the reader-response criticism of the late 1960s and early 1970s. This has become increasingly obvious with the rise of subsequent critical approaches whose practitioners have proved less interested in the close reading of texts than in the way literature represents, reproduces, and/or resists prevailing ideologies concerning gender, class, and race. In a retrospective essay entitled "The Turns of Reader-Response Criticism" (1990), Mailloux has suggested that, from the perspective of hindsight, the "close reading" of formalists and "Fish's early 'affective stylistics'" seem surprisingly similar. Indeed, Mailloux argues, the early "reader talk of . . . Iser and Fish enabled the continuation of the formalist practice of close reading. Through a vocabulary focused on a text's manipulation of readers, Fish was especially effective in extending and diversifying the formalist practices that continued business as usual within literary criticism" (48).

Since the mid-1970s, however, reader-response criticism (once commonly referred to as the "School of Fish") has diversified and taken on a variety of new forms, some of which truly *are* incommensurate with formalism, with its considerable respect for the integrity and power of the text. For instance, "subjectivists" like David Bleich, Norman Holland, and Robert Crosman have assumed what Mailloux calls the "absolute priority of individual selves as creators of texts" (*Conventions* 31). In other words, these critics do not see the reader's response as one "guided" by the text but rather as one motivated by deep-seated, personal, psychological needs. What they find in texts is, in Holland's phrase, their own "identity theme." Holland has argued that as readers we use "the literary work to symbolize and finally to replicate ourselves. We work out through the text our own characteristic patterns of desire" ("UNITY" 816). Subjective critics, as you may already have guessed, often find themselves confronted with the following question: If all interpretation is a function of private, psychological identity, then why have so many readers interpreted, say, Shakespeare's *Hamlet* in the same way? Different subjective critics have answered the question differently. Holland simply has said that common identity themes exist, such as that involving an oedipal fantasy.

Meanwhile, Fish, who in the late 1970s moved away from reader-response criticism as he had initially helped define it, came up with a different answer to the question of why different readers tend to read the same works the same way. His answer, rather than involving common individual identity themes, involved common *cultural* identity. In "Interpreting the *Variorum*" (1976), he argues that the "stability of interpretation among readers" is a function of shared "interpretive strategies." These strategies, which "exist prior to the act of reading and therefore determine the shape of what is read," are held in common by "interpretive communities" such as the one constituted by American college students reading a novel as a class assignment (*Text* 167, 171). In developing the model of interpretive communities, Fish truly has made the break with formalist or New Critical predecessors, becoming in the process something of a social, structuralist, reader-response critic. Recently, he has been engaged in studying reading communities and their interpretive conventions in order to understand the conditions that give rise to a work's intelligibility.

Fish's shift in focus is in many ways typical of changes that have taken place within the field of reader-response criticism — a field that, because of those changes, is increasingly being referred to as "reader-*oriented*" criticism. Less and less common are critical analyses examining the transactional interface between the text and its individual reader. Increasingly, reader-oriented critics are investigating reading communities, as the reader-oriented cultural critic Janice A. Radway has done in her study of female readers of romance paperbacks (*Reading the Romance,* 1984). They are also studying the changing reception of literary works across time; see, for example, Mailloux in his "pragmatic readings" of American literature in *Interpretive Conventions* (1982) and *Rhetorical Power* (1989).

An important catalyst of this gradual change was the work of Hans Robert Jauss, a colleague of Iser's whose historically oriented reception theory (unlike Iser's theory of the implied reader) was not available in English book form until the early 1980s. Rather than focusing on the implied, informed, or intended reader, Jauss examined actual past readers. In *Toward an Aesthetic of Reception* (1982), he argued that the reception of a work or author tends to depend upon the reading public's "horizons of expectations." He noted that, in the morally conservative climate of mid-nineteenth-century France, *Madame Bovary* was literally put on trial, its author Flaubert accused of glorifying adultery in passages representing the protagonist's fevered delirium via free indirect discourse, a mode of narration in which a third-person narrator tells us in an unfiltered way what a character is thinking and feeling.

As readers have become more sophisticated and tolerant, the popularity and reputation of *Madame Bovary* have soared. Sometimes, of course, changes in a reading public's horizons of expectations cause a work to be *less* well received over time. As American reception theorists influenced by Jauss have shown, Mark Twain's *Adventures of Huckleberry Finn* has elicited an increasingly ambivalent reaction from a reading public increasingly sensitive to demeaning racial stereotypes and racist language. The rise of feminism has prompted a downward revaluation of everything from Andrew Marvell's "To His Coy Mistress" to D. H. Lawrence's *Women in Love.*

Some reader-oriented feminists, such as Judith Fetterley, Patrocinio Schweickart, and Monique Wittig, have challenged the reader to become what Fetterley calls "the resisting reader." Arguing that literature written by men tends, in Schweickart's terms, to "immasculate" women, they have advocated strategies of reading that involve substituting masculine for feminine pronouns and male for female characters in order to expose the sexism inscribed in patriarchal texts. Other feminists, such as Nancy K. Miller in *Subject to Change* (1988), have suggested that there may be essential differences between the way women and men read and write.

That suggestion, however, has prompted considerable disagreement. A number of gender critics whose work is oriented toward readers and reading have admitted that there is such a thing as "reading like a woman" (or man), but they have also tended to agree with Peggy Kamuf that such forms of reading, like gender itself, are cultural rather than natural constructs. Gay and lesbian critics, arguing that sexualities have been similarly constructed within and by social discourse, have argued that there is a homosexual way of reading; Wayne Koestenbaum has defined "the (male twentieth-century first world) gay reader" as one who "reads resistantly for inscriptions of his condition, for texts that will confirm a social and private identity founded on a desire for other men. . . . Reading becomes a hunt for histories that deliberately foreknow or unwittingly trace a desire felt not by author but by reader, who is most acute when searching for signs of himself" (in Boone and Cadden, 176–77).

Given this kind of renewed interest in the reader and reading, some students of contemporary critical practice have been tempted to conclude that reader-oriented theory has been taken over by feminist, gender, gay, and lesbian theory. Others, like Elizabeth Freund, have suggested that it is deconstruction with which the reader-oriented approach has mixed and merged. Certainly, all of these approaches have informed and been informed by reader-response or reader-oriented theory. The case can be made, however, that there is in fact still a distinct reader-oriented approach to literature, one whose points of tangency are neither with deconstruction nor with feminist, gender, and so-called queer theory but rather with the new historicism and cultural criticism.

This relatively distinct form of reader theory is practiced by a number of critics, but is perhaps best exemplified by the work of scholars like Mailloux and Peter J. Rabinowitz. In *Before Reading: Narrative Conventions and the Politics of Interpretation* (1987), Rabinowitz sets forth four conventions or rules of reading, which he calls the rules of "notice," "signification," "configuration," and "coherence" — rules telling us which parts of a narrative are important, which details have a reliable secondary or special meaning, which fit into which familiar patterns, and how stories fit together as a whole. He then proceeds to analyze the misreadings and misjudgments of critics and to show that politics governs the way in which those rules are applied and broken. ("The strategies employed by critics when they read [Raymond Chandler's] *The Big Sleep*," Rabinowitz writes, "can teach us something about the structure of misogyny, not the misogyny of the novel itself, but the misogyny of the world outside it" [195].) In subsequent critical essays, Rabinowitz proceeds similarly, showing how a society's ideological assumptions about gender, race, and class determine the way in which artistic works are perceived and evaluated.

Mailloux, who calls his approach "rhetorical reception theory" or "rhetorical hermeneutics," takes a similar tack, insofar as he describes the political contexts of (mis)interpretation. In a recent essay on "Misreading as a Historical Act" (1993), he shows that a mid-nineteenth-century review of Frederick Douglass's slave *Narrative* by proto-feminist Margaret Fuller seems to be a misreading until we situate it "within the cultural conversation of the 'Bible politics' of 1845" (Machor 9). Woven through Mailloux's essay on Douglas and Fuller are philosophical pauses in which we are reminded, in various subtle ways, that all reading (including Mailloux's and our own) is culturally situated and likely to seem like *mis*reading someday. One such reflective pause, however, accomplishes more; in it, Mailloux reads the map of where reader-oriented criticism is today, affords a rationale for its being there, and plots its likely future direction. "However we have arrived at our present juncture," Mailloux writes,

the current talk about historical acts of reading provides a welcome opportunity for more explicit consideration of how reading is historically contingent, politically situated, institutionally
embedded, and materially conditioned; of how reading any text,
literary or nonliterary, relates to a larger cultural politics that goes
well beyond some hypothetical private interaction between an autonomous reader and an independent text; and of how our particular views of reading relate to the liberatory potential of literacy
and the transformative power of education. (5)

In the essay that follows, James Phelan shows how from its title
onward Conrad's "The Secret Sharer" puzzles and perplexes the
reader, leading us on in the hopes of answering questions like the following: Is the subject of this story a sharer who is secret? A sharer of
secrets? What kind of secrets?

Because the keeping or telling of secrets inevitably has ethical
implications, Phelan goes on to argue that the meanings we find in
Conrad's tale inevitably have ethical dimensions and implications. For
instance, we are put in the position of hoping, along with the
captain-narrator, that a man who has taken another man's life will escape and go free. (As Phelan puts it, we "try to be for Conrad what the
captain is for Leggatt — the wonderful somebody who understands"
[130]).

In the process of analyzing Conrad's text, Phelan makes some important distinctions between narratees and readers and, even more important, between "narrative audience" and "authorial audience." The
latter distinction is grounded in the two sides of every reader's "double
consciousness": the side that is absorbed in the narrative, believing in
its reality much as the characters believe in it, and the more critical, analytical side of our consciousness that knows the story is only a story.
To the extent that we read from the former perspective, we join the
"narrative audience;" the other side of our double consciousness
makes us part of the "authorial audience."

As members of the authorial audience trying to discover the secret
in Conrad's text — its revealing subtext — we find ourselves having to
choose between mutually exclusive beliefs: the belief that the captain
fantasized or hallucinated the existence of Leggatt and the belief that
the captain protects Leggatt because of his homosexual attraction to
him. And to accept the latter hypothesis, Phelan argues, puts us in the
position of accepting and approving of the homosexual bond that develops between the captain and Leggatt, for "the uncharacteristically

triumphant ending sends a strong signal about how this story endorses that bond and the actions it leads to." (139).

For many readers, this approval will involve secret sharing "in the sense of sharing in the secret and in the sense of sharing it secretly" (139). This statement brings Phelan's argument full circle, back to the ethics of reading a text that seems to promise the sharing of a secret. "If homosexuality must remain secret, how can it be genuinely valorized?" Phelan asks. "To participate, as the story asks us to do, in the secretiveness surrounding homosexuality is to be complicit with the forces that would repress homosexuality entirely" (140).

Phelan writes in a casual, even personal critical voice that involves us in his interpretive dilemmas, much as the captain implicates us in *his* ethical dilemma through *his* casual and personal mode of address. "I can't help wondering," Phelan comments while discussing the possible homosexual bond between the captain and Leggatt, "how much my perception of this secret is a consequence of my historical moment, in particular, the way in which the gay studies movement has made me and numerous other academic readers especially attuned to representations of same-sex desire" (139).

Phelan identifies his own approach as "rhetorical" reader-response criticism, thereby associating himself with those who believe that the text is "a meeting place for writer and reader," a place where the rhetorical "conventions, structures, and techniques" of the text encounter "the reader's beliefs, opinions, values, emotions, and knowledge." Thus, while according the author a definite and powerful role in the production of meaning, Phelan also sees meaning as being "intimately tied to subjectivity." He consequently finds "no grounds for establishing (or trying to establish) the single, definitive interpretation of a text." Phelan hastens to add that "readers can sometimes share reading experiences and interpretations. Indeed, by comparing similarities and differences in our experiences and interpretations, we may decide to revisit our experiences and revise our interpretations" (132).

Phelan uses the word *shared* advisedly when he speaks of the possibility of overlapping interpretations, for in "The Secret Sharer" he finds not only a good text on which to practice his rhetorical reader-response criticism but also a kind of parable about readers and their private experiences. These private experiences may themselves be not only shared but somehow validated by another — a double, a self at once other and the same, similar and different.

Ross C Murfin

READER-RESPONSE CRITICISM:
A SELECTED BIBLIOGRAPHY

Some Introductions to
Reader-Response Criticism

Beach, Richard. *A Teacher's Introduction to Reader-Response Theories.* Urbana: NCTE, 1993.

Fish, Stanley E. "Literature in the Reader: Affective Stylistics." *New Literary History* 2 (1970): 123–61. Rpt. in Fish, *Text* 21–67, and in Primeau 154–79.

Freund, Elizabeth. *The Return of the Reader: Reader-Response Criticism.* London: Methuen, 1987.

Holub, Robert C. *Reception Theory: A Critical Introduction.* New York: Methuen, 1984.

Leitch, Vincent B. *American Literary Criticism from the Thirties to the Eighties.* New York: Columbia UP, 1988.

Mailloux, Steven. "Learning to Read: Interpretation and Reader-Response Criticism." *Studies in the Literary Imagination* 12 (1979): 93–108.

———. "Reader-Response Criticism?" *Genre* 10 (1977): 413–31.

———. "The Turns of Reader-Response Criticism." *Conversations: Contemporary Critical Theory and the Teaching of Literature.* Ed. Charles Moran and Elizabeth F. Penfield. Urbana: NCTE, 1990. 38–54.

Rabinowitz, Peter J. "Whirl Without End: Audience-Oriented Criticism." *Contemporary Literary Theory.* Ed. G. Douglas Atkins and Laura Morrow. Amherst: U of Massachusetts P, 1989. 81–100.

Rosenblatt, Louise M. "Towards a Transactional Theory of Reading." *Journal of Reading Behavior* 1 (1969): 31–47. Rpt. in Primeau 121–46.

Suleiman, Susan R. "Introduction: Varieties of Audience-Oriented Criticism." Suleiman and Crosman 3–45.

Tompkins, Jane P. "An Introduction to Reader-Response Criticism." Tompkins ix–xxiv.

Reader-Response Criticism in
Anthologies and Collections

Flynn, Elizabeth A., and Patrocinio P. Schweickart, eds. *Gender and Reading: Essays on Readers, Texts, and Contexts.* Baltimore: Johns Hopkins UP, 1986.

Garvin, Harry R., ed. *Theories of Reading, Looking, and Listening.* Lewisburg: Bucknell UP, 1981. Essays by Cain and Rosenblatt.

Machor, James L., ed. *Readers in History: Nineteenth-Century American Literature and the Contexts of Response.* Baltimore: Johns Hopkins UP, 1993. Contains Mailloux essay "Misreading as a Historical Act: Cultural Rhetoric, Bible Politics, and Fuller's 1845 Review of Douglass's *Narrative.*"

Primeau, Ronald, ed. *Influx: Essays on Literary Influence.* Port Washington: Kennikat, 1977. Essays by Fish, Holland, and Rosenblatt.

Suleiman, Susan R., and Inge Crosman, eds. *The Reader in the Text: Essays on Audience and Interpretation.* Princeton: Princeton UP, 1980. See especially the essays by Culler, Iser, and Todorov.

Tompkins, Jane P., ed. *Reader-Response Criticism: From Formalism to Post-Structuralism.* Baltimore: Johns Hopkins UP, 1980. See especially the essays by Bleich, Fish, Holland, Prince, and Tompkins.

Reader-Response Criticism: Some Major Works

Bleich, David. *Subjective Criticism.* Baltimore: Johns Hopkins UP, 1978.

Booth, Stephen. *An Essay on Shakespeare's Sonnets.* New Haven: Yale UP, 1969.

Booth, Wayne C. *A Rhetoric of Irony.* Chicago: U of Chicago P, 1974.

Eco, Umberto. *The Role of the Reader: Explorations in the Semiotics of Texts.* Bloomington: Indiana UP, 1979.

Fish, Stanley Eugene. *Doing What Comes Naturally: Change, Rhetoric, and the Practice of Theory in Literary and Legal Studies.* Durham: Duke UP, 1989.

———. *Is There a Text in This Class? The Authority of Interpretive Communities.* Cambridge: Harvard UP, 1980. This volume contains most of Fish's most influential essays, including "Literature in the Reader: Affective Stylistics," "What It's Like to Read *L'Allegro* and *Il Penseroso,*" "Interpreting the *Variorum,*" "Is There a Text in This Class?" "How to Recognize a Poem When You See One," and "What Makes an Interpretation Acceptable?"

———. *Self-Consuming Artifacts: The Experience of Seventeenth-Century Literature.* Berkeley: U of California P, 1972.

———. *Surprised by Sin: The Reader in "Paradise Lost."* 2nd ed. Berkeley: U of California P, 1971.

Holland, Norman N. *5 Readers Reading.* New Haven: Yale UP, 1975.

————. "UNITY IDENTITY TEXT SELF." *PMLA* 90 (1975): 813–22.

Iser, Wolfgang. *The Act of Reading: A Theory of Aesthetic Response.* Baltimore: Johns Hopkins UP, 1978.

————. *The Implied Reader: Patterns of Communication in Prose Fiction from Bunyan to Beckett.* Baltimore: Johns Hopkins UP, 1974.

Jauss, Hans Robert. *Toward an Aesthetic of Reception.* Trans. Timothy Bahti. Intro. Paul de Man. Brighton, Eng.: Harvester, 1982.

Mailloux, Steven. *Interpretive Conventions: The Reader in the Study of American Fiction.* Ithaca: Cornell UP, 1982.

————. *Rhetorical Power.* Ithaca: Cornell UP, 1989.

Messent, Peter. *New Readings of the American Novel: Narrative Theory and Its Application.* New York: Macmillan, 1991.

Prince, Gerald. *Narratology.* New York: Mouton, 1982.

Rabinowitz, Peter J. *Before Reading: Narrative Conventions and the Politics of Interpretation.* Ithaca: Cornell UP, 1987.

Radway, Janice A. *Reading the Romance: Women, Patriarchy, and Popular Literature.* Chapel Hill: U of North Carolina P, 1984.

Rosenblatt, Louise M. *Literature as Exploration.* 4th ed. New York: MLA, 1983.

————. *The Reader, the Text, the Poem: The Transactional Theory of the Literary Work.* Carbondale: Southern Illinois UP, 1978.

Slatoff, Walter J. *With Respect to Readers: Dimensions of Literary Response.* Ithaca: Cornell UP, 1970.

Steig, Michael. *Stories of Reading: Subjectivity and Literary Understanding.* Baltimore: Johns Hopkins UP, 1989.

Exemplary Short Readings of Major Texts

Anderson, Howard. "*Tristram Shandy* and the Reader's Imagination." *PMLA* 86 (1971): 966–73.

Berger, Carole. "The Rake and the Reader in Jane Austen's Novels." *Studies in English Literature, 1500–1900* 15 (1975): 531–44.

Booth, Stephen. "On the Value of *Hamlet.*" *Reinterpretations of English Drama: Selected Papers from the English Institute.* Ed. Norman Rabkin. New York: Columbia UP, 1969. 137–76.

Easson, Robert R. "William Blake and His Reader in *Jerusalem.*" *Blake's Sublime Allegory.* Ed. Stuart Curran and Joseph A. Wittreich. Madison: U of Wisconsin P, 1973. 309–28.

Kirk, Carey H. "*Moby-Dick:* The Challenge of Response." *Papers on Language and Literature* 13 (1977): 383–90.

Leverenz, David. "Mrs. Hawthorne's Headache: Reading *The Scarlet Letter*." *Nathaniel Hawthorne, "The Scarlet Letter."* Ed. Ross C Murfin. Case Studies in Contemporary Criticism. Boston: Bedford–St. Martin's, 1991. 263–74.

Lowe-Evans, Mary. "Reading with a 'Nicer Eye': Responding to *Frankenstein*." *Mary Shelley, "Frankenstein."* Ed. Johanna M. Smith. Case Studies in Contemporary Criticism. Boston: Bedford–St. Martin's, 1992. 215–29.

Rabinowitz, Peter J. "'A Symbol of Something': Interpretive Vertigo in 'The Dead.'" *James Joyce, "The Dead."* Ed. Daniel R. Schwarz. Case Studies in Contemporary Criticism. Boston: Bedford–St. Martin's, 1994. 137–49.

Treichler, Paula. "The Construction of Ambiguity in *The Awakening*." *Kate Chopin, "The Awakening."* Ed. Nancy A. Walker. Case Studies in Contemporary Criticism. Boston: Bedford–St. Martin's, 1993. 308–28.

Other Works Referred to in "What Is Reader-Response Criticism?"

Booth, Wayne C. *A Rhetoric of Irony*. Chicago: U of Chicago P, 1974.

Culler, Jonathan. *Structural Poetics: Structuralism, Linguistics, and the Study of Literature*. Ithaca: Cornell UP, 1975.

Koestenbaum, Wayne. "Wilde's Hard Labor and the Birth of Gay Reading." *Engendering Men: The Question of Male Feminist Criticism*. Ed. Joseph A. Boone and Michael Cadden. New York: Routledge, 1990.

Richards, I. A. *Practical Criticism*. New York: Harcourt, 1929. Rpt. in *Criticism: The Major Texts*. Ed. Walter Jackson Bate. Rev. ed. New York: Harcourt, 1970. 575.

Wimsatt, William K., and Monroe C. Beardsley. *The Verbal Icon*. Lexington: U of Kentucky P, 1954. See especially the discussion of "The Affective Fallacy," with which reader-response critics have so sharply disagreed.

Reader-Reponse Approaches to Conrad

Higdon, David Leon. "'His Helpless Prey': Conrad and the Aggressive Text." *The Conradian* 12.2 (1987): 108–21.

Rosmarin, Adena. "Darkening the Reader: Reader-Response Criticism and *Heart of Darkness*." *Joseph Conrad, "Heart of Darkness."* Ed.

Ross C Murfin. *Case Studies in Contemporary Criticism*. Boston: Bedford–St. Martin's, 1989. 148–69.

Shires, Linda M. "The Privileged Reader and Narrative Methodology in *Lord Jim*." *Conradiana* 17.1 (1985): 19–30.

Talib, I. S. "Conrad's *Nostromo* and the Reader's Understanding of Anachronic Narratives." *Journal of Narrative Technique* 20.1 (1990): 1–21.

A READER-RESPONSE PERSPECTIVE

JAMES PHELAN

Sharing Secrets

"As long as I know that you understand. . . . But of course you do. It's a great satisfaction to have got somebody to understand. You seem to have been there on purpose. . . . It's very wonderful."

–LEGGATT TO THE CAPTAIN

Reading Secrets: Ethical Questions

"The Secret Sharer": Conrad's alliterative title plays peekaboo with any reader who pauses to puzzle over its meanings. Pondering matters of event and character, we can see the following significations emerge: a secret shared; a sharer who is secret; and a sharer who reveals a secret.[1] As a title, "The Secret Sharer" creates for the reader the expectation that the secret, the sharing, and the sharers will all be identified before story's end.[2] Pondering matters of telling and listening, we can glimpse other, less immediately apparent significations: "The Secret Sharer" names the narrator, the narratee (that is, the audience implicitly addressed by the narrator), and indeed Conrad and each of his readers. To narrate is to tell secrets; to read narrative is to share in them. "The Secret Sharer," *c'est moi — et lui et vous.*

---

[1]Mary Ann Dazey points out that the title is doubly ambiguous: the referent of *sharer* might be Leggatt or the captain; and *secret* can be either an adjective (modifying *sharer*) or part of a noun-noun compound analogous to such phrases as "Conrad aficionado" or "pizza lover."

[2]For a good discussion of the importance of titles in influencing readers' expectations, see Rabinowitz's *Before Reading*.

These significations about telling and listening (or writing and reading) in turn call attention to the ethical dimensions of Conrad's narrative, both in its events and in its telling and reception.[3] Secrets may be about matters honorable, shameful, or indifferent; may be revelations of virtue, vice, or mediocrity; but regardless of their content, secrets always carry some ethical implications. Furthermore, the keeping or telling of secrets always has an ethical dimension. We keep or tell secrets to inform or mislead, to titillate or ingratiate, to submit or dominate, repel or seduce, protect or hurt.

In the case of Conrad's narrative, the ethical dimensions of the action are everywhere apparent: the reader's involvement in "The Secret Sharer" is built on the conflict between the captain's responsibility to his crew and his decisions to keep Leggatt's existence a secret and to help him escape. The ethical dimensions of the telling, by contrast, are not so immediately evident. Strikingly, the occasion of the captain's narration is left unspecified. Conrad does not have him indicate any motive for his telling, identify his narratee, or locate himself in space. Even the one marker of the narrative situation Conrad supplies—its temporal location—lacks precision: the narrator comments that "at this distance of years" (41) he cannot be sure that Archbold was the name of the *Sephora*'s captain, but the distance is not measured by a specific number. Furthermore, although the narrator is very aware of himself as an actor and frequently comments on his behavior, that commentary almost never comes from his vantage point at the time of the narration.[4]

The unspecified occasion of narration is all the more noteworthy because Conrad had by 1909[5] already created several works in which the occasion and audience of the first-person narrator are explicitly defined—and made crucial to the effect of the whole narrative. To take just the two most celebrated cases, in *Heart of Darkness* and *Lord Jim,* Conrad includes information about Marlow, Marlow's audience, and the occasions of Marlow's narrations in order to influence substantially

[3]For an extended treatment of the ethical dimensions of writing and reading narrative, see Booth.

[4]It is this feature of the technique, I believe, that leads even such a perceptive critic as Steven Ressler to remark, "There is no retrospective sense, no time gap between the original events and their recounting" (97). In other words, though Ressler's claim runs counter to the narrator's remark about the "distance of years," it does capture the narrator's practice of presenting the events without commentary from his older, seemingly more mature self.

[5]Keith Carabine finds documentary evidence to support the view that Conrad wrote the story between December 3 and December 15, 1909.

the reader's understanding of Marlow's investment in the experiences of Kurtz and Jim. Indeed, our overall response to these texts involves the interaction of our responses to Marlow's narratives about Kurtz and Jim with our responses to Conrad's narratives about Marlow. In other words, by the time he wrote "The Secret Sharer," Conrad had already demonstrated that the technique of specifying narrative situations can extend the meaning and power of some narratives far beyond the meaning and power attendant on the straight narration of their primary sequences of events.

The material of "The Secret Sharer" certainly seems ripe for such treatment: a young and uncertain captain, trying to establish himself with a suspicious crew, harbors and protects a fugitive because the man seems to be his second self; through his determination to help the fugitive escape and with the fugitive's unexpected help, he manages to establish his authority with the crew, the ship, and himself. If Conrad had, say, employed Marlow to tell the captain's story to a group of veteran British seamen, Conrad could have made this tale *Lord Jim Revisited,* with Jim's traits split between the captain and Leggatt, with Marlow once again posing the ethical questions about what it means to be "one of us," and with Conrad's audience attending to the interaction between the captain's narrative and Marlow's quest for its meaning.

Why, then, would Conrad eschew the approach that he had employed so successfully before? What effects and purposes are likely to be guiding his choice of this different technique, which leaves the occasion and audience of the narration unspecified? More particularly, in this narrative of secrets, what is the relation between the ethical dimensions of the captain's story and the ethical dimensions of his telling? How do readers' efforts to participate in sharing the secrets of "The Secret Sharer" implicate them in the ethical dimensions of the story and its telling? Just what is at stake for us when we try to be for Conrad what the captain is for Leggatt—the wonderful somebody who understands? Before addressing these questions directly, I think it will be both appropriate and useful in this essay on secrets and unspecified narrative locations for me to reveal some details of my own "critical location."

Rhetorical Reader Response

The phrase *reader-response criticism* does not denote a single set of critical beliefs, methods, questions, assumptions, and principles. Instead, the phrase functions as a convenient terminological tent under which to gather a gallimaufry of critics interested in readers' roles in interpretation. Under this bigtop, one can find (at the least) the following groups:

1. Those who believe that individual readers determine the meaning of texts; for them, the text means what any reader says it does. Increasingly, members of this group are mingling autobiography with interpretive commentary.
2. Those who believe that groups of readers, who share key assumptions about the nature of texts and of interpretations, determine the meaning of texts; for them, the text means what the accepted interpretive strategies of the group reveal it to mean.
3. Those who believe that the meaning of texts is cocreated by authors and readers; for them, the meaning arises out of the interaction between what the author puts into the text and what the reader brings to it.
4. Those who believe that authors determine the meaning of texts but emphasize that meaning is not just cognitive but emotional, psychological, and ethical; for them, the meaning is a result of the author's agency, but meaning is not just understood in the intellect but also felt in the heart, the psyche, and the soul.

The text also covers those who synthesize selected principles of these four groups in different ways, such as those who emphasize the affective power of texts but see the individual reader or larger social forces as the main source of that power.

As my questions about Conrad's strategies suggest, I have sometimes kept company with the group that believes in the importance of authorial agency and sometimes with the group that believes in cocreation. The sign now hanging above my table in the tent reads "rhetorical reader response." This approach, like that of group 4, emphasizes "reader response" by calling attention to the multileveled quality of reading, the way in which experiencing a text involves the reader's beliefs, opinions, values, emotions, and knowledge. Furthermore, the approach is *rhetorical* because it views the text as a meeting place for writer and reader; the meeting comes about through the author's deployment of—and the reader's attention to—conventions, structures, techniques, and stylistic options. Rhetorical reading begins with a recognition of the otherness of the text, but it also knows that any response to that otherness has roots in the reader's subjectivity. This subjectivity, in turn, is not locatable in a single, coherent, stable self but rather arises from the multiplicity of roles, positions, and identities any self takes on; further, these roles, positions, and identities themselves arise from the interaction of a certain genetic endowment with numerous social and historical forces, many of which operate beyond the self's control.

Because I see reading as intimately tied to subjectivity, I see no grounds for establishing (or trying to establish) the single, definitive interpretation of a text; for the same reason, I see no clear boundary between authorial agency and reader response in the construction of interpretations. At the same time, because rhetorical reader response sees reading as an encounter with something beyond the self, and because it posits different selves as subject to many of the same social and historical forces, it believes that different readers can sometimes share reading experiences and interpretations. Indeed, by comparing similarities and differences in our experiences and interpretations, we may decide to revisit our experiences and revise our interpretations.[6]

Similarly, reading with a specific question in mind, whether that question is, "What are the gender politics of this text?" or "How does such-and-such a technique influence the ethical dimension of reading this text?" has the potential to alter not just the understanding but the experience of the text. The appeal of interpretations based on such questions depends on their capacity to effect such alterations, their capacity, in effect, to do something plausibly original with the elements of the text. In light of all these points, I offer the analysis in this essay not as the definitive interpretation of Conrad's narrative (not even the definitive reader-response interpretation) but as an interpretation with some potential to complicate other readers' experiences and interpretations. It marks one stage in my understanding and interpretation, a stage that is very much subject to alteration as I listen to other accounts, including those in this edition.

Audiences in Narrative

One way the rhetorical approach tries to account for the multi-leveled experience of reading is to recognize the multiple audience positions that narratives offer us. At the most basic level, we read and authors write as flesh-and-blood historical beings, with our particular sets of beliefs, values, prejudices, hobbyhorses, and crotchets. In creating a

[6]For more on this view of reader-response criticism, see Phelan, "Toward a Rhetorical Reader Response Criticism."

text, however, an author necessarily makes assumptions about her audience and then makes certain rhetorical choices on the basis of those assumptions. As readers interested in meeting the otherness of the text, we seek to recognize the implied sense of self (or selves)—or better, the implied complex subjectivity—conveyed by the author through those choices and assumptions. Further, we seek to go with those assumptions, to become members of the authorial audience, or, in an alternative formulation, to become the implied author's implied reader. We may of course also decide to resist or reject those assumptions, to become what Judith Fetterley has called resisting readers.

In addition, the writing and reading of fictional narratives depend on the operation of a double consciousness. In one part of their consciousnesses, authors and readers need to assent to the illusion that the narrative is not fiction but history or biography (we need to treat Leggatt and the captain as if they were real), while in another part of their consciousnesses, they need to maintain the tacit awareness that the narrative is fiction (of course we know that the captain and Leggatt are characters invented by Conrad). It is the authorial audience that retains the awareness of the fiction, and it is the narrative audience that occupies the position of the observer who believes in the reality of the narrative. From the rhetorical perspective, the satisfactory experience of fictional narrative depends on *simultaneously* entering the authorial and narrative audiences. Finally, in writing a narrative text, an author employs a narrator who in turn addresses a hypothetical audience, what I have above designated by the term *narratee*. The narratee, like the narrative audience, exists within the world of the fiction; the difference between the two is that the narratee is addressed by the narrator whereas the narrative audience observes that address.[7]

Detecting Secrets

Let us reapproach the ethical questions about "The Secret Sharer" by looking at Conrad's structuring of the action. Conrad evokes and guides the authorial and the narrative audiences' initial interests by intertwining two main instabilities. First, the uneasy relation between the captain and the crew. In command of his first ship, the young captain must prove both to his older, initially suspicious crew and to

[7]The classic formulation of the concepts of authorial and narrative audience is in Rabinowitz, "Truth in Fiction." The classic formulation of the concept of narratee is in Prince. I have recently tried to relate these concepts along the lines described here in "*Self-Help* for Narratee and Narrative Audience."

himself that he is a capable commander. As he says early in his account, "I wondered how far I should turn out faithful to that ideal conception of one's own personality every man sets up for himself secretly" (26). Second, the uncertainty of whether the captain will be able to keep Leggatt's presence a secret from the crew, from Archbold, from everyone.

Conrad's intertwining of these instabilities heightens the suspense we feel as the narrative and authorial audiences because they pull in opposite directions. The more the captain devotes himself to setting the crew at ease by working closely with them and otherwise following the conventions of command, the more he increases the chances for Leggatt's exposure. The more he gives in to his desire to protect Leggatt and his secret, the more he increases his crew's doubts about his ability. Reading the final episode is so intense partly because the two instabilities fully converge there, thus raising the conflict to its highest point. As the captain brings the boat near the shore of Koh-ring, he is simultaneously risking the two things he has been struggling mightily to maintain: Leggatt's secret existence and the effective command of the ship. Conrad's resolution of this climax is wonderfully efficient and—to the authorial audience—satisfying. The captain chooses to endanger the crew, the ship, and his own future for the sake of Leggatt; when he manages, with the assist from the hat he had given Leggatt, to turn the ship in time and to pick up the land breezes, the very dangerous course he has taken becomes incontrovertible evidence of his ability and his courage.

Even as Conrad's structuring of the action evokes this sequence of instability, suspense, and satisfaction, his narrative discourse deepens and complicates our involvement in the captain's story. As noted above, although Conrad indicates that the captain is looking back on his earlier experience, the captain only rarely speaks from his perspective at the time of the narration. Frequently this method of first-person, or "homodiegetic," narration[8] accompanies unreliable narration, that is, a telling in which a significant gap exists between the

[8]I introduce Gerard Genette's term *homodiegetic* because it is a more accurate descriptor than *first person*. As Genette points out, all narrators can say "I" and are in that sense first-person narrators. Homodiegetic narrators exist on the same narrative level as the events they tell, and thus, are typically both characters and narrators; heterodiegetic narrators, on the other hand, exist on a different narrative level from the characters and events they narrate about; they can comment on the action but typically cannot affect its outcome. Genette makes even a finer distinction, using the term *autodiegetic* for narrators who are protagonists and reserving *homodiegetic* for narrators who are secondary characters.

values and/or the understanding of the narrator and narrative audience and those of the implied author and authorial audience.[9] Although Conrad does not leave any clear signals that his norms are markedly different from the captain's,[10] both the narrative method and the focus on secrets invite us to ask whether there is more to this narrative than initially appears. More specifically, the technique and the subject matter encourage us to look for an important subtext, some secret whispered in the interstices of the narrative, perhaps even one that the captain himself may not be fully aware of. In other words, the technique and the subject matter authorize the authorial audience to search for a subtext.[11]

The search yields two possibilities I want to consider here. First, the captain has been having hallucinations and Leggatt exists only as his fantasy. Second, the captain's fellow feeling for Leggatt arises less from their common background and values than from their mutual sexual attraction.[12] The first possibility, hinted at in the captain's question of whether Leggatt is "visible to other eyes than mine" (51) is intriguing because it suggests a way of rereading the captain's psychology. Rather than a reasonably healthy man facing a difficult set of circumstances, he becomes a seriously unhealthy one whose anxieties about his new command lead him to invent an imaginary friend whom he fully understands and whom he can shelter and protect. Viewed in this light, the narrative is a study in the development, complication, and final resolution of this anxiety.

This hypothesis, however, is difficult to sustain because it must explain away too much recalcitrant evidence. The greatest recalcitrance is provided by Archbold's visit, which provides independent confirmation of Leggatt's existence and of the main lines of his story. Other,

[9]Although frequently cited without attribution now, the distinction between reliable and unreliable narration was first made by Wayne Booth in *The Rhetoric of Fiction*.

[10]In this connection, it is worth noting that despite considerable debate about the captain's decision to protect Leggatt, most critics assume that (on the axis of values at least) the captain is a reliable narrator. Noteworthy exceptions are Troy and Murphy.

[11]Identifying a subtext always has the attraction of making us feel that we are especially astute readers, the ones who "get it," as opposed to, say, the benighted narrator and those flesh-and-blood readers who remain tied to the view of the narrative audience, unable to join us in the authorial. Before declaring that a possible subtext is part of the authorial design, it is helpful to remember that the pull of this attraction is quite strong and that the search for subtexts, if conducted with sufficient ingenuity, can almost always turn up a delicious finding. In other words, we may sometimes decide, as we go fishing under the overt text, that some of what we catch should be thrown back.

[12]Other possible hidden meanings are suggested by Johnson and Garber's wonderful, playful essay exemplifying the strategies of psychoanalytic interpretation.

more minor, evidence includes the steward's hearing Leggatt's movement at a time when the captain is away from his cabin and the appearance of the captain's white hat floating in the sea after Leggatt leaves.
Of course it would be possible to argue that these events are also part
of the captain's fantasy, that the captain has used Archbold's visit as
the basis for his creation of Leggatt and that, after the event, he has
imaginatively recreated the version of that visit—and virtually everything else—that we get. In a reader-response criticism that emphasizes
the reader's role in creating the meaning of texts, these arguments
might be sufficient to allow the hypothesis to stand. Within a rhetorical reader-response approach, however, some significant problems arise.
Since the technique gives us the captain's experience as he feels it at the
time of the action, how do we explain, without even a covert clue from
Conrad, that the captain encounters Leggatt before he encounters
Archbold? More generally, the problem with this hypothesis is that it
makes the subtext almost a complete secret, something that is pointed
to only by the captain's single moment of doubt, a moment otherwise
well explained as a vivid sign of the strain the captain is feeling.

By contrast, the hypothesis that the authorial audience is supposed
to recognize the secret of the homosexual attraction is quite persuasive.
The text abounds in evidence—some covert, some not so covert—
that invites us to catch on to the secret. The captain's first glimpse of
Leggatt is charged with a sexual electricity: ". . . I saw at once something elongated and pale floating very close to the ladder. Before I
could form a guess a faint flash of phosphorescent light, which seemed
to issue suddenly from the naked body of a man, flickered in the sleeping water with the elusive, silent play of summer lightning in a night
sky" (28). Other elements of the scene also invite attention to its sexual undertones, even as the surface of the text attends more to Leggatt's apparent rising from the dead, his transformation from corpse
into living man. The captain's gaze follows the line of Leggatt's naked
body from foot to neck: "With a gasp I saw revealed to my stare a pair
of feet, the long legs, a broad livid back immersed right up to the neck
in a greenish cadaverous glow" (28). When the captain thinks that the
naked man is a "headless corpse," he involuntarily drops the cigar he is
smoking out of his mouth: a loss of potency and heat. When
he realizes that the man is still alive, the heat returns: "the horrid,
frost-bound sensation which had gripped me about the chest" passed
off (29).

More generally, the captain's consistent gazing upon Leggatt's
body suggests that a likely source of their "mysterious communica-

tion" is their mutual, unspoken recognition of their attraction: "I, . . . coming back on deck, saw the naked man from the sea sitting on the main-hatch, glimmering white in the darkness, his elbows on his knees and his head in his hands" (30). Later the captain says of Leggatt that, ". . . with his face nearly hidden, he must have looked exactly as I used to look in that bed. I gazed upon my other self for a while . . ." (38). Furthermore, the captain arranges matters so that he must bathe before Leggatt's gaze: "I took a bath and did most of my dressing, splashing, and whistling softly for the steward's edification, while the secret sharer of my life stood drawn up bolt upright in that little space" (40). After this description, we may feel compelled to ask: If he did *most* of the dressing, splashing, and whistling for the steward's edification, for whom did he do the rest of it?[13]

This evidence speaks strongly of the captain's attraction, but what of Leggatt's? The narrative perspective necessarily limits our access to his thoughts and feelings, but his part in the "mysterious communication" between the two, especially his confidence that the captain would understand everything, suggests that he too feels the unspoken bond. And one of his early speeches strongly suggests that the attraction is mutual: referring to his naked arrival at the ladder of the *Sephora,* he tells the captain, "I didn't mind being looked at [by you]. I—I liked it. And then you speaking to me so quietly—as if you had expected me—made me hold on a little longer" (37).

As the story continues, the evidence for the secret becomes less covert. The first night, the captain reports that "[w]e stood leaning over my bed-place, whispering side by side, with our dark heads together and our backs to the door" (34). Later, he tells us that at night "I would smuggle him into my bed-place, and we would whisper together, with the regular footfalls of the officer of the watch passing and repassing over our heads. It was an infinitely miserable time" (49). Why "infinitely miserable"? Perhaps because of sexual frustration. Perhaps their intimacy stopped at whispering, for fear that other expressions of it might become loud enough to alert the watch and expose them both. The ellipsis in my quotation of Leggatt's comment about the captain's understanding contains this description: "And in the same whisper, as if we two whenever we talked had to say things to each other which were not fit for the world to hear" (52): What is this

[13]The captain himself uses the word *queer* (in scare quotes): "I don't know whether the steward had told them that I was 'queer' only, or downright drunk" (39); but as far as I have been able to determine, this word did not have the associations with homosexuality in 1909 that it does in contemporary usage.

but what Oscar Wilde called the love that dare not speak its name? Finally, the captain's overt description of their final, significantly nonverbal communication is charged with the language of desire: "Our hands met gropingly, lingered united in a steady, motionless clasp for a second. . . . No word was breathed by either of us when they separated" (56).

The hypothesis encounters no significant recalcitrance, and attending to this subtext has significant consequences for our response. As flesh-and-blood readers, we have our own, sometimes highly charged, responses to representations of homosexuality, responses that range from homophobia to celebratory identification. In addition, as members of the authorial audience, attending to this secret alters our understanding of the action. Part of the captain's anxiety about his acceptance by the crew now becomes anxiety over whether they will suspect his sexual orientation. Archbold's talk about why he never liked Leggatt can now be seen as rooted in—may even be a coded way of voicing—Archbold's suspicion that Leggatt was homosexual. The captain's initial negative response to Leggatt's request that they maroon him on one of the islands becomes the response of the selfish, unfulfilled lover. His need to take the ship as close to Koh-ring as possible then becomes his way of atoning for this selfishness. Leggatt's words, "I know that you understand" (52), come to encompass the whole situation: why Leggatt decided to come on board, why he confided in the captain, why their bond is so strong, why they don't speak about it overtly or act on it differently, why he must leave. The captain's giving Leggatt his hat becomes a substitute for giving him a ring or any other token of remembrance and identification that one lover gives to another. Leggatt's leaving the hat in the water becomes his way of giving the ring back, and a powerful symbol of their unconsummated relationship: the good that they do each other does not depend on possession.

The ethics of attending to the secret of homosexual attraction are fairly complex.[14] The narrative's treatment of the relationship certainly

[14]Peter J. Rabinowitz has argued that some texts that contain secrets (his main example is Nella Larsen's *Passing*) are "fragile" because their appeal depends on their creation of two authorial audiences, one that does not get the secret and one that does. Once the secret becomes generally known, the power and appeal of the texts are, if not entirely lost, then altered. His essay offers a fascinating exploration of the ethics of teaching fragile texts. I do not think that "The Secret Sharer" is a fragile text in Rabinowitz's sense because I think that its power and appeal remain even after the secret is revealed. Furthermore, as will become clearer in the next section of this essay, I also think that this particular secret is only a part of the text's power and appeal.

valorizes it: the action is structured so that the authorial audience's pleasure and satisfaction in the story depend on our acceptance and approval of the bond between the captain and Leggatt. Furthermore, the uncharacteristically triumphant ending sends a strong signal about how this story endorses that bond and the actions it leads to. And as I suggested earlier, Conrad's handling of the telling, in effect, makes the authorial audience yet another "secret sharer"—in the sense of sharing in the secret and sharing it secretly. That is, we not only share the secret but do so without any explicit revelation of it. It is debatable whether the captain realizes that his narration reveals the secret. This point is worth dwelling on not for the sake of trying to settle the question but for the sake of assessing the captain's self-understanding after the events. If he is deliberately conveying the secret to readers astute enough to perceive it, then he becomes more self-aware and sophisticated as a narrator than his silence about the narrative occasion suggests. If, however, he is inadvertently revealing the secret, then we recognize that although he may have passed a critical test of his captaincy, he still needs to face other fundamental questions of identity.

Conrad's relation to the homosexual secret is even harder to pin down. If we opt for the understanding of the captain as in control of his narrative, we will also see Conrad as carefully in control behind the captain. If, however, we see the captain's revelation as unwitting, we may decide that Conrad has planned it that way or that Conrad himself is not fully aware of the homosexual subtext. In fact, articulating the secret and specifying the evidence for it helps to illuminate one of the fault lines in rhetorical reader response—the one running between the authorial and the flesh-and-blood audiences. On the one hand, the evidence points to a design on Conrad's part that the authorial audience needs to discern; indeed, without such a pattern of evidence, I would not suggest that this secret is a plausible one. On the other hand, I can't help wondering how much my perception of this secret is a consequence of my historical moment, in particular, the way in which the gay studies movement has made me and numerous other academic readers especially attuned to representations of same-sex desire. Is the secret constructed by the implied Conrad or the flesh-and-blood critic? I don't fully know. Furthermore, within rhetorical reader response, there is a sense in which it is not all that important to know. As I noted earlier, when the situated subjectivity of the reader encounters the otherness of the text, the analyst cannot always definitively locate the boundaries that mark off flesh-and-blood and authorial audiences—or more generally, reader, text, and author—from each other. The synergy among these different elements of the rhetorical transaction is precisely what rhetorical reader response wants to acknowledge.

In any case, Conrad's strategy of suggesting that there is a secret in the captain's narration without calling explicit attention to any particular secret can be seen as a sign of his confidence in his readers. In this view, Conrad is not only complimenting his audience but subtly influencing us to share his positive view of the captain and Leggatt.

Nevertheless, even this very positive construction of the ethical dimension of reading this story is complicated by the very reliance upon secrets itself. If homosexuality must remain secret, how can it be genuinely valorized? To participate, as the story asks us to do, in the secretiveness surrounding homosexuality is to be complicit with the forces that would repress homosexuality entirely. For this reason, I find it hard not to become a partially resistant reader of Conrad's text. But the nature of that resistance is itself further complicated by other responses that arise from Conrad's technique for representing the dynamic between the captain and Leggatt.

Guilty Secrets

As some readers have no doubt already noticed, there has been a conspicuous absence from my discussion to this point: I have not said anything about Leggatt's taking the life of another man. I use the phrase *taking the life* rather than *murdering* because Conrad's treatment of the event allows for our reasonable doubt. Leggatt tells his own story, making clear that the man died at his hands but not taking full responsibility for the death:

> "We closed just as an awful sea made for the ship. All hands saw it coming and took to the rigging, but I had him by the throat, and went on shaking him like a rat, the men above us yelling, 'Look out! look out!' Then a crash as if the sky had fallen on my head. They say that for over ten minutes hardly anything was to be seen of the ship. . . . It was a miracle that they found us, jammed together behind the forebits. It's clear that I meant business, because I was holding him by the throat still when they picked us up." (32)

The most striking feature of Conrad's handling of this event is that the captain never explicitly says what he thinks about it, and never directs the narratee how to think about it. In reading the report of his conversation with Archbold, we can infer that he has been unwilling to admit Leggatt's role in the man's death. "Don't you think," he suggests, "that the heavy sea . . . might have killed the man?" But Archbold has none of that: "Good God! . . . The sea! No man killed by the sea ever looked like that." And to demonstrate, "he advanced his head close to mine and thrust his tongue out at me so suddenly that I couldn't help starting back" (42). Though the captain starts back here, he never reaches the place where he assesses Leggatt's conduct for himself or the reader.

Instead, the captain assumes that the narratee will share his acceptance, his willingness to think that Leggatt's ending another man's life is less important than Leggatt's current plight and less important than Leggatt's bonding with him. Since the narratee is unspecified and since Conrad does not clearly depict Leggatt as a murderer, we are also likely to feel, as both flesh-and-blood and authorial readers, the pull of the captain's assumptions. To be the secret sharer of this narrative is to adopt—at least for the moments when we project ourselves into the narratee's position—these assumptions; to be the secret sharer of the narrative is also to endorse the captain's plan to protect Leggatt. It is, I find, a rather uncomfortable ethical position.

Even while as narratees we feel the pull of the captain's assumptions, we remain aware of other complex considerations in the authorial audience position. On the one hand, the captain's assumptions are defensible: Leggatt's plight is serious and the mutual understanding he and the captain share is impressive. On the other hand, the assumptions are questionable: Leggatt may be a murderer, and the captain's efforts to keep him hidden clearly interfere with the captain's performance of his primary responsibilities. In this way, hiding Leggatt's existence becomes the captain's *guilty* secret, a guilt made all the more complicated by the captain's unspoken homosexual attraction. Indeed, Conrad is presenting us with a situation in which the two main internal "threats" to a company of sailors—homosexuality and murder—become located, albeit not clearly realized, in the captain's second self. Once we recognize this dimension of the situation, the captain's identification with Leggatt puts him in even greater conflict with his responsibility to the crew. Although the captain seems in one way to have no trouble with the ethics of his behavior, he (and we) also know that he could not successfully defend himself to his crew on ethical grounds. As readers, we become the sharers of the captain's guilty secret, with the added burden or not being sure we can justify it to ourselves. Moreover, once Conrad makes us such secret sharers, once we are in this position of reading guilty secrets, we are at least temporarily in the uncomfortable position of living with them, carrying guilty secrets in our consciousness.

The increasing intensity of the narrative, then, depends not just on Conrad's skillful complication and then convergence of the instabilities, not just on our increasing recognition of the subtextual secret, but also on the complication of the reader's feelings of sharing and living with guilty secrets. Conrad's handling of the visit from Archbold and of the crew of the *Sephora* nicely illustrates the point. The key instability in the scene, with which the captain's narration is primarily concerned, is whether the captain can successfully protect Leggatt. At the same time, details such as the exchange between the captain and the first mate emphasize that Leggatt is indeed a secret to feel guilty about. The mate comments that the story he has heard about Leggatt "beats all these tales we hear about murders in Yankee ships." He also reports the crew's reaction to the idea that Leggatt might be hiding on the ship: "Our chaps took offence. 'As if we would harbour a thing like that,' they said. 'Wouldn't you like to look for him in our coal-hole?' Quite a tiff" (46). At this point, the tension between our efforts to read from the narratee position, where we remain sympathetic to the captain, and from the authorial-audience position, where we recognize the responsibility to the crew, is running high. If the suggestion that Leggatt is on the ship provokes this reaction among "our chaps," we can only imagine what their actually discovering him would provoke. Even as we recognize that the crew's position is problematic in its assumption that Leggatt is guilty, the mate's comments also function both to underline the captain's need for secrecy and to deepen the guilt associated with the secret.

By the time the captain is bringing the boat to the shore of Koh-ring, we are being pulled in different directions: toward compassion for Leggatt and hope for the captain and toward further guilt that the captain is recklessly endangering the crew and the ship by acting primarily on his own concerns, and these feelings are mingled with the fear that he will end up grounding the ship. Fear, hope, and guilt all come together in the moment when the captain violently speaks to and shakes the first mate—a moment which, as many critics note (see especially Leiter), doubles Leggatt's act during the crisis on the *Sephora*. As the captain shouts at the mate, our feelings may move us to be shouting to ourselves, "Shake some sense into the mate! No, don't touch him at all! Bring the ship all the way in! How can you value the secret over the ship? Listen to the mate! Forget the mate!"

In this context, Conrad's successful resolution of the instabilities brings at first a very welcome release from the conflict of our feelings. The release seems all the more satisfying when we reflect that the captain now never has to reveal his secret; the torment that made him feel as if he "had come creeping quietly as near insanity as any man who has not actually gone over the board" (51) is permanently over. But further reflection brings back some uneasiness. For some reason, the captain has decided to reveal the secret, and to some extent relive the torment, by telling the story. Our release is not thereby ruined, but the captain's fragility is underlined, as is his great good fortune in having events work out this way: the ending could so easily have been different. But after such a reading experience, after such discomfort and such welcome release, that alternate conclusion is one we may want, at least for a while, to keep secret.[15]

WORKS CITED

Booth, Wayne C. *The Company We Keep: An Ethics of Fiction*. Berkeley: U of California P, 1988.

———. *The Rhetoric of Fiction*. Rev. ed. Chicago: U of Chicago P, 1983.

Carabine, Keith. "'The Secret Sharer': A Note on the Date of Its Composition." *Conradiana* 19.3 (1987): 209–13.

Dazey, Mary Ann. "Shared Secret or Secret Sharing in Joseph Conrad's 'The Secret Sharer.'" *Conradiana* 18.3 (1986): 201–03.

Fetterley, Judith. *The Resisting Reader*. Bloomington: Indiana UP, 1978.

Genette, Gerard. *Narrative Discourse: An Essay on Method*. Trans. Jane Lewin. Ithaca: Cornell UP, 1980.

Johnson, Barbara, and Marjorie Garber. "Secret Sharing: Reading Conrad Psychoanalytically." *College English* 49 (1987): 628–40.

Leiter, Louis H. "Echo Structures: Conrad's 'The Secret Sharer.'" *Twentieth-Century Literature* 5.4 (1960): 159–75.

Murphy, Michael. "'The Secret Sharer': Conrad's Turn of the Winch." *Conradiana* 18.3 (1986): 1983–200.

Phelan, James. "*Self-Help* for Narratee and Narrative Audience: How I —and You?—Read 'How.'" *Style* (forthcoming).

———. "Toward a Rhetorical Reader Response Criticism: The Difficult, the Stubborn, and the Ending of *Beloved*." *Modern Fiction Studies* 39 (1993): 709–28.

[15]I wish to acknowledge the helpful comments of Elizabeth Preston, Susan Swinford, Mark Conroy, Peter J. Rabinowitz, and Rick Livingston on an earlier version of this essay.

Prince, Gerald. "Introduction to the Study of the Narratee." *Reader Response Criticism: From Formalism to Post-Structuralism*. Ed. Jane Tompkins. Baltimore: Johns Hopkins UP, 1980. 7–25.

Rabinowitz, Peter J. *Before Reading: Narrative Conventions and the Politics of Interpretation*. Ithaca: Cornell UP, 1987.

———. "'Betraying the Sender': The Rhetoric and Ethics of Fragile Texts." *Narrative* 2 (1994): 201–13.

———. "Truth in Fiction: A Reexamination of Audiences." *Critical Inquiry* 4 (1977): 121–41.

Ressler, Steve. *Joseph Conrad: Consciousness and Integrity*. New York: New York UP, 1988.

Troy, Mark. "'. . . of no particular significance except to myself': Narrative Posture in Conrad's 'The Secret Sharer.'" *Studia Neophilologica* 56 (1984): 35–50.

The New Historicism
and
"The Secret Sharer"

WHAT IS THE NEW HISTORICISM?

The title of Brook Thomas's *The New Historicism and Other Old-Fashioned Topics* (1991) is telling. Whenever an emergent theory, movement, method, approach, or group gets labeled with the adjective *new*, trouble is bound to ensue, for what is new today is either established, old, or forgotten tomorrow. Few of you will have heard of the band called "The New Kids on the Block." New Age bookshops and jewelry may seem "old hat" by the time this introduction is published. The New Criticism, or formalism, is just about the oldest approach to literature and literary study currently being practiced. The new historicism, by contrast, is *not* as old-fashioned as formalism, but it is hardly new, either. The term *new* eventually and inevitably requires some explanation. In the case of the new historicism, the best explanation is historical.

Although a number of influential critics working between 1920 and 1950 wrote about literature from a psychoanalytic perspective, the majority took what might generally be referred to as the historical approach. With the advent of the New Criticism, however, historically oriented critics almost seemed to disappear from the face of the earth. The dominant New Critics, or formalists, tended to treat literary works as if they were self-contained, self-referential objects. Rather than basing their interpretations on parallels between the text and historical contexts (such as the author's life or stated intentions in writing the work), these critics concentrated on the relationships *within* the text that give it its form and meaning. During the heyday of the New Criticism, concern about the interplay between literature and history virtually disappeared from literary discourse. In its place was a concern about intratextual repetition, particularly of images or symbols but also of rhythms and sound effect.

About 1970 the New Criticism came under attack by reader-response critics (who believe that the meaning of a work is not inherent in its internal form but rather is cooperatively produced by the reader and the text) and poststructuralists (who, following the philosophy of Jacques Derrida, argue that texts are inevitably self-contradictory and that we can find form in them only by ignoring or suppressing conflicting details or elements). In retrospect it is clear that, their outspoken opposition to the New Criticism notwithstanding, the reader-response critics and poststructuralists of the 1970s were very much *like* their formalist predecessors in two important respects: for the most part, they ignored the world beyond the text and its reader, and, for the most part, they ignored the historical contexts within which literary works are written and read.

Jerome McGann first articulated this retrospective insight in 1985, writing that "a text-only approach has been so vigorously promoted during the last thirty-five years that most historical critics have been driven from the field, and have raised the flag of their surrender by yielding the title 'critic,' and accepting the title 'scholar' for themselves" (*Inflections* 17). Most, but not all. The American Marxist Fredric Jameson had begun his 1981 book *The Political Unconscious* with the following two-word challenge: "Always historicize!" (9). Beginning about 1980, a form of historical criticism practiced by Louis Montrose and Stephen Greenblatt had transformed the field of Renaissance studies and begun to influence the study of American and English Romantic literature as well. And by the mid-1980s, Brook Thomas was working on an essay in which he suggests that classroom discussions of Keats's "Ode on a Grecian Urn" might begin with questions such as the following: Where would Keats have seen such an urn? How did a Grecian urn end up in a museum in England? Some very important historical and political realities, Thomas suggests, lie behind and inform Keats's definitions of art, truth, beauty, the past, and timelessness.

When McGann lamented the surrender of "most historical critics," he no doubt realized what is now clear to everyone involved in the study of literature. Those who had *not* yet surrendered — had not yet "yield[ed] the title 'critic'" to the formalist, reader-response, and post-structuralist "victors" — were armed with powerful new arguments and were intent on winning back long-lost ground. Indeed, at about the same time that McGann was deploring the near-complete dominance of critics advocating the text-only approach, Herbert Lindenberger was sounding a more hopeful note: "It comes as something of a surprise," he wrote in 1984, "to find that history is making a powerful comeback" ("New History" 16).

We now know that history was indeed making a powerful comeback in the 1980s, although the word is misleading if it causes us to imagine that the historical criticism being practiced in the 1980s by Greenblatt and Montrose, McGann and Thomas, was the same as the historical criticism that had been practiced in the 1930s and 1940s. Indeed, if the word *new* still serves any useful purpose in defining the historical criticism of today, it is in distinguishing it from the old historicism. The new historicism is informed by the poststructuralist and reader-response theory of the 1970s, plus the thinking of feminist, cultural, and Marxist critics whose work was also "new" in the 1980s. New historicist critics are less fact- and event-oriented than historical critics used to be, perhaps because they have come to wonder whether the truth about what really happened can ever be purely and objectively known. They are less likely to see history as linear and progressive, as something developing toward the present or the future ("teleological"), and they are also less likely to think of it in terms of specific eras, each with a definite, persistent, and consistent *Zeitgeist* ("spirit of the times"). Consequently, they are unlikely to suggest that a literary text has a single or easily identifiable historical context.

New historicist critics also tend to define the discipline of history more broadly than it was defined before the advent of formalism. They view history as a social science and the social sciences as being properly historical. In *Historical Studies and Literary Criticism* (1985), McGann speaks of the need to make "sociohistorical" subjects and methods central to literary studies; in *The Beauty of Inflections: Literary Investigations in Historical Method and Theory* (1985), he links sociology and the future of historical criticism. "A sociological poetics," he writes, "must be recognized not only as relevant to the analysis of poetry, but in fact as central to the analysis" (62). Lindenberger cites anthropology as particularly useful in the new historical analysis of literature, especially anthropology as practiced by Victor Turner and Clifford Geertz.

Geertz, who has related theatrical traditions in nineteenth-century Bali to forms of political organization that developed during the same period, has influenced some of the most important critics writing the new kind of historical criticism. Due in large part to Geertz's anthropological influence, new historicists such as Greenblatt have asserted that literature is not a sphere apart or distinct from the history that is relevant to it. That is what the old criticism tended to do: present the background information you needed to know before you could fully appreciate the separate world of art. The new historicists have used what Geertz would call "thick description" to blur distinctions, not only between history and the other social sciences but also between background and foreground, historical and literary materials, political and poetical events. They have erased the old boundary line dividing historical and literary materials, showing that the production of one of Shakespeare's historical plays was a political act and historical event, while at the same time showing that the coronation of Elizabeth I was carried out with the same care for staging and symbol lavished on works of dramatic art.

In addition to breaking down barriers that separate literature and history, history and the social sciences, new historicists have reminded us that it is treacherously difficult to reconstruct the past as it really was, rather than as we have been conditioned by our own place and time to believe that it was. And they know that the job is utterly impossible for those who are unaware of that difficulty and insensitive to the bent or bias of their own historical vantage point. Historical criticism must be "conscious of its status as interpretation," Greenblatt has written (*Renaissance* 4). McGann obviously concurs, writing that "historical criticism can no longer make any part of [its] sweeping picture unselfconsciously, or treat any of its details in an untheorized way" (*Studies* 11).

Unselfconsciously and *untheorized* are the key words in McGann's statement. When new historicist critics of literature describe a historical change, they are highly conscious of, and even likely to discuss, the *theory* of historical change that informs their account. They know that the changes they happen to see and describe are the ones that their theory of change allows or helps them to see and describe. And they know too that their theory of change is historically determined. They seek to minimize the distortion inherent in their perceptions and representations by admitting that they see through preconceived notions; in other words, they learn to reveal the color of the lenses in the glasses that they wear.

Nearly everyone who wrote on the new historicism during the 1980s cited the importance of the late Michel Foucault. A French philosophical historian who liked to think of himself as an archaeologist of human knowledge, Foucault brought together incidents and phenomena from areas of inquiry and orders of life that we normally regard as being unconnected. As much as anyone, he encouraged the new historicist critic of literature to redefine the boundaries of historical inquiry.

Foucault's views of history were influenced by the philosopher Friedrich Nietzsche's concept of a *wirkliche* ("real" or "true") history that is neither melioristic (that is, "getting better all the time") nor metaphysical. Like Nietzsche, Foucault didn't see history in terms of a continuous development toward the present. Neither did he view it as an abstraction, idea, or ideal, as something that began "In the beginning" and that will come to THE END, a moment of definite closure, a Day of Judgment. In his own words, Foucault "abandoned [the old history's] attempts to understand events in terms of . . . some great evolutionary process" (*Discipline and Punish* 129). He warned a new generation of historians to be aware that investigators are themselves "situated." It is difficult, he reminded them, to see present cultural practices critically from within them, and because of the same cultural practices, it is extremely difficult to enter bygone ages. In *Discipline and Punish: The Birth of the Prison* (1975), Foucault admitted that his own interest in the past was fueled by a passion to write the history of the present.

Like Marx, Foucault saw history in terms of power, but his view of power probably owed more to Nietzsche than to Marx. Foucault seldom viewed power as a repressive force. He certainly did not view it as a tool of conspiracy used by one specific individual or institution against another. Rather, power represents a whole web or complex of forces; it is that which produces what happens. Not even a tyrannical aristocrat simply wields power, for the aristocrat is himself formed and empowered by a network of discourses and practices that constitute power. Viewed by Foucault, power is "positive and productive," not "repressive" and "prohibitive" (Smart 63). Furthermore, no historical event, according to Foucault, has a single cause; rather, it is intricately connected with a vast web of economic, social, and political factors.

A brief sketch of one of Foucault's major works may help clarify some of his ideas. *Discipline and Punish* begins with a shocking but accurate description of the public drawing and quartering of a Frenchman who had botched his attempt to assassinate King Louis XV in 1757. Foucault proceeds by describing rules governing the daily life of modern Parisian felons. What happened to torture, to punishment as public spectacle? he asks. What complex network of forces made it disappear? In working toward a picture of this "power," Foucault turns up many interesting puzzle pieces, such as the fact that in the early years of the nineteenth century, crowds would sometimes identify with the prisoner and treat the executioner as if *he* were the guilty party. But Foucault sets forth a related reason for keeping prisoners alive, moving punishment indoors, and changing discipline from physical torture into mental rehabilitation: colonization. In this historical period, people were needed to establish colonies and trade, and prisoners could be used for that purpose. Also, because these were politically unsettled times, governments needed infiltrators and informers. Who better to fill those roles than prisoners pardoned or released early for showing a willingness to be rehabilitated? As for rehabilitation itself, Foucault compares it to the old form of punishment, which began with a torturer extracting a confession. In more modern, "reasonable" times, psychologists probe the minds of prisoners with a scientific rigor that Foucault sees as a different kind of torture, a kind that our modern perspective does not allow us to see as such.

Thus, a change took place, but perhaps not as great a change as we generally assume. It may have been for the better or for the worse; the point is that agents of power didn't make the change because humanity is evolving and, therefore, more prone to perform good-hearted deeds. Rather, different objectives arose, including those of a new class of doctors and scientists bent on studying aberrant examples of the human mind. And where do we stand vis-à-vis the history Foucault tells? We are implicated by it, for the evolution of discipline as punishment into the study of the human mind includes the evolution of the "disciplines" as we now understand that word, including the discipline of history, the discipline of literary study, and now a discipline that is neither and both, a form of historical criticism that from the vantage point of the 1980s looked "new."

Foucault's type of analysis has been practiced by a number of literary critics at the vanguard of the back-to-history movement. One of them is Greenblatt, who along with Montrose was to a great extent responsible for transforming Renaissance studies in the early 1980s and revitalizing historical criticism in the process. Greenblatt follows Foucault's lead in interpreting literary devices as if they were continuous with all other representational devices in a culture; he therefore turns to scholars in other fields in order to better understand the workings of literature. "We wall off literary symbolism from the symbolic structures operative elsewhere," he writes, "as if art alone were a human creation, as if humans themselves were not, in Clifford Geertz's phrase, cultural artifacts" (*Renaissance* 4).

Greenblatt's name, more than anyone else's, is synonymous with the new historicism; his essay entitled "Invisible Bullets" (1981) has been said by Patrick Brantlinger to be "perhaps the most frequently cited example of New Historicist work" ("Cultural Studies" 45). An English professor at the University of California, Berkeley — the early academic home of the new historicism — Greenblatt was a founding editor of *Representations,* a journal published by the University of California Press that is still considered today to be *the* mouthpiece of the new historicism.

In *Learning to Curse* (1990), Greenblatt cites as central to his own intellectual development his decision to interrupt his literary education at Yale University by accepting a Fulbright fellowship to study in England at Cambridge University. There he came under the influence of the great Marxist cultural critic Raymond Williams, who made Greenblatt realize how much — and what — was missing from his Yale education. "In Williams' lectures," Greenblatt writes, "all that had been carefully excluded from the literary criticism in which I had been trained — who controlled access to the printing press, who owned the land and the factories, whose voices were being repressed as well as represented in literary texts, what social strategies were being served by the aesthetic values we constructed — came pressing back in upon the act of interpretation" (2).

Greenblatt returned to the United States determined not to exclude such matters from his own literary investigations. Blending what he had learned from Williams with poststructuralist thought about the indeterminacy or "undecidability" of meaning, he eventually developed a critical method that he now calls "cultural poetics." More tentative and less overtly political than cultural criticism, it involves what Thomas calls "the technique of montage. Starting with the analysis of a particular historical event, it cuts to the analysis of a particular literary text. The point is not to show that the literary text reflects the historical event but to create a field of energy between the two so that we come to see the event as a social text and the literary text as a social event" ("New Literary Historicism" 490). Alluding to deconstructor Jacques Derrida's assertion that "there is nothing outside the text," Montrose explains that the goal of this new historicist criticism is to show the "historicity of texts and the textuality of history" (Veeser 20).

The relationship between the cultural poetics practiced by a number of new historicists and the cultural criticism associated with Marx-

ism is important, not only because of the proximity of the two approaches but also because one must recognize the difference between
the two to understand the new historicism. Still very much a part of
the contemporary critical scene, cultural criticism (sometimes called
"cultural studies" or "cultural critique") nonetheless involves several
tendencies more compatible with the old historicism than with the
thinking of new historicists such as Greenblatt. These include the tendency to believe that history is driven by economics; that it is deter-
minable even as it determines the lives of individuals; and that it is progressive, its dialectic one that will bring about justice and equality.

Greenblatt does not privilege economics in his analyses and views
individuals as agents possessing considerable productive power. (He
says that "the work of art is the product of a negotiation between a
creator or class of creators . . . and the institutions and practices of a
society" [*Learning* 158]; he also acknowledges that artistic productions are "intensely marked by the private obsessions of individuals,"
however much they may result from "collective negotiation and exchange" [*Negotiations* vii].) His optimism about the individual, however, should not be confused with optimism about either history's direction or any historian's capacity to foretell it. Like a work of art, a
work of history is the negotiated product of a private creator and the
public practices of a given society.

This does not mean that Greenblatt does not discern historical
change, or that he is uninterested in describing it. Indeed, in works
from *Renaissance Self-Fashioning* (1980) to *Shakespearean Negotiations*
(1988), he has written about Renaissance changes in the development
of both literary characters and real people. But his view of change —
like his view of the individual — is more Foucauldian than Marxist.
That is to say, it is not melioristic or teleological. And, like Foucault,
Greenblatt is careful to point out that any one change is connected
with a host of others, no one of which may simply be identified as
cause or effect, progressive or regressive, repressive or enabling.

Not all of the critics trying to lead students of literature back to
history are as Foucauldian as Greenblatt. Some even owe more to
Marx than to Foucault. Others, like Thomas, have clearly been more
influenced by Walter Benjamin, best known for essays such as "Theses
on the Philosophy of History" and "The Work of Art in the Age of
Mechanical Reproduction." Still others — McGann, for example —
have followed the lead of Soviet critic Mikhail Bakhtin, who viewed literary works in terms of discourses and dialogues between the official,
legitimate voices of a society and other, more challenging or critical

voices echoing popular or traditional culture. In the "polyphonic" writings of Rabelais, for instance, Bakhtin found that the profane language of Carnival and other popular festivals offsets and parodies the "legitimate" discourses representing the outlook of the king, church, and socially powerful intellectuals of the day.

Moreover, there are other reasons not to consider Foucault the single or even central influence on the new historicism. First, he critiqued the old-style historicism to such an extent that he ended up being antihistorical, or at least ahistorical, in the view of a number of new historicists. Second, his commitment to a radical remapping of the relations of power and influence, cause and effect, may have led him to adopt too cavalier an attitude toward chronology and facts. Finally, the very act of identifying and labeling *any* primary influence goes against the grain of the new historicism. Its practitioners have sought to "decenter" the study of literature, not only by overlapping it with historical studies (broadly defined to include anthropology and sociology) but also by struggling to see history from a decentered perspective. That struggle has involved recognizing (1) that the historian's cultural and historical position may not afford the best purview of a given set of events and (2) that events seldom have any single or central cause. In keeping with these principles, it may be appropriate to acknowledge Foucault as just one of several powerful, interactive intellectual forces rather than to declare him the single, master influence.

Throughout the 1980s it seemed to many that the ongoing debates about the sources of the new historicist movement, the importance of Marx or Foucault, Walter Benjamin or Bakhtin, and the exact locations of all the complex boundaries between the new historicism and other "isms" (Marxism and poststructuralism, to name only two) were historically contingent functions of the new historicism *newness*. In the initial stages of their development, new intellectual movements are difficult to outline clearly because, like partially developed photographic images, they are themselves fuzzy and lacking in definition. They respond to disparate influences and include thinkers who represent a wide range of backgrounds; like movements that are disintegrating, they inevitably include a broad spectrum of opinions and positions.

From the vantage point of the 1990s, however, it seems that the inchoate quality of the new historicism is characteristic rather than a function of newness. The boundaries around the new historicism remain fuzzy, not because it hasn't reached its full maturity but because, if it is to live up to its name, it must always be subject to revision and redefinition as historical circumstances change. The fact that so many critics we label new historicist are working right at the border of Marxist, poststructuralist, cultural, postcolonial, feminist, and now even a new form of reader-response (or at least reader-oriented) criticism is evidence of the new historicism's multiple interests and motivations, rather than of its embryonic state.

New historicists themselves advocate and even stress the need to perpetually redefine categories and boundaries — whether they be disciplinary, generic, national, or racial — not because definitions are unimportant but because they are historically constructed and thus subject to revision. If new historicists like Thomas and reader-oriented critics like Steven Mailloux and Peter Rabinowitz seem to spend most of their time talking over the low wall separating their respective fields, then maybe the wall is in the wrong place. As Catherine Gallagher has suggested, the boundary between new historicists and feminists studying "people and phenomena that once seemed insignificant, indeed outside of history: women, criminals, the insane" often turns out to be shifting or even nonexistent (Veeser 43).

If the fact that new historicists all seem to be working on the border of another school should not be viewed as a symptom of the new historicism's newness (or disintegration), neither should it be viewed as evidence that new historicists are intellectual loners or divisive outriders who enjoy talking over walls to people in other fields but who share no common views among themselves. Greenblatt, McGann, and Thomas all started with the assumption that works of literature are simultaneously influenced by and influencing reality, broadly defined. Whatever their disagreements, they share a belief in referentiality — a belief that literature refers to and is referred to by things outside itself — stronger than that found in the works of formalist, poststructuralist, and even reader-response critics. They believe with Greenblatt that the "central concerns" of criticism "should prevent it from permanently sealing off one type of discourse from another or decisively separating works of art from the minds and lives of their creators and their audiences" (*Renaissance* 5).

McGann, in his introduction to *Historical Studies and Literary Criticism,* turns referentiality into a rallying cry:

> What will not be found in these essays . . . is the assumption, so common in text-centered studies of every type, that literary works are self-enclosed verbal constructs, or looped intertextual fields of autonomous signifiers and signifieds. In these essays, the question of referentiality is once again brought to the fore. (3)

In "Keats and the Historical Method in Literary Criticism," he suggests a set of basic, scholarly procedures to be followed by those who have rallied to the cry. These procedures, which he claims are "practical derivatives of the Bakhtin school," assume that historicist critics will study a literary work's "point of origin" by studying biography and bibliography. The critic must then consider the expressed intentions of the author, because, if printed, these intentions have also modified the developing history of the work. Next, the new historicist must learn the history of the work's reception, as that body of opinion has become part of the platform on which we are situated when we study the work at our own particular "point of reception." Finally, McGann urges the new historicist critic to point toward the future, toward his or her *own* audience, defining for its members the aims and limits of the critical project and injecting the analysis with a degree of self-consciousness that alone can give it credibility (*Inflections* 62).

In his introduction to a collection of new historical writings on *The New Historicism* (1989), H. Aram Veeser stresses the unity among new historicists, not by focusing on common critical procedures but, rather, by outlining five "key assumptions" that "continually reappear and bind together the avowed practitioners and even some of their critics":

1. that every expressive act is embedded in a network of material practices;
2. that every act of unmasking, critique, and opposition uses the tools it condemns and risks falling prey to the practice it exposes;
3. that literary and non-literary texts circulate inseparably;
4. that no discourse, imaginative or archival, gives access to unchanging truths nor expresses inalterable human nature;
5. finally, that a critical method and a language adequate to describe culture under capitalism participate in the economy they describe. (xi)

These same assumptions are shared by a group of historians practicing what is now commonly referred to as "the new cultural history." Influenced by *Annales*-school historians in France, post-Althusserian Marxists, and Foucault, these historians share with their new historicist counterparts not only many of the same influences and assumptions but also the following: an interest in anthropological and sociological subjects and methods; a creative way of weaving stories and anecdotes about the past into revealing thick descriptions; a tendency to focus on nontraditional, noncanonical subjects and relations (historian Thomas Laqueur is best known for *Making Sex: Body and Gender from the Greeks to Freud* [1990]); and some of the same journals and projects.

Thus, in addition to being significantly unified by their own interests, assumptions, and procedures, new historicist literary critics have participated in a broader, interdisciplinary movement toward unification virtually unprecedented within and across academic disciplines. Their tendency to work along disciplinary borderlines, far from being evidence of their factious or fractious tendencies, has been precisely what has allowed them to engage historians in a conversation certain to revolutionize the way in which we understand the past, present, and future.

In the essay that follows, Michael Levenson shows how even a work as apparently distant from historical concerns as "The Secret Sharer" engages in active negotiation with the encompassing social world. Levenson locates Conrad's tale between the historical event that incited it and the immediate cultural conditions — including, and perhaps especially, the publishing conditions — that prevailed at the time the tale was written.

The historical event recalled by "The Secret Sharer" was the murder of John Francis, a black crewman on the *Cutty Sark*, by Sidney Smith, the first mate. The captain of the *Cutty Sark* subsequently let Smith escape, whereupon the crew mutinied and the captain committed suicide. Levenson suggests that this isolated historical episode typified the overarching "social dilemma" Conrad saw facing the world of his own day. "In the years leading up to 'The Secret Sharer,'" Levenson writes, "Conrad had been increasingly preoccupied with the fatal passage of political failure from the old authoritative oppressors to their modern opponents." The "impasse of modernity," in Conrad's view, lay in the choice between "autocracy" and the "disorder" of the "modern capitalist state" (164).

As a new historicist, Levenson is interested in relating literary texts to the rich density of social life, but he is wary of seeing art as merely a reflection of social and economic circumstances. As a rule, new historicists characteristically maintain that like any other artifact in the social realm, a work of literature deflects as well as reflects its surroundings, and Levenson is no exception to the rule. What Conrad did in writing "The Secret Sharer," Levenson argues, was to "revise" the historical (as well as the psychological) force of the *Cutty Sark* episode, thereby imagining his way beyond the impasse of choosing between a tyrannical old order and liberal but weak leadership. In the narrating captain, who allows Leggatt to escape, Conrad depicts not a tragic, suicidal "victim of his own gift of sympathy" (166) but, rather, someone who represents a more positive historical force and possibility: a sympathetic, nonautocratic leader who nonetheless acts on authentic conviction. In the captain of the *Sephora* — an invented character with no apparent historical counterpart — Conrad gives us not a tough-minded authority figure representing the positive aspects of the old autocratic order but a weak leader who submits to the will of "his steward, his second mate, his wife" (166).

Conrad, as Levenson points out, was interested throughout his career in the evolution of leadership in a changing, mechanizing, increasingly democratized world. Steamships governed by ineffectual captains became "compelling figures for the failures of modernity, for the disregard of the individual gesture" (168). Levenson sees Conrad's hopes for and worries about his own art figured in these stories as well: the steamship serves as a metaphor for a publishing industry increasingly driven by profit-turning plots and producing "a dull literary uniformity with no appetite for imaginative risk" (169). Seen against the background of this social and cultural emergency, in particular the failure of serious artists to find a secure livelihood, the writing of "The Secret Sharer" appears to have been a strong-willed reaction to a dire threat. "The captain who refuses to surrender to the shallow norms of his crew," writes Levenson, "is at one with the author who resists the temptations" of a mass readership (173).

Space does not permit a preview of the arguments Levenson makes once he begins analyzing the crosscurrents of biography, history, and fiction at their points of juncture in "The Secret Sharer." Suffice it to say that Levenson's reading of a story, its historical contexts, the sociohistorical impasse underlying those contexts, and the way in which that impasse affected the life of the story's author and the fiction he produced typifies the kind of "thick description" we associate with the new historicism. Through that thick description, Levenson not only reads the relationship between fiction and the past but also suggests the power of the novelist to affect the future by creating a world of believable possibility in which the usual oppositions and choices of history (such as the choice between tyranny and disorder) do not pertain. "One might speak," Levenson writes, "of the Conradian ship as a theater of possibility that does not reflect the social world so much as it keeps alive possibilities languishing there" (166).

Ross C Murfin

THE NEW HISTORICISM:
A SELECTED BIBLIOGRAPHY

The New Historicism: Further Reading

Brantlinger, Patrick. "Cultural Studies vs. the New Historicism." *English Studies/Cultural Studies: Institutionalizing Dissent.* Ed. Isaiah Smithson and Nancy Ruff. Urbana: U of Illinois P, 1994. 43–58.

Cox, Jeffrey N., and Larry J. Reynolds, eds. *New Historical Literary Study.* Princeton: Princeton UP, 1993.

Dimock, Wai-Chee. "Feminism, New Historicism, and the Reader." *American Literature* 63 (1991): 601–22.

Howard, Jean. "The New Historicism in Renaissance Studies." *English Literary Renaissance* 16 (1986): 13–43.

Lindenberger, Herbert. *The History in Literature: On Value, Genre, Institutions.* New York: Columbia UP, 1990.

———. "Toward a New History in Literary Study." *Profession: Selected Articles from the Bulletins of the Association of Departments of English and the Association of the Departments of Foreign Languages.* New York: MLA, 1984. 16–23.

Liu, Alan. "The Power of Formalism: The New Historicism." *English Literary History* 56 (1989): 721–71.

McGann, Jerome. *The Beauty of Inflections: Literary Investigations in Historical Method and Theory.* Oxford: Clarendon–Oxford UP, 1985.

———. *Historical Studies and Literary Criticism.* Madison: U of Wisconsin P, 1985. See especially the introduction and the essays in the following sections: "Historical Methods and Literary Interpretations" and "Biographical Contexts and the Critical Object."

Montrose, Louis Adrian. "Renaissance Literary Studies and the Subject of History." *English Literary Renaissance* 16 (1986): 5–12.

Morris, Wesley. *Toward a New Historicism.* Princeton: Princeton UP, 1972.

New Literary History 21 (1990). "History and . . ." (special issue). See especially the essays by Carolyn Porter, Rena Fraden, Clifford Geertz, and Renato Rosaldo.

Representations. This quarterly journal, printed by the University of California Press, regularly publishes new historicist studies and cultural criticism.

Thomas, Brook. "The Historical Necessity for — and Difficulties with — New Historical Analysis in Introductory Courses." *College English* 49 (1987): 509–22.

———. *The New Historicism and Other Old-Fashioned Topics*. Princeton: Princeton UP, 1991.

———. "The New Literary Historicism." *A Companion to American Thought*. Ed. Richard Wightman Fox and James T. Klappenberg. New York: Basil Blackwell, 1995.

———. "Walter Benn Michaels and the New Historicism: Where's the Difference?" *Boundary 2* 18 (1991): 118–59.

Veeser, H. Aram, ed. *The New Historicism*. New York: Routledge, 1989. See especially Veeser's introduction, Louis Montrose's "Professing the Renaissance," Catherine Gallagher's "Marxism and the New Historicism," and Frank Lentricchia's "Foucault's Legacy: A New Historicism?"

Wayne, Don E. "Power, Politics and the Shakespearean Text: Recent Criticism in England and the United States." *Shakespeare Reproduced: The Text in History and Ideology*. Ed. Jean Howard and Marion O'Connor. New York: Methuen, 1987. 47–67.

Winn, James A. "An Old Historian Looks at the New Historicism." *Comparative Studies in Society and History* 35 (1993): 859–70.

The New Historicism: Influential Examples

The new historicism has taken its present form less through the elaboration of basic theoretical postulates and more through certain influential examples. The works listed represent some of the most important contributions guiding research in this area.

Bercovitch, Sacvan. *The Rites of Assent: Transformations in the Symbolic Construction of America*. New York: Routledge, 1993.

Brown, Gillian. *Domestic Individualism: Imagining Self in Nineteenth-Century America*. Berkeley: U of California P, 1990.

Dollimore, Jonathan. *Radical Tragedy: Religion, Ideology and Power in the Drama of Shakespeare and His Contemporaries*. Brighton, Eng.: Harvester, 1984.

Dollimore, Jonathan, and Alan Sinfield, eds. *Political Shakespeare: New Essays in Cultural Materialism*. Manchester, Eng.: Manchester UP, 1985. This volume occupies the borderline between new historicist and cultural criticism. See especially the essays by Dollimore, Greenblatt, and Tennenhouse.

Gallagher, Catherine. *The Industrial Reformation of English Fiction*. Chicago: U of Chicago P, 1985.

Goldberg, Jonathan. *James I and the Politics of Literature*. Baltimore: Johns Hopkins UP, 1983.

Greenblatt, Stephen J. *Learning to Curse: Essays in Early Modern Culture*. New York: Routledge, 1990.

———. *Marvelous Possessions: The Wonder of the New World*. Chicago: U of Chicago P, 1991.

———. *Renaissance Self-Fashioning from More to Shakespeare*. Chicago: U of Chicago P, 1980. See chapter 1 and the chapter on *Othello* titled "The Improvisation of Power."

———. *Shakespearean Negotiations: The Circulation of Social Energy in Renaissance England*. Berkeley: U of California P, 1988. See especially "The Circulation of Social Energy" and "Invisible Bullets."

Liu, Alan. *Wordsworth, the Sense of History*. Stanford: Stanford UP, 1989.

Marcus, Leah. *Puzzling Shakespeare: Local Reading and Its Discontents*. Berkeley: U of California P, 1988.

McGann, Jerome. *The Romantic Ideology*. Chicago: U of Chicago P, 1983.

Michaels, Walter Benn. *The Gold Standard and the Logic of Naturalism: American Literature at the Turn of the Century*. Berkeley: U of California P, 1987.

Montrose, Louis Adrian. "'Shaping Fantasies': Figurations of Gender and Power in Elizabethan Culture." *Representations* 2 (1983): 61–94. One of the most influential early new historicist essays.

Mullaney, Steven. *The Place of the Stage: License, Play, and Power in Renaissance England*. Chicago: U of Chicago P, 1987.

Orgel, Stephen. *The Illusion of Power: Political Theater in the English Renaissance*. Berkeley: U of California P, 1975.

Sinfield, Alan. *Literature, Politics, and Culture in Postwar Britain*. Berkeley: U of California P, 1989.

Tennenhouse, Leonard. *Power on Display: The Politics of Shakespeare's Genres*. New York: Methuen, 1986.

Foucault and His Influence

As I point out in the introduction to the new historicism, some new historicists would question the "privileging" of Foucault implicit in this section heading ("Foucault and His Influence") and the following one ("Other Writers and Works"). They might cite the greater importance of one of those other writers or point out that to cite a central influence or a definitive cause runs against the very spirit of the movement.

Foucault, Michel. *The Archaeology of Knowledge*. Trans. A. M. Sheridan Smith. New York: Harper, 1972.

———. *Discipline and Punish: The Birth of the Prison*. 1975. Trans. Alan Sheridan. New York: Pantheon, 1978.

———. *The History of Sexuality*. Vol. 1. Trans. Robert Hurley. New York: Pantheon, 1978.

———. *Language, Counter-Memory, Practice*. Ed. Donald F. Bouchard. Trans. Donald F. Bouchard and Sherry Simon. Ithaca: Cornell UP, 1977.

———. *The Order of Things: An Archaeology of the Human Sciences*. New York: Vintage, 1973.

———. *Politics, Philosophy, Culture*. Ed. Lawrence D. Kritzman. Trans. Alan Sheridan et al. New York: Routledge, 1988.

———. *Power/Knowledge*. Ed. Colin Gordon. Trans. Colin Gordon et al. New York: Pantheon, 1980.

———. *Technologies of the Self*. Ed. Luther H. Martin, Huck Gutman, and Patrick H. Hutton. Amherst: U of Massachusetts P, 1988.

Dreyfus, Hubert L., and Paul Rabinow. *Michel Foucault: Beyond Structuralism and Hermeneutics*. Chicago: U of Chicago P, 1983.

Sheridan, Alan. *Michel Foucault: The Will to Truth*. New York: Tavistock, 1980.

Smart, Barry. *Michel Foucault*. New York: Ellis Horwood and Tavistock, 1985.

Other Writers and Works of Interest to New Historicist Critics

Bakhtin, M. M. *The Dialogic Imagination: Four Essays*. Ed. Michael Holquist. Trans. Caryl Emerson. Austin: U of Texas P, 1981. Bakhtin wrote many influential studies on subjects as varied as Dostoyevsky, Rabelais, and formalist criticism. But this book, in part due to Holquist's helpful introduction, is probably the best place to begin reading Bakhtin.

Benjamin, Walter. "The Work of Art in the Age of Mechanical Reproduction." 1936. *Illuminations*. Ed. Hannah Arendt. Trans. Harry Zohn. New York: Harcourt, 1968.

Fried, Michael. *Absorption and Theatricality: Painting and Beholder in the Works of Diderot*. Berkeley: U of California P, 1980.

Geertz, Clifford. *The Interpretation of Cultures*. New York: Basic, 1973.

———. *Negara: The Theatre State in Nineteenth-Century Bali*. Princeton: Princeton UP, 1980.

Goffman, Erving. *Frame Analysis*. New York: Harper, 1974.

Jameson, Fredric. *The Political Unconscious: Narrative as a Socially Symbolic Act.* Ithaca: Cornell UP, 1981.

Koselleck, Reinhart. *Futures Past.* Trans. Keith Tribe. Cambridge: MIT P, 1985.

Said, Edward. *Orientalism.* New York: Columbia UP, 1978.

Turner, Victor. *The Ritual Process: Structure and Anti-Structure.* Chicago: Aldine, 1969.

Young, Robert. *White Mythologies: Writing History and the West.* New York: Routledge, 1990.

Historical and New Historicist
Approaches to Conrad and "The Secret Sharer"

Bivona, Daniel. "Conrad's Bureaucrats: Agency, Bureaucracy and the Problem of Intention." *Novel* 26 (1993): 151–69.

Brantlinger, Patrick. *Rule of Darkness: British Literature and Imperialism. 1830–1914.* Ithaca: Cornell UP, 1988.

Dawson, Anthony B. "In the Pink: Self and Empire in 'The Secret Sharer.'" *Conradiana* 22 (1990): 185–96.

Demory, Pamela H. "Nostromo: Making History." *Texas Studies in Literature and Language* 35 (1993): 316–46.

Fleishman, Avrom. *Conrad's Politics: Community and Anarchy in the Fiction of Joseph Conrad.* Baltimore: Johns Hopkins UP, 1967.

Jameson, Fredric. *The Political Unconscious: Narrative as a Socially Symbolic Act.* Ithaca: Cornell UP, 1981.

McClure, John A. *Kipling & Conrad, the Colonial Fiction.* Cambridge: Harvard UP, 1981.

North, Michael. *The Dialect of Modernism: Race, Language, and Twentieth-Century Literature.* New York: Oxford UP, 1994.

Parry, Benita. *Conrad and Imperialism: Ideological Boundaries and Visionary Frontiers.* London: Macmillan, 1983.

Reilly, Jim. *Shadowtime: History and Representation in Hardy, Conrad, and George Eliot.* London: Routledge, 1993.

Said, Edward W. *Culture and Imperialism.* New York: Knopf, 1993.

Thomas, Brook. "Preserving and Keeping Order by Killing Time in *Heart of Darkness*." *Joseph Conrad, "Heart of Darkness."* Ed. Ross C Murfin. 2nd ed. Case Studies in Contemporary Criticism. Boston: Bedford–St. Martin's, 1996.

Watt, Ian P. *Conrad in the Nineteenth Century.* Berkeley: U of California P, 1979.

White, Andrea. *Joseph Conrad and the Adventure Tradition.* Cambridge: Cambridge UP, 1993. Contains a reading of "The Secret Sharer."

A NEW HISTORICIST PERSPECTIVE

MICHAEL LEVENSON

Secret History in "The Secret Sharer"

The lure of the psychological is so pronounced in "The Secret Sharer" that it requires a resolute act of will to give any historical perspective, new or otherwise, its due measure. From the first proposed title, "The Second Self," to the insistent evocation of psychic doubleness, the tale invites readings that focus on the mystery of personality, the threats and the opportunities of self-division, the strenuous labor of integration. Although no one can deny the salience of these issues, it is well to remember that even the most mysterious personalities live within a social world. "The Secret Sharer" emerges from a complex public history, and to a complex public history it returns. The premise of this essay, as of the style of reading on which it relies, is that literature's psychological insight loses none of its force when restored to the concrete conditions of its social emergence.

In the early fall of 1909 Conrad had a visit from one Captain Charles Marris, a "man out of the Malay Seas," who clearly stirred strong memories of the author's own early sailing days. The encounter, Conrad wrote, was "like the raising of a lot of dead—dead to me, because most of them live out there and even read my books and wonder who [the] devil has been around taking notes." He then adds, "They shall have some more of the stories they like" (*Letters* 277–78). For some time readers have recognized the episode as the immediate impetus for "The Secret Sharer," but it is worth noting the distinctive turn of Conrad's reflections on his work. His pride in his representational accuracy ("taking notes") and his keen consciousness of audience ("the stories they like") make clear that he fully accepts the worldly character of his literary vocation. His fiction regularly begins in the memory of some lived event, and it always unfolds with deep concern for its effect on the readers. Between the world that receives the work and the world that incited it, there stands the tale, which can never be reduced to its historical surroundings, but which everywhere reveals their traces.

"History" will enter our understanding of "The Secret Sharer" in two places. The first is the acknowledged source of the story, the brutal murder that occurred in 1880 on board the *Cutty Sark,* the legendary sea clipper, then struggling to sustain its cherished reputation in the age of steam. According to Basil Lubbock's history of the *Cutty Sark*, the ship's first mate, Sidney Smith, a "hard-fibred despotic" character, had taken a fierce dislike to a black crewman named John Francis (182).[1] The two seem to have clashed from early in the voyage, and then, after the ship passed through a storm of hurricane force, Francis apparently disregarded a clear order to alter course. Smith became enraged, the two fought, and following a struggle for a capstan bar, the mate struck Francis so violently that he fell senseless and, after lying comatose for three days, finally died.

At this point, as in "The Secret Sharer," the mate was confined to quarters, but when the ship arrived at Anjer, the captain, J. S. Wallace, quietly allowed him to escape in order to join the crew of an American ship, the *Colorado*. In Lubbock's reconstruction of the narrative, the crew of the *Cutty Sark* became infuriated as soon as the escape was known and refused to obey any of the captain's orders. Captain Wallace himself must have been overcome by guilt and shame, because when the *Cutty Sark* was four days out of Anjer, Wallace, after carefully indicating the ship's course to the helmsman, stepped to the rail and jumped to his death in the shark-infested waters.[2]

The story came to Conrad as a tale of oppression and revolt, of excessive and then weak authority, leading to mutinous social chaos, and in this respect the incident mirrors the large-scale social failure that he takes as the fate of modern Europe. In the years leading up to "The Secret Sharer" Conrad had been increasingly preoccupied with the fatal passage of political failure from the old authoritative oppressors to their modern opponents. Savage autocracy (in the aspect of czarist Russia) must be eradicated at last, but its prevailing alternative (the modern capitalist state) risked a new chaos in the mad pursuit of "material interests." If Conrad suddenly thought back to the *Cutty Sark* three decades after the event, it may well have been because the episode took the shape of the social dilemma (autocracy or disorder) that a skeptical Conrad formulated as the impasse of modernity.

Others, of course, were looking to socialism as an escape from the impasse. But for Conrad, to whom "the efforts of mankind to work its

---

[1]Although Conrad thoroughly elides the racial context of the murder, it nevertheless leaves its mark on the tale. When Leggatt narrates the murderous strangling, he recalls that "I was holding him by the throat still when they picked us up. He was black in the face (32).

[2]Norman Sherry has noted how Conrad had earlier used Wallace's hauntingly well-prepared self-destruction as the basis for Captain Brierly's suicide in *Lord Jim* (269).

own salvation present a sight of alarming comicality" ("Autocracy" 108), socialism offered no solution. And yet, he too refused to surrender to the morose social prospect. "The Secret Sharer" in a secret way tells us much about Conrad's affirmative response to this historical crisis. It does so through its acts of fidelity to the original event and still more through its strong acts of historical revision. One of the more revealing transformative acts appeared in a late letter to A. T. Saunders, in which Conrad willingly identifies the *Cutty Sark* incident as his source and then characterizes it as the narrative of a ship's mate who "had the misfortune to kill a man on deck. But his skipper had the decency to let him swim ashore on the Java coast as the ship was passing through Anjer Straits" (qtd. in Sherry 295). Here in the very act of describing his story's social origin, Conrad strikingly transforms that origin. His formulation de-emphasizes the crime, named here as a "misfortune," and justifies Captain Wallace's official failure by interpreting it as an "act of decency."

Within the tale itself, the central revisionary gesture is the decision to split the *Cutty Sark* and its Captain Wallace in two by creating another ship with a second captain (the story's narrator), and in so doing to revise the historical (as well as the psychological) force of the episode. Left in its "original" form, the incident could easily suggest a wretched human tragedy: Captain Wallace as the victim of his own gift of sympathy. But Conrad reserves sympathy for his narrator, while Archbold, the captain of the *Sephora*, remains a feeble tyrant incapable of "decency." Leggatt recalls that when he asked for a chance to swim to freedom, Archbold

> "refused, looking more sick than ever. He was afraid of the men, and also of that old second mate of his who had been sailing with him for years—a grey-headed old humbug; and his steward, too, had been with him devil knows how long—seventeen years or more—a dogmatic sort of loafer who hated me like poison, just because I was the chief mate. No chief mate ever made more than one voyage in the *Sephora*, you know. Those two old chaps ran the ship. Devil only knows what the skipper wasn't afraid of . . . —of what the law would do to him—of his wife, perhaps." (35)

Leggatt has asked, in effect, to repeat the historical circumstance that gave rise to the fiction he inhabits—Captain Wallace's release of Smith—and if Conrad has Archbold weakly refuse, it is because Conrad seeks to reconsider the terms of social authority and power. By inventing a new ship with a new captain, he invents a place outside the original account, a place that becomes, as it were, a theater in which Conrad can ask his personages to perform new historical roles. In the act of "decency" extended to his murderous mate, Wallace of the *Cutty Sark* had catastrophically renounced his responsibility, and it is fair to assume that his suicide was the result of this impossible conflict. But Conrad in "The Secret Sharer" is not concerned with tragic impossibility. By placing his narrator on that second ship and by separating Wallace's legal authority and his imaginative sympathy, he confuses the terms of conflict, unsettles the moral demands, and so opens the closed impasse of the historical record.

What has always made it so difficult to gauge the force of Conrad's social critique is that a ship's community stands in such unsteady relation to the social practices enacted on land. While he is often eager to tease out the thought of the ship as a social microcosm, he is too canny to belabor the metaphor. Often the most powerful suggestion resides in the failure of the metaphor, because in failing to correspond precisely to the present social world, the sailing community becomes an alternative to a phase of historical decay. Here one might speak of the Conradian ship as a theater of possibility that does not reflect the social world so much as it keeps alive possibilities languishing there.

When Archbold has returned to his own ship, the narrator's mate remarks that Leggatt's story "beats all these tales we hear about murders in Yankee ships," to which the narrator brusquely replies, "I don't think it beats them. I don't think it resembles them in the least" (46). This is a telling exchange. The captain refuses to sort the case within available categories, insisting instead on the moral singularities that cannot be resolved via the prevailing system of guilt and punishment. In denying "resemblance" he is refusing the act of abstract classification on which the legal/moral system relies. Through the choice of solidarity with Leggatt he repudiates the universalizing claims of the modern social order—that is, he repudiates the rational, impersonal, bureaucratic administration of justice. The "spiritless tenacity" (41) of Archbold, the dull, pitiless desire to bring Leggatt to justice, stands as an emblem of an exhausted modernity which can offer no persuasive self-justification but which doggedly persists in its conventional routines. Caught in the snares of the commonplace, this weak captain yields to his steward, his second mate, his wife, and so exemplifies what Conrad so deeply scorns in the moral life of his epoch: the loss of authentic conviction in favor of feeble submission to the will of others. Within the reign of moral formula and social convention, it becomes nearly impossible to recognize the claims of *difference*. So Archbold complains that he was "forced to take [Leggatt] on. He looked very smart, very gentlemanly, and all that. But do you know—I never liked him, somehow. I am a plain man. You see, he wasn't exactly the sort for the chief mate of a ship like the *Sephora*" (43).

No one could say that the narrator was similarly "forced" to take on Leggatt, and once one escapes the confines of a strictly psychological reading of the tale, his embrace of Leggatt can be more fully appreciated as a radical social provocation, a refusal of the prevailing norms of common opinion that have rendered Archbold so helpless. The high price of this refusal is an isolation that quickly incites suspicion and incomprehension. The narrator well understands the risk, admitting that "it's to no commander's advantage to be suspected of ludicrous eccentricities" (48). Indeed, his antic behavior, his agitation, and his self-doubt raise the same question for both the reader and the crew: What kind of captain is this?

Within the terms of the Conradian critique of modernity, captaincy becomes a defining figure, an embodied register of social and cultural health. Throughout Conrad's fiction the captain's burden lies in the need to assume the responsibilities of an immediate authority that is not dispersed through the elaborate web of bureaucratic impersonality but rather is located in the most direct intersubjective relations of human beings. On the open sea a ship's community is at once distant from the land-based rule of law and near to the anarchy of natural disaster. Emphasizing both of these circumstances, Conrad identifies the captain as the autocratic source of order. Frequently, in conditions of social or natural danger, all hope for community survival will rest with this one man, who must transform individual weakness into collective strength. The strong captain exemplifies an older code of honor that Conrad regards as threatened by the advent of a leveling modernity.

Yet, the strain in this imaginative project occurs in Conrad's effort to distinguish the successful "autocratic realm of the ship" (*Mirror* 17) from the horrors of modern European political autocracy. In this light the eccentricity of the captain-narrator can be seen not as a weakness that must be overcome but as a condition of success that must be preserved. He represents himself initially as "the only stranger on board" (26) and later as the "strange new captain" (49); indeed the language of "strangeness" persists throughout the tale. This emphasis is so relentless that it can easily take on a deceptive obviousness, because it can be all too easily linked to a personal rather than a social condition. And yet "strangeness" is for Conrad nearly an essential attribute of captaincy. The power that he abhors is the heavy lowering of the strong hand, the crushing weight of authority, so fully epitomized for him in the "fantastic bulk" ("Autocracy" 86) of the czarist state. What he offers in "The Secret Sharer" is another image of power: the power of withdrawal, of reticence, power not as a ponderous presence but as a beguiling distance. Conrad's fiction is rife with aloof, self-enclosed captains who succeed by retreating into some impenetrable interior space and who leave the ship's community to its own organic rhythms, until at a moment of crisis the reticence turns into a saving control. So with the young captain here—his strong final assertion of command does not diminish but preserves his distance from his shipmates. His task is not to overcome social distance in favor of an easy camaraderie; rather, it is to transform the strangeness of eccentricity into a strange authority.

But such is also the task of the Conradian artist,[3] and during the years leading up to "The Secret Sharer," the intimate connection between captaincy and artistry became one of his most cherished insights. It is not a matter of the captain simply as an emblem for the writer; indeed it is often just as plausible to reverse the terms and to see writing as an allegory for sailing. Each is a vocation of high dignity; each illuminates the other; each gives metaphors for the other. In *The Mirror of the Sea* (1905), pondering the disappearance of the sailing ship in the new age of steam, Conrad writes that

> the sailing of any vessel afloat is an art whose fine form seems already receding from us on its way to the overshadowed Valley of Oblivion. The taking of a modern steamship about the world (though one would not minimize its responsibilities) has not the same quality of intimacy with nature, which, after all, is an indispensable condition to the building up of an art. It is less personal and a more exact calling; less arduous, but also less gratifying in the lack of close communion between the artist and the medium of his art. . . . It is not an individual temperamental achievement, but simply the skilled use of a captured force, merely another step forward upon the way of universal conquest. (31–31)

Steam and steamships thus become compelling figures for the failures of modernity, for the disregard of individual gesture in favor of the mechanically impersonal routine of "universal conquest." The com-

---

[3]In an early and influential reading of the tale, R. W. Stallman spoke of it as an allegory of "man's aesthetic or artistic conscience" (284). Daniel R. Schwarz extended this insight in making the argument that the "captain's use of Leggatt has its analogy in the creative process of art" (9).

mand of a sailing ship, on the other hand, "like all true art," allows the "peculiarities" of individual vocation to display themselves and arouses an inspiration as great as that of "any man who ever put brush to canvas" (*Mirror* 31).

Here we come to the second historical opening into "The Secret Sharer": the cultural predicament of self-styled "serious artists" faced with the increasingly dominant machinery of mass publishing, a machinery that resembles the inexorable advance of steam upon the ocean. Only a few years later young modernist artists would firmly establish their confident solidarity and would daringly taunt the unresponsive cultural milieu. But in 1908 and 1909 the market forces of the publishing world seemed to have assumed terrifying powers, capable of repressing "high" cultural endeavor. (Witness the failure of Thomas Hardy's "A Sunday Morning Tragedy" to find a publisher.) Conrad anguished over his own failure to secure a stable family life through a writing career. His finances were precarious and constantly preoccupying; his letters return repeatedly to the exhausting financial constraint. Early in 1909 he ruefully observes that "all my immortal works (12 in all) have brought me last year something under five pounds in royalties" (*Letters* 187), and dryly confesses his powerlessness within the profit-hungry publishing milieu ("editors are not falling over each other in their eagerness to get at my stuff") (*Letters* 244).

Within this difficult context, the deep analogy between art and captaincy took on a new implication, as Conrad increasingly suspected that in his writing life he faced the specter of cultural steam—the specter, that is, of a dull literary uniformity with no appetite for imaginative risk. As his debts steadily mounted and as *Under Western Eyes* languished, he became oppressively conscious of the raw activity of text production, noting, at once mockingly and enviously, that he was not like Ford Madox Ford, "who can dash off 4000 words in 2 hours or there abouts" (*Letters* 277). The sheer physical demands of writing came to repel him: "There is *no* moment in the day when I don't hate the sight of pen and ink" (*Letters* 272). And even as he modestly demured when J. G. Huneker compared him to Flaubert, he admitted that "there is one point in which I resemble that great man; it is in the desperate, heart breaking toil and effort of the writing, the days of wrestling as with a dumb devil for every line of my creation" (*Letters* 235). Here is the other aspect of the guiding analogy: not the resemblance between the triumph of art and the mastery of a sailing ship's command, but now between the bitter struggle to produce sentences and the strenuous toil of the sailing laborer. In one of his reminiscences in the *English Review* Conrad writes revealingly of "the intimacy and the strain of a creative effort in which mind and will and conscience are engaged to the full, hour after hour, day after day, away from the world, and to exclusion of all that makes life really lovable and gentle —something for which a material parallel can only be found in the everlasting sombre stress of the westward passage round Cape Horn" (*Personal Record* 98–99).

During the months leading up to the writing of "The Secret Sharer," Conrad experienced a severe creative crisis that would ultimately lead to a violent personal breakdown. His ambitious novel *Under Western Eyes* (then still called by its protagonist's name, *Razumov*) had grown wildly beyond its initial conception, and as it grew, so grew the author's torment over his work. In 1909 Conrad frequently felt close to the collapse of his literary career. The writer's isolation, which in his more confident moods had appeared to allow the opportunity for splendid gestures of individual will, now seemed to him the crippling outcome of cultural neglect. When Ford assumed the editorship of the *English Review* in 1908, it appeared as if literary seriousness had found a secure home; indeed, Ford later said that he took up the *Review* in order to provide a forum for Conrad's work. Not only Conrad, but Thomas Hardy, H. G. Wells, D. H. Lawrence, Henry James, Ezra Pound, and Ford himself contributed to the early issues, and there briefly seemed reason to believe that such an enterprise might resist the encroachments of the profit-seeking steam. But by the summer of 1909 that collective effort had failed. Ford, who had poorly managed the finances, lost control of the journal, and just as unfortunately, he quarreled bitterly with his old friend and collaborator Conrad. The grounds of the quarrel were slight (Conrad's refusal to meet Willa Cather on short notice and his missing a deadline for an installment of his reminiscences) but the consequences for Conrad were serious. Intense feelings of being abandoned, left in the grip of his material hardship, unable to move the pen fast enough, vulnerable to slight and disrespect contributed to his agitating personal circumstance as he turned to write "The Secret Sharer."

The literary editor of the *Daily Mail* had proposed to pay Conrad five pounds per twelve hundred words for a series of short sketches. As the plan for "The Secret Sharer" first came to him, Conrad saw it as one of these unabashedly commercial squibs. With its one million readers, the *Daily Mail* represented the triumph of mass circulation, a "material interest," which like the steamship seemed bound for "universal conquest." Drawn as he necessarily was to the prospect of "a guinea a week at least," Conrad still could not overcome his distaste, realizing finally that he "hadn't the heart to throw [the story] away." "The Secret Sharer," as he aptly put it, "is the result of that reluctance" (*Letters* 297–98). The tale thus came into being as an act of stubborn resistance to that economic behemoth, the capitalist press, whose power Conrad at once admitted and despised.

Against this debilitating and demoralizing background, the composition of "The Secret Sharer" at the end of 1909 seemed a minor miracle. After months of hesitation, inefficiency, and self-doubt, the story fell onto the page with surprising speed—"12000 words in ten days," he proudly reported to Galsworthy (*Letters* 296)—and it seems clear that at this critical moment Conrad was as delighted by the material existence of the text (the sixty-four pages of typescript sent off to his agent) as he was by the content of the tale. Even before it becomes an object for our interpretation, we must recognize that "The Secret Sharer" was first of all a *thing* for Conrad, a heap of pages, a physical manifestation of the nearly exhausted creative will. Enthusiastically, he observed that he was "feeling as well" as he had felt in the *Lord Jim* days, "which were the last good ones" (*Letters* 298).

The production of the text, and in particular the creation of Leggatt as a second self, can then be seen as a response to the harsh challenge to "high" literature confronting Conrad after the failure of the *English Review*. All through the months leading up to "The Secret Sharer," he felt acutely the loss of cultural connection and the pain of near-total solitude. "No voices reach me here," he told Galsworthy in October (*Letters* 280). To read through the correspondence of this period is to be struck repeatedly with Conrad's attempt to nurture some form, almost any form, of cultural alliance. Left alone in his desperation, he made persistent, half-successful attempts to establish himself as a mentor to two literary protégés, Norman Douglas and Stephen Reynolds. He regarded Reynolds as "a son or younger brother" (*Letters* 215) and assumed responsibility for "saving" Douglas (who "has any amount of really good stuff in him" [*Letters* 261]) from dangerous influences. In these protective gestures we have notable counterparts to the relationship between the captain-narrator and Leggatt: in both realms, one finds the strenuous effort to fashion a small secure solidarity to stand against the large social failure. Within the immediate historical circumstance of 1909 the invention of Leggatt thus appears as an urgently willed response to the crisis of modernity. Like the captain of a sailing ship in the age of steam, Conrad saw himself faced with becoming a forgotten, unacknowledged, cultural laborer. Against this background "The Secret Sharer" offers an imaginary resolution to the real conflict: two radically estranged individuals discover one another and engage in saving acts of mutual validation—whatever else this connotes, it stands as Conrad's act of fictive reparation, performed under the pressure of historical need.

A persistent crux in the interpretation of "The Secret Sharer" has been the shifting valence toward the figure of Leggatt: Is he a threat that must be subdued or an ideal that must be respected? This question is how the difficulty has been posed, but given the historical pressures (on both captains and writers) we should recognize that before there can be any question of Leggatt's moral or psychological value ("ideal" or "dangerous"), he stands bluntly and powerfully as simply another being, a counterpart, who makes human relationship possible. Conrad's first title, "The Second Self," captures well this perception that prior to any moral relationship, and partly in defiance of such a relationship, stands the primordial tie between one self and a second, between these two subjectivities who build an intersubjectivity. When Leggatt describes his confinement on the *Sephora,* he recalls the "confounded lonely time" and admits that when first seen by the captain-narrator, he "didn't mind being looked at. . . . I wanted to be seen, to talk with somebody" (37–38). This, of course, is what the captain wants too. The root desire for acknowledgment, the yearning merely to be seen, to be recognized as a full being—this is what has been denied both men and what they recover in their secret sharing.

Yet even as the tale projects its vision of a mutually confirming intersubjectivity, it marks the limits of an imagined partnership. The collaboration of Leggatt and the narrator, much like the collaboration of Conrad and Ford, is not an end in itself; it is the necessary means to the great end and most cherished hope: the direct encounter between a confident self and a responsive world. Leggatt must swim off to his own uncertain future, while the narrator accepts the radical individuality of his command.

> Already the ship was drawing ahead. And I was alone with her. Nothing! no one in the world should stand now between us, throwing a shadow on the way of silent knowledge and mute affection, the perfect communion of a seaman with his first command. (59)

"Communion" resonates here, as it vividly presents the heightened, elevated, even spiritual character of the moment of vocation. The dignified stress of labor is what the writer and the captain share, even as their dignity is always at risk, as modern labor threatens to descend into the hollow routines of profit and loss. Attempting to stare down the mean contrivances of modernity, Conrad builds a consoling image of a brief solidarity that lasts just long enough to prepare for the triumph of self-will. The captain who refuses to surrender to the shallow norms of his crew is at one with the author who resists the temptations of the *Daily Mail*.

In Conrad's broadly pessimistic historical view, although an age of autocracy was at last fully giving way to an epoch of democracy, this change was no cause for rejoicing. He saw modern history as preeminently the reign of a profit-obsessed democracy, "which has elected to pin its faith to the supremacy of material interests" ("Autocracy" 107), steamships, and newspapers. All that was left of Europe, Conrad thought, was "an armed and trading continent, the home of slowly maturing economical contests for life and death, and of loudly proclaimed world-wide ambitions" ("Autocracy" 112). The sea was not outside this new web of power, nor was the sea of print. But from inside the net, the captain and the writer sought to preserve themselves from "the fascination of a material advantage" ("Autocracy" 111) and the degradation of human labor. Necessarily they looked to others for solidarity—not all others in the "world-wide" imperium, but a few others, shipmates and writing comrades. And yet the compelling logic of "The Secret Sharer," like the cultural context pressing hard against it, suggests that even the small community is too large to sustain. Sharing becomes a secret, a private partnership, so private it may scarcely seem more than conversation with oneself. One can only hope, or fancy, that this sharing is enough. Even when the sharer swims away, or the collaborator quarrels, or the protégé strays, still the secret of acknowledgment lingers. In its whisper it teaches how little one can expect to have and then stirs the thought that so little is all one needs in order to work on, to write on, alone in history.

WORKS CITED

Conrad, Joseph. "Autocracy and War." *Notes on Life and Letters.* Garden City: Doubleday, 1921.

———. *The Collected Letters of Joseph Conrad.* Vol. 4. Eds. Frederick R. Karl and Laurence Davies. Cambridge: Cambridge UP, 1990.

———. *The Mirror of the Sea.* Garden City: Doubleday, 1926.

———. *A Personal Record.* Garden City: Doubleday, 1923.

Lubbock, Basil. *The Log of the "Cutty Sark."* Boston: Lauriat, 1925.

Schwarz, Daniel R. *Conrad: The Later Fiction*. London: Macmillan, 1982.

Sherry, Norman. *Conrad's Eastern World*. Cambridge: Cambridge UP, 1966.

Stallman, R. W. "Conrad and 'The Secret Sharer.'" *The Art of Joseph Conrad*. Michigan State UP, 1960.

Feminist and Gender
Criticism and
"The Secret Sharer"

WHAT ARE FEMINIST
AND GENDER CRITICISM?

Among the most exciting and influential developments in the field of literary studies, feminist and gender criticism participate in a broad philosophical discourse that extends far beyond literature, far beyond the arts in general. The critical *practices* of those who explore the representation of women and men in works by male or female, lesbian or gay writers inevitably grow out of and contribute to a larger and more generally applicable *theoretical* discussion of how gender and sexuality are constantly shaped by and shaping institutional structures and attitudes, artifacts and behaviors.

Feminist criticism was accorded academic legitimacy in American universities "around 1981," Jane Gallop claims in her book *Around 1981: Academic Feminist Literary Theory* (1992). With Gallop's title and approximation in mind, Naomi Schor has since estimated that "around 1985, feminism began to give way to what has come to be called gender studies" (275). Some would argue that feminist criticism became academically legitimate well before 1981. Others would take issue with the notion that feminist criticism and women's studies have been giving way to gender criticism and gender studies, and with the either/or distinction that such a claim implies. Taken together, however, Gallop and Schor provide us with a useful fact — that of feminist criticism's historical precedence — and a chronological focus on the early to mid-1980s, a period during which the feminist approach was unquestionably influential and during which new interests emerged, not all of which were woman centered.

During the early 1980s, three discrete strains of feminist theory and practice — commonly categorized as French, North American, and British — seemed to be developing. French feminists tended to focus their attention on language. Drawing on the ideas of the psychoanalytic philosopher Jacques Lacan, they argued that language as we commonly think of it — as public discourse — is decidedly phallocentric, privileging what is valued by the patriarchal culture. They also spoke of the possibility of an alternative, feminine language and of *l'écriture féminine:* women's writing. Julia Kristeva, who is generally seen as a pioneer of French feminist thought even though she dislikes the feminist label, suggested that feminine language is associated with the maternal and derived from the pre-oedipal fusion between mother and child. Like Kristeva, Hélène Cixous and Luce Irigaray associated feminine writing with the female body. Both drew an analogy between women's writing and women's sexual pleasure, Irigaray arguing that just as a woman's *"jouissance"* is more diffuse and complex than a man's unitary phallic pleasure ("woman has sex organs just about everywhere"), so "feminine" language is more diffuse and less obviously coherent than its "masculine" counterpart (*This Sex* 101–03).

Kristeva, who helped develop the concept of *l'écriture féminine,* nonetheless urged caution in its use and advocacy. Feminine or feminist writing that resists or refuses participation in "masculine" discourse, she warned, risks political marginalization, relegation to the outskirts (pun intended) of what is considered socially and politically significant. Kristeva's concerns were not unfounded: the concept of *l'écriture féminine* did prove controversial, eliciting different kinds of criticism from different kinds of feminist and gender critics. To some, the concept appears to give writing a biological basis, thereby suggesting that there is an *essential* femininity, and/or that women are *essentially* different from men. To others, it seems to suggest that men can write as women, so long as they abdicate authority, sense, and logic in favor of diffusiveness, playfulness, even nonsense.

While French feminists of the 1970s and early 1980s focused on language and writing from a psychoanalytic perspective, North American critics generally practiced a different sort of criticism. Characterized by close textual reading and historical scholarship, it generally took one of two forms. Critics like Kate Millett, Carolyn Heilbrun, and Judith Fetterley developed what Elaine Showalter called the "feminist critique" of "male constructed literary history" by closely examining canonical works by male writers, exposing the patriarchal ideology implicit in such works and arguing that traditions of systematic masculine dominance are indelibly inscribed in our literary tradition. Fetterley urged women to become "resisting readers" — to notice how biased most of the classic texts by male authors are in their language, subjects, and attitudes and to actively reject that bias as they read, thereby making reading a different, less "immasculating" experience. Meanwhile, another group of North American feminists, including Showalter, Sandra Gilbert, Susan Gubar, and Patricia Meyer Spacks, developed a different feminist critical model — one that Showalter referred to as "gynocriticism." These critics analyzed great books by women from a feminist perspective, discovered neglected or forgotten women writers, and attempted to recover women's culture and history, especially the history of women's communities that nurtured female creativity.

The North American endeavor to recover women's history — for example, by emphasizing that women developed their own strategies to gain power within their sphere — was seen by British feminists like Judith Newton and Deborah Rosenfelt as an endeavor that "mystifies" male oppression, disguising it as something that has created a special world of opportunities for women. More important from the British standpoint, the universalizing and "essentializing" tendencies of French theory and a great deal of North American practice disguised women's oppression by highlighting sexual difference, thereby seeming to suggest that the dominant system may be impervious to change. As for the North American critique of male stereotypes that denigrate women, British feminists maintained that it led to counterstereotypes of female virtue that ignore real differences of race, class, and culture among women.

By now, the French, North American, and British approaches have so thoroughly critiqued, influenced, and assimilated one another that the work of most Western practitioners is no longer easily identifiable along national boundary lines. Instead, it tends to be characterized according to whether the category of *woman* is the major focus in the exploration of gender and gender oppression or, alternatively, whether the interest in sexual difference encompasses an interest in other differences that also define identity. The latter paradigm encompasses the work of feminists of color, Third World (preferably called postcolonial) feminists, and lesbian feminists, many of whom have asked whether the universal category of woman constructed by certain French and North American predecessors is appropriate to describe women in minority groups or non-Western cultures.

These feminists stress that, while all women are female, they are something else as well (such as African American, lesbian, Muslim Pakistani). This "something else" is precisely what makes them — including their problems and their goals — different from other women. As Armit Wilson has pointed out, Asian women living in Great Britain are expected by their families and communities to preserve Asian cultural traditions; thus, the expression of personal identity through clothing involves a much more serious infraction of cultural rules than it does for a Western woman. Gloria Anzaldúa has spoken personally and eloquently about the experience of many women on the margins of Eurocentric North American culture. "I am a border woman," she writes in *Borderlands = La Frontera: The New Mestiza* (1987). "I grew up between two cultures, the Mexican (with a heavy Indian influence) and the Anglo. . . . Living on the borders and in margins, keeping intact one's shifting and multiple identity and integrity is like trying to swim in a new element, an 'alien' element" (i).

Instead of being divisive and isolating, this evolution of feminism into femin*isms* has fostered a more inclusive, global perspective. The era of recovering women's texts, especially texts by white Western women, has been succeeded by a new era in which the goal is to recover entire cultures of women. Two important figures of this new era are Trinh T. Minh-ha and Gayatri Spivak. Spivak, in works such as *In Other Worlds: Essays in Cultural Politics* (1987) and *Outside in the Teaching Machine* (1993), has shown how political independence (generally looked upon by metropolitan Westerners as a simple and beneficial historical and political reversal) has complex implications for "subaltern" or subproletarian women.

The understanding of woman not as a single, deterministic category but rather as the nexus of diverse experiences has led some white, Western, "majority" feminists like Jane Tompkins and Nancy K. Miller to advocate and practice "personal" or "autobiographical" criticism. Once reluctant to reveal themselves in their analyses for fear of being labeled idiosyncratic, impressionistic, and subjective by men, some feminists are now openly skeptical of the claims to reason, logic, and objectivity that male critics have made in the past. With the advent of more personal feminist critical styles has come a powerful new interest in women's autobiographical writings, manifested in essays such as "Authorizing the Autobiographical" by Shari Benstock, which first appeared in her influential collection *The Private Self: Theory and Practice of Women's Autobiographical Writings* (1988).

Traditional autobiography, some feminists have argued, is a gendered, "masculinist" genre; its established conventions call for a life-plot that turns on action, triumph through conflict, intellectual self-discovery, and often public renown. The body, reproduction, children, and intimate interpersonal relationships are generally well in the background and often absent. Arguing that the lived experiences of women and men differ — women's lives, for instance, are often characterized by interruption and deferral — Leigh Gilmore has developed a theory of women's self-representation in her book *Autobiographics: A Feminist Theory of Self-Representation.*

Autobiographics was published in 1994, well after the chronological divide that, according to Schor, separates the heyday of feminist criticism and the rise of gender studies. Does that mean that Gilmore's book is a feminist throwback? Is she practicing gender criticism instead, the use of the word *feminist* in her book's subtitle notwithstanding? Or are both of these questions overly reductive? As implied earlier, many knowledgeable commentators on the contemporary critical scene are skeptical of the feminist/gender distinction, arguing that feminist criticism is by definition gender criticism and pointing out that one critic whose work *everyone* associates with feminism (Julia Kristeva) has problems with the feminist label while another critic whose name is continually linked with the gender approach (Teresa de Lauretis) continues to refer to herself and her work as feminist.

Certainly, feminist and gender criticism are not polar opposites but, rather, exist along a continuum of attitudes toward sex and sexism, sexuality and gender, language and the literary canon. There are, however, a few distinctions to be made between those critics whose writings are inevitably identified as being toward one end of the continuum or the other.

One distinction is based on focus: as the word implies, *feminists* have concentrated their efforts on the study of women and women's issues. Gender criticism, by contrast, has not been woman centered. It has tended to view the male and female sexes — and the masculine and feminine genders — in terms of a complicated continuum, much as we are viewing feminist and gender criticism. Critics like Diane K. Lewis have raised the possibility that black women may be more like white men in terms of familial and economic roles, like black men in terms of their relationships with whites, and like white women in terms of their relationships with men. Lesbian gender critics have asked whether lesbian women are really more like straight women than they are like gay (or for that matter straight) men. That we refer to gay and lesbian studies as gender studies has led some to suggest that gender studies is a misnomer; after all, homosexuality is not a gender. This objection may easily be answered once we realize that one purpose of gender criticism is to criticize gender as we commonly conceive of it, to expose its insufficiency and inadequacy as a category.

Another distinction between feminist and gender criticism is based on the terms "gender" and "sex." As de Lauretis suggests in *Technologies of Gender* (1987), feminists of the 1970s tended to equate gender with sex, gender difference with sexual difference. But that equation doesn't help us explain "the differences among women, . . . the differences *within women*." After positing that "we need a notion of gender that is not so bound up with sexual difference," de Lauretis provides just such a notion by arguing that "gender is not a property of bodies or something originally existent in human beings"; rather, it is "the product of various social technologies, such as cinema" (2). Gender is, in other words, a construct, an effect of language, culture, and its institutions. It is gender, not sex, that causes a weak old man to open a door for an athletic young woman. And it is gender, not sex, that may cause one young woman to expect old men to behave in this way, another to view this kind of behavior as chauvinistic and insulting, and still another to have mixed feelings (hence de Lauretis's phrase "differences *within women*") about "gentlemanly gallantry."

Still another related distinction between feminist and gender criticism is based on the *essentialist* views of many feminist critics and the *constructionist* views of many gender critics (both those who would call themselves feminists and those who would not). Stated simply and perhaps too reductively, the term "essentialist" refers to the view that women are essentially different from men. "Constructionist," by contrast, refers to the view that most of those differences are characteristics not of the male and female sex (nature) but, rather, of the masculine and feminine genders (nurture). Because of its essentialist tendencies, "radical feminism," according to the influential gender critic Eve Kosofsky Sedgwick, "tends to deny that the meaning of gender or sexuality has ever significantly changed; and more damagingly, it can make future change appear impossible" (*Between Men* 13).

Most obviously essentialist would be those feminists who emphasize the female body, its difference, and the manifold implications of that difference. The equation made by some avant-garde French feminists between the female body and the *maternal* body has proved especially troubling to some gender critics, who worry that it may paradoxically play into the hands of extreme conservatives and fundamentalists seeking to reestablish patriarchal family values. In her book *The Reproduction of Mothering* (1978), Nancy Chodorow, a sociologist of gender, admits that what we call "mothering" — not having or nursing babies but mothering more broadly conceived — is commonly associated not just with the feminine gender but also with the female sex, often considered nurturing by nature. But she critically examines the common assumption that it is in women's nature or biological destiny to "mother" in this broader sense, arguing that the separation of home and workplace brought about by the development of capitalism and the ensuing industrial revolution made mothering *appear* to be essentially a woman's job in modern Western society.

If sex turns out to be gender where mothering is concerned, what differences *are* grounded in sex — that is, nature? *Are* there *essential* differences between men and women — other than those that are purely anatomical and anatomically determined (for example, a man can exclusively take on the job of feeding an infant milk, but he may not do so from his own breast)? A growing number of gender critics would answer the question in the negative. Sometimes referred to as "extreme constructionists" and "postfeminists," these critics have adopted the viewpoint of philosopher Judith Butler, who in her book *Gender Trouble* (1990) predicts that "sex, by definition, will be shown to have been gender all along" (8). As Naomi Schor explains their position, "there is nothing outside or before culture, no nature that is not always and already enculturated" (278).

Whereas a number of feminists celebrate women's difference, postfeminist gender critics would agree with Chodorow's statement that men have an "investment in difference that women do not have" (Eisenstein and Jardine 14). They see difference as a symptom of oppression, not a cause for celebration, and would abolish it by dismantling gender categories and ultimately destroying gender itself. Since gender categories and distinctions are embedded in and perpetuated through language, gender critics like Monique Wittig have called for the wholesale transformation of language into a nonsexist, and nonheterosexist, medium.

Language has proved the site of important debates between feminist and gender critics, essentialists and constructionists. Gender critics have taken issue with those French feminists who have spoken of a feminine language and writing and who have grounded differences in language and writing in the female body.[1] For much the same reason, they have disagreed with those French-influenced Anglo-American critics who, like Toril Moi and Nancy K. Miller, have posited an essential relationship between sexuality and textuality. (In an essentialist sense, such critics have suggested that when women write, they tend to break the rules of plausibility and verisimilitude that men have created to evaluate fiction.) Gender critics like Peggy Kamuf posit a relationship only between *gender* and textuality, between what most men and women *become* after they are born and the way in which they write. They are therefore less interested in the author's sexual "signature" — in whether the author was a woman writing — than in whether the author was (to borrow from Kamuf) "Writing like a Woman."

Feminists like Miller have suggested that no man could write the "female anger, desire, and selfhood" that Emily Brontë, for instance, inscribed in her poetry and in *Wuthering Heights* (*Subject* 72). In the view of gender critics, it is and has been possible for a man to write like a woman, a woman to write like a man. Shari Benstock, a noted feminist critic whose investigations into psychoanalytic and poststructuralist theory have led her increasingly to adopt the gender approach, poses the following question to herself in *Textualizing the Feminine* (1991): "Isn't it precisely 'the feminine' in Joyce's writings and Derrida's that carries me along?" (45). In an essay entitled "Unsexing Language: Pronominal Protest in Emily Dickinson's 'Lay this Laurel,'" Anna Shannon Elfenbein has argued that "like Walt Whitman, Emily Dickinson crossed the gender barrier in some remarkable poems," such as "We learned to like the Fire / By playing Glaciers — when a Boy — " (Berg 215).

It is also possible, in the view of most gender critics, for women to read as men, men as women. The view that women can, and indeed

---

[1]Because feminist/gender studies, not unlike sex/gender, should be thought of as existing along a continuum of attitudes and not in terms of simple opposition, attempts to highlight the difference between feminist and gender criticism are inevitably prone to reductive overgeneralization and occasional distortion. Here, for instance, French feminism is made out to be more monolithic than it actually is. Hélène Cixous has said that a few men (such as Jean Genet) have produced "feminine writing," although she suggests that these are exceptional men who have acknowledged their own bisexuality.

have been forced to, read as men has been fairly noncontroversial. Everyone agrees that the literary canon is largely "androcentric" and that writings by men have tended to "immasculate" women, forcing them to see the world from a masculine viewpoint. But the question of whether men can read as women has proved to be yet another issue dividing feminist and gender critics. Some feminists suggest that men and women have some essentially different reading strategies and outcomes, while gender critics maintain that such differences arise entirely out of social training and cultural norms. One interesting outcome of recent attention to gender and reading is Elizabeth A. Flynn's argument that women in fact make the best interpreters of imaginative literature. Based on a study of how male and female students read works of fiction, she concludes that women come up with more imaginative, open-ended readings of stories. Quite possibly the imputed hedging and tentativeness of women's speech, often seen by men as disadvantages, are transformed into useful interpretive strategies — receptivity combined with critical assessment of the text — in the act of reading (Flynn and Schweickart 286).

In singling out a catalyst of the gender approach, many historians of criticism have pointed to Michel Foucault. In his *History of Sexuality* (1976, tr. 1978), Foucault distinguished sexuality (that is, sexual behavior or practice) from sex, calling the former a "technology of sex." De Lauretis, who has deliberately developed her theory of gender "along the lines of . . . Foucault's theory of sexuality," explains his use of "technology" this way: "Sexuality, commonly thought to be a natural as well as a private matter, is in fact completely constructed in culture according to the political aims of the society's dominant class" (*Technologies* 2, 12). Foucault suggests that homosexuality as we now think of it was to a great extent an invention of the nineteenth century. In earlier periods there had been "acts of sodomy" and individuals who committed them, but the "sodomite" was, according to Foucault, "a temporary aberration," not the "species" he became with the advent of the modern concept of homosexuality (42–43). By historicizing sexuality, Foucault made it possible for his successors to consider the possibility that all of the categories and assumptions that currently come to mind when we think about sex, sexual difference, gender, and sexuality are social artifacts, the products of cultural discourses.

In explaining her reason for saying that feminism began to give way to gender studies "around 1985," Schor says that she chose that date "in part because it marks the publication of *Between Men*," a seminal book in which Eve Kosofsky Sedgwick "articulates the insights of feminist criticism onto those of gay-male studies, which had up to then pursued often parallel but separate courses (affirming the existence of a homosexual or female imagination, recovering lost traditions, decoding the cryptic discourse of works already in the canon by homosexual or feminist authors)" (276). Today, gay and lesbian criticism is so much a part of gender criticism that some people equate it with the gender approach, while others have begun to prefer the phrase "sexualities criticism" to "gender criticism."

Following Foucault's lead, some gay and lesbian gender critics have argued that the heterosexual/homosexual distinction is as much a cultural construct as is the masculine/feminine dichotomy. Arguing that sexuality is a continuum, not a fixed and static set of binary oppositions, a number of gay and lesbian critics have critiqued heterosexuality as a norm, arguing that it has been an enforced corollary and consequence of what Gayle Rubin has referred to as the "sex/gender system." (Those subscribing to this system assume that persons of the male sex should be masculine, that masculine men are attracted to women, and therefore that it is natural for masculine men to be attracted to women and unnatural for them to be attracted to men.) Lesbian gender critics have also taken issue with their feminist counterparts on the grounds that they proceed from fundamentally heterosexual and even heterosexist assumptions. Particularly offensive to lesbians like the poet-critic Adrienne Rich have been those feminists who, following Doris Lessing, have implied that to make the lesbian choice is to make a statement, to act out feminist hostility against men. Rich has called heterosexuality "a beachhead of male dominance" that, "like motherhood, needs to be recognized and studied as a political institution" ("Compulsory Heterosexuality" 143, 145).

If there is such a thing as reading like a woman and such a thing as reading like a man, how then do lesbians read? Are there gay and lesbian ways of reading? Many would say that there are. Rich, by reading Emily Dickinson's poetry as a lesbian — by not assuming that "heterosexual romance is the key to a woman's life and work" — has introduced us to a poet somewhat different from the one heterosexual critics have made familiar (*Lies* 158). As for gay reading, Wayne Koestenbaum has defined "the (male twentieth-century first world) gay reader" as one who "reads resistantly for inscriptions of his condition, for texts that will confirm a social and private identity founded on a desire for other men. . . . Reading becomes a hunt for histories that deliberately foreknow or unwittingly trace a desire felt not by author but by reader, who is most acute when searching for signs of himself" (Boone and Cadden 176–77).

Lesbian critics have produced a number of compelling reinterpretations, or in-scriptions, of works by authors as diverse as Emily Dickinson, Virginia Woolf, and Toni Morrison. As a result of these provocative readings, significant disagreements have arisen between straight and lesbian critics and among lesbian critics as well. Perhaps the most famous and interesting example of this kind of interpretive controversy involves the claim by Barbara Smith and Adrienne Rich that Morrison's novel *Sula* can be read as a lesbian text — and author Toni Morrison's counterclaim that it cannot.

Gay male critics have produced a body of readings no less revisionist and controversial, focusing on writers as staidly classic as Henry James and Wallace Stevens. In Melville's *Billy Budd* and *Moby-Dick,* Robert K. Martin suggests, a triangle of homosexual desire exists. In the latter novel, the hero must choose between a captain who represents "the imposition of the male on the female" and a "Dark Stranger" (Queequeg) who "offers the possibility of an alternate sexuality, one that is less dependent upon performance and conquest" (5).

Masculinity as a complex construct producing and reproducing a constellation of behaviors and goals, many of them destructive (like performance and conquest) and most of them injurious to women, has become the object of an unprecedented number of gender studies. A 1983 issue of *Feminist Review* contained an essay entitled "Anti-Porn: Soft Issue, Hard World," in which B. Ruby Rich suggested that the "legions of feminist men" who examine and deplore the effects of pornography on women might better "undertake the analysis that can tell us why men like porn (not, piously, why this or that exceptional man does *not*)" (Berg 185). The advent of gender criticism makes precisely that kind of analysis possible. Stephen H. Clark, who alludes to Ruby Rich's challenge, reads T. S. Eliot "as a man." Responding to "Eliot's implicit appeal to a specifically masculine audience — "'You! hypocrite lecteur! — mon semblable, — mon *frère!*'" — Clark concludes that poems like "Sweeney Among the Nightingales" and "Gerontion," rather than offering what they are usually said to offer — "a social critique into which a misogynistic language accidentally seeps" — instead articulate a masculine "psychology of sexual fear and desired retaliation" (Berg 173).

Some gender critics focusing on masculinity have analyzed "the anthropology of boyhood," a phrase coined by Mark Seltzer in an article in which he comparatively reads, among other things, Stephen Crane's *Red Badge of Courage*, Jack London's *White Fang*, and the first *Boy Scouts of America* handbook (Boone and Cadden 150). Others have examined the fear men have that artistry is unmasculine, a guilty worry that surfaces perhaps most obviously in "The Custom-House," Hawthorne's lengthy preface to *The Scarlet Letter*. Still others have studied the representation in literature of subtly erotic disciple-patron relationships, relationships like the ones between Nick Carraway and Jay Gatsby, Charlie Marlow and Lord Jim, Doctor Watson and Sherlock Holmes, and any number of characters in Henry James's stories. Not all of these studies have focused on literary texts. Because the movies have played a primary role in gender construction during our lifetimes, gender critics have analyzed the dynamics of masculinity (vis-à-vis femininity and androgyny) in films from *Rebel Without a Cause* to *Tootsie* to last year's Best Picture. One of the "social technologies" most influential in (re)constructing gender, film is one of the media in which today's sexual politics is most evident.

Necessary as it is, in an introduction such as this one, to define the difference between feminist and gender criticism, it is equally necessary to conclude by unmaking the distinction, at least partially. The two topics just discussed (film theory and so-called "queer theory") give us grounds for undertaking that necessary deconstruction. The alliance I have been creating between gay and lesbian criticism on one hand and gender criticism on the other is complicated greatly by the fact that not all gay and lesbian critics are constructionists. Indeed, a number of them (Robert K. Martin included) share with many feminists the *essentialist* point of view; that is to say, they believe homosexuals and heterosexuals to be essentially different, different by nature, just as a number of feminists believe men and women to be different.

In film theory and criticism, feminist and gender critics have so influenced one another that their differences would be difficult to define based on any available criteria, including the ones outlined above. Cinema has been of special interest to contemporary feminists like Minh-ha (herself a filmmaker) and Spivak (whose critical eye has focused on movies including *My Beautiful Laundrette* and *Sammie and Rosie Get Laid*). Teresa de Lauretis, whose *Technologies of Gender* (1987) has proved influential in the area of gender studies, continues to publish film criticism consistent with earlier, unambiguously feminist works in which she argued that "the representation of woman as spectacle — body to be looked at, place of sexuality, and object of desire — so pervasive in our culture, finds in narrative cinema its most complex expression and widest circulation" (*Alice* 4).

Feminist film theory has developed alongside a feminist performance theory grounded in Joan Riviere's recently rediscovered essay "Womanliness as a Masquerade" (1929), in which the author argues that there is no femininity that is *not* masquerade. Marjorie Garber, a contemporary cultural critic with an interest in gender, has analyzed the constructed nature of femininity by focusing on men who have apparently achieved it — through the transvestism, transsexualism, and other forms of "cross-dressing" evident in cultural productions from Shakespeare to Elvis, from "Little Red Riding Hood" to *La Cage aux Folles*. The future of feminist and gender criticism, it would seem, is not one of further bifurcation but one involving a refocusing on femininity, masculinity, and related sexualities, not only as represented in poems, novels, and films but also as manifested and developed in video, on television, and along the almost infinite number of waystations rapidly being developed on the information highways running through an exponentially expanding cyberspace.

Bonnie Kime Scott begins the essay that follows by summarizing a conversation between two characters, David and Penelope, in a review essay entitled "Mr. Conrad: A Conversation" by the novelist Virginia Woolf. Among other things, Woolf's characters debate the lack of "intimacy" in Conrad's fiction. David concludes that this shortcoming is due to a lack of women characters, whereas Penelope resists the notion that intimacy is dependent on women and that "the feminine" must always be represented via women characters.

Stating that her use of Woolf's review is "part of the project of reclamation that remains necessary to resituate women in modernism," Scott compares David's objection to the lack of women in Conrad's fiction to "1970s-style feminist critique" and Penelope's broader interest in the feminine and its representation to Irigaray's version of French feminism (199, 198). Beginning with the former line of argument, Scott points out that "The Secret Sharer" has even fewer women than do most of Conrad's novels and tales; "[t]he only woman even mentioned" during the course of the story "is the wife of Archbold, the captain of the *Sephora*" (201). Scott reveals that Conrad "attributed some of the success" of "The Secret Sharer" to "its very lack of women," writing in a letter to his publisher that "'The Secret Sharer' between you and me is, *it*. Eh? No damned tricks with girls" (200). Conrad's use of the story's one female character, Scott goes on to suggest, is roughly the same as her husband's use of her: "Archbold uses his wife as an adjunct to an ideology that demands his pitiless fulfillment of the law." The older captain "becomes a figure for the law of the father," Scott asserts (202), thus making use (as many feminist critics have) of the psychoanalytic theory of Jacques Lacan.

Following her 1970s-style feminist critique of "The Secret Sharer," Scott pursues a line of argument like the one suggested by Woolf's Penelope. Scott analyzes the feminine more generally, commenting that the young captain's relationship with his "fugitive, second self — Leggatt — is fostered entirely" on a ship, that is, "in avoidance of females, yet in occupation of feminine spaces." The young captain's "construction of intimacy, both with the ship and with Leggatt," Scott writes, "permits [him] to assume a sense of manhood that is narrowly controlled and alien to much of the universe, including actual women" (203).

In this phase of her argument, Scott pays a great deal of attention to language, showing how feminine pronouns and personifications make this virtually womanless story one that is, nonetheless, steeped in what could be called a feminine language complete with "metaphors of gestation," "maternal emblem[s]," and even a "prebirth scenario." (Leggatt's shipboard ascent "via a cord from the sea" is read as "a creative move that usurps procreation by the mother," an act of usurpation that Scott at one point suggests "may be the whole intent of the work.") The young captain, Scott argues, is "like a mother who is invested in her child's development"; furthermore, "[c]aring for Leggatt places the captain-narrator in the . . . feminine position of being constantly divided between public and private selves (205–06).

Scott's reading of "the feminine" and "the maternal," however, should not simply be connected with the sort of French feminism practiced by Irigaray. What Scott is ultimately talking about is not a true *l'écriture féminine* but rather the construction of masculinity in (and out of) the absence of women, the process of male bonding that Sedgwick has described in her work on male homosocial relationships. Indeed, Scott practices gender criticism and even utilizes the approach called "queer theory" in arguing that "[t]he final casting off of Leggatt and the critics' casting off of the homosexual theme can be seen in the light of 'homosexual panic,' as discussed by Eve Sedgwick in the context of gay-bashing" (206).

Leggatt is ultimately cast off, Scott argues, because a feeling of responsibility toward the ship and its crew draws the young captain back from his desire for another man. This conclusion of "The Secret Sharer" has generally "been regarded as a happy ending," one indicating the captain's positive masculine development; however, Scott's critical take is distinctly different. "Unlike the texts of [Oscar] Wilde and [Herman] Melville," she writes, "Conrad's story has beautiful young male survivors," but they have "masked and cast aside homosexual identification. Instead they survive, playing the role of self-possessed, commanding, solitary men." (207). We end "The Secret Sharer," in other words, with the sort of simple, directed captain that did not please either of the characters in Woolf's early feminist dialogue.

Ross C Murfin

FEMINIST AND GENDER CRITICISM: A SELECTED BIBLIOGRAPHY

French Feminist Theory

Cixous, Hélène. "The Laugh of the Medusa." Trans. Keith Cohen and Paula Cohen. *Signs* 1 (1976): 875–93.

Cixous, Hélène, and Catherine Clément. *The Newly Born Woman.* Trans. Betsy Wing. Minneapolis: U of Minnesota P, 1986.

Irigaray, Luce. *An Ethics of Sexual Difference.* Trans. Carolyn Burke and Gillian C. Gill. Ithaca: Cornell UP, 1993.

———. *This Sex Which Is Not One.* Trans. Catherine Porter with Carolyn Burke. Ithaca: Cornell UP, 1985.

Jones, Ann Rosalind. "Inscribing Femininity: French Theories of the Feminine." *Making a Difference: Feminist Literary Criticism.* Ed. Gayle Green and Coppélia Kahn. London: Methuen, 1985. 80–112.

———. "Writing the Body: Toward an Understanding of *L'Écriture féminine.*" Showalter, *The New Feminist Criticism* 361–77.

Kristeva, Julia. *Desire in Language: A Semiotic Approach to Literature and Art.* Ed. Leon S. Roudiez. Trans. Thomas Gora, Alice Jardine, and Roudiez. New York: Columbia UP, 1980.

Marks, Elaine, and Isabelle de Courtivron, eds. *New French Feminisms: An Anthology.* Amherst: U of Massachusetts P, 1980.

Moi, Toril, ed. *French Feminist Thought: A Reader.* Oxford: Basil Blackwell, 1987.

Feminist Theory: Classic Texts, General Approaches, Collections

Abel, Elizabeth, and Emily K. Abel, eds. *The "Signs" Reader: Women, Gender, and Scholarship*. Chicago: U of Chicago P, 1983.

Barrett, Michèle, and Anne Phillips. *Destabilizing Theory: Contemporary Feminist Debates*. Stanford: Stanford UP, 1992.

Beauvoir, Simone de. *The Second Sex*. 1953. Trans. and ed. H. M. Parshley. New York: Bantam, 1961.

Benstock, Shari. *Textualizing the Feminine: On the Limits of Genre*. Norman: U of Oklahoma P, 1991.

Butler, Judith. *Gender Trouble: Feminism and the Subversion of Identity*. New York: Routledge, 1990.

de Lauretis, Teresa, ed. *Feminist Studies/Critical Studies*. Bloomington: Indiana UP, 1986.

Felman, Shoshana. "Women and Madness: The Critical Phallacy." *Diacritics* 5 (1975): 2–10.

Fetterley, Judith. *The Resisting Reader: A Feminist Approach to American Fiction*. Bloomington: Indiana UP, 1978.

Fuss, Diana. *Essentially Speaking: Feminism, Nature and Difference*. New York: Routledge, 1989.

Gallop, Jane. *Around 1981: Academic Feminist Literary Theory*. New York: Routledge, 1992.

———. *The Daughter's Seduction: Feminism and Psychoanalysis*. Ithaca: Cornell UP, 1982.

Greenblatt, Stephen, and Giles Gunn, eds. *Redrawing the Boundaries: The Transformation of English and American Literary Studies*. New York: MLA, 1992.

hooks, bell. *Feminist Theory: From Margin to Center*. Boston: South End, 1984.

Kolodny, Annette. "Dancing through the Minefield: Some Observations on the Theory, Practice, and Politics of a Feminist Literary Criticism." Showalter, *The New Feminist Criticism* 144–67.

———. "Some Notes on Defining a 'Feminist Literary Criticism.'" *Critical Inquiry* 2 (1975): 78.

Lovell, Terry, ed. *British Feminist Thought: A Reader*. Oxford: Basil Blackwell, 1990.

Meese, Elizabeth, and Alice Parker, eds. *The Difference Within: Feminism and Critical Theory*. Philadelphia: John Benjamins, 1989.

Miller, Nancy K., ed. *The Poetics of Gender.* New York: Columbia UP, 1986.

Millett, Kate. *Sexual Politics.* Garden City: Doubleday, 1970.

Rich, Adrienne. *On Lies, Secrets, and Silence: Selected Prose, 1966–1979.* New York: Norton, 1979.

Showalter, Elaine. "Toward a Feminist Poetics." Showalter, 125–43.

———, ed. *The New Feminist Criticism: Essays on Women, Literature, and Theory.* New York: Pantheon, 1985.

Stimpson, Catherine R. "Feminist Criticism." Greenblatt and Gunn 251–70.

Warhol, Robyn, and Diane Price Herndl, eds. *Feminisms: An Anthology of Literary Theory and Criticism.* New Brunswick, NJ: Rutgers UP, 1991.

Weed, Elizabeth, ed. *Coming to Terms: Feminism, Theory, Politics.* New York: Routledge, 1989.

Woolf, Virginia. *A Room of One's Own.* New York: Harcourt, 1929.

Women's Writing and Creativity

Abel, Elizabeth, ed. *Writing and Sexual Difference.* Chicago: U of Chicago P, 1982.

Berg, Temma F., ed. *Engendering the Word: Feminist Essays in Psychosexual Poetics.* Co-ed. Anna Shannon Elfenbein, Jeanne Larsen, and Elisa Kay Sparks. Urbana: U of Illinois P, 1989.

DuPlessis, Rachel Blau. *The Pink Guitar: Writing as Feminist Practice.* New York: Routledge, 1990.

Finke, Laurie. *Feminist Theory, Women's Writing.* Ithaca: Cornell UP, 1992.

Gilbert, Sandra M., and Susan Gubar. *The Madwoman in the Attic: The Woman Writer and the Nineteenth-Century Literary Imagination.* New Haven: Yale UP, 1979.

Homans, Margaret. *Bearing the Word: Language and Female Experience in Nineteenth-Century Women's Writing.* Chicago: U of Chicago P, 1986.

Jacobus, Mary, ed. *Women Writing and Writing about Women.* New York: Barnes, 1979.

Miller, Nancy K. *Subject to Change: Reading Feminist Writing.* New York: Columbia UP, 1988.

Newton, Judith Lowder. *Women, Power and Subversion: Social Strategies in British Fiction, 1778–1860*. Athens: U of Georgia P, 1981.

Poovey, Mary. *The Proper Lady and the Woman Writer: Ideology as Style in the Works of Mary Wollstonecraft, Mary Shelley, and Jane Austen*. Chicago: U of Chicago P, 1984.

Showalter, Elaine. *A Literature of Their Own: British Women Novelists from Brontë to Lessing*. Princeton: Princeton UP, 1977.

Spacks, Patricia Meyer. *The Female Imagination*. New York: Knopf, 1975.

Feminism, Race, Class, and Nationality

Anzaldúa, Gloria. *Borderlands = La Frontera: The New Mestiza*. San Francisco: Spinsters/Aunt Lute, 1987.

Christian, Barbara. *Black Feminist Criticism: Perspectives on Black Women Writers*. New York: Pergamon, 1985.

hooks, bell. *Ain't I a Woman? Black Women and Feminism*. Boston: South End, 1981.

———. *Black Looks: Race and Representation*. Boston: South End, 1992.

Kaplan, Cora. *Sea Changes: Essays on Culture and Feminism*. London: Verso, 1986.

Moraga, Cherríe, and Gloria Anzaldúa. *This Bridge Called My Back: Writings by Radical Women of Color*. New York: Kitchen Table, 1981.

Newton, Judith, and Deborah Rosenfelt, eds. *Feminist Criticism and Social Change: Sex, Class, and Race in Literature and Culture*. New York: Methuen, 1985.

Pryse, Marjorie, and Hortense Spillers, eds. *Conjuring: Black Women, Fiction, and Literary Tradition*. Bloomington: Indiana UP, 1985.

Robinson, Lillian S. *Sex, Class, and Culture*. 1978. New York: Methuen, 1986.

Smith, Barbara. "Towards a Black Feminist Criticism." Showalter, *The New Feminist Criticism* 168–85.

Feminism and Postcoloniality

Emberley, Julia. *Thresholds of Difference: Feminist Critique, Native Women's Writings, Postcolonial Theory*. Toronto: U of Toronto P, 1993.

Minh-ha, Trinh T. *Woman, Native, Other: Writing Postcoloniality and Feminism*. Bloomington: Indiana UP, 1989.

Mohanty, Chandra Talpade, Ann Russo, and Lourdes Torres, eds. *Third World Women and the Politics of Feminism*. Bloomington: Indiana UP, 1991.

Schipper, Mineke, ed. *Unheard Words: Women and Literature in Africa, the Arab World, Asia, the Caribbean, and Latin America*. London: Allison, 1985.

Spivak, Gayatri Chakravorty. *In Other Worlds: Essays in Cultural Politics*. New York: Methuen, 1987.

———. *Outside in the Teaching Machine*. New York: Routledge, 1993.

Wilson, Armit. *Finding a Voice: Asian Women in Britain*. 1979. London: Virago, 1980.

Women's Self-Representation and Personal Criticism

Benstock, Shari, ed. *The Private Self: Theory and Practice of Women's Autobiographical Writings*. Chapel Hill: U of North Carolina P, 1988.

Gilmore, Leigh. *Autobiographics: A Feminist Theory of Self-Representation*. Ithaca: Cornell UP, 1994.

Martin, Biddy, and Chandra Talpade Mohanty. "Feminist Politics: What's Home Got to Do with It?" *Life/Lines: Theorizing Women's Autobiography*. Ed. Bella Brodski and Celeste Schenck. Ithaca: Cornell UP, 1988.

Miller, Nancy K. *Getting Personal: Feminist Occasions and Other Autobiographical Acts*. New York: Routledge, 1991.

Smith, Sidonie. *A Poetics of Women's Autobiography: Marginality and the Fictions of Self-Representation*. Bloomington: Indiana UP, 1988.

Feminist Film Theory

de Lauretis, Teresa. *Alice Doesn't: Feminism, Semiotics, Cinema*. Bloomington: Indiana UP, 1986.

Doane, Mary Ann. *Re-vision: Essays in Feminist Film Criticism*. Frederick: U Publications of America, 1984.

Modleski, Tania. *Feminism without Women: Culture and Criticism in a "Postfeminist" Age*. New York: Routledge, 1991.

Mulvey, Laura. *Visual and Other Pleasures.* Bloomington: Indiana UP, 1989.

Penley, Constance, ed. *Feminism and Film Theory.* New York: Routledge, 1988.

Studies of Gender and Sexuality

Boone, Joseph A., and Michael Cadden, eds. *Engendering Men: The Question of Male Feminist Criticism.* New York: Routledge, 1990.

Butler, Judith. *Gender Trouble: Feminism and the Subversion of Identity.* New York: Routledge, 1990.

Chodorow, Nancy. *The Reproduction of Mothering: Psychoanalysis and the Sociology of Gender.* Berkeley: U of California P, 1978.

Claridge, Laura, and Elizabeth Langland, eds. *Out of Bounds: Male Writing and Gender(ed) Criticism.* Amherst: U of Massachusetts P, 1990.

de Lauretis, Teresa. *Technologies of Gender: Essays on Theory, Film, and Fiction.* Bloomington: Indiana UP, 1987.

Doane, Mary Ann. "Masquerade Reconsidered: Further Thoughts on the Female Spectator." *Discourse* 11 (1988–89): 42–54.

Eisenstein, Hester, and Alice Jardine, eds. *The Future of Difference.* Boston: G. K. Hall, 1980.

Flynn, Elizabeth A., and Patrocinio P. Schweickart, eds. *Gender and Reading: Essays on Readers, Texts, and Contexts.* Baltimore: Johns Hopkins UP, 1986.

Foucault, Michel. *The History of Sexuality: Volume I: An Introduction.* Trans. Robert Hurley. New York: Random, 1978.

Kamuf, Peggy. "Writing like a Woman." *Women and Language in Literature and Society.* New York: Praeger, 1980. 284–99.

Laqueur, Thomas. *Making Sex: Body and Gender from the Greeks to Freud.* Cambridge: Harvard UP, 1990.

Riviere, Joan. "Womanliness as a Masquerade." 1929. *Formations of Fantasy.* Ed. Victor Burgin, James Donald, and Cora Kaplan. London: Methuen, 1986. 35–44.

Rubin, Gayle. "Thinking Sex: Notes for a Radical Theory of the Politics of Sexuality." Abelove, Barale, and Halperin 3–44.

———. "The Traffic in Women: Notes on the 'Political Economy' of Sex." *Toward an Anthropology of Women.* Ed. Rayna R. Reiter. New York: Monthly Review, 1975. 157–210.

Schor, Naomi. "Feminist and Gender Studies." *Introduction to Scholarship in Modern Languages and Literatures.* Ed. Joseph Gibaldi. New York: MLA, 1992. 262–87.

Sedgwick, Eve Kosofsky. *Between Men: English Literature and Male Homosocial Desire.* New York: Columbia UP, 1988.

———. "Gender Criticism." Greenblatt and Gunn 271–302.

Lesbian and Gay Criticism

Abelove, Henry, Michèle Aina Barale, and David Halperin, eds. *The Lesbian and Gay Studies Reader.* New York: Routledge, 1993.

Butters, Ronald, John M. Clum, and Michael Moon, eds. *Displacing Homophobia: Gay Male Perspectives in Literature and Culture.* Durham: Duke UP, 1989.

Craft, Christopher. *Another Kind of Love: Male Homosexual Desire in English Discourse, 1850–1920.* Berkeley: U of California P, 1994.

de Lauretis, Teresa. *The Practice of Love: Lesbian Sexuality and Perverse Desire.* Bloomington: Indiana UP, 1994.

Dollimore, Jonathan. *Sexual Dissidence: Augustine to Wilde, Freud to Foucault.* Oxford: Clarendon, 1991.

Fuss, Diana, ed. *Inside/Out: Lesbian Theories, Gay Theories.* New York: Routledge, 1991.

Garber, Marjorie. *Vested Interests: Cross-Dressing and Cultural Anxiety.* New York: Routledge, 1992.

Halperin, David M. *One Hundred Years of Homosexuality and Other Essays on Greek Love.* New York: Routledge, 1990.

The Lesbian Issue. Special issue, *Signs* 9 (1984).

Martin, Robert K. *Hero, Captain, and Stranger: Male Friendship, Social Critique, and Literary Form in the Sea Novels of Herman Melville.* Chapel Hill: U of North Carolina P, 1986.

Munt, Sally, ed. *New Lesbian Criticism: Literary and Cultural Readings.* New York: Harvester Wheatsheaf, 1992.

Rich, Adrienne. "Compulsory Heterosexuality and Lesbian Existence." Abel and Abel 139–68.

Stimpson, Catherine R. "Zero Degree Deviancy: The Lesbian Novel in English." *Critical Inquiry* 8 (1981): 363–79.

Weeks, Jeffrey. *Sexuality and Its Discontents: Meanings, Myths, and Modern Sexualities.* London: Routledge, 1985.

Wittig, Monique. "The Mark of Gender." Miller, *The Poetics of Gender* 63–73.

———. "One Is Not Born a Woman." *Feminist Issues* 1.2 (1981): 47–54.

———. *The Straight Mind and Other Essays.* Boston: Beacon, 1992.

Queer Theory

Butler, Judith. *Bodies That Matter: On the Discursive Limits of "Sex."* New York: Routledge, 1993.

Cohen, Ed. *Talk on the Wilde Side: Towards a Genealogy of Discourse on Male Sexualities.* New York: Routledge, 1993.

de Lauretis, Teresa, ed. Issue on Queer Theory. *differences* 3.2 (1991).

Sedgwick, Eve Kosofsky. *Epistemology of the Closet.* Berkeley: U of California P, 1991.

———. *Tendencies.* Durham: Duke UP, 1993.

Sinfield, Alan. *Cultural Politics — Queer Reading.* Philadelphia: U of Pennsylvania P, 1994.

———. *The Wilde Century: Effeminacy, Oscar Wilde, and the Queer Moment.* New York: Columbia UP, 1994.

Warner, Michael, ed. *Fear of a Queer Planet: Queer Politics and Social Theory.* Minneapolis: U of Minnesota P, 1993.

Feminist and Gender Approaches to Conrad

Brodie, Susan Lundvall. "Conrad's Feminine Perspective." *Conradiana* 16 (1984): 141–54.

DeKoven, Marianne. *Rich and Strange: Gender, History, Modernism.* Princeton: Princeton UP, 1991.

Klein, Karen. "The Feminine Predicament in Conrad's *Nostromo.*" *Brandeis Essays in Literature.* Ed. John Hazel Smith. Waltham, MA: Brandeis English and American Literature Department, 1983. 101–16.

London, Bette. *The Appropriate Voice: Narrative Authority in Conrad, Forster, and Woolf.* Ann Arbor: U of Michigan P, 1990.

Smith, Johanna. "'Too Beautiful Altogether': Patriarchal Ideology in *Heart of Darkness.*" *Joseph Conrad, "Heart of Darkness."* Ed. Ross C Murfin. 2nd ed. Case Studies in Contemporary Criticism. Boston: Bedford–St. Martin's, 1996.

Straus, Nina Pelikan. "The Exclusion of the Intended from Secret Sharing in Conrad's *Heart of Darkness.*" *Novel* 20 (1987): 123–37.

Sullivan, Zoreh T. "Enclosure, Darkness, and the Body: Conrad's Landscape." *The Centennial Review* 25 (1981): 59–79.

Torgovnick, Marianna. *Gone Primitive: Savage Intellects, Modern Lives.* Chicago: U of Chicago P, 1990.

A FEMINIST AND GENDER PERSPECTIVE

BONNIE KIME SCOTT

Intimacies Engendered
in Conrad's "The Secret Sharer"

In "Mr Conrad: A Conversation," the most experimental of her numerous review essays on the works of Joseph Conrad, Virginia Woolf constructs an intimate conversation between a man and a woman, David and Penelope. Their talk concerns Conrad, who by the 1923 date of Woolf's essay was becoming a "classic" modern writer.[1] Penelope's name suggests the stay-at-home female hero of Homer's *Odyssey,* whose situation contrasts with that of her seafaring husband, a precursor to many of Conrad's male heroes. Penelope anticipates a sorority of young women Woolf would introduce more deliberately in her extended fictional essay *A Room of One's Own* (1929). Like Woolf herself, the Penelopes of England were educated inexpensively at home—they had the run of their fathers' libraries. Penelopes were directed in their reading by university-educated men such as the David in this essay, or St. John Hirst in Woolf's first and most Conradian novel, *The Voyage Out* (1915). David has placed Conrad in Penelope's canon by writing about his novels in letters to her. What is to be learned from this unusual narrative scenario? Might it provide an allegory of feminist reading?

Woolf's narrator remarks that Penelope's limited knowledge qualifies her as an ideal conversationalist on books. More education might have stinted her enthusiasm or "diverted [it] less fortunately into the creation of books of her own" ("Mr Conrad: A Conversation" 376). Though positive on its surface, this comment presents problems to a feminist reader. Though enthusiasm is attractive in a social situation, how adequate is it to literary analysis? Shouldn't Penelope have been trained for something more than lively conversation that engages a male? Or should we have attended more to the conversation of women of her sort? Perhaps Woolf is embedding a self-reflexive joke about

---

[1]Woolf's essay, written for the *Nation & Athenaeum,* reviewed *Almayer's Folly, Tales of Unrest, An Outcast of the Islands, The Nigger of the "Narcissus," Typhoon, Lord Jim, Youth,* and *Romance*—all in J. M. Dent's uniform edition of 1923. "The Secret Sharer" is not mentioned, but falls within the temporal range of these works.

having written books of her own on the basis of a comparable education. Why shouldn't Penelope have books of her own? Should we identify Penelope's views as Woolf's, or as a representative woman's point of view on Conrad? Woolf's playful narrative indirection has aroused feminist controversy,[2] but it opens numerous questions for a feminist reading of "The Secret Sharer."

Whereas David sees Conrad as a "romantic" with "a mind of one facet," Penelope decisively if amusingly rejects this as "a confection of cobwebs spun while you shave, chiefly with a view to saving yourself the trouble of investigating and possibly admiring, the work of a living contemporary . . ." (377). As an outsider to literary production (unlike Woolf), Penelope lacks a competitive motive for discrediting Conrad. She credits him with greatness on the basis that he is "many and complex," not the man of a single facet who emerges from David's reading. To her, Conrad's novels set the "man of words" against the type of the sea captain who insists "the world, the temporal world, rests on a very few simple ideas." The combined whole is better than some of the parts. One aspect of Conrad's writing that she does not respect is the "grand deliberate manner which has in it the seeds of pomposity and monotony." For her the multiple facets of Conrad have formal integrity: "The beauty of surface has always a fibre of morality within" (378). A comparable formal duality would be the aim of Lily Briscoe, the woman artist of Woolf's 1927 novel, *To the Lighthouse:* "Beautiful and bright it should be on the surface . . . but beneath the fabric must be clamped together with bolts of iron" (171). Penelope is admiring the aspects of Conrad's art that got him into F. R. Leavis's *The Great Tradition:* modernist form and humanistic moral concern. But no single point of view prevails.

It is over a supposed lack of "intimacy" that the dialogue between David and Penelope really gets interesting. David considers that this lack might spring from Conrad's formality in using a language that is not his own, or from displaying the attitudes of an aristocrat. Finally, however, David decides that the deficit arises from "the fact that there are no women in his books" (379). This remark aligns David with 1970s-style feminist critique. He faults Conrad for failing to create

---

[2]The most notable exchange is between Elaine Showalter and Toril Moi. In *A Literature of Their Own* Showalter, whose values were progressive and realist, finds a retreat from feminism in Woolf's tactics of indirection and her presumed sensitivity to male listeners. Moi finds in Woolf's narrative form nothing less than a subversion of patriarchy.

complex, autonomous women.[3] Much of the feminist criticism of Conrad to date has been concerned with the limitations of his female characters and the ideology complicit with their narrative constructions. Although Penelope might have been expected to raise this objection to women's representation, she moves on to another feminist category, the feminine: "There are the ships, the beautiful ships. . . . They are more feminine than his women, who are either mountains of marble or the dreams of a charming boy over the photograph of an actress. But surely a great novel can be made out of a man and a ship, a man and a story, a man and death and dishonour?" (379). Penelope resists David's limited conception that intimacy is dependent on women, but she poses a new array of questions. She senses that Conrad has replaced women with other things: ships, stories, moral tests, and the archetypal encounter with death. Penelope's repetition of the word *man*, however, may encourage us to think that men have become a Conradian obsession.

In this dialogue between a man and a woman, Woolf touches on numerous issues, exalting the ideas of neither participant, and expecting her audience to work the questions through. This anticipates the "woman-analysis" which was proposed by Luce Irigaray in an attempt to move away from isolation and silencing of women in Western discourse and which is mirrored in the analytical sessions designed by Freud and Jacques Lacan (148). In 1923, Woolf's essay did not get the response she hoped for, and she felt "slightly dashed" that "no one has mentioned it." She imagines that several of the men in her Bloomsbury circle had not "quite approved" (379n). I have led off my essay on Conrad by reviving the literary criticism of a slightly later female modernist. This move is part of the project of reclamation that remains necessary to resituate women in modernism, and to challenge masculine bias in the theory as well as the canon of modernism.[4] While Woolf's novels and her essay *A Room of One's Own* are now relatively well known, her other essays have only begun to yield another modernism. Women's book reviews in general have a great deal to contribute to our understanding of untapped potentials and unacknowledged contexts of modernist writing. At the same time, it is important to acknowledge that we have additional historically conditioned concerns today.

---

[3]For strongly argued essays that update and apply this tradition of feminist scholarship to Conrad's *Heart of Darkness,* see Straus, Smith, and London.

[4]See my introduction to *The Gender of Modernism* (1–3).

"No Damned Tricks with Girls"

Feminist critique of women characters in "The Secret Sharer"
could hardly be more limited by the materials of a story. Even if the
women characters of *Heart of Darkness* fulfill Conrad's stereotypical
female categories[5] and are manipulated to satisfy the moral needs of its
narrator, at least there are a number of them: the imperialist idealist
aunt who arranges Marlow's job in the Congo (26–27); two women
knitting at the portals of the company office in a city that made him
"think of a white sepulchre" (24); the powerful native woman, reso-
nant with the fecundity of the jungle, who is Kurtz's lover (76–77);
and Kurtz's virginal "Intended," denied insight into "the horror" (85)
when Marlow reports back to her in Europe (93).[6]

In writing to his publisher Edward Garnett, Conrad attributed
some of the success of "The Secret Sharer" to its very lack of women:

> *The Secret Sharer* between you and me is, *it*. Eh? No damned tricks
> with girls there. Eh? Every word fits and there's not a single uncer-
> tain note. Luck my boy. Pure luck. (*Letters* 243)

His confiding remarks to this regular and intimate correspondent
come in the context of one male author writing to another. The
"girls" refers most immediately to the focal woman of "Freya of the
Seven Isles," a story published alongside "The Secret Sharer" and "A
Smile of Fortune" to make up the collection *'Twixt Land and Sea*.
"Freya" was not as well received by Garnett or the general public.
Conrad eventually dismissed the story as part of his emergence from a
period of convalescence. In my reading, "Freya" clearly merits David's
"romantic" label. The title character is a golden goddess to the com-
peting men who admire her; embowered in foliage, she fulfills a familiar Conradian fertility image. She is not idealized by the narrator, how-

---

[5]Cedric Watts lists five types—a considerable increase over Woolf's two: exotic se-
ductresses, "associated with fecund jungle" and capable of "weakening or incapacitating
the men who embrace them," an example being Kurtz's native consort; noble idealists,
romantic figures who "preserve their faith in the men they love" but "are ignorant of
those men or of the harsh realities of the world," a group including Kurtz's "intended";
statuesquely beautiful objects of male desire, associated with his "most disappointingly
conventional writing"; seemingly subjugated women "strongly dominated by men" but
capable of striking back; and a Victorian type: "idealistic women who have had disillu-
sioning experience of the world" but try to make it a better place (179–80).

[6]On ideological uses of female characters, and particularly the intended and the na-
tive woman, see Johanna M. Smith (passim), Marianne DeKoven (97), and Nina Pelikan
Straus (134). Straus's "The Exclusion of the Intended from Secret Sharing in Conrad's
Heart of Darkness evokes "The Secret Sharer," and the exclusion of women she notes in
Heart of Darkness certainly applies to the story.

ever, who credits her with good sense about the excesses of her lover. The romance of Jasper and Freya is triangulated with his love of a beautiful white sailing ship. Subtract the ship, and the romance falters. "The Secret Sharer" suggests that when you subtract the woman, the romance goes on. Conrad's remarks to Garnett suggest further that it was by the art of subtraction, making each note certain (rather like Ezra Pound's modernist formula, "to use absolutely no word that does not contribute to the presentation" [59]), that he could do "it"—the orgasmic ideal of literary expression. "The Secret Sharer," shared with Garnett, is the very stuff of intimacy, rhythmically punctuated by "Eh."

The only woman even mentioned in "The Secret Sharer" is the wife of Archbold, the captain of the *Sephora*. She figures merely as a presence on board during its crisis: a fierce storm and, in the midst of it, Leggatt's murder of a man who was insolent to him while he was setting a reefed foresail to save the ship. In his first intimate conversation with the unnamed young captain-narrator of the ship to which he escapes, Leggatt speculates about her possible influence on the *Sephora*'s captain. Archbold does not have Leggatt's respect on several counts—he is supposedly dominated by his second mate and steward, and is fearful of "what the law would do to him—of his wife perhaps" (201). In their conversations, Leggatt regularly plays on attitudes shared with his audience of one, the younger captain whose ship Leggatt has boarded; the first subject for agreement is marked by "Oh, yes!" working much as the "Eh!" does in Conrad's correspondence. They seem to agree that having his wife along says a lot about Archbold, and that it is not good:

> "Oh, yes! she's on board. Though I don't think she would have meddled. She would have been only too glad to have me out of the ship in any way. The 'brand of Cain' business, don't you see. That's all right. I was ready enough to go off wandering on the face of the earth—and that was price enough to pay for an Abel of that sort." (35)

Another shared assumption is that anything his wife might have said to Archbold would be meddling. Leggatt assumes, stereotypically, that the Old Testament law of the Bible would appeal to her. This squares with the representation of women's values in *Heart of Darkness,* where missionary impulses support the imperial ideology of both the aunt and the Intended. But although Archbold called Leggatt's murderous act "a nice little tale for a quiet tea party"—selecting for his sarcasm a

proper, civilized event usually presided over by a woman—on this occasion the older captain's priority is upholding the law.

The day after Leggatt tells the young captain about the wife
aboard the *Sephora*, Archbold twice brings up the topic in relating his
own account. Implicity, her presence made both the terrible weather
and the murder that much worse for the *Sephora*'s chief officer. He
identifies the *Sephora* further as "an English ship," as if having a
woman on board invokes national standards and pride. (Behind this is
the attitude that England is morally superior to other nations, which is
echoed later in the first mate's comment that the incident "[b]eats all
these tales we hear about murders in Yankee ships" (46). The young
captain dismisses this line of discussion, as he does most attempts at
intimate conversation by his officers.[7]) Archbold uses his wife as an
adjunct to an ideology that demands his pitiless fulfillment of the
law. This is the single-faceted reasoning that Woolf, through Penelope, detects in Conrad's captains. Archbold becomes a figure for the
law of the father. Leggatt and the captain, in attacking his reasoning
and reaching their own understanding, engage in a Freudian oedipal
struggle to oust the father. But the law, whether taken from the biblical legend of Cain and Abel or the statutes enforced by Archbold, remains phallocratic and out of the realm of women. As the post-
Freudian theory of Jacques Lacan has suggested, it is through the
name of the father and his law that one enters the command of symbolic language.

A Man and a Ship

The study of men's intimacy on board ships, suggested in the Woolf
essay, is particularly applicable to "The Secret Sharer." The captain-
narrator pursues first and last an intimacy with the body of his ship, his
first command. It is a feminine love object, and conventionally so in
the language of the sea, down to the feminine pronouns and body
parts long used for ships. The central drama of the story, the captain's
cherishing of a fugitive, second self—Leggatt—is fostered entirely in
this context, in avoidance of females, yet in occupation of feminine
spaces. The ship is both the captain's first love and the mother of his
second self. Jungian archetypal theory and its feminist appropriations
have proven useful in exploring the feminine in Conrad's landscapes,

---

[7]In *Heart of Darkness,* Marianna Torgovnick identifies an ideology of British moral
superiority to Belgium in their African imperial methods (143–45).

and particularly in *Heart of Darkness*.[8] Significantly, "The Secret Sharer" is a first-person narration, making it comparable in conception to Marlow's narrative, which comes in for no small appreciation by Woolf. The captain-narrator is equally susceptible to the detection of ideological bias. His construction of intimacy, both with the ship and with Leggatt, permits the captain to assume a sense of manhood that is narrowly controlled and alien to much of the universe, including actual women, natural places and events, and even his crew.

As the story opens, the narrator gazes deliberately at various aspects of the scene around his ship, revealing much about his attitude toward relationships. He shows little awareness of human beings, and less knowledge. Fishing stakes could be taken as evidence of local industry and written about in a connective manner. Instead he constructs metaphors of fences that divide, and a fantasy of a nomad tribe that deserts him. Only the remote sea and sky meet, to be captured by him aesthetically. Though he knows the name of the "Paknam pagoda," he does not let us know why he calls it "great." Its contribution to the narrative is the large mound of trees that diversifies the horizon, providing rest to his eyes. He applies the feminine pronoun to the third human artifact, a tugboat that has just connected men on board with people back home by delivering the mail: "the tug steaming right into the land became lost to my sight, hull and funnel and masts, as though the impassive earth had swallowed her up without an effort, without a tremor" (25). We learn nothing about any mail he may have received; indeed the captain's past is almost entirely withheld.

The captain-narrator is reticent about several additional pieces of human evidence. He refers obscurely to "something which did away with the solemnity of perfect solitude" (25) as if not wanting to interfere with the aesthetics of his highly figurative, precisely directed initial description. We must wait for a pedestrian dialogue with his first and second mates to learn that the captain has spotted a ship anchored inside some offshore islands, and longer still to get "information" that the second mate has learned from the tugboat skipper. The second mate's timing is interesting for its provision of a "surprise" (a word registered twice by the narrator). This unnamed officer, who gradually gathers the epithet "sneering young cub," has given the first mate

---

[8]Zoreh T. Sullivan offers a powerful reading of the maternal body in *Heart of Darkness*, using the paradigms of Erich Neumann's *Great Mother* and Carl Jung's *Symbols of Transformation*, among other sources; Marianna DeKoven sustains this sort of analysis. James F. White identifies twenty-three Jungian phrases with a submerged "fertility theme" in "The Secret Sharer."

time to appear foolish with his standard "Bless my soul!" and his need
to account for things. After the second mate efficiently recites the data
about the *Sephora,* including its name, draft, origin, and cargo, the
captain's initial description seems, in comparison, highly abstract and
out of touch with reality. It comes as no surprise later that the captain
does not recollect for sure the name of the *Sephora*'s captain. His own
name and the names of his ship and crew are likewise withheld, perhaps again for the sake of abstraction; this lack enhances the importance of Leggatt's name. The captain-narrator's view of what is important determines that we learn nothing of the reasons for his sudden
hiring as captain, or of his relationships ashore. He rejoices that he has
chosen not "the unrest of the land" but the "untempted life" of the
sea, which presents "no disquieting problems" (28). Might women
thus be dismissed from his life and narrative art? If nothing else, he has
hit on a pattern of carefully selected images, substituting artistic emotion for personal emotion; these were criteria for modernism encouraged by Ezra Pound's imagism and T. S. Eliot's "Tradition and the
Individual Talent," and in line with the stress placed on figurative language by the New Critics who held sway into the 1970s.

As the night deepens, the captain deliberately establishes an exclusive partnership with his femininely constructed ship. Feminine pronouns dominate his first thoughts about her.

> She floated at the starting-point of a long journey, very still in an
> immense stillness, the shadows of her spars flung far to the east-
> ward by the setting sun. At the moment I was alone on her decks.
> There was not a sound in her. (25)

They have as a mutual task "measuring our fitness for a long and arduous enterprise, the appointed task of both our existences" (25). This
communion with his ship is repeatedly inhibited: "Fast alongside a
wharf, littered like any ship in port with a tangle of unrelated things,
invaded by unrelated shore people, I had hardly seen her yet properly"
(27). Like a couple on a honeymoon tour, they will use their maiden
voyage to establish a working relationship. On board, the captain's
delicate sense of solitude is interrupted by the spotting of the *Sephora,*
by the noises and motions of the crew, and most seriously by the visit
of "the naked man from the sea," Leggatt. The captain makes the odd
decision to take the night watch himself, so as to be alone with his
ship. His language, gaze, and physical contact bestow on the ship a
human, increasingly feminine body. Thus at first he describes his
"hand resting lightly on my ship's rail as if on the shoulder of a trusted

friend" (25). Alone with his ship late at night "as she lay cleared for sea, the stretch of her main-deck seemed to me very fine under the stars. Very fine, very roomy for her size, and very inviting. I descended the poop and paced the waist" (27). Gaining confidence as he imagines the "passage," he decides to go get a cigar, as if congratulating himself for his masculine promise, or preparing for intercourse.

"The naked man from the sea"

Once Leggatt appears at the foot of the rope ladder, the feminine is shifted toward metaphors of gestation, where the captain is more a midwife or even a mother than a patriarchal figure.[9] Leggatt ascends via a cord from the sea—a maternal emblem in Jungian terms, but more specifically here evoking the voyage from the ovary, in a wash of seminal fluid, to the womb. Getting somewhat ahead of the prebirth scenario, the captain looks Leggatt over as the parent might a newborn, commenting upon the quality of his features and his likeness to himself. In effect, he brings forth himself in a creative move that usurps procreation by the mother; indeed that may be the whole intent of the work. The captain introduces Leggatt into a presymbolic gestation period in his womb-shaped stateroom, where Leggatt repeatedly assumes a fetal position and they communicate by touch as well as sparse speech. Leggatt is clad for dormacy in one of the captain's sleeping suits and is nearly always veiled in the tissue of bed curtains or garments hanging in a recessed part of the cabin. The captain brings tinned food and provides his own morning coffee for Leggatt's in-utero nourishment.

The captain is an exceptionally empathetic listener, like a mother who is invested in her child's development. The captain fills in Leggatt's brusque, disconnected sentences, as a parent might supplement

---

[9]James F. White offers the "human fertility" as a third, deep theme of "The Secret Sharer." This begins with "matchmaking" and "first embrace" with the ship (the "hand resting lightly on my ship's rail"), and proceeds through twenty-three stages, identified with images in the text, to birth and afterbirth (the captain's hat, lost in the sea by the newly launched Leggatt). James Joyce deliberately devised a text that would mimic fetal stages of development for the "Oxen of the Sun" chapter of his *Ulysses*, one of the monuments of modernism. Both authors could be diagnosed as exhibiting womb envy, or as appropriating feminine biological processes for their creative purposes. See Susan Stanford Friedman's essay, "Creativity and the Childbirth Metaphor." Friedman sees a fundamental historical separation over the childbirth metaphor. Women are traditionally assigned to reproduction, and men to the production of literary work (75–76). Male metaphors intensify difference between mind and body, whereas women's metaphors reconstitute women's fragmented selves into (pro)creative units (93).

or divert the expressions of a child. Almost no explanation of Leggatt's violent deed is required. Instead the captain-narrator assigns to Leggatt qualities of "self-possession" and "intellect." These are masculine traits, expressed in abstract language of the symbolic. They are what both young men would have learned at Conway, the training school they shared. The captain supplies the idea that Leggatt murdered a man in "a fit of temper." It is also a mother's tendency to join forces with her child against a misunderstanding world. The condemning crew and captain become a distant "they," easily dismissed. In this all-male reconfiguration, "they" can incorporate women, heterosexuals, and natives on shore. In his level of accepting the statements of his interlocutor, the captain resembles Conrad's earlier narrator, Marlow, as he covers the "horror" of Kurtz's narrative in *Heart of Darkness.* Caring for Leggatt places the captain-narrator in the disempowering, feminine position of being constantly divided between public and private selves, of needing to measure up to the expectations of masculine order posed by his two mates and the steward, and of needing to nurture a dependent in the motherly mode described above. He is justifiably concerned about the impression he is making on his professional associates.

While the captain may not have a wife on board, he does develop a distracting, intimate relationship with a man, and this homosexual configuration provides another way of engendering the story. Leggatt and the captain were trained at Conway, an all-male school; they have spent years on voyages, almost exclusively in the company of men. John Batchelor insists that *erotics* is the wrong word for the male ties in both *Lord Jim* and "The Secret Sharer." In admitting that Conrad's evocation of "intense bonding, all the more intense for being fleeting, surreptitious and wordless" resembles "the odd quality of the impersonal sexual encounter found in Genet and other male homosexual writers," he insists that "the resemblance is in the oddness, the surreptitiousness, and the intensity rather than in the sexuality" (188). The final casting off of Leggatt and the critics' casting off of the homosexual theme can be seen in the light of "homosexual panic," as discussed by Eve Sedgwick in the context of gay-bashing (19–21). In an early confrontation of the critics' avoidance of the theme, Bruce Harkness supplied a long list of evidence of a "Hyacinthine archetype" encountered through Leggatt. Convincing gestures and symbols include Leggatt's invitation of the gaze, beginning when he is nude and seemingly headless in the water; concern that the steward (himself attuned to feminine duties) might detect something "queer"; their whispering together in bed; and a series of touches culminating in their tumble together in the sail locker. The two men are closeted together repeatedly. In her *Epistemology of the Closet,* Eve Sedgwick cites two 1891 texts, Oscar Wilde's *Portrait of Dorian Gray* and Herman Melville's own story of intimacy at sea, *Billy Budd,* for "their startling erotic congruence." These works "set the terms for a modern homosexual identity." Interestingly, they coincided with "inaugural discourses of modern homo/sexuality—in law, in the crisis of female status, in the career of imperialism" (48–49). These are the same discourses that we have seen operating in "The Secret Sharer," as they did a decade earlier in *Heart of Darkness.* Sedgwick also suggests that "the modernist impulse toward abstraction . . . owes an incalculable part of its energy precisely to turn-of-the-century male homo/heterosexual definitional panic"; she includes Conrad in a long list of authors who invested the "desired male body" in figurative language (167).

Immediately after situating Leggatt in his stateroom, the captain gives narrative evidence of wanting to get back to sole command. Told that the wind has risen, he states, "I was going out to make the acquaintance of my ship." But mysterious communication, and an indication of mutual desire, expressed on their lips, intervene. "I pointed to the recessed part where the little camp-stool awaited him and laid my finger on my lips. He made a gesture—somewhat vague—a little mysterious, accompanied by a faint smile, as if of regret." There follows an admission of incomplete communion with his ship: "This is not the place to enlarge upon the sensations of a man who feels for the first time a ship move under his feet to his own independent word. In my case they were not unalloyed" (47). Leggatt is that alloy; he has moved the captain in an unexpected direction.

Only when Leggatt has departed "to take his punishment: a free man, a proud swimmer striking out for a new destiny" can the captain take command of his chosen destiny: "I was alone with her. Nothing! no one in the world should stand now between us, throwing a shadow on the way of silent knowledge and mute affection, the perfect communion of a seaman with his first command" (59). The final unity and resolution are formally neat and satisfying. The masculinized captain now rules the feminine body of his ship and has command of the language expected by his officers. This ending has traditionally been regarded as happy. Unlike the texts of Wilde and Melville, Conrad's story has beautiful young male survivors. But the captain and Leggatt have masked and cast aside homosexual identification. Instead they survive, playing the role of self-possessed, commanding, solitary men.

"When I say a man —"

Had he finished describing his murder victim instead of being interrupted by the captain, Leggatt might have given a new dimension to the "others" of this story. In the original tale that became a basis for Conrad's tale, the murdered man was "negro." Conrad's story *The Nigger of the "Narcissus"* copes more directly with the history of enforced black labor on ships. In another instance, the beautiful ship of "Freya," painted over in white by its new owner, is rumored to have originally been a slave ship. In *Playing in the Dark: Whiteness and the Literary Imagination,* Toni Morrison argues that "the fabrication of an Africanist persona is reflexive; an extraordinary mediation of the self; a powerful exploration of the fears and desires that reside in the writerly conscious" (17). The suppression of the politics of race, whether by Conrad, his narrator, or his critics, adds additional layers to the previously noted suppressions of women and homosexuality. There is no lack of symbolic blackness in this text. In most cases blackness applies to the alien female sex as well as to a racial other. Feminists reading the African landscape of *Heart of Darkness* could refer to Freud's concept of woman being "a dark continent."

"The Secret Sharer" closes with the captain's close scrape with Koh-ring, a passage featuring many references to blackness. Its double peaks suggest breasts to James F. White in his reading of the fertility archetype throughout "The Secret Sharer." The captain's only solution may be to cast out Leggatt to seek nurture there. But once into the close encounter, the captain must use every ounce of what would seem a maturing masculinity to escape a native population, a feminine jungle, a homosexual relationship, and the destruction of himself and his cherished ship.

The story leaves us to confront what the captain avoids. Though in command of his words and in touch with his first command, the captain has been reduced before our eyes to a few simple ideas and a narrow path that avoids both heterosexual and homosexual relations. He has had a brief experience of the multiplicity afforded by taking on feminine and homosexual roles. Doubling back to Woolf's conversational essay, which provided my introduction to a problematic feminist reading of this story, I doubt that ultimately the captain would please either David or Penelope: indeed, he has rejected conversation and difference to follow a singular path. If, however, we question this ending, we still must ask whether we are reading against a masculinist grain of Conrad, or discovering the multiplicity of a feminist fiber within.

WORKS CITED

Batchelor, John. *The Life of Joseph Conrad*. Oxford: Blackwell, 1994.

Conrad, Joseph. Author's Note. *'Twixt Land and Sea*. By Joseph Conrad. Garden City: Doubleday, 1924. vii–x.

———. *Heart of Darkness*. Ed. Ross C Murfin. 2nd ed. Case Studies in Contemporary Criticism. Boston: Bedford–St. Martin's, 1996.

———. *Letters from Conrad: 1895–1924*. London: Nonsuch, 1928.

DeKoven, Marianne. *Rich and Strange: Gender, History, Modernism*. Princeton: Princeton UP, 1991.

Friedman, Susan Stanford. "Creativity and the Childbirth Metaphor: Gender Difference in Literary Discourse." *Speaking of Gender*. Ed. Elaine Showalter. New York: Routledge, 1989. 73–100.

Harkness, Bruce. "The Secret of 'The Secret Sharer' Bared." *Joseph Conrad: Critical Assessments*. Vol. 3. Ed. Keith Carabine. Mountfield, Eng.: Helm Information, 1992. 301–308.

Irigaray, Luce. *This Sex Which Is Not One*. Trans. Catherine Porter with Carolyn Burke. Ithaca: Cornell UP, 1985.

London, Bette. *The Appropriate Voice: Narrative Authority in Conrad, Forster, and Woolf*. Ann Arbor: U of Michigan P, 1990.

Meyers, Jeffrey. *Joseph Conrad: A Biography*. New York: Scribner's, 1991.

Moi, Toril. *Sexual/Textual Politics: Feminist Literary Theory*. London: Methuen, 1985.

Morrison, Toni. *Playing in the Dark: Whiteness and the Literary Imagination*. Cambridge: Harvard UP, 1992.

Pound, Ezra. "A Retrospect." *A Modernist Reader*. Ed. Peter Faulkner. London: Batsford, 1986. 59–71.

Scott, Bonnie Kime. Introduction. *The Gender of Modernism: A Critical Anthology*. By Bonnie Kime Scott. Bloomington: Indiana UP, 1990. 1–18.

Sedgwick, Eve Kasofsky. *Epistemology of the Closet*. Berkeley: U of California P, 1990.

Showalter, Elaine. *A Literature of Their Own: British Women Novelists from Brontë to Lessing*. Princeton: Princeton UP, 1977.

Smith, Johanna. "'Too Beautiful Altogether': Patriarchal Ideology in *Heart of Darkness*." *Joseph Conrad, Heart of Darkness*. Ed. Ross C Murfin. 2nd ed. Case Studies in Contemporary Criticism. Boston: Bedford–St. Martin's, 1996. 179–95.

Straus, Nina Pelikan. "The Exclusion of the Intended from Secret Sharing in Conrad's *Heart of Darkness*." *Novel* 20 (1987): 123–37.

Sullivan, Zoreh T. "Enclosure, Darkness, and the Body: Conrad's Landscape." *The Centennial Review* 25 (1981): 59–79.

Torgovnick, Marianna. *Gone Primitive: Savage Intellects, Modern Lives.* Chicago: U of Chicago P, 1990.

Watts, Cedric. *A Preface to Conrad.* 2nd ed. London: Longman, 1993.

White, James F. "The Third Theme in 'The Secret Sharer.'" *Conradiana* 21.1 (1989): 37–46.

Woolf, Virginia. *The Essays of Virginia Woolf, Volume II: 1912–1918.* Ed. Andrew McNeillie. San Diego: Harcourt, 1987.

———. "Lord Jim." In Woolf, *The Essays of Virginia Woolf, Volume II.* 140–43.

———. "Mr Conrad: A Conversation." *The Essays of Virginia Woolf, Volume III: 1919–1924.* Ed. Andrew McNeillie. San Diego: Harcourt, 1988. 376–80.

———. "Mr Conrad's 'Youth.'" In Woolf, *The Essays of Virginia Woolf, Volume II.* 158–60.

———. *To the Lighthouse.* San Diego: Harcourt, 1981.

Deconstruction
and
"The Secret Sharer"

WHAT IS DECONSTRUCTION?

Deconstruction has a reputation for being the most complex and forbidding of contemporary critical approaches to literature, but in fact almost all of us have, at one time, either deconstructed a text or badly wanted to deconstruct one. Sometimes when we hear a lecturer effectively marshal evidence to show that a book means primarily one thing, we long to interrupt and ask what he or she would make of other, conveniently overlooked passages that seem to contradict the lecturer's thesis. Sometimes, after reading a provocative critical article that *almost* convinces us that a familiar work means the opposite of what we assumed it meant, we may wish to make an equally convincing case for our former reading of the text. We may not think that the poem or novel in question better supports our interpretation, but we may recognize that the text can be used to support *both* readings. And sometimes we simply want to make that point: texts can be used to support seemingly irreconcilable positions.

To reach this conclusion is to feel the deconstructive itch. J. Hillis Miller, the preeminent American deconstructor, puts it this way: "Deconstruction is not a dismantling of the structure of a text, but a demonstration that it has already dismantled itself. Its apparently solid ground is no rock but thin air" ("Stevens' Rock" 341). To deconstruct a text isn't to show that all the high old themes aren't there to be found in it. Rather, it is to show that a text — not unlike DNA with its double helix — can have intertwined, opposite "discourses" — strands of narrative, threads of meaning.

Ultimately, of course, deconstruction refers to a larger and more complex enterprise than the practice of demonstrating that a text can have contradictory meanings. The term refers to a way of reading texts practiced by critics who have been influenced by the writings of the French philosopher Jacques Derrida. It is important to gain some understanding of Derrida's project and of the historical backgrounds of his work before reading the deconstruction that follows, let alone attempting to deconstruct a text.

Derrida, a philosopher of language who coined the term *deconstruction,* argues that we tend to think and express our thoughts in terms of opposites. Something is black but not white, masculine and therefore not feminine, a cause rather than an effect, and so forth. These mutually exclusive pairs or dichotomies are too numerous to list but would include beginning/end, conscious/unconscious, presence/ absence, and speech/writing. If we think hard about these dichotomies, Derrida suggests, we will realize that they are not simply oppositions; they are also hierarchies in miniature. In other words, they contain one term that our culture views as being superior and one term viewed as negative or inferior. Sometimes the superior term seems only subtly superior (*speech, cause*), but at other times we know immediately which term is culturally preferable (*presence, beginning,* and *consciousness* are easy choices). But the hierarchy always exists.

Of particular interest to Derrida, perhaps because it involves the language in which all the other dichotomies are expressed, is the hierarchical opposition "speech/writing." Derrida argues that the "privileging" of speech, that is, the tendency to regard speech in positive terms and writing in negative terms, cannot be disentangled from the privileging of presence. (Postcards are written by absent friends; we read Plato because he cannot speak from beyond the grave.) Furthermore, according to Derrida, the tendency to privilege both speech and presence is part of the Western tradition of *logocentrism,* the belief that in some ideal beginning were creative *spoken* words, such as "Let there be light," spoken by an ideal, *present* God.[1] According to logocentric

---

[1]Derrida sometimes uses the word *phallogocentrism* to indicate that there is "a certain indissociability" between logocentrism and the "phallocentrism" (Derrida, *Acts* 57) of a culture whose God created light, the world, and man before creating woman — from Adam's rib. "Phallocentrism" is another name for patriarchy. The role that deconstruction has played in feminist analysis will be discussed later.

tradition, these words can now be represented only in unoriginal speech or writing (such as the written phrase in quotation marks above). Derrida doesn't seek to reverse the hierarchized opposition between speech and writing, or presence and absence, or early and late, for to do so would be to fall into a trap of perpetuating the same forms of thought and expression that he seeks to deconstruct. Rather, his goal is to erase the boundary between oppositions such as speech and writing, and to do so in such a way as to throw into question the order and values implied by the opposition.

Returning to the theories of Ferdinand de Saussure, who invented the modern science of linguistics, Derrida reminds us that the association of speech with present, obvious, and ideal meaning — and writing with absent, merely pictured, and therefore less reliable meaning — is suspect, to say the least. As Saussure demonstrated, words are *not* the things they name and, indeed, they are only arbitrarily associated with those things. A word, like any sign, is what Derrida has called a "deferred presence"; that is to say, "the signified concept is never present in itself," and "every concept is necessarily . . . inscribed in a chain or system, within which it refers to another and to other concepts" ("Différance" 138, 140). Neither spoken nor written words have present, positive, identifiable attributes themselves. They have meaning only by virtue of their difference from other words (*red, read, reed*) and, at the same time, their contextual relationship to those words. Take *read* as an example. To know whether it is the present or past tense of the verb — whether it rhymes with *red* or *reed* — we need to see it in relation to some other words (for example, *yesterday*).

Because the meanings of words lie in the differences between them and in the differences between them and the things they name, Derrida suggests that all language is constituted by *différance,* a word he has coined that puns on two French words meaning "to differ" and "to defer": words are the deferred presences of the things they "mean," and their meaning is grounded in difference. Derrida, by the way, changes the *e* in the French word *différence* to an *a* in his neologism *différance;* the change, which can be seen in writing but cannot be heard in spoken French, is itself a playful, witty challenge to the notion that writing is inferior or "fallen" speech.

In *Dissemination* (1972) and *De la grammatologie* [*Of Grammatology*] (1967), Derrida begins to redefine writing by deconstructing some old definitions. In *Dissemination,* he traces logocentrism back to Plato, who in the *Phaedrus* has Socrates condemn writing and who, in all the great dialogues, powerfully postulates the metaphysical longing for origins and ideals that permeates Western thought. "What Derrida does in his reading of Plato," Barbara Johnson points out in her translator's introduction to *Dissemination,* "is to unfold dimensions of Plato's *text* that work against the grain of (Plato's own) Platonism" (xxiv). Remember: that is what deconstruction does, according to Miller; it shows a text dismantling itself.

In *Of Grammatology,* Derrida turns to the *Confessions* of Jean-Jacques Rousseau and exposes a grain running against the grain. Rousseau — who has often been seen as another great Western idealist and believer in innocent, noble origins — on one hand condemned writing as mere representation, a corruption of the more natural, childlike, direct, and therefore undevious speech. On the other hand, Rousseau acknowledged his own tendency to lose self-presence and blurt out exactly the wrong thing in public. He confesses that by writing at a distance from his audience, he often expressed himself better: "If I were present, one would never know what I was worth," Rousseau admitted (Derrida, *Of Grammatology* 142). Thus, Derrida shows that one strand of Rousseau's discourse made writing seem a secondary, even treacherous supplement, while another made it seem necessary to communication.

Have Derrida's deconstructions of *Confessions* and the *Phaedrus* explained these texts, interpreted them, opened them up and shown us what they mean? Not in any traditional sense. Derrida would say that anyone attempting to find a single, homogeneous, or universal meaning in a text is simply imprisoned by the structure of thought that would oppose two readings and declare one to be right and not wrong, correct rather than incorrect. In fact, any work of literature that we interpret defies the laws of Western logic, the laws of opposition and noncontradiction. From deconstruction's point of view, texts don't say "A and not B." They say "A and not-A." "Instead of a simple 'either/or' structure," Johnson explains,

> deconstruction attempts to elaborate a discourse that says *neither* "either/or" *nor* "both/and" nor even "neither/nor," while at the same time not totally abandoning these logics either. The word deconstruction is meant to undermine the either/or logic of the opposition "construction/destruction." Deconstruction is both, it is neither, and it reveals the way in which both construction and destruction are themselves not what they appear to be. (Johnson, *World* 12–13)

Although its ultimate aim may be to criticize Western idealism and logic, deconstruction began as a response to structuralism and to formalism, another structure-oriented theory of reading. Using Saussure's theory as Derrida was to do later, European structuralists attempted to create a *semiology,* or science of signs, that would give humankind at once a scientific and a holistic way of studying the world and its human inhabitants. Roland Barthes, a structuralist who later shifted toward poststructuralism, hoped to recover literary language from the isolation in which it had been studied and to show that the laws that govern it govern all signs, from road signs to articles of clothing. Claude Lévi-Strauss, a structural anthropologist who studied everything from village structure to the structure of myths, found in myths what he called *mythemes,* or building blocks, such as basic plot elements. Recognizing that the same mythemes occur in similar myths from different cultures, he suggested that all myths may be elements of one great myth being written by the collective human mind.

Derrida did not believe that structuralists had the concepts that would someday explain the laws governing human signification and thus provide the key to understanding the form and meaning of everything from an African village to Greek myth to Rousseau's *Confessions.* In his view, the scientific search by structural anthropologists for what unifies humankind amounts to a new version of the old search for the lost ideal, whether that ideal be Plato's bright realm of the Idea or the Paradise of Genesis or Rousseau's unspoiled Nature. As for the structuralist belief that texts have "centers" of meaning, in Derrida's view that derives from the logocentric belief that there is a reading of the text that accords with "the book as seen by God." Jonathan Culler, who thus translates a difficult phrase from Derrida's *L'Écriture et la différence* [*Writing and Difference*] (1967) in his book *Structuralist Poetics* (1975), goes on to explain what Derrida objects to in structuralist literary criticism:

[When] one speaks of the structure of a literary work, one does so from a certain vantage point: one starts with notions of the meaning or effects of a poem and tries to identify the structures responsible for those effects. Possible configurations or patterns that make no contribution are rejected as irrelevant. That is to say, an intuitive understanding of the poem functions as the "centre". . . : it is both a starting point and a limiting principle. (244)

Deconstruction calls into question assumptions made about literature by formalist, as well as by structuralist, critics. Formalism, or the
New Criticism as it was once commonly called, assumes a work of literature to be a freestanding, self-contained object, its meanings found
in the complex network of relations that constitute its parts (images,
sounds, rhythms, allusions, and so on). To be sure, deconstruction is
somewhat like formalism in several ways. Both formalism and deconstruction are text-oriented approaches whose practitioners pay a great
deal of attention to rhetorical *tropes* (forms of figurative language including allegory, symbol, metaphor, and metonymy). And formalists,
long before deconstructors, discovered counterpatterns of meaning in
the same text. Formalists find ambiguity: deconstructors find undecidability. On close inspection, however, the formalist understanding of
rhetorical tropes or figures is quite different from that of deconstruction, and undecidability turns out to be different from the ambiguity
formalists find in texts.

Formalists, who associated literary with figurative language, made
qualitative distinctions between types of figures of speech; for instance,
they valued symbols and metaphors over metonyms. (A metonym is a
term standing for something with which it is commonly associated or
contiguous; we use metonymy when we say we had "the cold plate"
for lunch.) From the formalist perspective, metaphors and symbols are
less arbitrary figures than metonyms and thus rank more highly in the
hierarchy of tropes: a metaphor ("I'm feeling blue") supposedly involves a special, intrinsic, nonarbitrary relationship between its two
terms (the feeling of melancholy and the color blue); a symbol ("the
river of life") allegedly involves a unique fusion of image and idea.

From the perspective of deconstruction, however, these distinctions are suspect. In "The Rhetoric of Temporality" Paul de Man deconstructs the distinction between symbol and allegory; elsewhere, he,
Derrida, and Miller have similarly questioned the metaphor/metonymy
distinction, arguing that all figuration is a process of linguistic substi-
tution. In the case of a metaphor (or symbol), they claim, we have forgotten what juxtaposition or contiguity gave rise to the association
that now seems mysteriously special. Derrida, in "White Mythology,"
and de Man, in "Metaphor (*Second Discourse*)," have also challenged
the priority of literal over figurative language, and Miller has gone so
far as to deny the validity of the literal/figurative distinction, arguing
that all words are figures because all language involves *catachresis,* "the
violent, forced, or abusive importation of a term from another realm
to name something which has no proper name" (Miller, *Ariadne* 21).

The difference between the formalist concept of literary ambiguity and the deconstructive concept of undecidability is as significant as the gap between formalist and deconstructive understandings of figurative language. Undecidability, as de Man came to define it, is a complex notion easily misunderstood. There is a tendency to assume it refers to readers who, when forced to decide between two or more equally plausible and conflicting readings, throw up their hands and decide that the choice can't be made. But undecidability in fact debunks this whole notion of reading as a decision-making process carried out on texts by readers. To say we are forced to choose or decide, or that we are unable to do so, is to locate the problem of undecidability falsely within ourselves, rather than recognizing that it is an intrinsic feature of the text.

Undecidability is thus different from ambiguity, as understood by formalists. Formalists believed that a complete understanding of a literary work is possible, an understanding in which ambiguities will be resolved objectively by the reader, even if only in the sense that they will be shown to have definite, meaningful functions. Deconstructors do not share that belief. They do not accept the formalist view that a work of literary art is demonstrably unified from beginning to end, in one certain way, or that it is organized around a single center that ultimately can be identified and defined. Neither do they accept the concept of irony as simply saying one thing and meaning another thing that will be understood with certainty by the reader. As a result, deconstructors tend to see texts as more radically heterogeneous than do formalists. The formalist critic ultimately makes sense of ambiguity; undecidability, by contrast, is never reduced, let alone mastered by deconstructive reading, although the incompatible possibilities between which it is impossible to decide can be identified with certainty.

For critics practicing deconstruction, a literary text is neither a sphere with a center nor an unbroken line with a definite beginning and end. In fact, many assumptions about the nature of texts have been put in question by deconstruction, which in Derrida's words "dislocates the borders, the framing of texts, everything which should preserve their immanence and make possible an internal reading or merely reading in the classical sense of the term" ("Some Statements" 86). A text consists of words inscribed in and inextricable from the myriad discourses that inform it; from the point of view of deconstruction, the boundaries between any given text and that larger text we call language are always shifting.

It was that larger text that Derrida was referring to when he made his famous statement *"there is nothing outside the text"* (*Grammatology* 158). To understand what Derrida meant by that statement, consider the following: we know the world through language, and the acts and practices that constitute that "real world" (the Oklahoma City bombing, the decision to marry) are inseparable from the discourses out of which they arise and as open to interpretation as any work of literature. Derrida is not alone in deconstructing the world/text opposition. De Man viewed language as something that has great power in individual, social, and political life. Geoffrey Hartman, who was closely associated with deconstruction during the 1970s, wrote that "nothing can lift us out of language" (xii).

Once we understand deconstruction's view of the literary text — as words that are part of and that resonate with an immense linguistic structure in which we live and move and have our being — we are in a better position to understand why deconstructors reach points in their readings at which they reveal, but cannot decide between, incompatible interpretive possibilities. A text is not a unique, hermetically sealed space. Perpetually open to being seen in the light of new contexts, any given text has the potential to be different each time it is read. Furthermore, as Miller has shown in *Ariadne's Thread: Story Lines* (1992), the various "terms" and "famil[ies] of terms" we use in performing our readings invariably affect the results. Whether we choose to focus on a novel's characters or its realism, for instance, leads us to different views of the same text. "No one thread," Miller asserts, "can be followed to a central point where it provides a means of overseeing, controlling, and understanding the whole" (21).

Complicating matters still further is the fact that the individual words making up narratives — the words out of which we make our mental picture of a character or place — usually have several (and often have conflicting) meanings due to the complex histories of their usage. (If your professor tells the class that you have written a "fulsome report" and you look up the word *fulsome* in a contemporary dictionary, you will learn that it can mean either "elaborate" or "offensive"; if, for some reason, you don't know what *offensive* means, you will find out that it can equally well describe your favorite quarterback and a racist joke.) "Each word," as Miller puts it, "inheres in a labyrinth of branching interverbal relationships"; often there are "forks in the etymological line leading to bifurcated or trifurcated roots." Deconstructors often turn to etymology, not to help them decide whether a statement means this or that, but rather as a way of revealing the coincidence of several meanings in the same text. "The effect of etymological retracing," Miller writes, "is not to ground the work solidly but to render it unstable, equivocal, wavering, groundless" (*Ariadne* 19).

Deconstruction is not really interpretation, the act of choosing between or among possible meanings. Derrida has glossed de Man's statement that "there is no need to deconstruct Rousseau" by saying that "this was another way of saying: there is always already deconstruction, at work *in* works, especially *literary* works. It cannot be applied, after the fact and from outside, as a technical instrument. Texts deconstruct *themselves* by themselves" (Derrida, *Memoires* 123). If deconstruction is not interpretation, then what is it? Deconstruction may be defined as reading, as long as reading is defined as de Man defined it — as a process involving moments of what he called *aporia* or terminal uncertainty, and as an act performed with full knowledge of the fact that all texts are ultimately unreadable (if reading means reducing a text to a single, homogeneous meaning). Miller explains unreadability by saying that although there are moments of great lucidity in reading, each "lucidity will in principle contain its own blind spot requiring a further elucidation and exposure of error, and so on, ad infinitum. . . . One should not underestimate, however, the productive illumination produced as one moves through these various stages of reading" (*Ethics* 42, 44).

Miller's point is important because, in a sense, it deconstructs or erases the boundary between the readings of deconstructors and the interpretations of more traditional critics. It suggests that all kinds of critics have had their moments of lucidity; it also suggests that critics practicing deconstruction know that their *own* insights — even their insights into what is or isn't contradictory, undecidable, or unreadable in a text — are hardly the last word. As Art Berman writes,

> In *Blindness and Insight* de Man demonstrates that the apparently well-reasoned arguments of literary critics contain contradiction at their core; yet there is no alternative path to insight. . . . The readers of criticism recognize the blindness of their predecessors, reorganize it, and thereby gain both the insight of the critics and a knowledge of the contradiction that brings forth insight. Each reader, of course, has his own blindness; and the criticism of criticism is not a matter of rectifying someone else's mistakes. (Berman 239–40)

When de Man spoke of the resistance to theory he referred generally to the antitheoretical bias in literary studies. But he might as well
have been speaking specifically of the resistance to deconstruction, as
expressed not only in academic books and journals but also in popular
magazines such as *Newsweek*. Attacks on deconstruction became more
common and more personal some four years after de Man's death in
1983. That was the year that a Belgian scholar working on a doctoral
thesis discovered ninety-two articles that de Man had written during
World War II for the Brussels newspaper *Le Soir*, a widely read French-
language daily that had fallen under Nazi control during the German
occupation of Belgium. Ultimately, one hundred and seventy articles
by de Man were found in *Le Soir*; another ten were discovered in *Het
Vlaamsche Land*, a collaborationist newspaper published in Flemish.
These writings, which date from 1941 (when de Man was twenty-one
years old), ceased to appear before 1943, by which time it had become
clear to most Belgians that Jews were being shipped to death camps
such as Auschwitz.

De Man's wartime journalism consists mainly, but not entirely, of
inoffensive literary pieces. In one article de Man takes Germany's triumph in World War II as a given, places the German people at the
center of Western civilization, and foresees a mystical era involving
suffering but also faith, exaltation, and rapture. In another article, entitled "*Les Juifs dans la littérature actuelle*" ["Jews in Present-Day Literature"], de Man scoffs at the notion that Jewish writers have significantly influenced the literature of his day and, worse, considers the
merits of creating a separate Jewish colony that would be isolated from
Europe.

No one who had known de Man since his immigration to the
United States in 1948 had found him to be illiberal or anti-Semitic.
Furthermore, de Man had spent his career in the United States demys-
tifying or, as he would have said, "debunking" the kind of ideological
assumptions (about the relationship between aesthetics and national
cultures) that lie behind his most offensive Belgian newspaper writings. The critic who in *The Resistance to Theory* (1986) argued that literature must not become "a substitute for theology, ethics, etc."
(de Man 24) had either changed radically since writing of the magical
integrity and wholeness of the German nation and its culture or had
not deeply believed what he had written as a young journalist.

These points have been made in various ways by de Man's former
friends and colleagues. Geoffrey Hartman has said that de Man's later
work, the work we associate with deconstruction, "looks like a belated,

but still powerful, act of conscience" (26–31). Derrida, who like Hartman is a Jew, has read carefully de Man's wartime discourse, showing it to be "split, disjointed, engaged in incessant conflicts" (Hamacher, Hertz, and Keenan 135). "On the one hand," Derrida finds "*unpardonable*" de Man's suggestion that a separate Jewish colony be set up; "on the other hand," he notes that of the four writers de Man praises in the same article (André Gide, Franz Kafka, D. H. Lawrence, and Ernest Hemingway), not one was German, one (Kafka) *was* Jewish, and all four "represent everything that Nazism . . . would have liked to extirpate from history and the great tradition" (Hamacher, Hertz, and Keenan 145).

While friends asserted that some of de Man's statements were unpardonable, deconstruction's severest critics tried to use a young man's sometimes deplorable statements as evidence that a whole critical movement was somehow morally as well as intellectually flawed. As Andrej Warminski summed it up, "the 'discovery' of the 1941–42 writings is being used to perpetuate the old myths about so-called 'deconstruction'" (Hamacher, Hertz, and Keenan 389). Knowing what some of those myths are — and why, in fact, they *are* myths — aids our understanding in an indirect, contrapuntal way that is in keeping with the spirit of deconstruction.

In his book *The Ethics of Reading* (1987), Miller refutes two notions commonly repeated by deconstruction's detractors. One is the idea that deconstructors believe a text means nothing in the sense that it means whatever the playful reader *wants* it to mean. The other is the idea that deconstruction is "immoral" insofar as it refuses to view literature in the way it has traditionally been viewed, namely, "as the foundation and embodiment, the means of preserving and transmitting, the basic humanistic values of our culture" (9). Responding to the first notion, Miller points out that neither Derrida nor de Man "has ever asserted the freedom of the reader to make the text mean anything he or she wants it to mean. Each has in fact asserted the reverse" (10). As for the second notion — that deconstructors are guilty of shirking an ethical responsibility because their purpose is not to (re)discover and (re)assert the transcendent and timeless values contained in great books — Miller argues that "this line of thought" rests "on a basic misunderstanding of the way the ethical moment enters into the act of reading" (9). That "ethical moment," Miller goes on to argue, "is not a matter of response to a thematic content asserting this or that idea about morality. It is a much more fundamental 'I must' responding to the language of literature in itself. . . . Deconstruction is nothing more or less than good reading as such" (9–10). Reading itself, in other words, is an act that leads to further ethical acts, decisions, and behaviors in a real world involving relations to other people and to society at large. For these, the reader must take responsibility, as for any other ethical act.

A third commonly voiced objection to deconstruction is to its playfulness, to the evident pleasure its practitioners take in teasing out all the contradictory interpretive possibilities generated by the words in a text, their complex etymologies and contexts, and their potential to be read figuratively or even ironically. Certainly playfulness and pleasure are aspects of deconstruction. In his book *The Post Card* (1987), Derrida specifically associates deconstruction with pleasure; in an interview published in a collection of his essays entitled *Acts of Literature* (1992), he speculates that "it is perhaps this *jouissance* which most irritates the all-out adversaries of deconstruction" (56). But such adversaries misread deconstruction's "jouissance," its pleasurable playfulness. Whereas they see it as evidence that deconstructors view texts as tightly enclosed fields on which they can play delightfully useless little word games, Derrida has said that the "subtle and intense pleasure" of deconstruction arises from the "dismantl[ing]" of repressive assumptions, representations, and ideas — in short, from the "lifting of repression" (*Acts* 56–57). As Gregory S. Jay explains in his book *America the Scrivener: Deconstruction and the Subject of Literary History* (1990), "Deconstruction has been not only a matter of reversing binary oppositions but also a matter of disabling the hierarchy of values they enable and of speculating on alternative modes of knowing and of acting" (xii).

Far from viewing literature as a word-playground, Derrida, in Derek Attridge's words, "emphasizes . . . literature as an institution," one "not given in nature or the brain but brought into being by processes that are social, legal, and political, and that can be mapped historically and geographically" (*Acts* 23). By thus characterizing Derrida's emphasis, Attridge counters the commonest of the charges that have been leveled at deconstructors, namely, that they divorce literary texts from historical, political, and legal institutions.

In *Memoires for Paul de Man* (1986), Derrida argues that, where history is concerned, "deconstructive discourses" have pointedly and effectively questioned "the classical assurances of history, the genealogical narrative, and periodizations of all sorts" (15) — in other words, the tendency of historians to view the past as the source of (lost) truth and value, to look for explanations in origins, and to view as unified epochs (for example, the Victorian period, 1837–1901) what are in fact complex and heterogeneous times in history. As for politics, Derrida points out that de Man invariably "says something about institutional structures and the political stakes of hermeneutic conflicts," which is to say that de Man's commentaries acknowledge that conflicting interpretations reflect and are reflected in the politics of institutions (such as the North American university).

In addition to history and politics, the law has been a subject on which deconstruction has had much to say of late. In an essay on Franz Kafka's story "Before the Law," Derrida has shown that for Kafka the law as such exists but can never be confronted by those who would do so and fulfill its commands. Miller has pointed out that the law "may only be confronted in its delegates or representatives or by its effects on us or others" (*Ethics* 20). What or where, then, is the law itself? The law's presence, Miller suggests, is continually deferred by narrative, that is, writing about or on the law which constantly reinterprets the law in the attempt to reveal what it really is and means. This very act of (re)interpretation, however, serves to "defer" or distance the law even further from the case at hand, since the (re)interpretation takes precedence (and assumes prominence) over the law itself. (As Miller defines it, narrative would include everything from a Victorian novel that promises to reveal moral law, to the opinion of a Supreme Court justice regarding the constitutionality of a given action, however different these two documents are in the conventions they follow and the uses to which they are put.) Miller likens the law to a promise, "the validity of [which] does not lie in itself but in its future fulfillment," and to a story "divided against itself" that in the end "leaves its readers . . . still in expectation" (*Ethics* 33).

Because the facts about deconstruction are very different from the myth of its playful irreverence and irrelevance, a number of contemporary thinkers have found it useful to adapt and apply deconstruction in their work. For instance, a deconstructive theology has been developed. Architects have designed and built buildings grounded, as it were, in deconstructive architectural theory. In the area of law, the critical legal studies movement has, in Christopher Norris's words, effectively used "deconstructive thinking" of the kind de Man used in analyzing Rousseau's *Social Contract* "to point up the blind spots, conflicts, and antinomies that plague the discourse of received legal wisdom." Critical legal theorists have debunked "the formalist view of law," that is, the "view which holds law to be a system of neutral precepts and principles," showing instead how the law "gives rise to various disabling contradictions," such as "the problematic distinction between 'private' and 'public' domains." They have turned deconstruction into "a sophisticated means of making the point that all legal discourse is performative in character, i.e., designed to secure assent through its rhetorical power to convince or persuade" (Norris, *Deconstruction and the Interests* 17). Courtroom persuasion, Gerald Lopez has argued in a 1989 article in the *Michigan Law Review*, consists of storytelling as much as argument (Clayton 13).

In the field of literary studies, the influence of deconstruction may be seen in the work of critics ostensibly taking some other, more political approach. Barbara Johnson has put deconstruction to work for the feminist cause. She and Shoshana Felman have argued that chief among those binary oppositions "based on repression of differences with entities" is the opposition man/woman (Johnson, *Critical* x). In a reading of the "undecidability" of "femininity" in Balzac's story "The Girl with the Golden Eyes," Felman puts it this way: "the rhetorical hierarchization of the . . . opposition between the sexes is . . . such that woman's *difference* is suppressed, being totally subsumed by the reference of the feminine to masculine identity" ("Rereading" 25).

Elsewhere, Johnson, Felman, and Gayatri Spivak have combined Derrida's theories with the psychoanalytic theory of Jacques Lacan to analyze the way in which gender and sexuality are ultimately textual, grounded in language and rhetoric. In an essay on Edmund Wilson's reading of Henry James's story *The Turn of the Screw*, Felman has treated sexuality as a form of rhetoric that can be deconstructed, shown to contain contradictions and ambiguities that more traditional readings of sexuality have masked. Gay and lesbian critics have seen the positive implications of this kind of analysis, hence Eve Kosofsky Sedgwick's admission in the early pages of her book *Epistemology of the Closet* (1990): "One main strand of argument in this book is deconstructive, in a fairly specific sense. The analytic move it makes is to demonstrate that categories presented in a culture as symmetrical binary oppositions . . . actually subsist in a more unsettled and dynamic tacit relation" (9–10).

In telling "The Story of Deconstruction" in his book on contemporary American literature and theory, Jay Clayton assesses the current status of this unique approach. Although he notes how frequently deconstructive critics have been cited for their lack of political engagement, he concludes that deconstruction, "a movement accused of formalism and arid intellectualism, participates in the political turn of contemporary culture" (34). He suggests that what began as theory in the late 1960s and 1970s has, over time, developed into a method employed by critics taking a wide range of approaches to literature — ethnic, feminist, new historicist, Marxist — in addition to critics outside of literary studies per se who are involved in such areas as critical legal studies and critical race theory, which seeks to "sustain a complementary relationship between the deconstructive energies of Critical Legal Studies and the constructive energies of civil rights activism" (58).

Clayton cites the work of Edward Said as a case in point. Through 1975, the year that his *Beginnings: Intention and Method* was published, Said was employing a form of deconstructive criticism that, in Clayton's words, emphasized the "power" of texts "to initiate projects in the real world" (45–46). Said became identified with cultural and postcolonial criticism, however, beginning in 1978 with the publication of his book *Orientalism,* in which he deconstructs the East/West, Orient/Occident opposition. Said argues that Eastern and Middle Eastern peoples have for centuries been stereotyped by the Western discourses of "orientalism," a textuality that in no way reflects the diversity and differences that exist among the peoples it claims to represent. According to Said, that stereotyping not only facilitated the colonization of vast areas of the globe by the so-called West but also still governs, to a great extent, relations with the Arab and the so-called Eastern world. The expansion of Said's field of vision to include not just literary texts but international relations is powerfully indicative of the expanding role that deconstruction currently plays in developing contemporary understandings of politics and culture, as well as in active attempts to intervene in these fields.

In the essay that follows, the noted American deconstructor J. Hillis Miller characterizes Conradian narration as a form of "secret sharing," since through Conrad's narrators we not only see places we never have visited but also feel what the narrators subjectively have felt. In doing so, Miller goes a long way toward disproving the myth that deconstructors deny literature's referential power or moral relevance. He reveals Conrad's power to represent the world realistically; at the same time, he shows how ethical themes are subtly anticipated in apparently neutral depictions of the natural world.

Miller argues that if Conradian narration (and narration in general) involves sharing secrets, reading does as well. To receive a narrator's secrets is to incur an obligation "to judge, to decide, to act" not unlike the obligation of Conrad's captain-narrator to "decide whether to hide the fugitive Leggatt or turn him over to the law as embodied in the captain of the *Sephora*" (233). Calling "The Secret Sharer" a "curious form of testimony, witness, or deposition" by a captain who has "only sky and sea . . . for judges," Miller suggests that "the reader is implicitly put in the position of judge or jury." Was Leggatt "justified in strangling the mutinous crewman or was it unjustified manslaughter, voluntary or involuntary? What should his punishment be? We must also pass judgment on the narrator. Did he do right or wrong in harboring the fugitive murderer?" (237, 236)

By viewing reading as a private, ethical act — and in positing connections between reading and judgment, narration and the law — Miller develops ideas that he has set forth recently in *The Ethics of Reading* and that Derrida has explored in his reading of Kafka entitled "Before the Law." By stressing Conrad's great power to represent real places realistically — the power, as Conrad himself put it, to make us "see" — Miller also extends the work he has begun in his even more recent *Topographies*. But it is not just the newest, most recent version of deconstruction that is represented here. In "Sharing Secrets" Miller also makes the kind of deconstructive moves that he, de Man, and Derrida have long made, treating Conrad's text not as a nut containing a kernel of meaning that can be extracted via interpretive effort but as rhetoric — a narrative that branches, doubles back on itself, and dead-ends so often that contradictory readings are possible and moments of aporia, or "undecidability," are inevitable.

Miller's manner of deconstructing "The Secret Sharer" can perhaps best be anticipated by previewing sentences from the paragraph in which he reads Conrad's title: "What is a secret sharer? A secret *sharer*? A *secret* sharer? A different meaning arises depending on which word is stressed." Having shown two ways of reading two words, Miller focuses on the first of the two: "Just what is a secret, if there is such a thing? If there is such a thing, can it be shared? Does it remain a secret when it has been shared?" As for the second word, Miller writes: "*Shared* is related in meaning and etymology to *sheared,* as a ploughshare cuts the furrow, dividing the earth. To share something usually means to cut it into at least two pieces. . . . A secret, it would seem, cannot be cut in two in this way" (238). As he and Derrida have often done before, Miller turns to etymology to show how problematic the interpretation of a single, key word or phrase can be, thereby suggesting the impossibility of reading an entire text in a unitary way.

Miller subsequently explores the various secrets we may possibly share as we read (and then discuss or write about) "The Secret Sharer." In doing so he focuses on repeated words and variants on those words: he shows how they are used differently in different contexts and how they become increasingly enigmatic, secretive, even strange as a result, as any word does when it is repeated many times. He ultimately connects that strangeness with Sigmund Freud's notion of the uncanny and, beyond that, with the narrator's encounter with his *own* strangeness in a man who is in one sense the opposite of himself and in another sense his repetition or double. Through the encounter between a man representing the law (the captain-narrator) and another representing transgression (Leggatt), Miller suggests, "'The Secret Sharer' shows that law and order, the justice that validates command and hierarchy . . . must be periodically interrupted by some decisive act that reaffirms the law by breaking the law. Such an irruptive act always has something violent, dangerous, or illicit about it. Its emblems in "'The Secret Sharer' are Leggatt's act of murder and the narrator's secret hiding of Leggatt" (250).

It is somewhat unusual for a critic reading deconstructively to say something as declarative as "'The Secret Sharer' shows that . . . ." What Miller asserts 'The Secret Sharer' shows, however, is that stability and continuity may mean interruption, that breaking something may reaffirm it — in short, that opposites may be alike and apparent doubles utterly different. His assertion, in a sense, is the secret deconstruction finds in every text.

Ross C Murfin

DECONSTRUCTION: A SELECTED BIBLIOGRAPHY

Writings on Deconstruction

Arac, Jonathan, Wlad Godzich, and Wallace Martin, eds. *The Yale Critics: Deconstruction in America*. Minneapolis: U of Minnesota P, 1983. See especially the essays by Bové, Godzich, Pease, and Corngold.

Berman, Art. *From the New Criticism to Deconstruction: The Reception of Structuralism and Post-Structuralism*. Urbana: U of Illinois P, 1988.

Butler, Christopher. *Interpretation, Deconstruction, and Ideology: An Introduction to Some Current Issues in Literary Theory.* Oxford: Oxford UP, 1984.

Clayton, Jay. *The Pleasure of Babel: Contemporary American Literature and Theory.* New York: Oxford UP, 1993.

Culler, Jonathan. *On Deconstruction: Theory and Criticism after Structuralism.* Ithaca: Cornell UP, 1982.

———. *Structuralist Poetics: Structuralism, Linguistics, and the Study of Literature.* Ithaca: Cornell UP, 1975. See especially ch. 10.

Esch, Deborah. "Deconstruction." *Redrawing the Boundaries: The Transformation of English and American Literary Studies.* Ed. Stephen Greenblatt and Giles Gunn. New York: MLA, 1992. 374–91.

Feminist Studies 14 (1988). Special issue on deconstruction and feminism.

Hamacher, Werner, Neil Hertz, and Thomas Keenan. *Responses: On Paul de Man's Wartime Journalism.* Lincoln: U of Nebraska P, 1989.

Hartman, Geoffrey. "Blindness and Insight." *The New Republic,* 7 Mar. 1988: 26–31.

Jay, Gregory S. *America the Scrivener: Deconstruction and the Subject of Literary History.* Ithaca: Cornell UP, 1990.

Leitch, Vincent B. *American Literary Criticism from the Thirties to the Eighties.* New York: Columbia UP, 1988. See especially ch. 10, "Deconstructive Criticism."

———. *Cultural Criticism, Literary Theory, Poststructuralism.* New York: Columbia UP, 1992.

Loesberg, Jonathan. *Aestheticism and Deconstruction: Pater, Derrida, and de Man.* Princeton: Princeton UP, 1991.

Melville, Stephen W. *Philosophy beside Itself: On Deconstruction and Modernism.* Theory and History of Lit. 27. Minneapolis: U of Minnesota P, 1986.

Norris, Christopher. *Deconstruction and the Interests of Theory.* Oklahoma Project for Discourse and Theory no. 4. Norman: U of Oklahoma P, 1989.

———. *Deconstruction: Theory and Practice.* London: Methuen, 1982. Rev. ed. London: Routledge, 1991.

———. *Paul de Man, Deconstruction and the Critique of Aesthetic Ideology.* New York: Routledge, 1988.

Weber, Samuel. *Institution and Interpretation.* Minneapolis: U of Minnesota P, 1987.

Works by de Man, Derrida, and Miller

de Man, Paul. *Allegories of Reading.* New Haven: Yale UP, 1979. See especially ch. 1, "Semiology and Rhetoric," and ch. 7, "Metaphor (*Second Discourse*)."

———. *Blindness and Insight.* New York: Oxford UP, 1971. Minneapolis: U of Minnesota P, 1983. The 1983 edition contains important essays not included in the original edition.

———. "Phenomenality and Materiality in Kant." *Hermeneutics: Questions and Prospects.* Ed. Gary Shapiro and Alan Sica. Amherst: U of Massachusetts P, 1984. 121–44.

———. *The Resistance to Theory.* Minneapolis: U of Minnesota P, 1986.

———. *Romanticism and Contemporary Culture.* Ed. E. S. Burt, Kevin Newmarkj, and Andrzej Warminski. Baltimore: Johns Hopkins UP, 1993.

———. *Wartime Journalism, 1939–1943.* Lincoln: U of Nebraska P, 1989.

Derrida, Jacques. *Acts of Literature.* Ed. Derek Attridge. New York: Routledge, 1992.

———. "Différance." *Speech and Phenomena.* Trans. David B. Alison. Evanston: Northwestern UP, 1973. 129–60.

———. *Dissemination.* 1972. Trans. Barbara Johnson. Chicago: U of Chicago P, 1981. See especially the concise, incisive "Translator's Introduction," which provides a useful point of entry into this work and others by Derrida.

———. "Force of Law: The 'Mystical Foundation of Authority.'" Trans. Mary Quaintance. *Deconstruction and the Possibility of Justice.* Ed. Drucilla Cornell, Michel Rosenfeld, and David Gray Carlson. New York: Routledge, 1992. 3–67.

———. *Given Time. 1, Counterfeit Money.* Trans. Peggy Kamuf. Chicago: U of Chicago P, 1992.

———. *Margins of Philosophy.* Trans. Alan Bass. Chicago: U of Chicago P, 1982. Contains the essay "White Mythology: Metaphor in the Text of Philosophy."

———. *Memoires for Paul de Man.* Wellek Library Lectures. Trans. Cecile Lindsay, Jonathan Culler, and Eduardo Cadava. New York: Columbia UP, 1986.

———. *Of Grammatology.* 1967. Trans. Gayatri C. Spivak. Baltimore: Johns Hopkins UP, 1976.

———. "Passions." *Derrida: A Critical Reader.* Ed. David Wood. Cambridge: Basil Blackwell, 1992. 5–35.

————. *The Post Card: From Socrates to Freud and Beyond.* Trans. with intro. Alan Bass. Chicago: U of Chicago P, 1987.

————. "Some Statements and Truisms about Neo-logisms, Newisms, Postisms, and Other Small Seisisms." *The States of "Theory."* New York: Columbia UP, 1990. 63–94.

————. *Specters of Marx.* Trans. Peggy Kamuf. New York: Routledge, 1994.

————. *Writing and Difference.* 1967. Trans. Alan Bass. Chicago: U of Chicago P, 1978.

Miller, J. Hillis. *Ariadne's Thread: Story Lines.* New Haven: Yale UP, 1992.

————. *The Ethics of Reading: Kant, de Man, Eliot, Trollope, James, and Benjamin.* New York: Columbia UP, 1987.

————. *Fiction and Repetition: Seven English Novels.* Cambridge: Harvard UP, 1982.

————. *Hawthorne and History: Defacing It.* Cambridge: Basil Blackwell, 1991. Contains a bibliography of Miller's work from 1955 to 1990.

————. *Illustrations.* Cambridge: Harvard UP, 1992.

————. "Stevens' Rock and Criticism as Cure." *Georgia Review* 30 (1976): 3–31, 330–48.

————. *Typographies.* Stanford: Stanford UP, 1994.

————. *Versions of Pygmalion.* Cambridge: Harvard UP, 1990.

Essays on Deconstruction and Poststructuralism

Barthes, Roland. *S/Z.* Trans. Richard Miller. New York: Hill, 1974. In this influential work, Barthes turns from a structuralist to a poststructuralist approach.

Benstock, Shari. *Textualizing the Feminine: On the Limits of Genre.* Norman: U of Oklahoma P, 1991.

Bloom, Harold, et al., eds. *Deconstruction and Criticism.* New York: Seabury, 1979. Includes essays by Bloom, de Man, Derrida, Miller, and Hartman.

Chase, Cynthia. *Decomposing Figures.* Baltimore: Johns Hopkins UP, 1986.

Cohen, Tom. *Anti-Mimesis: From Plato to Hitchcock.* Cambridge: Cambridge UP, 1994.

Elam, Diane. *Feminism and Deconstruction: Ms. en Abyme.* New York: Routledge, 1994.

Felman, Shoshana. "Rereading Femininity." Special Issue on "Feminist Readings: French Texts/American Contexts," *Yale French Studies* 62 (1981): 19–44.

———. "Turning the Screw of Interpretation." *Literature and Psychoanalysis: The Question of Reading: Otherwise.* Special issue, *Yale French Studies* 55–56 (1978): 3–508. Baltimore: Johns Hopkins UP, 1982.

Harari, Josué, ed. *Textual Strategies: Perspectives in Post-Structuralist Criticism.* Ithaca: Cornell UP, 1979.

Johnson, Barbara. *The Critical Difference: Essays in the Contemporary Rhetoric of Reading.* Baltimore: Johns Hopkins UP, 1980.

———. *A World of Difference.* Baltimore: Johns Hopkins UP, 1987.

Krupnick, Mark, ed. *Displacement: Derrida and After.* Bloomington: Indiana UP, 1987.

Meese, Elizabeth, and Alice Parker, eds. *The Difference Within: Feminism and Critical Theory.* Philadelphia: John Benjamins, 1989.

Sedgwick, Eve Kosofsky. *Epistemology of the Closet.* Berkeley: U of California P, 1990.

Ulmer, Gregory L. *Applied Grammatology.* Baltimore: Johns Hopkins UP, 1985.

———. *Teletheory: Grammatology in the Age of Video.* New York: Routledge, 1989.

Deconstructive and Poststructuralist Approaches to Conrad

Bonney, William. *Thorns and Arabesques: Contexts for Conrad's Fiction.* Baltimore: Johns Hopkins UP, 1980.

Brooks, Peter. "An Unreadable Report: Conrad's *Heart of Darkness.*" *Reading for the Plot: Design and Intention in Narrative.* New York: Knopf, 1984.

Mansell, Darrell. "Trying to Bring Literature Back Alive: The Ivory in Joseph Conrad's *Heart of Darkness.*" *Criticism* 33 (1991): 205–15.

Miller, J. Hillis. "*Heart of Darkness* Revisited." *Joseph Conrad, "Heart of Darkness."* Ed. Ross C Murfin. 2nd ed. Case Studies in Contemporary Criticism. Boston: Bedford–St. Martin's, 1996.

Pecora, Vincent. "The Sounding Empire: Conrad's *Heart of Darkness.*" *Self and Form in Modern Narrative.* Baltimore: Johns Hopkins UP, 1989.

A DECONSTRUCTIVE PERSPECTIVE

J. HILLIS MILLER

Sharing Secrets

The moment of decision is a madness.
                                    –KIERKEGAARD

In an often quoted statement Conrad said, "My task which I am trying to achieve is, by the power of the written word, to make you hear, to make you feel—it is, before all, to make you *see*." What most immediately strikes the reader of "The Secret Sharer" is Conrad's extraordinary descriptive power. Conrad excels in what might be called a force not so much of representation as of presentation. He can use words to make things present. From the opening depiction of the Gulf of Siam as seen from a ship anchored at sunset off the mouth of the Meinam River all the way through to the climactic account of the ship's agonizingly slow reversal of direction just before it goes aground on Koh-ring Island, the reader is made almost to feel that he or she has been there and has had these experiences. The fact that the topographical names are of real places reinforces this verisimilitude.

This representational vividness is not limited to the outward appearances of sea and sky or the details of seafaring. Conrad succeeds also in making the reader feel as if he or she has been, so to speak, inside the narrator's skin and has experienced all of his subjective feelings as well as seen what he saw. The reader becomes the sharer of the narrator's secret feelings, just as the narrator says he was able to put himself inside Leggatt's feelings and thoughts when Leggatt told how he killed an insolent seaman: "I did not think of asking him for details, and he told me the story roughly in brusque, disconnected sentences. I needed no more. I saw it all going on as though I were myself inside that other sleeping-suit" (31).

"To make you *see*," as you can see, has a double meaning. It can refer to physical seeing or to seeing in the sense of having an intimate understanding, as when someone says, "Now I see." Seeing names not just detached vision from the outside. It also names a penetrating vision that gets inside what might be thought of as impenetrably hidden within the other person. Narration as the sharing of secrets might be an alternative way to express what Conrad means by saying he wants "to make you *see*." If Leggatt shares his secret with the narrator, the narrator shares the secret again, along with his own secrets (at least some of them), with the reader. The narrator's understanding of Leggatt occurs to a considerable degree by a wordless telepathy that has its uncanny side. The reader in turn is asked to understand things that, as in most works of fiction, are only implied, not fully spelled out. We are invited to have the kind of telepathic understanding of the narrator that the narrator has of Leggatt.

Just what it might mean to share a secret, or what kind of secret it is that can be shared, remains to be seen. It would seem that a kept secret would need to be kept jealously. An "open secret" is not really a secret, as the oxymoronic phrase implies. Nevertheless, "The Secret Sharer" depends on the assumption that some secrets can be shared without ceasing to be secret. The story suggests, moreover, that such sharing does more than impart knowledge; it also lays on the one who receives the secret an obligation, a responsibility to judge, to decide, to act. The narrator of "The Secret Sharer," for example, must decide whether to hide the fugitive Leggatt or to turn him over to the law as embodied in the captain of the *Sephora*, Leggatt's ship.[1] Moreover, he must do this instantaneously, precipitously, as is the case generally with ethical decisions. He does not have time to think it all out and weigh the pros and cons. Once he has decided and has hidden Leggatt in his cabin, he cannot go back on his decision, since to do so would be to admit his own guilt, his complicity in Leggatt's crime.[2] Even if he had infinite leisure to think over what he should do, his

---

[1] In *Under Western Eyes,* the composition of which Conrad interrupted in order to write "The Secret Sharer," the same situation is presented with a reverse outcome. Whereas the narrator of "The Secret Sharer" hides and protects Leggatt, in *Under Western Eyes* the hardworking ambitious student, Razumov, turns the revolutionary Victor Haldin over to the police when Haldin comes to his room seeking asylum after having assassinated an official of the repressive czarist regime. It seems as if Conrad was compelled to write the same story twice with opposite choices by the person on whom another person makes a demand.

[2] The alert reader will note the doubling of two letters that turns *legate* (meaning emissary, as in "papal legate"; it comes from the Latin *legare,* to depute, commission, charge) into a proper name: Leggatt. The pronunciation would be the same. The doubling of letters is not only another example of the doubling that is ubiquitous in the story, but by way of the pun on *legate* also defines Leggatt as an emissary of some sort and the narrator as the recipient or legatee of a charge transmitted to him by Leggatt. This legacy passes to readers of the story, or rather to me as a solitary reader, who must take sole responsibility for what I make of the story. *Legate, legacy,* and so on, are related etymologically to words like *legal* and *legislate* (from Latin *lex*) that have to do with lawmaking, law-giving. In some obscure way, Leggatt comes to the narrator bearing a legacy that has the force of law.

final decision would be precipitate, an interruption, irruptive, since a just, ethical decision can never be clearly made on the basis of pre-existing rules or laws. It is a leap in the dark, always at least implicitly violent, like Leggatt's murderous attack on the mutinous seaman, or his spontaneous decision to leap into the water off the deck of the *Sephora* — "Then a sudden temptation came over me. I kicked off my slippers and was in the water before I had made up my mind fairly (36)[3] — or like the narrator's decision to hide Leggatt. We must, therefore, pass judgment not only on Leggatt but also on the narrator. Does he do right or wrong in hiding the fugitive murderer Leggatt? On what basis does he make that decision? On what basis should we judge him?

What should *we* do, if anything, after we have read "The Secret Sharer"? Reading the story is a little like having our privacy invaded, just as Leggatt invades the narrator's privacy when he suddenly and unexpectedly enters his life. It puts on us an obligation to act in some way, but to act how? What should we do? Or, rather, what should *I* do, since the act of reading is a personal, individual, and secret event? Others can see that I hold the book in my hands and am running my eyes from line to line, but my thoughts and feelings are hidden, unless I choose to make them public, to bring them out into the open. In the same way, the narrator's story would have remained secret if he had not chosen to write it down and publish it so all the world might read it. My reading of "The Secret Sharer" would also remain secret unless I were to decide to talk about my reading, to teach the story, or to write an essay about it, such as this one. I have then told my own se-cret and have submitted my judgment of the story to the judgment of others. Literature, particularly storytelling in literature, as well as teaching and writing about literature, seem to have something essen-tially to do with the sharing of secrets.

To apply that notion here, however, raises some puzzling ques-tions. To whom is the narrator of "The Secret Sharer" speaking, or to whom or for whom is he writing? In other works by Conrad, for ex-ample *Lord Jim* or *Heart of Darkness,* an elaborate fiction gives the

[3]Readers of Conrad's *Lord Jim* will juxtapose Leggatt's jump to Jim's quite differ-ent jump from the *Patna.* Jim abandons the ship with all its passengers, the one thing a ship's officer is not supposed to do. "I had jumped . . . It seems," says Jim, as if it were an event that was not the result of conscious decision and that he cannot now even re-member. Nevertheless, he is held accountable for it by the law and disgraced for life as punishment for his act. How should we hold Leggatt accountable for the determining acts of *his* life?

narrator a name (Marlow) and a distinct individuality. These novels put the narrator in a described situation. They show him telling the story to specified auditors, motivated to do so by a particular demand for narration. All that specificity is missing in "The Secret Sharer." The story just begins. It starts with an abrupt sentence in the first person, past tense. This sentence transports the reader to a place and to an event that took place at some unidentified time in the past, though we are told later in the story that it was years earlier. "On my right hand there were lines of fishing-stakes resembling a mysterious system of half-submerged bamboo fences. . . ." To whom is the narrator addressing these words? Are we to imagine him as speaking or as writing? Where? When? Since no time, no situation of narration, and no specific auditors are given, it might even be possible to imagine that the narrator is talking to himself. He may be remembering these events in an inward musing reminiscence that we as readers have magically been given the power to overhear. It might be said that "The Secret Sharer," in its lack of a circumstantial accounting for its coming into existence, exposes the dependence of any confession on some external, technological device, some means of recording or inscription. A confession I make to myself is not a confession. Unless this story had been written down and published by a relay of handwriting, typesetting, and printing, it would have remained secret. It needs also to be remembered that "The Secret Sharer" is a fictive confession, a story that Conrad has made up. The only access to the secrets the story tells is by way of the story itself. If all copies of the story were to vanish, so too would vanish any means of reaching the secret it tells (or perhaps does not tell—that remains to be seen).

The narrator's confession, however, is curiously incomplete. Neither the narrator nor the ship he commands are given names. Those names are kept secret, whereas the name of the man he hides in his cabin is given, "Leggatt," along with the name of his ship, the "*Sephora*," and a possible name for its captain, "Archbold." The carefully guarded namelessness of the narrator and of his ship means that the narrator has confessed without confessing, since we can hardly hold him publicly responsible or haul him before the law if we do not even know his name, the exact date of the events, the name of his ship, and so on. In a court of law, such details would have been obtained first of all.

Nor will it do to assume that the story is straightforwardly autobiographical. We cannot take it for granted that the name of the narrator is the same as the name of the author on the title page: Joseph Conrad. We know from external biographical evidence that the events narrated in "The Secret Sharer" did not, so far as anyone knows, happen to Conrad, though they were based in part on real events that happened to other people.[4] But Conrad has apparently made up the central episode: the hiding of the fugitive. Or, to put this another way, absolutely no verification of this aspect of the tale exists. It is an impenetrable secret. Who knows? Maybe something of the sort did happen to Conrad back in the 1880s and he kept it secret all those years, until he wrote the story in 1910. The story itself is the only evidence we have, and it is no evidence one way or the other, since a work of fiction proves nothing about the historical existence of the things it names.

On the other hand, it may be that the best self-portrait is the portrait of another. An author is always revealing secrets about himself, even when he tells the stories of people most unlike himself. This idea would parallel the way the narrator of "The Secret Sharer," in spite of strongly identifying himself with Leggatt as his secret self, his double, his alter ego, nevertheless insists that "[h]e was not a bit like me, really" (34). In any case, the narrator of "The Secret Sharer" jealously preserves the situation of isolation from human judgment he describes at the beginning of the tale: "In this breathless pause at the threshold of a long passage we [he and his ship] seemed to be measuring our fitness for a long and arduous enterprise, the appointed task of both our existences to be carried out, far from all human eyes, with only sky and sea for spectators and for judges" (25). The narrator will be judged only by the sky and sea. In the same way, Leggatt refuses to be judged by the appointed civil authorities. "But you don't see me coming back to explain such things to an old fellow in a wig and twelve respectable tradesmen, do you?" he scornfully asks. "What can they know whether I am guilty or not—or of *what* I am guilty, either?" (52). The narrator at no point asks for an exonerating judgment from the reader. He says he wants only sky and sea for spectators and judges. Even so, by telling the story, he breaks that isolation, "far from all human eyes," though he does not tell us his name or the name of his ship. If we readers are only by accident, so to speak, overhearing the narrator musing to himself, that means we have been made stand-ins for the sky and sea, the real spectators and judges. The narrator, like Leggatt, has sidestepped the officially empowered legal authorities. He has gone over their heads to appeal first to the sky and sea and then indirectly, perhaps

[4]The best account of the factual background of "The Secret Sharer" is in Norman Sherry's "'The Secret Sharer': The Basic Fact of the Tale" (253–69).

even inadvertently, to us the readers, or rather to me as reader, since my reading is, at least initially, solitary and remains solitary unless I choose to reveal it to others.

You can see that "The Secret Sharer" is a curious form of testimony, witness, or deposition. The reader is implicitly put in the position of judge or jury. The phrase referring to the sky and sea as spectators and judges invites the reader to think of his or her duty as going beyond spectatorship to judgment. We must pass judgment on Leggatt. Was he justified in strangling the mutinous crewman or was it unjustified manslaughter, voluntary or involuntary? What should his punishment be? We must also pass judgment on the narrator. Did he do right or wrong in harboring the fugitive murderer, Leggatt? Is he fit for the command of a ship on a long and arduous voyage? The narrator's anxiety about whether he is fit to command is a primary motif in the story, as in other stories and novels by Conrad, such as "The Shadow Line," "Typhoon," or *The Nigger of the "Narcissus."* The narrator tells us that he was "untried as yet by a position of the fullest responsibility," and he says, "I wondered how far I should turn out faithful to that ideal conception of one's own personality every man sets up for himself secretly" (26).[5] Here is another form of doubling, not that of the narrator by Leggatt, but an internal doubling whereby the narrator is doubled by his ideal image of himself. That other self, not any external code, presides over his self-evaluation. It may be that for the narrator Leggatt is no more than a fortuitous external representation of that hidden secret self, that ideal conception of himself to which he must be faithful.

It is not certain beforehand how best to read "The Secret Sharer." Only an actual reading will tell, one that starts (as always should be the case) with questions. Let me begin at the beginning, with the title. It seems transparent enough, but just what does it mean? To whom or to what in the story does it refer? Like all titles, it functions as a clue. It is, the reader assumes, a synecdochic summing up in which the part stands for the whole and is presumably like the whole. A reader asks, "Why did he call it this?" A title is outside what it names, an alien or stranger to the text that may conceivably be related to it only ironically; and at the same time a title is part of the text, a member of the family of terms we use to understand it. A title is outside and inside at once. In "The Secret Sharer," though not of course with all works, the

[5]See Byron James Caminero-Santangelo's *Failing the Test: Narration and Legitimation in the Work of Joseph Conrad.*

title is actually repeated inside the story. The phrase is used more than once to define Leggatt when the narrator is hiding him in his cabin. He calls Leggatt early in the story "the secret sharer of my life" (40), then, soon after, "the secret sharer of my cabin" (43), and in its last sentence "the secret sharer of my cabin and of my thoughts" (60).

What is a secret sharer? A secret *sharer*? A *secret* sharer? A different meaning arises depending on which word is stressed. If *sharer* is stressed, *secret* is an adjective modifying *sharer*. Leggatt secretly shares the narrator's cabin, lives there with him, shares his thoughts. If *secret* is stressed, *secret* is a noun and *sharer* is another noun. Leggatt is someone who shares a secret or secrets. But does the title name only Leggatt? Its use as a title that sums up the whole story invites the reader to look for a wider reference. Does the narrator not, as I have already suggested, share Leggatt's secret when Leggatt tells his story, and then share it again with the reader in telling his story? Just what is a secret, if there is such a thing? If there is such a thing, can it be shared? Does it remain a secret when it has been shared? Is there such a thing as a shared secret? Does it not cease to be secret when it is shared? What does it mean to speak of a secret as "shared"? Divided, cut in two? As when we speak of a shared meal? All these questions are raised by an attempt to decide the exact force of the title. *Shared* is related in meaning and etymology to *sheared,* as a ploughshare cuts the furrow, dividing the earth. To share something usually means to cut it into at least two pieces, though it can also mean "to have in common," as when we say, "They shared a bed." A secret, it would seem, cannot be cut in two in this way. It is an indivisible whole, like a single person, is it not? When a secret becomes an open secret, shared promiscuously, it is hardly a secret any longer. Anyone with some small experience of life knows that when you say, "I'll tell you a secret, if you promise to keep it," you might as well be shouting it from the housetops or printing it on the front page of the *New York Times.*

As Jacques Derrida has recently demonstrated (in *Passions,* in *Given Time, I: Counterfeit Money,* and in a series of admirable seminars), a true secret, if there is such a thing, cannot be revealed. If it can be revealed it is not really a secret, or to put this another way, one must distinguish between those quasi-secrets that can be revealed, such as state secrets or secret recipes, and other more secret secrets that cannot by any means be revealed. Does "The Secret Sharer" hide a secret of that sort? What would the traces or marks of such a secret be? Even if it is an unpresentable and unrevealable secret, we would not know of its existence unless it manifested itself in indirect signs of some sort announcing its hidden existence. Something must say, "There is a secret there." That announcement would give another reading of the title. To share a secret might not mean to share it with another person, but to participate in the secret, to be subject to its force, even though the secret as such cannot be revealed. What would then be passed on from Leggatt to the narrator is not some identifiable secret that can be revealed but subjection to the irresistible force of a secret that cannot be revealed but that nevertheless imposes a pitiless obligation on those who come to be subject to it, to share in it.[6] There seems little we would like to know about "The Secret Sharer," however, that we cannot know. It seems as if the narrator tells all. He shares all the secrets with the reader. What remains still secret at the end of the story?

For one thing, the narrator's testimony is incomplete. He seems reluctant to tell us everything. If I were a lawyer for the prosecution I would have a few questions to ask him, beyond asking him to tell me his name, the name of his ship, and a few more particulars in the way of dates and facts. For example, the reader can never know Archbold's version of the murder (if Archbold is really his name), since the narrator explicitly refuses to give it: " . . . he had to raise his voice to give me his tale. It is not worth while to record that version" (42). Why not? One would have thoughts Archbold to be a valuable additional witness. Certainly he would have been called on in a court of law to tell his story. The narrator seems so certain that Leggatt told the truth that he discounts any other version. In doing so, he does keep a secret from the reader, a secret he or she can never know.

As a matter of fact, the narrator gives the reader the essence of Archbold's interpretation of what happened: Archbold sees the events as evidence of God's providence, not (as Leggatt sees them) as evidence of Leggatt's bravery in setting the reefed foresail in the midst of a terrible storm. "God's own hand in it," says Archbold. "Nothing less could have done it. I don't mind telling you that I hardly dared give the order" (43). Leggatt insists that his captain gave no such order, that he, Leggatt, acted on his own and saved the ship, just as he justifiably (or so he believes) took the law into his own hands when he killed the mutinous crewman. The latter was an "ill-conditioned snarling cur" (31). It might be noted that a few lines later Leggatt himself becomes doglike when he takes the crewman by the neck and "shak[es]

---

[6] I owe this reading of "secret sharer" to Kevin Yee.

him like a rat" (32). This doubling is redoubled much later when the narrator shakes the chief mate to get him to tend to the head-sheets when they are about to go aground: "'You go forward'—shake—'and stop there'—shake—'and hold your noise'—shake—'and see these head-sheets properly overhauled'—shake, shake—shake" (58). Leggatt obscurely doubles the rebellious crewman, as the narrator doubles Leggatt. Like the crewman, both Leggatt and the narrator transgress against convention or law. The covert similarity is hidden by the narrator's strong endorsement of Leggatt's judgment that the crewman was one of those "miserable devils that have no business to live at all. He wouldn't do his duty and wouldn't let anybody else do theirs." The narrator agrees. He tells the reader, "I knew well enough the pestiferous danger of such a character where there are no means of legal repression" (31). Readers of *The Nigger of the "Narcissus"* will remember the sullen, resentful, and mean-spirited Donkin: another Conradian character who malingers, complains, and refuses to do his duty.

What the narrator says of the crewman Leggatt kills would seem to support the idea that Conrad is an archconservative spokesperson for British ideas of hierarchy, duty, fidelity, imperial responsibility, the white man's burden, and so on, with the overtones of sexism and racism that are associated with such allegiances. Conrad's narrator asserts that onboard ship "there are no means of legal repression." In order to preserve the laws of duty, obedience, and so on, someone must act against the law, outside the law, in a strange kind of unlawful law-preserving or law-establishing violence.[7] "The Secret Sharer," in its confrontation of his disquieting aspect of the law, in particular law onboard ship, is analogous to Herman Melville's *Billy Budd*. To read them side by side would be instructive.

It is not exactly the case, however, that at sea "there are no means of legal repression": as the captain of the *Sephora* says to Leggatt, "I represent the law here" (35). A ship's captain is not the law, but he represents the law. This situation, however, is also the case onshore. The law is never present in person, but only in its representatives: the police, a lawyer, a judge, a jury. The whole apparatus of the law is not the law itself but a representation of another law. Thus the narrator's claim that there are no means of legal repression of an insubordinate

---

[7]See Walter Benjamin's "Critique of Violence" as the most troubling and searching investigation of this problem. See also Jacques Derrida's discussion of Benjamin's essay and related questions of the grounds of justice in "Force of Law: The 'Mystical Foundation of Authority.'"

crewman seems strangely problematic. Archbold, for example, does not hesitate to "arrest" Leggatt and keep him locked in his cabin.

In contrast to the narrator's judgment and Leggatt's self-evaluation, Archbold sees Leggatt as without question a murderer. He must be turned over "to the law" as soon as he can be got ashore. In fact Archbold is morbidly concerned with this responsibility: "His obscure tenacity on that point had in it something incomprehensible and a little awful; something, as it were, mystical. . . . Seven-and-thirty virtuous years at sea . . . seemed to have laid him under some pitiless obligation" (43). Why is this sense of obligation "incomprehensible," "awful," "mystical"? Perhaps because it is a sense of justice that leads beyond itself to injustice. It uses an appeal to law to justify the unjustified and unjustifiable. In any case, neither Leggatt nor the narrator feels that pitiless obligation. Their obligation is rather to their personal sense of justice, which may be equally incomprehensible, awful, even mystical (whatever Conrad may mean by such portentous terms). Which obligation should we credit? Which behavior should we approve of and imitate? Moral life is full of situations not entirely unlike Leggatt's or the narrator's. What would I have done in their places? What *should* I have done, and on the basis of what moral and public law, or secret and private one?

In order to try to formulate more exactly what might still be kept secret in the story, I turn now to its first paragraph. This paragraph is a striking example of the way the narrator's tale is not just objective description but at every turn a figurative transformation and an active intervention, as what I would call "rhetorical reading" must always be. The narrator's way with language gives the reader a model for his or her own activity. Along with the wonderfully vivid scene-setting that the opening paragraph has as its apparent main goal, it also unostentatiously sets up several other horizons of expectation that are crucial to the meaning of the narration that follows. First, it introduces the motif of doubling and redoubling. Second, it initiates the reader into a process whereby one thing stands for another or is like another. In this it serves as an introductory handbook on how to read parabolically. Third, it gives the reader the first example of something that is mysterious, incomprehensible—something not open to rational knowing. The very first sentence does all three of these things at once, besides being effective at making us *see:* "On my right hand there were lines of fishing-stakes resembling a mysterious system of half-submerged bamboo fences, incomprehensible in its division of the domain of tropical fishes, and crazy of aspect as if abandoned for ever by some nomad tribe of fishermen now gone to the other end of the ocean; for there was no sign of human habitation as far as the eye could reach" (24). This is an accurate description of a real place in the real world. It tells the reader that the water is quite shallow off the mouth of the River Meinam at the head of what used to be called the Gulf of Siam. And it tells us that there were bamboo fish weirs there, that is, fenced enclosures with narrow openings that trap schools of small fish when they swim in and cannot find their way out again. Such fish weirs, though not of bamboo, are still used in the shallow waters around Deer Isle, Maine, where I spend my summers. I have recently (in December 1994) seen such weirs, probably in this case of bamboo, in the shallow water on the western side of Taiwan, south of the city of Kaohsiung, much closer geographically to the ones Conrad describes than Deer Isle, Maine. Even though the narrator knows they are fish weirs, since he calls them "fishing-stakes," nevertheless he describes them (in a way that is characteristic of Conrad's art of description throughout his work) as if he does not quite understand them, as if they are "mysterious," "incomprehensible." They look like "half-submerged bamboo fences" whose purpose is inscrutable. Just as words can become strange, uncanny, when they are repeated over and over, so can ordinary things, when looked at in a certain way, seem to harbor some unfathomable secret, as the lives of the fishermen who made these "crazy" (in the sense of *dilapidated*, but also with a hint of *insane*) fish weirs is unknown. In a similar way, much later in the story, the narrator stresses what is mysterious about the human life on the islands where Leggatt is put ashore: "Unknown to trade, to travel, almost to geography, the manner of life they harbour is an unsolved secret" (53).[8]

The first sentence also introduces the theme of division, sharing, or doubling. The system of bamboo fences is incomprehensible in its *division* of the domain of tropical fishes. A little later in the paragraph, "two small clumps of trees, one on each side" of the river mouth are a small-scale doubling (24); another occurs when the narrator tells us that in the cuddy (that is, the room on the ship used as the officers' dining room), "two bunches of bananas hung from the beam symmetrically, one on each side of the rudder-casing." The next sentence makes explicit the parallel between the bananas and the doubling of the narrator by Leggatt: "two of [the] captain's sleeping-suits were simultaneously in use" (33).

---

[8] Since Conrad wrote this story, partly through colonization of the political or economic sort, partly through the work of many busy Western anthropologists, fewer and fewer places on the globe are unsolved secrets in this way.

To return to the first paragraph, the entire scene is later divided and then subdivided in a mirroring that anticipates and universalizes that of the two main characters. The narrator sees "the straight line of the flat shore joined to the stable sea, edge to edge, with a perfect and unmarked closeness . . ." (24). The doubling of shore and sea in its unmarked intimacy is like the intimate doubling of the narrator and Leggatt. What happens to the one seems almost to happen to the other. The narrator often feels he is outside himself and dwelling inside the skin or inside the sleeping-suit of the other man: "I was constantly watching myself, my secret self, as dependent on my actions as my own personality" (40); "That mental feeling of being in two places at once affected me physically as if the mood of secrecy had penetrated my very soul" (48). The doubling of sea and shore, that so distinctly anticipates the relation between the narrator and Leggatt, preparing the unaware reader, is doubled once more, however, in the description of the whole expanse of the earth, sea, and sky together. The great dome of the evening sky, an elemental and sublime[9] spectacle, doubles the sea and shore: "one levelled floor half brown, half blue under the enormous dome of the sky" (24).

Conrad's wording in this last phrase exemplifies another chief stylistic feature of this opening paragraph. It is a feature also present in Kant's celebrated example in *The Critique of Judgment* of the arching sky over the sea as, in its inhuman materiality, a correlate of sublime feelings. In Conrad as in Kant the sea and shore together become a "levelled floor" and the sky becomes a "dome." The whole scene becomes one gigantic architectural construction. It is as though it is not possible to confront directly a scene representing sublime feelings and then name it without turning its alien otherness into something more familiar and human, in this case a manmade dwelling. "Floor" and "dome" are examples of those original catachreses whereby we give

[9] I mean the word *sublime* in the strong, traditional sense of the word, as it is used from Longinus through Kant and Burke up to present-day theorists of the sublime such as Thomas Weiskel, Jean-François Lyotard, or Paul de Man. For all of these philosopher-critics the sublime, in one way or another, is a subjective feeling mingling fear and inordinate pleasure. Strictly speaking, no object is sublime, but the feeling of the sublime may be aroused or represented by some aspect of nature that exceeds human comprehension, something that is terrifying because it is unknown and unknowable. The sublime can only be named in figures that are illegitimate in the sense that they are not proper names and are not commensurate with the frightening unknowability they seek to make apparently nameable. An empty sea under the sky is one example Kant gives of the sublime, although like Conrad he sees this in architectural terms. It cannot be seen in its sheer materiality. See Paul de Man's "Phenomenality and Materiality in Kant."

names to what has no proper name and cover over what is wholly other by giving it familiar labels that make it seem something within which we can be at home.

This transformation of inhuman nature into the architectural human is present earlier in the paragraph when the narrator sees the "group of barren islets" as something "suggesting ruins of stone walls, towers, and blockhouses." The paragraph is a tissue of such comparisons. The fish weirs look "as if abandoned for ever by some nomad tribe of fishermen." Inland the curving river is intermittently visible in "gleams as of a few scattered pieces of silver," and the tug winding up that river eventually disappears "as though the impassive earth had swallowed her up without an effort, without a tremor." All these "as ifs," the reader can see, are humanizations of the inhuman nature they serve to name. The sky is like a dome, the sea and shore a floor. The islets are ruined buildings, the river is like silver coins, the earth is a huge beast that can swallow whole tugboats at a gulp. An imaginary narrative about nomad fishermen is invented to account for the crazy aspect of those fish weirs.

These figures show that the first paragraph—far from simply being wonderfully vivid description that makes the reader feel that he or she has been there—is the site of a strong verbal will to power on Conrad's part (or the narrator's part) which describes things by transforming them into something they are not. What might at first appear to be neutral description is a series of performative speech acts. These do not just describe. They posit. They do this on their own independent unauthorized say-so. In this they fulfill Aristotle's remark in the *Poetics* that a gift for metaphor is a mark of genius in a poet, the one thing he cannot learn from another (22.9.1459a).[10] It is as if the narrator were

---

[10]William Wordsworth, in the Preface of 1815, is true to Aristotle when he sees such metaphorical transformations as prime evidence of the poetic imagination. Speaking of the comparison of the old leech-gatherer in "Resolution and Independence" to a stone, a sea-beast, and a cloud, Wordsworth says, "In these images, the conferring, the abstracting, and the modifying powers of the Imagination, immediately and mediately acting, are all brought into conjunction. The stone is endowed with something of the power of life to approximate it to the sea-beast; and the sea-beast stripped of some of its vital qualities to assimilate it to the stone; which intermediate image is thus treated for the purpose of bringing the original image, that of the stone, to a nearer resemblance to the figure and condition of the aged Man; who is divested of so much of the indications of life and motion as to bring him to the point where the two objects unite and coalesce in just comparison. After what has been said, the image of the cloud need not be commented upon" (754). For Wordsworth, as for Conrad, the primary evidence of word power is the ability to use words in personifications of the inanimate and depersonifications of the animate.

saying, "Let these barren islets be seen as ruined towers, walls, and blockhouses . . ." and so on. If "The Secret Sharer" is obliquely the story of how the narrator grew up to the point where he was worthy of the solitude and independent responsibility of command, the verbal mastery of the first paragraph is evidence that he has long since achieved that right to command. He has command over words. He can use those words performatively to change what is there before him into something else: the sky into a dome, rocky islets into ruined cities, the sea and shore into a floor, the fish weirs into abandoned fences, the whole natural inhuman landscape into a humanized architectural scene of abandonment and desolation. What it might mean to say that these speech act transformations are unauthorized, or only secretly authorized, and how that might correspond to other unauthorized acts in the story remains to be seen.

One way to investigate this further is to recognize that the story throughout turns on a series of key words and word clusters that gain a peculiar meaning and force through repetition. Marvin Mudrick and other critics have objected to these repetitions, saying they are tedious and obvious. Such critics have missed the point. *Double, stranger, secret, ghostly, mysterious, conscience, understand*—the repetition of these words (and their variants) calls attention to them, singles them out by using them over and over in somewhat different verbal contexts. They thereby become strange, as any word does when it is repeated many times and its materiality, what gives it force, begins to show through its immaterial meaning: it becomes senseless sound or marks on the page.

The most salient example of this repetition is of the word *double,* though the same thing could be demonstrated with all the other words listed above: "In a moment he had concealed his damp body in a sleeping-suit of the same grey-stripe pattern as the one I was wearing and followed me like my double" (30); ". . . murmured my double, distinctly" (31); "My double gave me an inkling of his thoughts" (31); "My double there was no homicidal ruffian" (31); "he would think he was seeing double" (33); "My double followed my movements" (33); "anybody bold enough to open [the door] stealthily would have been treated to the uncanny sight of a double captain busy talking in whispers with his other self" (34); "My double breathed into my ear, anxiously" (37); "I took a peep at my double" (39) and so on and on, double after double, through many more doublings.

The careful reader will note that the word *double* appears first as an explicit trope, a simile. Dressed in a striped sleeping-suit like the one the narrator is wearing, Leggatt follows the narrator "*like* [his] double" (emphasis added). The first-time reader cannot tell at this point whether this is important or only a passing figure inserted for vividness. From then on, however, the simile, weakest of tropes, becomes a literal assertion. Leggatt is "my double," over and over again, as if the verbal similitude had the power to materialize itself. It is as though a simile could be a speech act, a way of doing things with words. It makes happen as literal fact what it initially names as an "as if." The insistent repetition matches the opening tropological transformations. It is another quite curious version of the performative will to power over words or the will to make use of words in acts of power.

The will in question is not that of a subjective ego in full possession of its free power of volition. The words rather seem to act on their own, or they promise to do so. Such word use is a process that creates the self. The narrator of "The Secret Sharer" ceases to be a stranger to himself and becomes worthy of command through his response to the demand made on him by Leggatt. That response operates through the narrative transformations that make up the verbal texture of "The Secret Sharer." The story does what it talks about.

Words repeated insistently, as they are by Conrad in this story, become detached, enigmatic. They seem to harbor a secret. The repetition of the key words makes them somehow uncanny. They become intruders into the sentences in which they are used so that they stand out rather than being fully assimilated into a local meaning.[11] In this they are like Leggatt himself, the ghostly guest who invades the narrator's ship as an alien presence. Such words in their repetition work as a repetitive speech act: *secret, secret, secret, secret; double, double, double, double;* in a mad and maddening refrain that has evidently much annoyed Mudrick and other such readers. They have not seen how the repetition mimes the story's central theme. The narrator himself more than once says that his sense of being double and living within two minds and bodies was almost a form of insanity: "all the time the dual working of my mind distracted me almost to the point of insanity" (40); "I think I had come creeping quietly as near insanity as any man

---

[11]William Carlos Williams long ago formulated this strange effect of certain word uses apropos of Marianne Moore's poetry, though with emphasis on the making material of words rather than on the uncanny draining away of meaning I am stressing. "Miss Moore," wrote Williams, "gets great pleasure from wiping soiled words or cutting them clean out, removing the aureoles that have been pasted about them or taking them bodily from greasy contexts. For the compositions which Miss Moore intends, each word should first stand crystal clear with no attachments; not even an aroma" (128).

who has not actually gone over the border" (51). To be of two minds, to be subject to a doubling repetition, is to be on the brink of insanity.

The collective force of this cluster of words, as they are repeated again and again in different combinations, is to make of the story a large-scale version of the kind of transformation effected by the performative tropes in the first paragraph. The scene of sea, sky, islets, and shore is turned into a sublimely desolate architectural construction; the literal story of the narrator's harboring a fugitive murderer is changed by the narrator's language into an uncanny story of doubling and repetition. The narrator's performative positings turn objective description into a testimony or confession addressed to me as reader. With the narrator's intervention, the episode becomes what it was not in itself: a narrative of the invasion of a safe domicile by a ghostly stranger who upsets the familiar economy of that home and puts a terrible burden of responsibility on its inhabitant. This is the traditional mission of such ghostly invaders in older versions of this narrative, as in "Sir Gawain and the Green Knight."

Sigmund Freud, citing Schelling, defines *uncanny* (*unheimlich*) as "the name for everything that ought to have remained . . . hidden and secret and has become visible" (27). Freud's essay is inexhaustibly rich and complex, not least in its contradictions. This is not the place to try to read it in detail. The word *uncanny* appears once in Conrad's story: anyone coming in "would have been treated to the uncanny sight of a double captain busy talking in whispers with his other self." In many ways, moreover, the story corresponds to key aspects of Freud's examples of the uncanny. Not only is doubling in itself uncanny (as are other forms of repetition) according to Freud, but Freud also stresses the gruesome aspects of the uncanny and their relation to sexual mutilation, as well as to ghost effects and to the invasion of the home by a spooky personage who represents something familiar that ought to be kept secret.

Leggatt appears first as a seemingly headless corpse in the water, "ghastly, silvery, fish-like" (29). Once he is hidden in the narrator's cabin he becomes a phantom presence there, attired "in the ghostly grey of [his] sleeping-suit" (31). That doubling presence makes "a scene of weird witchcraft; the strange captain having a quiet confabulation . . . with his own grey ghost" (33). At one point, the narrator says, "an irresistible doubt of his bodily existence flitted through my mind. Can it be, I asked myself, that he is not visible to other eyes than mine? It was like being haunted" (51). The narrator's success in keeping Leggatt hidden raises the question of whether others can see him at all.

The English word *uncanny* does not of course fully translate the German word *unheimlich*. Both, however, are double antithetical words. *Uncanny* comes from *can*, to know how, be able. *Canny* means not only shrewd, but "susceptible of human understanding; explicable; natural," whereas *uncanny* is the opposite: "exciting wonder and fear: inexplicable; strange, as in 'an uncanny laugh.'" But the second meaning of *uncanny* shows that it is not so much the opposite of *canny* as it is canny knowledge and insight carried to that hyperbolic point where it reverses itself and becomes uncanny: "so keen and perceptive as to seem preternatural, as in 'uncanny insight.'"[12] In the same way, as any reader of Freud's essay knows, the word *unheimlich* is uncanny in that it too reverses itself and comes to mean not something alien to the home, unhomey, but precisely something familiar to the home, a home secret that ought to have been kept hidden, but has come out of the closet, so to speak. "Thus 'heimlich,'" says Freud, "is a word the meaning of which develops towards an ambivalence, until it finally coincides with its opposite, 'unheimlich.' 'Unheimlich' is in some way or other a sub-species of 'heimlich'" (30). Understanding the uncanny means comprehending the incomprehensible, since the uncanny is by definition strange, inexplicable. If the reader has "The Secret Sharer" in mind, he or she will remember both the emphasis on what is mysterious and indescribable about Leggatt for the narrator and the counterstress on the total understanding that the narrator and Leggatt have of one another. Of Leggatt's story the narrator says, "There was something that made comment impossible in his narrative, or perhaps in himself; a sort of feeling, a quality, which I can't find a name for" (36). Naming is here opposed to wordless understanding. Though he cannot name it, he can understand it, as their ultimate exchange of affirmations asserts: "I understand"; "I only hope I have understood, too"; "You have. From first to last" (55).

The "individual instances" of the *unheimlich* Freud examines depend in large part on a resource of the German word not present in the English one. *Heim* means *home* in German. The group of *heim* words, including *unheimlich,* is associated with family relationships and with the domestic economy of the house — its division into separate rooms devoted to different uses; its doors, windows, closets, walls, and gates. The English word *uncanny* does not overtly have such associations. Freud's discussion of E. T. A. Hoffmann's "Sandman" is his most extended investigation of uncanny literary works. Conrad's story

---

[12]These definitions are drawn from *The American Heritage Dictionary*.

is also an admirable exploitation of the relation of the uncanny to the home and to the opposition between belonging to the home, being a familiar there, and being a stranger. A ship is like a large home with many rooms. The crew is, in a manner of speaking, one big family. The narrator stresses how they all know one another. He is the only stranger. He is an alien guest who nevertheless swells within the heart of the home, the captain's quarters, and has a right to be there. Leggatt enters the captain's quarters as the double of the narrator's strangeness, an inner strangeness within what is already strange.

Just what is the uncanny secret that is as familiar as one's own private part of the house? It must be a secret that is in danger of being exposed, or rather that is apparently exposed by the captain's narration though it ought to remain hidden, or perhaps still does remain hidden after all the narrator's confessional openness. The secret can hardly be Leggatt's act of murder, since that is known by all onboard the *Sephora*. It will ultimately be known to sailors all over that part of the world. The secret must be the narrator's complicity in that murder, his doubling of Leggatt's act by harboring him, and, the most hidden secret, the secret behind the secret: the occult ground or obligation that justifies that act and makes it the right thing to do.

Conrad repeatedly emphasizes the similarity between the narrator and Leggatt in their propensity to lawless transgression and consequent guilt. This similarity is most overt when the narrator's sense of identity with Leggatt makes him feel guilty too when Archbold comes seeking Leggatt: "I felt as if I, personally, were being given to understand that I, too, was not the sort that would have done for the chief mate of a ship like the *Sephora*. I had no doubt of it in my mind" (43); "I believe that he [Archbold] was not a little disconcerted by the reverse side of that weird situation, by something in me that . . . suggested a mysterious similitude to the young fellow he had distrusted and disliked from the first" (44). That "mysterious similitude" can be identified, at least in part. Both Leggatt and the narrator have the same social and class background. Both have been trained in the same naval school in preparation for assuming the loneliness of command and the responsibility of independent decision; such training was an essential part of the formation of those Englishmen who once dominated so much of the world. Both have taken the law into their own hands. Both have made an instantaneous decision or series of decisions that reaffirms the law by transgressing the law. Leggatt has killed an insubordinate crewman in order to save his ship in the storm and in order to maintain the hierarchy of command that is essential onboard ship. He has preserved law and order where, according to the narrator, "no means of legal repression" were available. The narrator has, in a spontaneous decision, repeated the murderer's crime by hiding him. In doing so he becomes an accessory after the fact, liable to the same punishment as Leggatt himself might receive from the law. Already the narrator has transgressed the ship's normal rules by taking the nighttime anchor watch himself. He doubles both of those transgressions again at the end of the story when he brings the ship dangerously close to shore, risking his ship and horrifying the crew, in order, on his "conscience," to bring Leggatt as close to shore as he can. The whole force of the story implies that these transgressions are absolutely necessary to make the narrator worthy of command. Only through those acts can he, at the end of the story, leave Leggatt "to take his punishment: a free man, a proud swimmer striking out for a new destiny." This separation allows the narrator to replace the homosocial relation to Leggatt with the heterosexual relation to his ship, which means he is no longer a stranger aboard: "Already the ship was drawing ahead. And I was alone with her. Nothing! no one in the world should stand now between us, throwing a shadow on the way of silent knowledge and mute affection, the perfect communion of a seaman with his first command" (59).

"The Secret Sharer" shows that law and order, the justice that validates command and hierarchy, cannot be maintained by the simple reaffirmation of rules and conventions that are already in place and remain in place. That justice must be periodically interrupted by some decisive act that reaffirms the law by breaking the law. Such an irruptive act always has something violent, dangerous, or illicit about it. Its emblems in "The Secret Sharer" are Leggatt's act of murder and the narrator's secret hiding of Leggatt. The ground for such acts remains secret. It is felt only by those on whom it imposes a "pitiless obligation," though that ground is absolutely compelling in the responsibility it lays on the one who receives its commands.

Conrad's name for this command is a traditional one, "conscience," twice repeated as the name for what drives the narrator to go so close to the shore: "It was now a matter of conscience to shave the land as close as possible" (56); hidden in the sail locker Leggatt was "able to hear everything—and perhaps he was able to understand why, on my conscience, it had to be thus close—no less" (58). In a brilliant recent book on Shakespeare, *Daemonic Figures*, Ned Lukacher has shown how the word *conscience* is at the confluence of the two great lines of the Western tradition: the Socratic and Hellenic tradition of the daemon, who commands me to act in a certain way, and the Christian tradition of the still small voice of conscience, the voice of God within the soul that imposes an implacable obligation to act in a certain way in witness of the truth, even if it is against the law. An example of the latter is the appeal to conscience by English Protestants under Catholic rule during the reign of Mary Tudor. They refused in the name of conscience to recant, even when that refusal meant they would be burned at the stake. In their case, as when the narrator risks his ship and all aboard, the call of conscience is stronger even than the wish to live, stronger than the appeal of any established law.[13]

The law can be preserved and reaffirmed only by acts that are apparently against the law. The ground for these acts remains private, hidden, secret, apparent only to those who are sensitive to it, who hear its call. It is apparent even then only in its inapparency. It is something that I cannot show to others, something that is, strictly speaking, unpresentable, unrepresentable, just as the narrator cannot find a word for that "sort of feeling, a quality" he senses in Leggatt. But if this secret ground of law-preserving and law-affirming transgression cannot be presented, it can be passed on to those who are fit to "understand," as the narrator understands Leggatt. It can be transmitted in a narration like "The Secret Sharer" that makes its demand on the reader for a similar understanding. The ultimate secret of "The Secret Sharer" remains a secret, but that by no means deprives it of power.

Near the beginning of this essay I asked, "Did the narrator do right or wrong in hiding the fugitive murderer Leggatt? On what basis did he make that decision? On what basis should we judge him?" Now I am in a position to answer those questions, after a fashion. Yes, he did right, he acted justly, but we cannot know the ground of that rightness and justice. We can only feel or "understand" its effect in another doubling—or perhaps, on the contrary, not feel it. (That cannot be known beforehand or safely predicted for a given reader.) The story itself gives the reader a model of an inaugural act that responds to a secret demand. The story is a violent tropological transformation that turns "the basic fact of the tale" into a story of testing and testimony. What led Conrad to make this transformation cannot be known. It remains secret. The basis of ethical decisions and acts, including the act of writing or reading, is the ultimate secret, the most secret secret.

---

[13]I owe the example of the Protestants' appeal to conscience in sixteenth-century England to an admirable lecture by Steven Mullaney, "Reforming Resistance: Class, Gender, and Legitimacy in Foxe's *Book of Martyrs*."

This secret cannot be revealed. It is not the object of a possible clear knowledge. Nevertheless, it is a secret I can share, though it remains secret. This secret can only be passed on to me as an obscure but commanding force that comes from something absolutely other. If it cannot be named, it can nevertheless be made into a story and so transferred to me when I read it as another strong demand for response and taking responsibility. An example of such a response would be teaching "The Secret Sharer" or writing an essay about it, such as this one.

WORKS CITED

Benjamin, Walter. "Critique of Violence." *Reflections: Essays, Aphorisms, Autobiographical Writings.* Trans. Edmund Jephcott. New York: Harcourt, 1978. 277–300.

Butcher, S. H. *Aristotle's Theory of Poetry and Fine Art, with a Critical Text and Translation of the Poetics.* New York: Dover, 1951. 87.

Caminero-Santangelo, Byron James. *Failing the Test: Narration and Legitimation in the Work of Joseph Conrad.* Diss. U of California, Irvine, 1993. Ann Arbor: UMI, 1993.

Conrad, Joseph. Preface. *The Nigger of the "Narcissus."* Garden City: Doubleday, 1959.

de Man, Paul. "Phenomenality and Materiality in Kant." *Hermeneutics: Questions and Prospects.* Ed. Gary Shapiro and Alan Sica. Amherst: U of Massachusetts P, 1984. 121–144.

Derrida, Jacques. "Force of Law: The 'Mystical Foundation of Authority'." Trans. Mary Quaintance. *Deconstruction and the Possibility of Justice.* Ed. Drucilla Cornell, Michel Rosenfeld, and David Gray Carlson. New York and London: Routledge, 1992. 3–67.

Freud, Sigmund. "The Uncanny." *Studies in Parapsychology.* New York: Collier, 1971.

Lukacher, Ned. *Daemonic Figures: Shakespeare and the Question of Conscience.* Ithaca, NY: Cornell UP, 1994.

Mullaney, Steven. "Reforming Resistance: Class, Gender, and Legitimacy in Foxe's *Book of Martyrs.*" University of California, Irvine. 13 Jan. 1995.

Sherry, Norman. "'The Secret Sharer': The Basic Fact of the Tale." *Conrad's Eastern World.* Cambridge: Cambridge UP, 1966. 253–69.

Williams, William Carlos. *Selected Essays.* New York: Random, 1954.

Wordsworth, William. *Poetical Works.* Ed. Thomas Hutchinson and Ernest de Selincourt. London: Oxford UP, 1966.

Glossary of Critical
and Theoretical Terms

Most terms have been glossed parenthetically where they first appear in the text. Mainly, the glossary lists terms that are too complex to define in a phrase or a sentence or two. A few of the terms listed are discussed at greater length elsewhere (*feminist criticism,* for instance); these terms are defined succinctly, and a page reference to the longer discussion is provided.

AFFECTIVE FALLACY   First used by William K. Wimsatt and Monroe C. Beardsley to refer to what they regarded as the erroneous practice of interpreting texts according to the psychological responses of readers. "The Affective Fallacy," they wrote in a 1946 essay later republished in *The Verbal Icon* (1954), "is a confusion between the poem and its *results* (what it *is* and what it *does*). . . . It begins by trying to derive the standards of criticism from the psychological effects of a poem and ends in impressionism and relativism." The affective fallacy, like the intentional fallacy (confusing the meaning of a work with the author's expressly intended meaning), was one of the main tenets of the New Criticism, or formalism. The affective fallacy has recently been contested by reader-response critics, who have deliberately dedicated their efforts to describing the way individual readers and "interpretive communities" go about "making sense" of texts.

See also: Authorial Intention, Formalism, Reader-Response Criticism.

AUTHORIAL INTENTION   Defined narrowly, an author's intention in writing a work, as expressed in letters, diaries, interviews, and conversations. Defined more broadly, "intentionality" involves unexpressed motivations, designs, and purposes, some of which may have remained unconscious.

The debate over whether critics should try to discern an author's intentions (conscious or otherwise) is an old one. William K. Wimsatt and

Monroe C. Beardsley, in an essay first published in the 1940s, coined the term "intentional fallacy" to refer to the practice of basing interpretations on the expressed or implied intentions of authors, a practice they judged to be erroneous. As proponents of the New Criticism, or formalism, they argued that a work of literature is an object in itself and should be studied as such. They believed that it is sometimes helpful to learn what an author intended, but the critic's real purpose is to show what is actually in the text, not what an author intended to put there.

See also: Affective Fallacy, Formalism.

BASE   *See* Marxist Criticism.

BINARY OPPOSITIONS   *See* Oppositions.

BLANKS   *See* Gaps.

CANON   Since the fourth century, used to refer to those books of the Bible that the Christian church accepts as being Holy Scripture. The term has come to be applied more generally to those literary works given special status, or "privileged," by a culture. Works we tend to think of as "classics" or the "Great Books" produced by Western culture—texts that are found in every anthology of American, British, and world literature—would be among those that constitute the canon.

Recently, Marxist, feminist, minority, and postcolonial critics have argued that, for political reasons, many excellent works never enter the canon. Canonized works, they claim, are those that reflect—and respect—the culture's dominant ideology and/or perform some socially acceptable or even necessary form of "cultural work." Attempts have been made to broaden or redefine the canon by discovering valuable texts, or versions of texts, that were repressed or ignored for political reasons. These have been published both in traditional and in nontraditional anthologies. The most outspoken critics of the canon, especially radical critics practicing cultural criticism, have called into question the whole concept of canon or "canonicity." Privileging no form of artistic expression that reflects and revises the culture, these critics treat cartoons, comics, and soap operas with the same cogency and respect they accord novels, poems, and plays.

See also: Cultural Criticism, Feminist Criticism, Ideology, Marxist Criticism.

CONFLICTS, CONTRADICTIONS   *See* Gaps.

CULTURAL CRITICISM   A critical approach that is sometimes referred to as "cultural studies" or "cultural critique." Practitioners of cultural criticism oppose "high" definitions of culture and take seriously popular cultural forms. Grounded in a variety of continental European influences, cultural criticism nonetheless gained institutional force in England, in 1964, with the founding of the Centre for Contemporary Cultural Studies at Birmingham University. Broadly interdisciplinary in its scope and approach, cultural criticism views the text as the locus and catalyst of a complex network of political and economic discourses. Cultural critics share with Marxist critics an interest in the ideological contexts of cultural forms.

DECONSTRUCTION   A poststructuralist approach to literature that is strongly influenced by the writings of the French philosopher Jacques Derrida. Deconstruction, partly in response to structuralism and formalism, posits the undecidability of meaning for all texts. In fact, as the deconstructionist critic J. Hillis Miller points out, "deconstruction is not a dismantling of the structure of a text but a demonstration that it has already dismantled itself." *See* "What Is Deconstruction?" pp. 211–27.

DIALECTIC   Originally developed by Greek philosophers, mainly Socrates and Plato, as a form and method of logical argumentation; the term later came to denote a philosophical notion of evolution. The German philosopher G. W. F. Hegel described dialectic as a process whereby a thesis, when countered by an antithesis, leads to the synthesis of a new idea. Karl Marx and Friedrich Engels, adapting Hegel's idealist theory, used the phrase "dialectical materialism" to discuss the way in which a revolutionary class war might lead to the synthesis of a new social economic order. The American Marxist critic Fredric Jameson has coined the phrase "dialectical criticism" to refer to a Marxist critical approach that synthesizes structuralist and poststructuralist methodologies.

See also: Marxist Criticism, Poststructuralism, Structuralism.

DIALOGIC   *See* Discourse.

DISCOURSE   Used specifically, can refer to (1) spoken or written discussion of a subject or area of knowledge; (2) the words in, or text of, a narrative as opposed to its story line; or (3) a "strand" within a given narrative that argues a certain point or defends a given value system.

More generally, "discourse" refers to the language in which a subject or area of knowledge is discussed or a certain kind of business is transacted. Human knowledge is collected and structured in discourses. Theology and medicine are defined by their discourses, as are politics, sexuality, and literary criticism.

A society is generally made up of a number of different discourses or "discourse communities," one or more of which may be dominant or serve the dominant ideology. Each discourse has its own vocabulary, concepts, and rules, knowledge of which constitutes power. The psychoanalyst and psychoanalytic critic Jacques Lacan has treated the unconscious as a form of discourse, the patterns of which are repeated in literature. Cultural critics, following Mikhail Bakhtin, use the word "dialogic" to discuss the dialogue *between* discourses that takes place within language or, more specifically, a literary text.

See also: Cultural Criticism, Ideology, Narrative, Psychoanalytic Criticism.

FEMINIST CRITICISM   An aspect of the feminist movement whose primary goals include critiquing masculine-dominated language and literature by showing how they reflect a masculine ideology; writing the history of unknown or undervalued women writers, thereby earning them their rightful place in the literary canon; and helping create a climate in which women's creativity may be fully realized and appreciated. *See* "What Are Feminist and Gender Criticism?" pp. 175–89.

FIGURE   *See* Metaphor, Metonymy, Symbol.

FORMALISM   Also referred to as the New Criticism, formalism reached its height during the 1940s and 1950s, but it is still practiced today. Formalists treat a work of literary art as if it were a self-contained, self-referential object. Rather than basing their interpretations of a text on the reader's response, the author's stated intentions, or parallels between the text and historical contexts (such as the author's life), formalists concentrate on the relationships *within* the text that give it its own distinctive character or form. Special attention is paid to repetition, particularly of images or symbols, but also of sound effects and rhythms in poetry.

Because of the importance placed on close analysis and the stress on the text as a carefully crafted, orderly object containing observable formal patterns, formalism has often been seen as an attack on Romanticism and impressionism, particularly impressionistic criticism. It has sometimes even been called an "objective" approach to literature. Formalists are more likely than certain other critics to believe and say that the meaning of a text can be known objectively. For instance, reader-response critics see meaning as a function either of each reader's experience or of the norms that govern a particular "interpretive community," and deconstructors argue that texts mean opposite things at the same time.

Formalism was originally based on essays written during the 1920s and 1930s by T. S. Eliot, I. A. Richards, and William Empson. It was significantly developed later by a group of American poets and critics, including R. P. Blackmur, Cleanth Brooks, John Crowe Ransom, Allen Tate, Robert Penn Warren, and William K. Wimsatt. Although we associate formalism with certain principles and terms (such as the "affective fallacy" and the "intentional fallacy" as defined by Wimsatt and Monroe C. Beardsley), formalists were trying to make a cultural statement rather than establish a critical dogma. Generally southern, religious, and culturally conservative, they advocated the inherent value of literary works (particularly of literary works regarded as beautiful art objects) because they were sick of the growing ugliness of modern life and contemporary events. Some recent theorists even suggest that the rising popularity of formalism after World War II was a feature of American isolationism, the formalist tendency to isolate literature from biography and history being a manifestation of the American fatigue with wider involvements.

See also: Affective Fallacy, Authorial Intention, Deconstruction, Reader-Response Criticism, Symbol.

GAPS   When used by reader-response critics familiar with the theories of Wolfgang Iser, refers to "blanks" in texts that must be filled in by readers. A gap may be said to exist whenever and wherever a reader perceives something to be missing between words, sentences, paragraphs, stanzas, or chapters. Readers respond to gaps actively and creatively, explaining apparent inconsistencies in point of view, accounting for jumps in chronology, speculatively supplying information missing from plots, and resolving problems or issues left ambiguous or "indeterminate" in the text.

Reader-response critics sometimes speak as if a gap actually exists in a text; a gap is, of course, to some extent a product of readers' perceptions. Different readers may find gaps in different texts, and different gaps in the same text. Furthermore, they may fill these gaps in different ways, which is why, a reader-response critic might argue, works are interpreted in different ways.

Although the concept of the gap has been used mainly by reader-response critics, it has also been used by critics taking other theoretical approaches. Practitioners of deconstruction might use "gap" when speaking of the radical contradictoriness of a text. Marxists have used the term to speak of everything from the gap that opens up between economic base and cultural superstructure to the two kinds of conflicts or contradictions to be found in literary texts. The first of these, they would argue, results from the fact that texts reflect ideology, within which certain subjects cannot be covered, things cannot be said, contradictory views cannot be recognized as contradictory. The second kind of conflict, contradiction, or gap within a text results from the fact that works don't just reflect ideology; they are also fictions that, consciously or unconsciously, distance themselves from the same ideology.

See also: Deconstruction, Ideology, Marxist Criticism, Reader-Response Criticism.

GENDER CRITICISM   Developing out of feminist criticism in the mid-1980s, this fluid and inclusive movement by its nature defies neat definition. Its practitioners include, but are not limited to, self-identified feminists, gay and lesbian critics, queer and performance theorists, and poststructuralists interested in deconstructing oppositions such as masculine/feminine, heterosexual/homosexual. This diverse group of critics shares an interest in interrogating categories of gender and sexuality and exploring the relationships between them, though it does not necessarily share any central assumptions about the nature of these categories. For example, some gender critics insist that all gender identities are cultural constructions, but others have maintained a belief in essential gender identity. Often gender critics are more interested in examining gender issues through a literary text than a literary text through gender issues. *See* "What Are Feminist and Gender Criticism?" pp. 175–89.

GENRE   A French word referring to a kind or type of literature. Individual works within a genre may exhibit a distinctive form, be governed by certain conventions, and/or represent characteristic subjects. Tragedy, epic, and romance are all genres.

Perhaps inevitably, the term *genre* is used loosely. Lyric poetry is a genre, but so are characteristic *types* of the lyric, such as the sonnet, the ode, and the elegy. Fiction is a genre, as are detective fiction and science fiction. The list of genres grows constantly as critics establish new lines of connection between individual works and discern new categories of works with common characteristics. Moreover, some writers form hybrid genres by combining the characteristics of several in a single work. Knowledge of genres helps critics to understand and explain what is conventional and unconventional, borrowed and original, in a work.

HEGEMONY   Given intellectual currency by the Italian communist Antonio Gramsci, the word (a translation of *egemonia*) refers to the pervasive system of assumptions, meanings, and values—the web of ideologies, in other words—that shapes the way things look, what they mean, and therefore what reality *is* for the majority of people within a given culture.

See also: Ideology, Marxist Criticism.

IDEOLOGY   A set of beliefs underlying the customs, habits, and/or practices common to a given social group. To members of that group, the beliefs seem obviously true, natural, and even universally applicable. They may seem just as obviously arbitrary, idiosyncratic, and even false to outsiders or members of another group who adhere to another ideology. Within a society, several ideologies may coexist, or one or more may be dominant.

Ideologies may be forcefully imposed or willingly subscribed to. Their component beliefs may be held consciously or unconsciously. In either case, they come to form what Johanna M. Smith has called "the unexamined ground of our experience." Ideology governs our perceptions, judgments, and prejudices—our sense of what is acceptable, normal, and deviant. Ideology may cause a revolution; it may also allow discrimination and even exploitation.

Ideologies are of special interest to sociologically oriented critics of literature because of the way in which authors reflect or resist prevailing views in their texts. Some Marxist critics have argued that literary texts reflect and reproduce the ideologies that produced them; most, however, have shown how ideologies are riven with contradictions that works of literature manage to expose and widen. Still other Marxists have focused on the way in which texts themselves are characterized by gaps, conflicts, and contradictions between their ideological and anti-ideological functions.

Feminist critics have addressed the question of ideology by seeking to expose (and thereby call into question) the patriarchal ideology mirrored or inscribed in works written by men—even men who have sought to counter sexism and break down sexual stereotypes. New historicists have been interested in demonstrating the ideological underpinnings not only of literary representations but also of our interpretations of them. Fredric Jameson, an American Marxist critic, argues that all thought is ideological, but that ideological thought that knows itself as such stands the chance of seeing through and transcending ideology.

See also: Cultural Criticism, Feminist Criticism, Marxist Criticism, New Historicism.

IMAGINARY ORDER One of the three essential orders of the psychoanalytic field (*see* Real and Symbolic Order), it is most closely associated with the senses (sight, sound, touch, taste, and smell). The infant, who by comparison to other animals is born premature and thus is wholly dependent on others for a prolonged period, enters the Imaginary order when it begins to experience a unity of body parts and motor control that is empowering. This usually occurs between six and eighteen months, and is called by Lacan the "mirror stage" or "mirror phase," in which the child anticipates mastery of its body. It does so by identifying with the *image* of wholeness (that is, seeing its own image in the mirror, experiencing its mother as a whole body, and so on). This sense of oneness, and also difference from others (especially the mother or primary caretaker), is established through an image or a vision of harmony that is both a mirroring and a "mirage of maturation" or false sense of individuality and independence. The Imaginary is a metaphor for unity, is related to the visual order, and is always part of human subjectivity. Because the subject is fundamentally separate from others and also internally divided (conscious/unconscious), the apparent coherence of the Imaginary, its fullness and grandiosity, is always false, a *mis*recognition that the ego (or "me") tries to deny by imagining itself as coherent and empowered. The Imaginary operates in conjunction with the Real and the Symbolic and is not a "stage" of development equivalent to Freud's "pre-oedipal stage," nor is it prelinguistic.

See also: Psychoanalytic Criticism, Real, Symbolic Order.

IMPLIED READER   A phrase used by some reader-response critics in place of the phrase "the reader." Whereas "the reader" could refer to any idiosyncratic individual who happens to have read or to be reading the text, "the implied reader" is *the* reader intended, even created, by the text. Other reader-response critics seeking to describe this more generally conceived reader have spoken of the "informed reader" or the "narratee," who is "the necessary counterpart of a given narrator."

See also: Reader-Response Criticism.

INTENTIONAL FALLACY   *See* Authorial Intention.

INTENTIONALITY   *See* Authorial Intention.

INTERTEXTUALITY   The condition of interconnectedness among texts. Every author has been influenced by others, and every work contains explicit and implicit references to other works. Writers may consciously or unconsciously echo a predecessor or precursor; they may also consciously or unconsciously disguise their indebtedness, making intertextual relationships difficult for the critic to trace.

Reacting against the formalist tendency to view each work as a freestanding object, some poststructuralist critics suggested that the meaning of a work emerges only intertextually, that is, within the context provided by other works. But there has been a reaction, too, against this type of intertextual criticism. Some new historicist critics suggest that literary history is itself too narrow a context and that works should be interpreted in light of a larger set of cultural contexts.

There is, however, a broader definition of intertextuality, one that refers to the relationship between works of literature and a wide range of narratives and discourses that we don't usually consider literary. Thus defined, intertextuality could be used by a new historicist to refer to the significant interconnectedness between a literary text and nonliterary discussions of or discourses about contemporary culture. Or it could be used by a poststructuralist to suggest that a work can be recognized and read only within a vast field of signs and tropes that is *like* a text and that makes any single text self-contradictory and "undecidable."

See also: Discourse, Formalism, Narrative, New Historicism, Poststructuralism, Trope.

MARXIST CRITICISM   An approach that treats literary texts as material products, describing them in broadly historical terms. In Marxist criticism, the text is viewed in terms of its production and consumption, as a product *of* work that does identifiable cultural work of its own. Following Karl Marx, the founder of communism, Marxist critics have used the terms *base* to refer to economic reality and *superstructure* to refer to the corresponding or "homologous" infrastructure consisting of politics, law, philosophy, religion, and the arts. Also following Marx, they have used the word *ideology* to refer to that set of cultural beliefs that literary works at once reproduce, resist, and revise.

METAPHOR   The representation of one thing by another related or similar thing. The image (or activity or concept) used to represent or "figure" something else is known as the "vehicle" of the metaphor; the thing represented is called the "tenor." In other words, the vehicle is what we substitute for the tenor. The relationship between vehicle and tenor can provide much additional meaning. Thus, instead of saying, "Last night I read a book," we might say, "Last night I plowed through a book." "Plowed through" (or the activity of plowing) is the vehicle of our metaphor; "read" (or the act of reading) is the tenor, the thing being figured. The increment in meaning through metaphor is fairly obvious. Our audience knows not only *that* we read but also *how* we read, because to read a book in the way that a plow rips through earth is surely to read in a relentless, unreflective way. Note that in the sentence above, a new metaphor—"rips through"—has been used to explain an old one. This serves (which is a metaphor) as an example of just how thick (another metaphor) language is with metaphors!

Metaphor is a kind of "trope" (literally, a "turning," that is, a figure of speech that alters or "turns" the meaning of a word or phrase). Other tropes include allegory, conceit, metonymy, personification, simile, symbol, and synecdoche. Traditionally, metaphor and symbol have been viewed as the principal tropes; minor tropes have been categorized as *types* of these two major ones. Similes, for instance, are usually defined as simple metaphors that usually employ *like* or *as* and state the tenor outright, as in "My love is like a red, red rose." Synecdoche involves a vehicle that is a *part* of the tenor, as in "I see a sail" meaning "I see a boat." Metonymy is viewed as a metaphor involving two terms commonly if arbitrarily associated with (but not fundamentally or intrinsically related to) each other. Recently, however, deconstructors such as Paul de Man and J. Hillis Miller have questioned the "privilege" granted to metaphor and the metaphor/metonymy distinction or "opposition." They have suggested that all metaphors are really metonyms and that all figuration is arbitrary.

See also: Deconstruction, Metonymy, Oppositions, Symbol.

METONYMY   The representation of one thing by another that is commonly and often physically associated with it. To refer to a writer's handwriting as his or her "hand" is to use a metonymic "figure" or "trope." The image or thing used to represent something else is known as the "vehicle" of the metonym; the thing represented is called the "tenor."

Like other tropes (such as metaphor), metonymy involves the replacement of one word or phrase by another. Liquor may be referred to as "the bottle," a monarch as "the crown." Narrowly defined, the vehicle of a metonym is arbitrarily, not intrinsically, associated with the tenor. In other words, the bottle just happens to be what liquor is stored in and poured from in our culture. The hand may be involved in the production of handwriting, but so are the brain and the pen. There is no special, intrinsic likeness between a crown and a monarch; it's just that crowns traditionally sit on monarchs' heads and not on the heads of university professors. More broadly, *metonym* and *metonymy* have been used by recent critics to refer to a wide range of figures and tropes. Deconstructors have questioned the distinction between metaphor and metonymy.

See also: Deconstruction, Metaphor, Trope.

NARRATIVE   A story or a telling of a story, or an account of a situation or of events. A novel and a biography of a novelist are both narratives, as are Freud's case histories.

Some critics use the word *narrative* even more generally; Brook Thomas, a new historicist, has critiqued "narratives of human history that neglect the role human labor has played."

NEW CRITICISM *See* Formalism.

NEW HISTORICISM First practiced and articulated in the late 1970s and early 1980s in the work of critics such as Stephen Greenblatt—who named this movement in contemporary critical theory—and Louis Montrose, its practitioners share certain convictions, primarily that literary critics need to develop a high degree of historical consciousness and that literature should not be viewed apart from other human creations, artistic or otherwise. They share a belief in referentiality—a belief that literature refers to and is referred to by things outside itself—that is fainter in the works of formalist, poststructuralist, and even reader-response critics. Discarding old distinctions between literature, history, and the social sciences, new historicists agree with Greenblatt that the "central concerns" of criticism "should prevent it from permanently sealing off one type of discourse from another, or decisively separating works of art from the minds and lives of their creators and their audiences."

See also: "What Is the New Historicism?" pp. 145–57; Authorial Intention, Deconstruction, Formalism, Ideology, Poststructuralism, Psychoanalytic Criticism.

OPPOSITIONS A concept highly relevant to linguistics, inasmuch as linguists maintain that words (such as *black* and *death*) have meaning not in themselves but in relation to other words (*white* and *life*). Jacques Derrida, a poststructuralist philosopher of language, has suggested that in the West we think in terms of these "binary oppositions" or dichotomies, which on examination turn out to be evaluative hierarchies. In other words, each opposition—beginning/end, presence/absence, or consciousness/unconsciousness—contains one term that our culture views as superior and one term that we view as negative or inferior.

Derrida has "deconstructed" a number of these binary oppositions, including two—speech/writing and signifier/signified—that he believes to be central to linguistics in particular and Western culture in general. He has concurrently critiqued the "law" of noncontradiction, which is fundamental to Western logic. He and other deconstructors have argued that a text can contain opposed strands of discourse and, therefore, can mean opposite things: reason *and* passion, life *and* death, hope *and* despair, black *and* white. Traditionally, criticism has involved choosing between opposed or contradictory meanings and arguing that one is present in the text and the other absent.

French feminists have adopted the ideas of Derrida and other deconstructors, showing not only that we think in terms of such binary oppositions as male/female, reason/emotion, and active/passive, but that we also associate reason and activity with masculinity and emotion and passivity with femininity. Because of this, they have concluded that language is "phallocentric," or masculine-dominated.

See also: Deconstruction, Discourse, Feminist Criticism, Poststructuralism.

PHALLUS The symbolic value of the penis that organizes libidinal development and that Freud saw as a stage in the process of human subjectivity. Lacan viewed the Phallus as the representative of a fraudulent power (male over female) whose "Law" is a principle of psychic division (conscious/unconscious) and sexual difference (masculine/feminine). The Symbolic order (*see* Symbolic Order) is ruled by the Phallus, which of itself has no inherent meaning *apart from* the power and meaning given to it by individual cultures and societies, and represented by the name of the father as lawgiver and namer.

POSTSTRUCTURALISM   The general attempt to contest and subvert structuralism initiated by deconstructors and certain other critics associated with psychoanalytic, Marxist, and feminist theory. Structuralists, using linguistics as a model and employing semiotic (sign) theory, posit the possibility of knowing a text systematically and revealing the "grammar" behind its form and meaning. Poststructuralists argue against the possibility of such knowledge and description. They counter that texts can be shown to contradict not only structuralist accounts of them but also themselves. In making their adversarial claims, they rely on close readings of texts and on the work of theorists such as Jacques Derrida and Jacques Lacan.

Poststructuralists have suggested that structuralism rests on distinctions between "signifier" and "signified" (signs and the things they point toward), "self" and "language" (or "text"), texts and other texts, and text and world that are overly simplistic, if not patently inaccurate. Poststructuralists have shown how all signifieds are also signifiers, and they have treated texts as "intertexts." They have viewed the world as if it *were* a text (we desire a certain car because it *symbolizes* achievement) and the self as the subject, as well as the user, of language; for example, we may shape and speak through language, but it also shapes and speaks through us.

See also: Deconstruction, Feminist Criticism, Intertextuality, Psychoanalytic Criticism, Semiotics, Structuralism.

PSYCHOANALYTIC CRITICISM   Grounded in the psychoanalytic theories of Sigmund Freud, it is one of the oldest critical methodologies still in use. Freud's view that works of literature, like dreams, express secret, unconscious desires led to criticism and interpreted literary works as manifestations of the authors' neuroses. More recently, psychoanalytic critics have come to see literary works as skillfully crafted artifacts that may appeal to *our* neuroses by tapping into our repressed wishes and fantasies. Other forms of psychological criticism that diverge from Freud, although they ultimately derive from his insights, include those based on the theories of Carl Jung and Jacques Lacan. *See* "What Is Psychoanalytic Criticism?" pp. 79–90.

READER-RESPONSE CRITICISM   An approach to literature that, as its name implies, considers the way readers respond to texts as they read. Stanley Fish describes the method by saying that it substitutes for one question, "What does this sentence mean?" a more operational question, "What does this sentence do?" Reader-response criticism shares with deconstruction a strong textual orientation and a reluctance to define a single meaning for a work. Along with psychoanalytic criticism, it shares an interest in the dynamics of mental response to textual cues. *See* "What Is Reader-Response Criticism?" pp. 112–23.

REAL   One of the three orders of subjectivity (*see* Imaginary Order and Symbolic Order), the Real is the intractable and substantial world that resists and exceeds interpretation. The Real cannot be imagined, symbolized, or known directly. It constantly eludes our efforts to name it (death, gravity, the physicality of objects are examples of the Real), and thus challenges both the Imaginary and the Symbolic orders. The Real is fundamentally "Other," the mark of the divide between conscious and unconscious, and is signaled in language by gaps, slips, speechlessness, and the sense of the uncanny. The Real is not what we call "reality." It is the stumbling block of the Imaginary (which thinks it can "imagine" anything, including the Real) and of the Symbolic, which tries to bring the Real under its laws (the Real exposes the "phallacy" of the Law of the Phallus). The Real is frightening; we try to tame it with laws and language and call it "reality."

See also: Imaginary Order, Psychoanalytic Criticism, Symbolic Order.

SEMIOLOGY, SEMIOTIC   *See* Semiotics.

SEMIOTICS   The study of signs and sign systems and the way meaning is derived from them. Structuralist anthropologists, psychoanalysts, and literary critics developed semiotics during the decades following 1950, but much of the pioneering work had been done at the turn of the century by the founder of modern linguistics, Ferdinand de Saussure, and the American philosopher Charles Sanders Peirce.

Semiotics is based on several important distinctions, including the distinction between "signifier" and "signified" (the sign and what it points toward) and the distinction between "langue" and "parole." *Langue* (French for "tongue," as in "native tongue," meaning language) refers to the entire system within which individual utterances or usages of language have meaning; *parole* (French for "word") refers to the particular utterances or usages. A principal tenet of semiotics is that signs, like words, are not significant in themselves, but instead have meaning only in relation to other signs and the entire system of signs, or langue.

The affinity between semiotics and structuralist literary criticism derives from this emphasis placed on langue, or system. Structuralist critics, after all, were reacting against formalists and their procedure of focusing on individual words as if meanings didn't depend on anything external to the text.

Poststructuralists have used semiotics but questioned some of its underlying assumptions, including the opposition between signifier and signified. The feminist poststructuralist Julia Kristeva, for instance, has used the word *semiotic* to describe feminine language, a highly figurative, fluid form of discourse that she sets in opposition to rigid, symbolic, masculine language.

See also: Deconstruction, Feminist Criticism, Formalism, Oppositions, Poststructuralism, Structuralism, Symbol.

SIMILE   *See* Metaphor.

SOCIOHISTORICAL CRITICISM   *See* New Historicism.

STRUCTURALISM   A science of humankind whose proponents attempted to show that all elements of human culture, including literature, may be understood as parts of a system of signs. Structuralism, according to Robert Scholes, was a reaction to "'modernist' alienation and despair."

Using Ferdinand de Saussure's linguistic theory, European structuralists such as Roman Jakobson, Claude Lévi-Strauss, and Roland Barthes (before his shift toward poststructuralism) attempted to develop a "semiology" or "semiotics" (science of signs). Barthes, among others, sought to recover literature and even language from the isolation in which they had been studied and to show that the laws that govern them govern all signs, from road signs to articles of clothing.

Particularly useful to structuralists were two of Saussure's concepts: the idea of "phoneme" in language and the idea that phonemes exist in two kinds of relationships: "synchronic" and "diachronic." A phoneme is the smallest consistently significant unit in language; thus, both "a" and "an" are phonemes, but "n" is not. A diachronic relationship is that which a phoneme has with those that have preceded it in time and those that will follow it. These "horizontal" relationships produce what we might call discourse or narrative and what Saussure called "parole." The synchronic relationship is the "vertical" one that a word has in a given instant with the entire system of language ("langue") in which it may generate meaning. "An" means what it means in English because those of us who speak the language are using it in the same way at a given time.

Following Saussure, Lévi-Strauss studied hundreds of myths, breaking them into their smallest meaningful units, which he called "mythemes." Removing each from its diachronic relations with other mythemes in a single myth (such as the myth of Oedipus and his mother), he vertically aligned those mythemes that he found to be homologous (structurally correspondent). He then studied the relationships within as well as between vertically aligned columns, in an attempt to understand scientifically, through ratios and proportions, those thoughts and processes that humankind has shared, both at one particular time and across time. One could say, then, that structuralists followed Saussure in preferring to think about the overriding langue or language of myth, in which each mytheme and mytheme-constituted myth fits meaningfully, rather than about isolated individual paroles or narratives. Structuralists followed Saussure's lead in believing what the poststructuralist Jacques Derrida later decided he could not subscribe to—that sign systems must be understood in terms of binary oppositions. In analyzing myths and texts to find basic structures, structuralists tended to find that opposite terms modulate until they are finally resolved or reconciled by some intermediary third term. Thus, a structuralist reading of *Paradise Lost* would show that the war between God and the bad angels becomes a rift between God and sinful, fallen man, the rift then being healed by the Son of God, the mediating third term.

See also: Deconstruction, Discourse, Narrative, Poststructuralism, Semiotics.

SUPERSTRUCTURE   *See* Marxist Criticism.

SYMBOL   A thing, image, or action that, although it is of interest in its own right, stands for or suggests something larger and more complex—often an idea or a range of interrelated ideas, attitudes, and practices.

Within a given culture, some things are understood to be symbols: the flag of the United States is an obvious example. More subtle cultural symbols might be the river as a symbol of time and the journey as a symbol of life and its manifold experiences.

Instead of appropriating symbols generally used and understood within their culture, writers often create symbols by setting up, in their works, a complex but identifiable web of associations. As a result, one object, image, or action suggests others, and often, ultimately, a range of ideas.

A symbol may thus be defined as a metaphor in which the "vehicle," the thing, image, or action used to represent something else, represents many related things (or "tenors") or is broadly suggestive. The urn in Keats's "Ode on a Grecian Urn" suggests many interrelated concepts, including art, truth, beauty, and timelessness.

Symbols have been of particular interest to formalists, who study how meanings emerge from the complex, patterned relationships between images in a work, and psychoanalytic critics, who are interested in how individual authors and the larger culture both disguise and reveal unconscious fears and desires through symbols. Recently, French feminists have also focused on the symbolic. They have suggested that, as wide-ranging as it seems, symbolic language is ultimately rigid and restrictive. They favor semiotic language and writing, which, they contend, is at once more rhythmic, unifying, and feminine.

See also: Feminist Criticism, Metaphor, Psychoanalytic Criticism, Trope.

SYMBOLIC ORDER One of the three orders of subjectivity (*see* Imaginary Order and Real), it is the realm of law, language, and society; it is the repository of generally held cultural beliefs. Its symbolic system is language, whose agent is the father or lawgiver, the one who has the power of naming. The human subject is commanded into this preestablished order by language (a process that begins long before a child can speak) and must submit to its orders of communication (grammar, syntax, and so on). Entrance into the Symbolic order determines subjectivity according to a primary law of referentiality that takes the male sign (phallus; *see* Phallus) as its ordering principle. Lacan states that both sexes submit to the Law of the Phallus (the law of order, language, and differentiation) but that their individual relation to the law determines whether they see themselves as—and are seen by others to be—either "masculine" or "feminine." The Symbolic institutes repression (of the Imaginary), thus creating the unconscious, which itself is structured like the language of the symbolic. The unconscious, a timeless realm, cannot be known directly, but it can be understood by a kind of translation that takes place in language—psychoanalysis is the "talking cure." The Symbolic is not a "stage" of development (as is Freud's "oedipal stage"), nor is it set in place once and for all in human life. We constantly negotiate its threshold (in sleep, in drunkenness) and can "fall out" of it altogether in psychosis.

See also: Imaginary Order, Psychoanalytic Criticism, Real.

SYNECDOCHE *See* Metaphor, Metonymy.

TENOR *See* Metaphor, Metonymy, Symbol.

TROPE A figure, as in "figure of speech." Literally a "turning," that is, a turning or twisting of a word or phrase to make it mean something else. Principal tropes include metaphor, metonymy, personification, simile, and synecdoche.

See also: Metaphor, Metonymy.

VEHICLE *See* Metaphor, Metonymy, Symbol.

About the Contributors

THE VOLUME EDITOR

Daniel R. Schwarz is Professor of English at Cornell University. His books include *Narrative and Representation in the Poetry of Wallace Stevens* (1993); *The Case for a Humanistic Poetics* (1991); *The Transformation of the English Novel, 1890–1930* (1989); *Reading Joyce's "Ulysses"* (1987); *The Humanistic Heritage: Critical Theories of the English Novel from James to Hillis Miller* (1986); *Conrad: The Later Fiction* (1982); *Conrad: "Almayer's Folly" through "Under Western Eyes"* (1980); *Disraeli's Fiction* (1979); and the forthcoming *Reconfiguring Modernism: Explorations in the Relationships, Between Modern Art and Modern Literature*. Additionally, he edited *The Dead* (1994) in Bedford's Case Studies in Contemporary Criticism series. He has lectured widely in the United States and abroad.

THE CRITICS

Michael Levenson is Professor of English at the University of Virginia. He is the author of *Modernism and the Fate of Individuality: Character and Form from Conrad to Woolf* (1991) and *A Genealogy of Modernism: A Study of English Literary Doctrine, 1908–1922* (1984).

J. Hillis Miller, Distinguished Professor of English and Comparative Literature at the University of California, Irvine, is the preeminent American deconstructionist critic. Among his many important studies of nineteenth- and twentieth-century literature are *Versions of Pygmalion* (1990), *The Linguistic Moment: From Wordsworth to Stevens* (1985), and *Fiction and Repetition: Seven English Novels* (1982).

James Phelan is Professor of English and Chair at Ohio State University, where he teaches courses in narrative and narrative theory. His books include *Narrative as Rhetoric* (1996), *Beyond the Tenure Track* (1991), *Reading People, Reading Plots* (1989), and *Worlds from Words* (1981). He is the editor of *Narrative*, the journal of the Society for the Study of Narrative Literature, as well as the co-editor (with Gerald Graff) of Bedford's *Adventures of Huckleberry Finn: A Case Study in Critical Controversy* (1995).

Bonnie Kime Scott is Professor of English and Women's Studies at the University of Delaware, where she teaches courses on modernism, feminist studies, and Irish Studies. She is author of *Joyce and Feminism* (1984), *James Joyce* (feminist readings series, 1987), and the two-volume study, *Refiguring Modernism* (1995), which focuses on Virginia Woolf, Djuna Barnes, and Rebecca West. She collected and edited *New Alliances in Joyce Studies* (1988) and the critical anthology, *The Gender of Modernism* (1990), and is at present editing the letters of Rebecca West.

THE SERIES EDITOR

Ross C Murfin, general editor of Case Studies in Contemporary Criticism, and volume editor of Conrad's *Heart of Darkness* and Hawthorne's *The Scarlet Letter* in the series, is provost and vice president for Academic Affairs at Southern Methodist University. He has taught at the University of Miami, Yale University, and the University of Virginia and has published scholarly studies on Joseph Conrad, Thomas Hardy, and D. H. Lawrence.